The
Girl Who Saved Them

BOOKS BY S.E. RUTLEDGE

A Promise to My Sister

S. E. Rutledge

The Girl Who Saved Them

bookouture

Published by Bookouture in 2025

An imprint of Storyfire Ltd.
Carmelite House
50 Victoria Embankment
London EC4Y 0DZ

www.bookouture.com

The authorised representative in the EEA is Hachette Ireland
8 Castlecourt Centre
Dublin 15 D15 XTP3
Ireland
(email: info@hbgi.ie)

Copyright © S.E. Rutledge, 2025

S.E. Rutledge has asserted her right to be identified
as the author of this work.

All rights reserved. No part of this publication may be reproduced, stored in any retrieval system, or transmitted, in any form or by any means, electronic, mechanical, photocopying, recording or otherwise, without the prior written permission of the publishers.

ISBN: 978-1-83618-475-1
eBook ISBN: 978-1-83618-474-4

This book is a work of fiction. Whilst some characters and circumstances portrayed by the author are based on real people and historical fact, references to real people, events, establishments, organizations or locales are intended only to provide a sense of authenticity and are used fictitiously. All other characters and all incidents and dialogue are drawn from the author's imagination and are not to be construed as real.

For my best friend and sister, Felicia

PROLOGUE

SEPTEMBER 3, 1939

LOUISE

A rifle from the Great War stands by the door, freshly cleaned but somehow still stained with the living nightmares it's been through, with the hell Father has suffered... The French government only declared war on Germany today, and already the war is standing at our door, waiting for Father to take it up again for the first time in twenty years, for his son, my only brother, to follow him to the battlefield.

"Please, don't cry," Fernand whispers softly, drawing me into his arms and nudging my blond hair aside to press a kiss to my temple.

I try to suppress the tears. But how can I contain my terror when that hideous rifle is just across the room, staring at me, an awful reminder of the wars of the past and those yet to come? *Will little André be the next son to follow his father to the next war?* The grim thought of my nephew, a boy of barely seven, eagerly trotting after Fernand with a gun makes me sick to my stomach.

Midnight has fallen, a dying fire in the hearth has left the silent house heavy with a bleak cold, and my little sister's absence only makes the quiet feel all the more empty. Fernand and I have been waiting up for her for hours. She is no doubt somewhere roaming Paris with her wild friends, getting into God knows what kind of trouble while we sit here on the eve of war... It's been this way ever since our mother passed away five years ago.

Sometimes I wonder if she even cares about this family...

As if summoned by thought, the door opens, making me tense, and Marie slips inside.

"Marie," Fernand calls quietly, hushing me before I can demand where she's been all this time. "Come sit down. I need to talk to you girls."

Her freckled cheeks flush as red as her hair, and for a moment I think she will ignore us and stomp upstairs to her room as her teenage temper would dictate. Instead, she sighs and slumps down into the armchair across from us, lips drawn in a frown. She doesn't look at us, as if *we* are the ones in the wrong.

"Father and I will be leaving soon," Fernand begins.

"You don't *have* to. You're leaving us," Marie mutters under her breath, glaring at the floor with her arms crossed.

Fernand squeezes my hand to stop me from reprimanding her, then rises to sit beside her. He settles an arm around her tense shoulders, and part of me resents the fact that she doesn't draw away from him, even in her anger. Marie hasn't let me hug her in years, not even after our mother died when we were fifteen and ten, young girls who didn't know how to live in a home without a mother, all of us lost and grieving.

"Yes, I do, Marie," Fernand says. "It doesn't mean I *want* to, but I have to. It's my job to take care of you all, and even if I'm not here I want you to know I'm doing everything I can to make sure you're safe." He insistently pulls her to her feet, directing her to sit stiffly beside me. "Now, I know you girls aren't the best of friends."

An understatement if there ever was one, I think, frowning, and Marie huffs.

"But you're my sisters, and you're the only ones I trust with this. I don't know how long Father and I will be gone..."

It could be forever... I shake that horrible thought away, blinking back tears. I don't want to think of that possibility, that my kind, soft-spoken father who enjoys warm tea and helping me make school lesson plans for my students, that my brother who always happily let his little sisters sleep in his bed when we were young if we'd had a nightmare, might never come home.

"Louise, Marie, I want you to take care of André while I'm gone. I know you're very different"—he looks between us, somber and yet with a hint of amusement—"but I know he'll be safe and loved with you girls, just as he would with his mother..."

Fernand's eyes shine in the firelight, glistening with tears he doesn't allow to fall, and I take his hand. He and our father have more in common than just their dark, unruly hair and spectacles. When Fernand's wife died, André was all he had left of her, and I know it hurts his heart to see his wife's eyes looking up at him from his son's face. Just as I see the pain in Father's eyes when he looks at me, my sun-kissed hair and dark eyes, for I am a nearly identical image of the woman he loved and lost.

"Of course we will," Marie says resolutely. It's true that Marie and I have always had our differences, but it seems we've finally found something we can agree on.

I nod in agreement. "We'll take care of him like our own."

Neither Marie nor I ask our brother to promise he'll come back, that André will not be made an orphan, and he doesn't promise it either. We all know it's not a promise he can definitely keep. But Marie and I can keep ours. No matter what comes, no matter how wide becomes the chasm between Marie and me—which, no matter what either of us do, has only seemed to deepen as the years pass—we will put it all aside to give André the love and home he needs.

Until Fernand comes home, a soft whisper in my mind says, and, for my own sake, I have to hold on to that small wisp of hope.

1

JUNE–JULY 1941

LOUISE

Even with Fernand and our father gone for more than eighteen months, the war still somehow felt so far away, so surreal. Like the moon. It was always there, a constant presence over our heads we grew so accustomed to that it became a universal truth, something that simply *was*, something that would never reach us.

But it came anyway...

Our government fled like cowards in June, declared Paris free for the taking nine months after *they* were the ones to declare war on Germany. Just a month after the Germans began their Blitzkrieg and days after our government ran, the Germans came in legions and tanks, arms raised in Hitler's salute. A curfew was put in place, though most could bribe their way into disregarding it, our radios and newspapers became filled with foreign voices and Nazi propaganda. There were soldiers everywhere; in the cafés, the cinemas, at doorways standing guard, walking the streets with comrades and sympathetic Parisians as if they'd always lived here, as if they were not intruders posing as tourists.

I took to ignoring them, unlike Marie, who made no attempt to hide her disdain. After a while, I simply stopped seeing them. Their presence, as the war had once been, became just another universal fact. They simply *were*. They existed among us and that was the way life was. But the days soon became weeks, and weeks bled into months, and the Germans made sure we couldn't disregard them anymore, especially where the Jews were concerned.

Aside from the ever-rising cost of food, medicine, clothing, paper, and everything else, the trust and companionship that once ran deeply within our community has been degraded to suspicious glances and carefully chosen words. Sympathizers denounce other Parisians to the German authorities, people who were their friends, neighbors, and colleagues. Those who voice opposition to the Reich or sympathy to the Jews could find themselves under arrest. And so, everyone learns to guard their tongue in the presence of a former friend and German soldier alike.

"Louise! It's wonderful to see you!"

I've just slipped ten francs to one of the farmers in the market square in exchange for extra rice, over the allowed rations, when the cheerful voice startles me. I turn, and am relieved to catch sight of my old friend, Yvonne, and her baby son, Daniel.

I return her smile, glancing back at the farmer to make sure he is discreetly adding a few extra cups of rice to my bag.

"We're on our way to get breakfast. Would you like to join us? It's been a while since we talked. I want to hear all about you. Maybe you've got someone new in your life? Plenty of handsome men now," Yvonne says sweetly, perhaps a bit too loudly.

Her suggestive comment isn't lost on anyone in the vicinity. The farmer glares with tired eyes, a woman acquiring her rations bristles silently, and a few German soldiers nearby smirk.

If I didn't know Yvonne any better, I'd think she meant it. But I've grown up with her for twenty years, since we were two, and I know the way she's biting her lip means she's anxious. I quickly gather my flour, cheese, and meat rations, curious about what Yvonne wants to tell me.

The morning is still young, and, while the city is alive with soldiers and civilians, the small café Yvonne picks for our early meal is all but empty. Despite the heat, we sit at a table on the outdoor patio at the back of the café, tucked into a corner in the shade. Here, we are invisible from the main street.

We settle into an easy conversation as we await a cup of coffee. When it arrives, we split it, which leaves each of us with perhaps a few mouthfuls. Prices are rising too high for common people like Yvonne and I to indulge even in simple treats, so we stretch our money as thin as it will go.

For a while, we reminisce over our younger days; when we were little girls who snuck into our mothers' cosmetic bags to try their ruby lipstick, who stood on each other's knees to reach the shelves in the library because we were too embarrassed to ask the handsome assistant for his help, before the war when we dolled ourselves up for our first dates and never imagined the turmoil of the world could reach us in our little sphere of bliss.

Oh, how I miss those days so much... Life of today compared to the past is dull and depressing. How I long to teach at the primary school again, see my students eagerly smiling up at me, sit with my father and read late into the night, hear André burst through the front door unannounced and make him a quick lunch to take to Fernand in his tailor shop. How I long for the simplicity of peaceful days, when I was only a brand-new teacher and my most troubling concern was whether Marie would join us for supper rather than running across the city with her friends... I am only twenty-two, Marie barely seventeen, and yet I feel ancient, like a relic beaten down by all the ages.

After a while, silence settles between us, and Yvonne steals a few glances around before her eyes turn seriously on me. She whispers, "If there was a way to fight... would you?"

I tense. My first instinct is to feign disgust at the mere thought of retaliation, but I bite my tongue. One must never let one's guard slip. Anyone, even your closest friends and family, could be the ones to turn you in; but I know Yvonne. She would not ask me this question lightly.

What are you up to? I wonder, holding her gaze. "In what way?" I ask quietly.

Violence is out of the question. That kind of confrontation gets people killed. But what other kind of resistance is there? How does one fight without arms?

"Escape routes," Yvonne says. "A resistance group was established in Belgium earlier this month, and now here in Paris. It's being called the Comet Line. The Allies are losing airmen all over Europe, but not all of them are killed. Some are surviving and escaping into civilian homes. We want to establish escape routes, the largest there's ever been! From Belgium, to France, and down to Spain. If we do this right, we can get those airmen to safety."

Weightlessness washes over me in terror and excitement.

She leans toward me earnestly. "I trust you, Louise, I know you won't say anything. If you want to, you can forget I ever said anything, and we'll never speak of it again. But aren't you tired of being helpless?"

Aren't we all... Thousands of our men and boys are gone, dead or missing, vanished like ghosts into memory, and we are left to wonder what has become of them. Our government has been replaced by the Nazis' Vichy puppet. Fernand and Father... they're gone too. And now we are alone. There is no one left to protect us. I'm terrified to speak freely in the city of my childhood, cautious of my fellow citizens and the foreign soldiers. This isn't living. I'm only existing, like an immobile star that dreams of the day it can fall from the heavens and become a comet, blazing a trail across the darkness to create something breathtaking. God, how I wish I could do something worthwhile, something that will matter in a hundred years.

André... The thought of my nephew stops this treacherous train of thought. Since my mother died, I have tried to fill the void she left behind. Not that I have ever truly been able to make our home as warm and happy as she did, but, in all things, my family has been my only concern.

My eyes flicker to her son, the innocent child who could be caught in the crossfire if something goes wrong. "His father would want this," Yvonne whispers in a broken voice, catching my gaze directed at her baby.

Yvonne married an Englishman. The last she heard of him was a year ago, a letter informing her he was missing after the Battle of Dunkirk. She's holding out hope that he's still alive, perhaps as a prisoner or in hiding. Maybe joining the Comet Line is her way of honoring him, of hoping, doing for his men what she hopes others will do for him.

Maybe, if I had no sister or nephew to care for, no brother or father to wait for... But I have a family I love, who I am responsible for, family I could never endanger in this way... But how do I refuse when she too has someone to look after and someone to wait for?

"I... I need to think about it," I say hesitantly.

She smiles. "Of course. There's no rush. This is all still fairly new. The first soldiers haven't even been moved yet, but they will need places to hide, people to give them food, clothes, and documents. My home is the perfect secluded place for visitors."

As quickly as the topic came, it fades back into inconsequential conversation no one would suspect followed a discussion of escape routes and Allied soldiers.

I think of nothing but the Comet Line and the ordinary civilians risking everything to aid the Allies in the weeks following our meeting. At first, I try to think of a way to turn Yvonne down as I teach my private class of children at home, as I make supper and clean, as I listen to Marie complain about her supervisor at the mail office. Then, without my consciously realizing it, my thoughts start to change.

We have a cellar. It's big enough to hold several people, at least six or seven.

I speak English. Father taught me when I was young. That would certainly be helpful in dealing with soldiers who might not speak French or German.

Marie and I already trade with the farmers and in the market square. They all know us; we always trade for extra rations. No one would be suspicious to see us with more supplies than anyone else.

But how could I keep Marie and André out of it? How could I risk my life and possibly their lives? How could I turn away the people who need my help for the sake of comfort?

I agonize over the possibilities for weeks; what involvement would mean for André and Marie. Would uprooting our entire lives be worth the risk to save the soldiers trying to save us? God knows I hope someone has saved my brother and father, has taken them to safety and given them food and warm beds. I never had the chance to help them, but I do have the chance to save someone else's brother, some other child's father. And are their families not back home, terrified for their men lost among the enemy, hoping someone will protect them? What would become of us if everyone decided they would let someone else with less to lose do the job? Then, there would be no resistance and the Germans would take the world without anyone so much as raising a finger. And what kind of future would that be for André?

If I don't, who will? In the end, it is this thought that makes my decision, but there would be no way to keep it secret from Marie. Keeping her in the dark would only endanger her. The only way to ensure her safety as well as André's is to tell her the truth.

"How could you?" Marie demands after we put André to bed. "Did you not think of André? What would Fernand say? You can't just risk everything for strangers!"

"They need our help. If I don't, there may not be anyone else who will."

"There's plenty of fools who will throw their lives away for a cause," she snaps.

"I am not a fool. *They* are the ones risking their lives to save us. They need me, they are our men." I try to reason with her, but she will have none of it.

"No! I am a Frenchwoman; our men are dead, missing, or have their tails between their legs! I don't care about Allied soldiers—leave that to women with nothing to lose."

"And what if *everyone* thought that way? Then no one would stand up against Hitler. Remember, Mother always taught us to care about everyone—"

"You're not *her*!" she seethes venomously. "You always forget that. We can't do this!"

"*We* are not doing anything. *I* am," I tell her sternly, ignoring the pang in my heart. She's seemed to resent me since our mother died. "I will hide these men, and you will have nothing else to do with it. I only want you to know so, in case the worst should happen, you can take André and get away.

Fernand and Father are alive out there somewhere, I know it, and, God willing, there will be someone to save them too."

This silences her for a long time, but the fire in her eyes isn't quelled. "No," she finally says, using the stern tone I know means she won't be swayed. "I know you, Louise. You're not going to change your mind, and I won't let you do this alone. You can care about the Allies, but I only care about you and André. It'll be easier if we're both involved."

Our hushed argument after that statement lasts until the crackling fire in the hearth is naught but glowing embers, but Marie remains immovable. Despite my pleas, reasonings, and threats, she won't listen, and I have to admit defeat when she whispers, "You know what we're getting into, and so do I."

All our lives, we've had our differences, but if we're similar in one way it is in our stubbornness. Neither of us will be swayed, and we both know it. And so, when I go to meet Yvonne to offer my life and home to the Comet Line, Marie comes with me and offers the same.

2

MARCH 25, 1944

LOUISE

Three years ago, when I was only an excited teacher eager to pass my knowledge down to the next generations, I never could have imagined the danger I'd be getting myself into. Who would have thought all those hours spent learning English from my father would be used to help fugitive soldiers? Who would have thought all my time spent studying geography would be used to smuggle those soldiers to safehouses along the way to Spain?

I wouldn't usually act as a guide along the escape routes. I'm only ever a hostess to soldiers for a few days or weeks at the most, but there's been a disruption in our chain of command. Our leaders in Paris were arrested in January, and ever since then common citizens of the Line have been grasping at straws, trying to operate on our own without much success. For Marie and me, it has meant going hungry to feed the already weakened pilots in the cellar, walking on eggshells in our own home and city, terrified for our lives the longer we have no one to give us aid and direction.

First it was Andrée de Jongh the Germans arrested in January last year, then her father a few months later. Jacques Le Grelle took charge of our operations in Paris, a man known as Jacques Cartier took over in Brussels, and Jean-François Nothomb had to try to continue coordinating contact between Brussels and Paris. Jacques Cartier drowned, Le Grelle and Nothomb were arrested last January, hours apart, and it seems that every day Line members are being caught by SS and Gestapo.

I signal for the four British pilots following me to stop, crouching low to the ground at the sound of rustling grass. I might have dismissed it as a rabbit or bird a few hours ago, but we're only a mile or so from Angerville, and the first dim signs of morning are lightening the horizon. This time, as I strain my ears, I catch what I dreaded to hear. The faint voice of a man speaking in German.

"Get down," I whisper, crawling into a dip in the earth. "There might be a patrol close to us. I haven't heard dogs, so that's good. Cover yourselves and stay quiet."

They try to do as I ask, but they are tired and slow. We left Paris before curfew to reach the safehouse of a farmer called Sam sixty miles away, and I've only given them a few breaks in the last eleven hours. I help them camouflage their exhausted faces and bodies with dirt and weeds until they've vanished into the earth.

The voice is closer. Others have joined the first, as has the loud squelching of their boots.

My heart races, pounding so furiously I wonder if it's the sound drawing the patrol directly toward us. I cover myself quickly, wishing the season were later in the year so my blond hair might blend in with the withered grass.

"No one move," I whisper, sounding much calmer than I am. The ground doesn't so much as breathe.

"Nein! Of course I'm sure," a German says from somewhere above.

"You're always sure," another snickers in annoyance.

"Because I heard something!"

Six sets of muddy black boots halt directly in my line of sight, making my chest ache with terror, and I squeeze my eyes shut, not daring to breathe.

God, please don't let them find us, let them walk away. We're so close to the safehouse.

I know what the Nazis do to people who aid the Allies, and I don't know if I could survive such gruesome torture. It wouldn't be my own pain that would make me speak. They would find Marie and André, then use them as weapons to force the truth out of me.

The boots move closer, so near the tip of my nose I can pick out every individual scuff on the black leather. The barrel of a rifle prods the brush, sending a bird scuttling from its refuge.

"You see? The boy keeps crying wolf, but all I see are birds and rabbits."

"It wasn't a bird, I heard—" the first man begins to protest.

Another man cuts him off in exasperation. "You hear too many things. Maybe the Eastern Front made you delusional. Let's go, our watch will be over soon."

Tears of utter relief spill down my cheeks as they start in the direction of Angerville. We wait, unmoving, listening to see if they return, and when I'm finally sure they're gone I get up.

"Don't worry, there's not much further to go," I whisper in assurance to the four pilots, each of whom stare back at me with eyes brimming with fear, gratitude, and relief.

Light is breaking over the horizon, shattering the cover of night. Flat farmland and pastures stretch further than I can see, cattle graze and mill idly in groups. Thankfully, no lights emanate from behind the windows of farmhouses. Hours such as these when the stars still glint faintly overhead, and the roosters still sleep soundly, are too early for anyone to wake.

The thought of the bed waiting for me in the safehouse makes my eyes grow heavy, and I rub them clear, glancing back down to the nook in the hill to make sure the soldiers cannot be seen where I've hidden them. Satisfied, I hasten across the pasture and to Sam's safehouse, slipping through the door when it immediately opens to receive me.

"Did you have a safe journey, Amia?" Sam asks, bolting the door.

He doesn't know my real name, nor do I know his. Should any of us be betrayed, it's better we don't have the information the Gestapo wants. So, like all our members, Marie and I are known only by code names. Amia and Cora Pettit.

"It could have been better." I sigh, stifling a yawn. "A German patrol passed us a little way outside of Angerville, but they didn't see us. I made sure we weren't followed here."

He nods, then limps to the stove and pours two cups of tea. It is cool by now, but I drink it gratefully, then follow him back outside. Two horses have already been tied to a wagon piled high with hay, and regard us with mild vexation as Sam climbs up and grabs the reins and I haul myself onto the itchy straw.

"They're a few yards over the hill, look to the left of the fence post that's leaning over."

Sam directs the horses across the field to the place I've indicated. The cattle, finally taking notice of us, amble closer, and I toss handfuls of hay to encourage them to follow. When we reach the hill, several dozen cows have gathered around to graze, giving me plenty of cover to scurry back down the slope to where the men lie.

"Come on, let's be quick. Lie down in the back of the cart

and we'll cover you up. Only about a hundred yards to go, then you can eat and sleep."

A few minutes later, blocked by the cows, Sam and I have tossed hay over the four airmen curled up in the cart and begun the slow, bumpy ride back to the house.

Inside, Sam puts on another kettle for tea and the soldiers settle on a worn sofa and pair of rickety wooden chairs, picking bits of straw out of their hair and clothes. Their pilot uniforms have been exchanged for simple brown and gray trousers, jackets, and shirts, and they've been provided with false documents.

From my place at the window, I look sympathetically at the youngest pilot, who couldn't be any older than Marie—now only twenty, and yet the steadiness in his eyes hides that he is little more than a child.

You gave everything to protect us. Now we will do the same for you.

They were shot down over Belgium a month ago, and they've been with Marie and me for almost two weeks. They should've been smuggled into Spain by now, but the Comet Line hasn't been able to do very much lately. Even in the Line's early years, there were betrayals beyond count; safehouses raided, infiltrators turning over helpers to the Gestapo, others unwillingly betrayed when those under torture broke and gave up more names. Our leaders seem to disappear overnight, and those who take their place never last for long.

It's a miracle Marie and I haven't been caught in three years... My resolve, as it always does when the implications of our involvement with the Comet Line grow too dire, wavers at the thought of André. No doubt he is sound asleep in his bed, oblivious to the fact that Marie is likely waiting up for me, that I am miles from home, that our lives hang precariously in the balance of caution and chance... Part of me wishes I'd never agreed to this, that I had Marie's resolve to let others carry this burden.

But the other part of me hopes my brother and father met someone who saved them and is certain my mother—who taught her children to love thy neighbor as thyself—would be proud of her daughters, believes in my heart that, despite the danger, this is what is right. Even if Marie hates me for it...

3

MARCH 27, 1944

MARIE

"I gave you twenty francs," I mutter crossly, not taking the offered sack of flour when the grocer tries to hand it to me. He's only added one extra cup, not the three I paid for.

He shrugs. "Prices are up. Do you want it, or are they going to have a problem?" He nods to the group of German soldiers standing across the market square.

I glare at him. "And are you going to explain to them why there's extra flour in this sack? Or should I go crying that you're trying to bribe a poor little girl? Who do you think they'll believe?"

Playing sweet and innocent never fails. Men, whether they be German police looking for troublemakers or market dealers trying to swindle more than we can afford, will see a pretty young girl and just that. They assume she's too naive to be a liar and too weak to be a threat.

The grocer frowns but doesn't budge. Only when I turn as if to approach the soldiers does he relent. "Fine!" he hisses, dumping another cup into the sack. "But that's all the extra I can afford. Now go."

I smirk inwardly to myself. I wouldn't risk drawing attention to the farmers and black-market dealers Parisians rely on for much-needed food. His arrest would harm everyone he provides with extra rations, but he clearly believed I wouldn't care about the consequences if I reported him to the Nazis. I place the flour into my bicycle's basket and slip back into the crowd of shoppers, mentally taking note of the francs left in my purse, just twenty-seven. If I'm lucky, it will get me a few extra eggs. Despite the allowed amounts of goods listed on the ration card, everything is scarce, and costs are growing higher by the day. A few years ago, it was just the luxuries no one could get: ice cream, cigarettes, silk. Now, it seems one cannot find a pinch of sugar without handing over half a day's wages.

Louise was finally able to get the four British soldiers out of the city two days ago. Four grown men and three others are impossible to feed with the rations for three people, especially now that buying anything extra is unaffordable. Rather than split what little food we had and risk the men getting any weaker, Louise chose to go hungry for days at a time to give them her rations.

She's too selfless for her own good. Louise has always tried to do right by everyone else, often at her own expense, even when the world has gone to shambles. *Mother cared about everyone too, would have given the shoes off her feet in the dead of winter if someone else needed them...*

The once-familiar city of Paris I've called home all my life is unrecognizable now, a twisted reality even a madman could never have imagined. The streets are filled with thin and dirty citizens bargaining for whatever they can like vagrants. Foreign soldiers and officers with vivid swastika armbands occupy the cafés, cinemas, and parks, never wanting for anything. Storefronts display a fraction of the goods they did before the invasion, and posters plastered on windows and walls spew nothing but German propaganda. A poster of a boy with rosy cheeks has been all but ruined by rain, one of the old STO program posters the Vichy government started spreading to encourage people to go to Germany for labor in exchange for our prisoners of war. *For you. For yours. For our prisoners* it reads, beneath the boy's smiling face.

Yes, send three of us to Germany in exchange for one prisoner. What a splendid idea! Give Hitler three more slave laborers for one person they've already worked beyond usefulness, I think bitterly, scowling at the poster.

The Vichy government decided they would require men to enlist in the STO and work in Germany. At first, they put up colorful posters and encouraged people to voluntarily join the program, but that didn't fool anyone. The program was law for French citizens, and the facade soon crumbled into open threats to meet the Nazis' demands for manpower. They deported thousands of men to Germany over the following few years, but thousands of others ran away to the resistance to escape the summons. In their despicable attempts to appease the Nazis, they forced our remaining men who weren't dead or rotting in POW camps into servitude to the Reich or into hiding.

All three of my friends, Roger, Léon, and Victor, were called up in 1940. We'd been friends for years and I was the honorary little sister of the group. Perhaps that is what made me so strong-willed—or pigheaded, as Louise would say. They disappeared to the resistance the same day they received their STO summons. They came to bid me a hasty goodbye in the night, ruffling my hair and promising they'd stay safe. I never heard from them again.

We used to sneak into venues and theaters to sample the cuisine and watch the shows. They introduced me to the local farmers when they went to work, and we'd spend hours hiking around the countryside, building stick huts, catching birds and rabbits, and challenging one another to wrestling matches. I won our fights a few times, but, in true older-brother fashion, they made me work for my victories. Those days of childish fun and teenage troublemaking are only a few years gone, yet sometimes it feels like a lifetime has passed since my boys joined the resistance and I got caught up in my own silent fight, hiding fugitive soldiers with Louise and carrying coded messages on my mail route.

"Marie! How are you?" The cloying voice makes my stomach churn, and I curse myself for being too distracted to see my old friend, Jeanne, approach. I'd rather avoid her altogether these days.

To think there was a time I was excited to let her drag me off for a day at the salon, or to convince her to jump into the river with me and ruin our freshly curled hair and pretty makeup...

"Jeanne," I greet her with as sincere a smile as I can muster, forcing myself to also greet the burly man she walks arm in arm with.

The German Gestapo nods to me wordlessly, his face indifferent, and casts an impatient glance at his young, smiling lover, who seems determined to chat. I'm fairly certain he's old enough to be her father, and it sickens me deep in my bones.

"It's a beautiful day. Carl and I have just come from Butte-du-Chapeau-Rouge. You remember that park, don't you? It's been so long since you and I last went."

Because you prefer the company of Nazis.

Jeanne and I used to walk through the Chapeau-Rouge Park after school years ago and toss breadcrumbs from our lunches to the birds. But Jeanne—like everyone—has shown how fickle she really is, where her priorities truly lie, and most people's true colors are hideous.

"Yes, it's been some time," I agree.

Jeanne is undeterred by my short answers, conversing pleasantly as if it's the most natural thing in the world to hang off the arm of the enemy. I bite back the scornful names I'd like to call her, pretending I don't notice the pearls around her neck, or her white blouse that has an almost iridescent sheen and must be some expensive, foreign silk. No doubt gifts from her Nazi lover.

And a Gestapo, no less, I think, barely suppressing my disgust. *An ordinary soldier, I may have been able to forgive her for, but Gestapo... I think even the devil would look upon the Gestapo and shudder.*

When I finally manage to make my escape, agreeing but never intending to meet up with Jeanne when I have some free time as she suggests, I continue home. I slow down when I realize my pace has quickened furiously, not wanting to draw any attention to myself.

Damn paranoid Nazis. They see threats everywhere even where they don't exist, in the way someone walks, in the way a man steps outside to have a cigar, in the way a woman shares her rations with a friend. As Shakespeare said, suspicion always haunts the guilty mind.

Several officers occupy the patio of a café, sipping cups of coffee, and fluffy croissants many don't have the ingredients to make sit untouched on their plates. They don't know what it's like to be hungry, to be forced to go without while foreign invaders live like kings. One German sits along the sidewalk where I pass inches from him, but his attention isn't on the commonfolk. He is turned toward another soldier nearby, making some brief exchange I don't understand.

I snatch the croissant from his plate and slip it discreetly beneath the rest of my rations, never faltering in my steps nor letting the smirk touch my lips.

Let him consider it a small price for all the trouble he and his government have caused us. He doesn't need it as much as André.

. . .

When I get home Louise's soft voice is drifting from the sitting room, speaking once again in German, and the children eagerly echo back whatever she said.

Away from the scrutiny of soldiers, Parisians, and Louise, I scowl as I put our rations away in the kitchen with perhaps more force than necessary. She and Father always enjoyed academia, but teaching the German language was never part of her curriculum when she taught at the primary school. Now, aside from all the other subjects, most days she gives the children lessons in German, and I can't stand to hear the foreign words infecting our one sanctuary from the occupiers.

It's like admitting defeat, teaching the next generation the language of our invaders, because we must accept this is the way life simply is now. Louise used to try to teach me as well, but I adamantly refused. We have been forced to submit to their every whim, and I won't let them take control over my words as well.

I poke my head into the sitting room, looking for André.

Twelve children, mostly girls and a few boys, sit on the rug before the hearth and Louise, sounding out German words one syllable at a time. André sits at the back of the group, the tallest of the children at twelve years old, with the same unruly hair as Fernand, distractedly gazing out the window.

Before Louise can draw his attention, I tap him on the shoulder and quietly indicate for him to follow me back to the kitchen.

"I got you something. What's our rule?" I smirk mischievously, holding my pinky out.

He grins, linking his finger in a promise. "Don't tell Louise."

I give him the croissant I relieved the soldier of, and he thanks me happily before running upstairs, where he can eat it without Louise asking any questions. It's no infraction to steal from a German in my eyes, but Louise would have a fit, even if a small slight like that would only get me in trouble. The trouble she was determined to get into could harm all of us, not just her. How angry I had been at her, how foolish I thought she was to even consider it. I have never changed my mind about that, and I care no more for the resistance now than I did back then. Louise can worry about aiding the Allies, and I will help her if I must, but keeping her out of trouble and ensuring André stays safe like we promised Fernand is all I care about.

4

APRIL 3, 1944

LOUISE

"Ja! Very good, well done, everyone!" I smile proudly, glad to see my students enthusiastically encouraging each other. "We'll pick up our lesson tomorrow morning."

We started the day with a mathematic lesson, and even my youngest students are progressing quickly at the same level as the older children. Afterwards, we briefly covered the French Revolution and the rise of Napoleon, then moved on to German lessons.

I know Marie disapproves, but when war has a tight grip on every corner of the world being able to understand the words of your enemy is invaluable. I've been their teacher for the last four years—first for a year at the primary school, and then for the last three years as a private tutor. I loved the primary school, but after the invasion the pay became too dismal to justify staying. Though it broke my heart to leave, staying home made it easier to take care of André, and parents who didn't trust the Nazis not to infect the school's curriculum with their propaganda were eager to enroll their children with me instead.

The children depart, André runs outside to play with the other boys, and I have the afternoon to clean and try to piece together a meal from what little rations we have.

As I am measuring flour Marie brought home last week for a loaf of bread, there is a knock at the door. My heart stutters and I nearly expect the shouts of SS or Gestapo, until I remember they would have just broken the door down with their rifles.

"Yes, come in!" I call out, quickly washing my hands.

Yvonne is in the sitting room when I come to meet my guest, examining the flashcards the children and I made for studying.

"Yvonne. I was about to start baking. Would you like some coffee? I still have some left from last month's rations."

"That would be lovely, thank you."

Yvonne wanders to the kitchen window as I put on the kettle, and draws the floral curtains closed. "Are we alone?' she asks, glancing toward the door as if expecting someone to appear.

"Yes. Marie went out after she got home from work; André is outside playing with his friends."

She nods. "Good. I have some news to tell you. Good news, but Line business."

I check the hallway to make sure André hasn't returned before I close the door, then silently pour Yvonne and me a bit of coffee and join her at the table.

"I've had word from Michelle," Yvonne begins. "There was a meeting last month in Madrid. A British diplomat and a few others met to discuss the future of the Line. We have new leaders in Paris and Brussels now."

"Thank God." I heave a shuddering sigh, sinking back into my chair. "I was beginning to worry what might become of us."

Without leaders, with our members being betrayed and arrested every day, the Comet Line has been on the brink of collapse, even with our longest-serving members like Michelle Dumon still aiding operations.

Yvonne sips her steaming coffee. "I don't know what his real name is, but an agent we're calling Thomas Rutland will be leading us here in Paris with Michelle and Max. As of now, Max will still be our designated guide from the city to Tours."

Max—known by very few as anything other than this, his code name—has been the guide from Paris to Tours for the last two years.

"So, this must mean we'll be moving more men than usual," I state grimly, drumming my fingers against the table as I glance back at the flour on the counter. After months of the Comet Line being unable to move any soldiers, and with the soldiers continuing to be shot down over the continent, there will no doubt be twice the number of men we need to smuggle to Spain. The longer they're in hiding, the greater the threat of capture becomes.

"As quickly as possible." Yvonne nods. "Some soldiers will come by foot and stay in the farmhouses. Dozens of men all showing up at the station is bound to look suspicious. The first six are supposed to be here in two weeks, all Americans. Michelle wants you and me to host three of them each."

"So soon? Marie and I won't have much time to get any extra rations together."

"Don't worry, they'll only be in Paris for a few days while word is being sent to Tours."

I don't voice my concerns to Yvonne, but I cannot ignore the warning twist in my stomach as we finish our coffee and move on to washing the dishes. The feeling is one I've grown accustomed to in the last three years of risking my life and family every day to help the men who've given everything to help us. It's strange to be so accustomed to the presence of danger that it has become ordinary. Like the moon and stars, like the Germans occupying our city, taking multiple lives into my hands every second of my life has become something that simply *is*.

André chooses this moment to loudly burst into the house,

cutting off our conversation as he barrels into the kitchen, grabs the cap he discarded on the floor earlier, and shouts a quick goodbye before running back out to his friends.

"Boys." Yvonne chuckles, grabbing the broom to sweep up the dirt he tracked across my clean floors.

"Speaking of, where is Daniel?"

"I've left him with my mother for the day," Yvonne says. "She sees him every weekend, but she can never spoil him enough."

All talk of resistance fades into ordinary topics of a grandmother who can never seem to visit her grandson enough, the newest fashion trends, the rising prices, and jokes made at the expense of the Germans and their desperate attempts to paint the war in their favor.

With the Allies in the west and the Soviets holding the line in the east, Germany has few allies left in this fight. We can only pray the end of this madness is near, that our loved ones are still surviving somewhere, and life will once again return to the days of peace and ease before the war.

5

APRIL 10–15, 1944

MARIE

After finishing my mail route, I ride south through the city into the open countryside, breathing deeply the refreshing scent of grass and wildflowers, and I let myself forget why I'm coming this way.

Azure forget-me-nots, yellow tulips and daffodils, violet pansies, and wild lavender grow for miles, reaching to the warmth of the sun, inspiring memories of happier days. Like my mother, flowers were always my favorite part of nature. When I was young, I fancied myself a budding florist, and Mother would let me help her plant her garden. She'd weave beautiful flower crowns for me, and when she laid them in my red hair she'd kiss my freckled cheeks and say all I needed was wings and I'd look like a fairy.

But that all feels like it was lifetimes ago. A farmhouse comes into view, and I must focus again on the present. When Louise told me, after we'd finally got rid of the previous four soldiers, that we'd be hiding three more, I could barely suppress a scream of frustration.

All week, we've been hoarding as much extra food as we can. Every day, I ride out to the farmers with different excuses as to why I need to buy more rations: rats got into our meat, our cheese was spoiled in the sun, a spilled pot of water ruined our flour. It's a wonder none of them have ever suspected anything —or maybe they do and simply don't care.

A small, elderly man appears at the door when I knock. I've known him since I was a teenager, back when my boys would come to till the earth for him and I followed behind dropping seeds into the holes. Jeanne even came with us once. She was absolutely distraught when we ended up having a mud fight, though her mood improved when we teamed up against the boys, tackling them to the ground and smearing mud in their hair in retaliation for our dirtied clothes, and the day ended with laughter and the old farmer reprimanding us.

"Oh, Marie!" He gives a tired smile. "Well, don't stand there dawdling, girl, come in. What are you doing out here?"

"I need extra flour this month," I say, pulling two diamond rings from my pocket and setting them in his extended hand.

"Indeed," he muses, rolling the jewels between his fingers. "Where did you get these?"

"An old friend," I say simply, if somewhat bitterly.

I'd already spent my wages in the market when Louise informed me that we'd need to start preparing for the arrival of more men, so certain avenues had to be taken. Jeanne was so pleased when I came to visit her in the Lutetia Hotel and offered to help pick her outfit for a lavish evening event with her Gestapo officer, Carl. I pocketed some rings, her pearl necklace, and a few pendants and bracelets, but she never noticed. Her collection of gifts was verging on a hoard.

One could almost think her Nazi loves her. A shame he doesn't treat his wife with as much devotion as his French mistress.

. . .

When I return home with the extra flour, having avoided the notice of nosy civilians by sneaking in through the back door of the kitchen, Yvonne is at the sink drying dishes. Little Daniel, who just turned four, sits on the floor under the table, playing with cardboard cutouts of airplanes.

"Hello, Marie. May I help you with that?" Yvonne asks, smiling, nodding to the flour.

"No," I say shortly. She's an amiable woman, like Louise, but I don't have the patience to mask my dislike of her right now, and I turn my back to shove the flour into a cupboard.

It's her fault we're in this situation to begin with. If only she could have just kept her business to herself, I wouldn't have to steal from backstabbing friends to afford rations for soldiers who could get us all killed.

"Louise is cleaning upstairs. André had the house in a right state today," Yvonne goes on, chuckling. "Dirt and leaves tracked through every room. I'm not looking forward to the day when Daniel starts making those sorts of big messes. If only they'd stay little forever!"

If only you'd have thought of your son before you got involved in the resistance...

"Yes, too bad," I mutter, my temper for the day already frayed. "And one day they'll grow up and drag their friends into their messes too."

If Yvonne notices my subtle jab, she doesn't acknowledge it. She's too mild-mannered to rise to such insults, like Louise. Part of me wishes she'd snap, just for the sake of proving that she has feelings when it comes to the danger we're all in.

Louise's heels patter down the stairs. "Yvonne, look at what I've just found!" She hurries into the kitchen, blond hair tied back in a ribbon and a smudge of dust on her rosy cheek. She doesn't notice me as she presents an open book to Yvonne.

Yvonne gasps in astonishment. "You still have them!" she exclaims, gently lifting a delicate orange poppy preserved between the pages. "I thought you said the book disappeared!"

Louise lifts a fragile daisy, and, though I can't see her face, I can hear the sad smile in her voice as she speaks. "It was in my parents' room. My father must have been looking at them."

I remember those flowers... Our mother loved anything colorful and beautiful, and grew a little flower garden regardless of the season. After she died, Louise tried to maintain Mother's flowers, but they withered. Father cried when they started to die. I remember sitting at the window, watching Louise and Yvonne clip the last of the bright blossoms and press them between the pages of a book, so there would always be the memory—and I hated them for it. Louise had made it *her* duty to fill the motherly role, abdicating her place as my sister, and such a burdensome task was for a mother figure to do. And that didn't involve me.

"Marie, where are *your* flowers?" Daniel calls, peeking from under the table.

His voice startles me from my thoughts. I realize my eyes have begun to burn, and my chest aches like a raw wound. I swiftly turn away, pretending to be busy as Louise takes notice of me.

"How was your day, Marie?" she asks softly, but I ignore her.

Thankfully, André chooses this moment to burst inside, flushed, hair ruffled, and the knees of his pants streaked with dirt.

"André! Look at you! Those are your good pants!" Louise groans.

"Will you come play football with us? The teams are uneven, we need more players! Please?" André begs, using his chocolate-brown eyes to pleading perfection like a puppy.

"I want to play!" Daniel grins, jumping up.

"Daniel, love, you're too little," Yvonne says. "Let the older boys play."

"That's alright, mademoiselle!" André smiles, heaving a giggling little Daniel onto his shoulders. "I'm the captain, so he can help me come up with game plays, and, Aunt Louise, he can help you keep score. And Aunt Marie can be on my team!"

"Well, it certainly sounds like you've got everything all worked out." Yvonne laughs.

Louise smiles, finally relenting in the face of André's and Daniel's pleading eyes. "Alright, but don't think you're getting out of a bath later, young man. You're a mess," she says pointedly.

André whoops in victory and I take a deep, steadying breath before reluctantly following them outside. I want nothing less than to play in the noisy street right now. I want to be alone. I want to hug my brother and let myself cry. I want my parents back. I want my friends back, those who ran away and the one who cozies up to the enemy. I want to go to bed, sleep, and hopefully wake up to realize the last few miserable years were only dreams. If only I were so lucky...

Saturday, as it has for the last few years, finds me once again biking through the city, delivering the mail. It's midday by the time I make it to City Hall, my bicycle still piled high with letters and packages, and the bell towering above the brick building chimes twelve o'clock. Sunlight glints blindingly off the windows bearing classical pediments, and the statues, columns, and rounded arches of the building designed by Gabriel Davioud is a pleasant, simplistic change from the ornamental Baroque and Rococo styles of the past.

Several people are waiting in line at the clerk's desk when I enter the vast, tiled room, and other employees and German officers stand in separate groups discussing matters of business.

A few officers glance in my direction, eyeing the stack of papers and parcels I'm carrying. I put on my best oblivious face, fiddling absent-mindedly with one of my braids which make me look younger than twenty. Dismissively, they turn away.

Yes, ignore me, I'm no threat. Just a girl who couldn't possibly be up to no good.

When I reach the desk, I give the blond clerk a timid smile. "Hello, sir," I say, setting the mail before him. "Lovely day to travel."

"Miss Cora," Henry, one of our Line members, greets me, and says, in recognition of the code phrase, "Have you seen the paper this morning?"

I saw the propaganda headlines, more lies about another German victory in some battle, but I shake my head anyway. "I'm afraid not. I've been so busy today."

"Well then, here you are." He grabs the newspaper from his desk. "You can have it. I've already read it twice this morning."

I smile, tucking the folded newspaper under my arm. Between the pages, there will be six documents I am to bring to Yvonne, then the old photographer will take the soldiers' photos and make their papers look as legitimate as possible, so, hopefully, they hold up even under Gestapo scrutiny should it come to that.

Tomorrow already, I think grimly. *The first six Americans will arrive in Paris tomorrow, and then two days later Louise and I must bring three of them to stay in our cellar...*

I give myself twenty minutes between receiving the documents and starting toward Yvonne's home to ensure I am not being followed. I turn down Rue Manin, and immediately regret it; it's too late to block my face when Jeanne, seated alone on the patio of a café beneath a forest-green awning, spots me. I force myself not to sneer as she waves me over with a smile.

I'd rather dine with a Nazi. They may be the enemy, but they were never friends.

"Marie, you must join us." Jeanne grins. A new pearl necklace is fastened around her neck.

"Perhaps another time. I have a lot of work today," I simper apologetically, indicating my full basket of mail. *Not all of us rely on our German lovers for money and food. What a good little housedog you make, Jeanne, a pretty shiny collar and all. Where has your master gone?*

"Oh please, you must!" Jeanne insists. "What's a few minutes?"

Just as I make to refuse again, her Gestapo officer emerges from the café.

"There you are, Carl." Jeanne smiles at him. "I was just asking Marie to join us. That would be alright, wouldn't it? Won't you tell her she's more than welcome?"

He glances between us in annoyance. Momentarily, I think he may slap his whining pet, but he simply takes a seat beside her. "Yes, do join us," he says, more as a command than an invitation.

My grip tightens around the handles of my bike, suddenly damp with sweat, and I am determined not to look at the newspaper in my basket. I relent, "As long as I'm not imposing."

I've never wanted to engage in any conversation less as Jeanne tries to draw me into prattle of our schooldays, the newest fashion trends, and makeup brands like we used to talk about. The Gestapo sitting beside her is a difficult wall to ignore, as is the way his hand boldly roams across her thigh as he ignores our chat and sips his coffee. It's almost as if nothing has changed for her since the invasion. As if she is not wearing a fine Dior coral dress, as if she does not live in luxury with maids while I bargain on the black market for two more eggs.

Oh, to hurl their coffee over that expensive dress and perfect uniform. My fingers twitch with longing to do just that. "This has been wonderful, Jeanne, but I'm afraid—" I start, only for her officer to cut me off coolly.

"Jeanne tells me you work in the mail office," he states, and I nearly shrink under his cold gaze. "I imagine you come across interesting correspondence."

Does he know? My mind quickly turns over what must be the hundreds of coded letters I've delivered to resistance members over the last three years. I clench my fists, feeling them begin to tremble. *No, he couldn't know. We'd be speaking in an interrogation cell if he did. Calm down.*

"Some," I concede meekly. "I once came across one postmarked all the way from Rome."

"Fascinating," he mutters sardonically. "And do you come across anything *irregular?*"

"Well... no. I don't think so, I'm not quite sure what that means."

He seems unimpressed, but not suspecting of my mask of naivety. His gaze flickers to my bicycle. My heart leaps into my throat as he reaches and grabs the newspaper Henry gave to me.

Breathe! I scream at myself, but my racing mind cannot convince my body to cooperate, and I watch in horror as Jeanne's officer examines the propaganda headline with a smirk, sending fervent prayers to any god listening not to let the documents slip out.

"Resistance fighters try to be clever, using unfortunate couriers to carry their messages. Makes no difference to us, we find them all eventually. The war will be done with soon, no underground resistance movements will survive much longer," he says, gauging my reaction. "What do you think of that?"

I think you're losing. I think the Allies are butchering your men and now you're trying to cover your weakness with bold lies of German victories. I think you'll be dead soon.

"I'm happily awaiting the day."

"As you should. Life will be much easier then," he says, holding the newspaper out. "Familiarize yourself. It's quite informative."

"I will," I manage, forcing myself not to snatch my death warrant back too hastily. "Thank you for inviting me to join you, but I'm behind on work. My, how the time goes in good company."

Not until I've rounded the corner of the street do I let out a shuddering breath. My knees are suddenly no more than wisps of air, and I slump onto a bench. The newspaper is still clutched at my side, the corner of a document barely poking from between the pages.

That was too close. Damn it, Louise! Why did we have to get involved in this? I don't want to be another martyr who should have just minded their own family!

When I have calmed my breathing, I head to the limits of the nineteenth arrondissement, where Yvonne's small house is situated along the Canal Saint-Denis. She is crouched among the flowerbeds of her garden with Daniel, who smiles widely, dirt smeared on his chubby cheeks. "Hi, Marie! Look! I'm planting flowers!"

"Hello, Daniel! Yvonne, I have your mail for you."

Yvonne pulls off her gardening gloves, smiling. "Wonderful. I was starting to worry about you, you were supposed to be here almost an hour ago."

"Unforeseen delay," I say shortly, handing her the folded newspaper, glad to be rid of it.

"Daniel, love, would you be a dear and plant the rest of Maman's seeds for her?"

Daniel grins, and drops seeds into the soil as Yvonne slips into the house, leaving me no choice but to follow her as she talks. "I wish you'd been here on time. You could have met Pierre. I was hoping to introduce you, since he'll be the Americans' guide to Tours."

"Pierre?" I wonder trepidatiously. "I thought Max was going to be their guide."

Yvonne shrugs. "He was, but we're expecting more men

than usual to be arriving in the next month, and they need to be moving as quickly as possible. Pierre is helping with travel."

It's reasonable. Too many soldiers hiding in the city at once puts them all at risk of discovery, and they can't be evacuated in large groups as it would draw too much attention. It makes sense that the Line would need more than one operative guide. But no matter how logical the arrangement is, something doesn't feel right; it's as if a few pieces of a completed puzzle have suddenly rotated and no longer fit correctly.

"Who is the guide?" I ask.

"Pierre Boulain."

"I've never heard of him before. Why weren't Louise and I told?"

"It wasn't decided on until a few days ago," Yvonne says, slipping the documents under a loose floorboard beneath a rug. "He was here to discuss the plans with me. He stayed a bit longer so he could meet you, but he had to leave. You missed him by a few minutes."

Somehow, that revelation relieves me more than escaping Jeanne and her officer did.

"You told him I was coming?"

"Yes, of course. I can't host all six men, and he knows you and Louise will be coming back in a few days to take three of them after the photographer gets their documents in order."

Blanching, I stare at her wide-eyed in disbelief. "Why would you do that? He's a guide, he doesn't need to know who is hosting anyone or where. Did you mention us by name?"

"Of course not." Yvonne bristles at the insinuation. "He knows you as Amia and Cora, but that's beside the point. Pierre has been a member of the Line for a long while now. He's done this kind of work with us before. He's completely trustworthy. Max will be busy with other trips out of the city, so Pierre is filling in for him."

Despite her assurances, I can't shake the heaviness that has settled over my chest. Louise and I have worked with Max countless times before. He's been one of the Line's most successful and trusted guides. But I've lost count of how many Comet Line members have been betrayed by spies or traitors who only wish to save their own skin. No doubt hundreds of ordinary people like Louise and me are now rotting in prisons or graves, cursing themselves for trusting the stranger who claimed to be a friend... One learns to be suspicious, and a certain distance must be maintained for the sake of safety.

Maybe Pierre is a genuine ally, but how am I to know for certain? Until I can be sure he poses no danger to my family, I want him to remain a stranger to us. But if I tell Yvonne, she'll talk to Louise, and Louise won't listen to me. They're both unbearably trusting and will no doubt shrug off my concerns.

"What time will the men be arriving tomorrow?" I ask nonchalantly.

"First thing in the morning," Yvonne says.

Then we'll be here first thing in the evening instead of in two days.

Louise will believe me when I tell her we're meant to change the plans, and we can retrieve the men before Boulain comes to meet us. Right now, he only knows us by our code names, and I'd rather keep it that way. A name means nothing if there is no face to pin it to. And if it turns out that I'm only paranoid and he's trustworthy, then there's no harm done.

6

APRIL 16, 1944

LOUISE

The abrupt change in plans was odd, since there seemed to be no obvious reason for it. When Marie returned home yesterday, she informed me that Yvonne had got word from Michelle, instructing us to retrieve the Americans this evening. Since we'll be taking three of the soldiers, Marie, Yvonne, and I will each escort one of them through the city, giving the impression of ordinary couples taking an evening stroll. Sometimes hiding in plain sight is more effective than staying in the shadows. We take different routes every time, being sure to avoid anywhere where people might recognize us and be suspicious.

The evening is warm as Marie and I make our way across the city. Curfew is a few hours away, but the streets are alive with couples sharing meals, families taking strolls and buying tickets to the cinema, everyone enjoying the lingering pleasure of their evenings before the Germans mingling in the crowds enforce the rules of occupation once more.

It takes several minutes after knocking on the door for Yvonne to peek outside, brows shooting up in surprise. "Oh!

Louise, Marie! Well… come in," she stammers, stepping aside. "What are you doing here?"

"What do you mean?" I ask. "We're here to take three of them with us."

Yvonne frowns. "You weren't supposed to be here until Tuesday."

I glance at Marie, waiting for an explanation, but she wears an expression of confusion.

"Oh my, I'm so sorry. I must have mixed the days up!" Marie pleads innocence. "We were talking about when they would arrive and when we would come and then the new guide and… oh, I'm sorry about this!"

Even I almost believe her, but I recognize the disingenuous frown and doe eyes.

Why did she lie to me?

"Well, I suppose we could move the men early? The photographer has already finished their documents, right?" Marie simpers.

Yvonne bites her lip worryingly, glancing down the hall to her son's room. "I can't tonight. Daniel is in bed. I'd planned to bring him to my mother so I could help you with the men. I can't leave him by himself, especially at this hour, and not with men still in the attic."

"We'll be fine, we can do it on our own," Marie says in assurance. "The city is busy tonight; we'll blend in easily."

Yvonne looks to me in question and I cast Marie a look of displeasure, silently demanding an explanation. "We shouldn't risk coming here this late again," I finally concede. "Someone might notice and report us."

"Alright, if you're sure." Yvonne nods and disappears into the attic.

Once she's out of sight, I turn quickly on Marie. "Why did you tell me the plans changed? It seems you're the only one who knew about it."

"Can't we concentrate on the more pressing issue at the moment?" she snaps quietly. "We can talk when we're not out in the open with three reasons to be executed."

I bite my tongue, ignoring her jab at the Allied men we're supposed to protect. She's never hidden her disapproval of our work, and I've become used to her snide comments.

After a moment of quiet shuffling above our heads, Yvonne returns with three men in tow. They all wear plain commoner clothing and they've been able to shave, but the exhaustion is evident in their slumped shoulders and heavy eyes. The tallest of them, a handsome, dark-haired man resembling the American actor James Stewart, stares back at me, and the intensity in his deep, ocean-blue eyes makes my heart skip several beats.

"Gentlemen, this is Amia and Cora. They will be your hostesses for the time being," Yvonne says, gesturing to Marie and me. "Girls, this is Robert, George, and William."

William is the one who has yet to look away from me, and I find I must forcibly tear my gaze away to acknowledge the other men.

"Gentlemen," I greet them in English. "I hope your journey has been safe."

Their faces brighten at the sound of their native language, and they nod.

"Mademoiselle, it's a pleasure to meet you." William smiles, and I am stunned by the perfection of his French accent and words.

"You are French, sir?" I ask.

"No," he says, this time in English, and it suits his languid voice much better. "American, born and raised in Nebraska, but I speak French. It's made life easier lately."

Positively lovely... I quickly shake away the intruding thought of William's voice to focus on the present and give them instructions. Walk confidently. Don't talk and risk your accents being heard. Don't look around too much, or you'll look nervous, and thus suspicious. Stay beside Marie and me and let us manage any issues when and if they arise.

Just as we are preparing to leave, Yvonne takes my hand and squeezes it tightly.

"Be careful, Louise," she whispers.

I pat her hand in assurance. "Of course. We always are. Pugna Quin Percutias."

Fight without arms. It is the Comet Line's motto, an oath, an assurance that one doesn't need weapons or violence to resist, only a mind and heart of strong will.

"Pugna Quin Percutias," she repeats, then tiptoes down the hall to ensure Daniel is still safe and sound asleep.

Marie offers her arm to Robert, who barely looks seventeen, and I take William's, while George walks beside him. We space our departures, then rejoin one another on the street, hearts pounding. No matter how many times I lead Allied soldiers down the German-infested streets without being caught, I wonder if this is the day our luck will run out. Marie carries on in French, smiling and making comments about the picture we supposedly saw at the cinema, while Robert, who doesn't understand a word of what she's saying, smiles and nods obliviously.

"I suppose we ought to make conversation too," William says, tucking my arm further into his own.

"That would be wise," I agree quietly, letting my gaze wander over the crowd for anyone who might be paying us too much attention. "Where did you learn to speak French?"

"University," William says. "I took some classes when I was studying medicine, and then I traveled abroad for a few months with a friend back in '38. Never imagined I'd visit a second time like this. And how did you learn English?"

"My father taught me. He learned from a friend of his in the trenches of the Great War."

"That's remarkable. My father also fought in the trenches,

for eight months. Terrible times, but he said it gave him a much better appreciation for life."

"I suppose it does for all of us. I've learned to appreciate the simple things now that they've become so scarce." I glance up at William, and his deep blue eyes hold mine in a trance. We should probably be speaking of more trivial things for the sake of our guise, but there is something gentle and inviting about him, something that compels even a stranger to bare their heart to him. "I think, in peacetime, we forget what our fathers have seen and never want us to."

William nods in agreement. "I do believe you're right. My father was... very upset that I was joining the air force. I imagine it's difficult to watch your son run headfirst into war when he's still too young and dumb to truly understand what it means."

The image of my father's devastated face, when Fernand told us he was going to war, reenters my mind. Father's gentle face crumpled, and he cried as if Fernand had said he was to be executed. He understood the dreadful cost of war, paid with blood and the sons of our country, and never thought the day would come that his own son might suffer as he did.

"Well, we'll get you home. Then your father can give you a proper dressing-down."

William chuckles. "He gave up trying to discipline me years ago. Although, all his lessons have started to sink in lately. And it only took twenty-nine years! Better late than never, I suppose."

The attention of three Germans standing vigilant on the steps of a bank turns toward us, and their suspicious, appraising faces makes my grip around William's arm stiffen slightly. Before I can think of something to put them at ease, Marie laughs, a girlish noise that sounds frivolous coming from her, then her voice drops to a low and sultry tone as she speaks to Robert, but loud enough to reach the Germans' ears and bring a blush to my cheeks. The suggestive way she leans and murmurs words in his ear that only ladies of the night should know amuses the soldiers, and they chuckle, gesturing and jeering among themselves.

"Clever girl. Quick thinking, too," William mutters as we pass the soldiers, who don't spare us another glance.

"She's a good actor," I say, frowning. *And a good liar...*

Once we are safely home, and William, George, and Robert are hidden in the cellar, I allow myself to breathe easily. Marie, however, remains tense, her eyes narrowed. I follow her to the kitchen and halt at the door, crossing my arms over my chest.

"Well, we're no longer out in the open," I begin. "Care to explain yourself?"

Marie scoffs. "Oh, don't talk to me like that. I'm not a child, and I won't be spoken to like one."

I hold my breath for a few seconds, trying to control my rising frustration. "I'm speaking to you as your sister. And I want to know why you put our plans in jeopardy today. Do you realize what your impulsiveness could have cost us?"

"*My* impulsiveness?" Marie demands in disbelief.

"Please, let's not rehash that conversation." I sigh heavily, rubbing my eyes. "Joining the Line is not a decision I made on a whim." *Unlike you*, I add silently. *You'd barely thought about it for an hour when you decided to dive in headfirst beside me.* "Tell me what happened today."

"Did you know there was supposed to be a new guide?" she asks. "Yvonne said his name is Pierre Boulain."

"No, I wasn't aware. I know of him, though. Pierre has been a member of the Line for a long time. He's guided several groups before."

"I know, Yvonne told me. But did you know she told him about us? She even told him what day we were supposed to be there for them. He doesn't need to know us. You know as well as

I do it's more dangerous for us the more people involved. That's the whole point of code names and personally knowing as few members as possible."

"It's not as if she's told a stranger."

"She might as well have," Marie huffs, crossing her arms. "We've never met him. It bothers me that she told him our plans. It's not his business who hides who. If he's a guide, all he needs to know is how many men he's escorting and when. Knowing anything else puts everyone else at risk. I had a bad feeling about it."

"You risked the police catching us for a *bad feeling*? What if a patrol stopped us? Two of them don't even speak French, and Yvonne wasn't there to help us! Do you realize how dangerous this was? I can't believe you'd risk something like this without even telling me first."

She glares. "It's not as if you'd have listened to me. I wasn't going back to meet Boulain. If Yvonne wants to act like a fool, fine. It's on her and Daniel's heads, not ours."

"Marie!" I snap. "How could you be so—"

She brushes past me as if I were a ghost and disappears up the stairs.

So careless! So unfeeling! I want to scream after her, unable to believe the way she disregards me. Not for the first time, I wonder how people as kind and loving as our parents could have raised such an angry heathen of a girl. She was always rebellious but, when our mother passed away a few months after her tenth birthday, it was like an entirely different girl took her place. A girl who couldn't bear to look at me or hear me sing, a girl who glared with contempt at every meal I made, every dress I mended for her. A girl in whose eyes I could see the accusation, "you're *not* our mother." Sometimes, I think the day our mother died was when Marie and I truly and irrevocably lost each other.

Shaking the thoughts away, I gather bread and cheese for

the men. The wooden stairs groan with age as I descend into the darkness, letting the lamps upstairs light my path.

"I've brought you supper." I attempt to smile at them. "You must be famished."

They murmur their thanks and descend on the rations first as a feral pack would its prey, but quickly remember themselves. The youngest, Robert, flushes under my gaze and regains his manners.

"It's been a while since we've had a decent meal," William offers with an apologetic smile, and the candlelight makes his eyes glow, sharply defining his handsome features.

Despite the twinge of hurt in my heart and my irritation with Marie, I find myself genuinely smiling back at him, and feel my heart lighten.

7

APRIL 18–22, 1944

MARIE

In usual fashion after another of our arguments—of which there have been manyLouise and I haven't spoken to one another for the last two days. She's still angry that I lied to her about the plans changing, and I find her indignation both ironic and frustrating.

As I sort through the letters in the mail office, my heart clenches at the sight of mine and Louise's code names. I normally come across at least one letter intended for another Comet Line member—it's easy to send coded messages through me—but it doesn't make the task easier no matter how often I do it. Usually I can tell by the writing who a letter has come from, but I don't recognize the long, scrawling handwriting on this envelope. I tuck it into my pocket and hurry to finish organizing the mail.

A few hours into my route, my curiosity about the mysterious sender of the letter becomes too much to ignore. I've nearly delivered mail to the wrong people, distracted as I am by the thought of the letter. My anxiety is obvious, and, if anyone suspects me of being up to no good, I can't be caught with anything connected to the Comet Line.

Suddenly, a blaring siren jolts me. The alarm rolls over me in waves of dread, high pitches dying into low tones that seem to warn of the end of time. Without another coherent thought, I jerk my bike around and flee, weaving through frightened civilians as they try to gather their bearings and escape the streets. Amid the chaos, children scream as their parents drag them, pointing up to the sky.

Overhead, the black silhouettes of Allied planes rumble across the sky, and, suddenly, black dots are hurtling toward the ground with deadly intent. The first explosion couldn't be more than a mile off, and it rattles the earth and the wheels of my bike. Mail flies out of my basket, forgotten in the whirl of panic, but I don't stop. I am blind and deaf to anything but the thunder of my heart and the mental pathway home that I've mapped out.

Louise is waiting at the door when I arrive. Her terrified eyes settle on me with relief. "Marie, hurry! Get inside!" she shouts, and I throw my bike down and dash inside. Louise slams and bars the door, barely breathing, then drags me down to the cellar.

"I've already brought water and rations down. André is safe. He's scared, but he's fine," she babbles nervously. "Are you alright, Marie? The planes sound so close to us. Are you hurt?"

The flicker of a candle catches my attention. "What—"

"There was nothing to be done." Louise sighs, rubbing her eyes wearily.

In one corner, André sits wrapped in a quilt and casting curious glances at the other side of the chilly room. The three Americans appear almost relaxed, like the sound of bombs and airplanes hasn't bothered them for a long time, and they cast uncertain glances at André.

I scowl at Louise, snatching her wrist quickly.

"I know," she whispers. "Please, not now. He's terrified

enough. I've already explained that he can't say anything about them."

André never should have known about them! They never should have been here at all!

I want to shake her until she sees sense, berate her for the compromising positions she's been putting us in since she made this life-threatening decision on our behalf. For now, I bite back all my scathing words and sit next to André.

"Are you alright?" I ask, winding a protective arm around his shoulders.

Another bomb shakes the cellar, making the ground groan like some long-dormant beast awakening, and André buries his head between his knees. Louise settles on the other side of him and rubs comforting circles over his back.

"We're safe here. Don't worry, nothing is going to happen to you," she says soothingly, but he refuses to look at either of us.

We try to coax him from his fearful position and assure him everything will be alright, but he refuses to move. As the cellar walls quake and the siren blares, André's shoulders shake with silent tears, and no words or hugs will bring him peace.

Fernand, I wish you were here... The image of André curled in upon himself is painfully familiar. When André's mother died seven years ago, he would cry for hours, and no one but Fernand and his soothing but firm words could comfort him. There is such power in a father's strength that sometimes it's all that can make a sad, confused little boy feel safe.

There is a hesitant shuffling. One of the Americans has moved closer, and sits down across from us. I can't remember his name. I've never bothered to learn any of their names.

"Bonjour," he greets André. "André, is it?"

The foreign voice makes André tense, but then curiosity triumphs over his fear and he peeks up.

"Hello, young man," the American tries again, holding his hand out. "My name is William Chappell."

Tentatively, after a quick glance between Louise and me, André shakes William's hand. While I try to silently discourage him, Louise gives a soft, encouraging smile, and my fingers twitch with the urge to slap her.

"That's a strong grip you've got there," William says. "You must be the strongest boy your age. How old are you? Sixteen?"

André's lips quirk. "Twelve," he corrects.

"Only twelve? I never would have guessed. You certainly look like the man of the house. You must have dug this basement all by yourself to protect your aunts." William grins. "You know, we've got a basement in America."

"You have a bomb cellar too?" André asks in astonishment.

"Oh, no, not for that, thank God. Sometimes we have big tornadoes and have to hide in the basement. But I'm sure that wouldn't bother you much."

"You're from America? Are you a soldier?"

William nods. "I'm from Nebraska, and I'm a pilot."

"My dad's a soldier, but he doesn't fly planes."

"Well, *I* think the bravest men are the ones on the ground. Like you and your father. It's easy to be up in the air, not so much to be down here where the greatest danger is."

To my surprise, André flashes a toothy smile. He lowers his knees, straightening up. Fascinated by a man from the mysterious land across the Atlantic, he seems to easily forget his fear, and badgers William with dozens of questions. William is happy to oblige, regaling him with stories of tornadoes, racing horses with his cousins, and learning to fly jets and shoot guns.

I should be glad he is distracting André, but I can't help the bitterness that stings my heart. Fernand should be the one to make his son feel better, Louise and I should be the ones who know how to make him feel protected, not some stranger soldier.

But he's not coddling him, I think. William hasn't once said that everything will be alright, or that he's safe, like a mother would do for her child. He talks to him as he would to another man, makes him feel like a protector rather than the one who needs protecting. It's in a mother's nature to nurture and shield through her love, but a father's instinct is more stern, guided by a need to make his child strong when the time comes to face the world beyond their parents' protection.

Fernand, please come home. A boy needs his father just as he does his mother. No matter how much Louise and I love him, we are no substitutes for either.

At last, once half the day has gone, the bombs stop, the sirens go silent, and André must be ordered to come back upstairs rather than remaining to talk with the Americans, practically fidgeting with curiosity. Louise reiterates the importance of secrecy and makes him swear to never utter a word to anyone about them.

Once he's gone upstairs to his bedroom, Louise turns to me expectantly, as if waiting for a grenade with the pin pulled to explode. Hours ago, I would have taken the opportunity to scream at her for her idiocy, but right now I don't even want to look at her. I storm out the door to gather up the bit of mail that managed to make it home with me. It's one thing to hide Allied soldiers, but another entirely for André to know about them. He's just a boy, and he might accidentally say something he shouldn't. One slip of the tongue is all it would take to get us all killed.

And she lectures me *on putting us in danger.*

The next day passes in a similar fashion. Although the bombers don't come near Paris, the sirens are sounded and we spend hours in the cellar, listening to the radio for news. The bombing yesterday was barely three miles from us in Noisy-le-Sec and killed almost five hundred people.

The news of the casualties made the Americans look more gloomy and wretched than usual. As the days drag on and we are repeatedly rushing to barricade ourselves in the cellar, the Americans grow somber. They seem torn between excitement and concern. On one hand, the Allies are close, fighting the Germans and claiming more victories. On the other, we are all stuck in the middle beneath their war, sitting ducks waiting for a bomb to be dropped on us.

By the fourth day after the first bombs fell, there have been two additional air raids and, according to the radio, over a thousand are dead.

To my dismay, William is once again sitting close to us, listening to André's stories about playing football in the streets and helping Fernand in his tailor shop before he left for war. The other men respect the distance there should be and refrain from approaching or speaking unless spoken to. Louise allows William to sit at her side as he converses with André, ignoring the disapproving frown I shoot in her direction.

She shouldn't let André get attached to them. Once we finally get rid of them, we'll never see them again. Though, it may be a while before they can leave now. The bombings may have interrupted the escape routes, and we'll have to wait for word from—

The letter! I nearly gasp aloud when I suddenly remember the letter addressed to Cora and Amia from a few days ago. In all the chaos of the Allied bombings, I completely forgot about it.

Louise glances questioningly at me, but I offer no explanation as I scurry to my bedroom upstairs. The house is dim, but the faint sunlight is such a jarring contrast to the pitch black and few candles that it stings my temples. My perception of time is sensitive and skewed like my vision, and a quick glance out the window at the setting sun tells me it's dusk and not dawn.

The clothes I was wearing the first day of the bombings are still where I clumsily discarded them, beside the oak dresser in my bedroom. In my haste to take the opportunity between sirens to don clean clothes, I forgot to bring them down to be washed. I open the letter and scan the bottom of the page, to see that the signature is Yvonne's code name.

Dear Amia and Cora,

I've spoken with Pierre and, now that everything is in order, we can start the trip. Please bring your three suitcases to my home on the 23rd. There are still quite a few things left to pack! Pierre has booked the earliest train possible, so be sure to be here once curfew is lifted. I look forward to seeing you then.

Sincerely, Rose

Pierre's name inked onto the page makes a shudder roll down my spine, and I fight the urge to crumple it in my fist.

Yvonne is communicating directly with Pierre Boulain, but we've heard nothing from any other Line leaders... Pierre likely returned to see her on the day that Louise and I were originally supposed to come for the Americans. Perhaps that was when he and Yvonne worked out a date and time to arrange for us to meet with the six Americans. I wonder if any of the Line's leaders have been informed of this arrangement?

It's half past seven. The time that lies between now and when curfew is lifted tomorrow when Pierre wants to meet is less than twelve hours... If Louise sees this letter from Yvonne, she'll want to bring the men in the cellar to meet with Pierre, or at least go by herself to confirm the plans still stand, and then Pierre will find out who she is.

With all the soldiers that have been arriving recently and the many more that are sure to come, the Line will want to get them all out of Paris as soon as possible, especially if they wish to avoid being delayed by more air raids and because the longer they remain in one place the greater their risk of being caught. I doubt the instructions in this letter have changed. If they have, Yvonne will come to us in person rather than sending another letter and risking us not receiving it in time.

But I'm not willing to risk that yet. We still have no idea who Pierre is, and I don't like the thought of acting on orders not explicitly from one of the Line's leaders. No good can come of it; I know that well enough if the terrible months when our organization's leaders were arrested, and the Nazis were hunting our members down like hounds, are anything to go by.

Louise has perfected the role of homemaker over the years, but with that comes the motherly heart that wants to believe the best of everyone. It's a dangerous mindset to have when you're the one surrounded by wolves and hiding a steak behind your back. Yvonne, like Louise, has faith in too many people, and perhaps a bit of God's good grace if they've managed to remain undiscovered by the authorities, who, by now, I must believe are either negligent or stupid.

Louise is strong, but not in the way she needs to be. If we're caught, it's not just her life and mine at stake. It is André, our friends, the soldiers she cares so much about. We don't need another mother figure to rely on for love and coddling. We need what Fernand and Father were, fierce protectors and providers who have no qualms about putting their own needs aside, no reservations against doing whatever it takes to ensure their family stays safe.

But I'm suited for that role. Louise thinks me inconsiderate and callous, but someone must be. If Louise is too gentle to do it, then I will. Some days, it means stealing from the enemy, and often I have considered leaving for labor, like Roger, Léon, and Victor were called up for. I only know it means prioritizing my family over any resistance or soldiers Louise is sitting in the cellar with and waiting for reliable instructions from resistance members I know we can trust.

I lock the door in case Louise wanders up to see what had

me in such a hurry, unlatch the window, letting the warm air fill the room, then strike a match to light a candle. I dip one corner of the letter into the flame, watching silently as it catches, and the air feeds its heat and carries the scent of burning paper away as it crumbles delicately beneath my fingers.

8

APRIL 25, 1944

LOUISE

My students haven't returned to lessons since before the first bombing. It's understandable that parents are reluctant to let their children out of their sight with the threat of Allied bombs falling on the city; I haven't let André wander far from the house either.

However, despite the lack of regular contact with his friends and the hours I've insisted he is home within, André doesn't seem to mind. Ever since he discovered the Americans in the cellar, he frequently asks to bring them their meals, and he enjoys talking to William. He's also begun to show more interest in our daily lessons, a miracle I wish I could tell Fernand about. William's stories about studying at university to become a doctor and traveling around the world as a student and a pilot have enthralled André the way even I could never manage. Particularly, he's shown a keen interest in learning English. For the sake of maintaining his newfound enthusiasm for knowledge, I've begun to teach him the basics of the language.

I glance expectantly to the kitchen door, but there is no sign of André fidgeting impatiently and waiting to follow me to the cellar. He's been in his room all morning. Since devouring his breakfast like a boy starved, he has been pleasantly quiet, buried in the English textbooks I gave him.

Best not to bother him, I decide, being mindful not to catch my heels on the stairs as I slip into the cellar with the men's rations.

A muffled voice babbles down below, unintelligible at first, then I catch the slowly spoken English words, "My name... is André."

William's quiet, languid voice follows, sending a shiver down my spine. "Very good!"

A candle burns close to the floor, the single flame casting soft light over André and William sitting across from each other. I hesitate, the breath catching in my throat at the scene before me, and I watch silently as André demonstrates his newly learned words and William smiles encouragingly. I cannot find my voice to scold André for coming down without me, trying as I am to swallow the lump in my throat.

It's like watching a father and son... like looking back in time and seeing Fernand grinning with pride as André showed him the first pair of shoes he made.

My presence catches William's attention. He smiles sheepishly but doesn't interrupt André as he talks eagerly. I haven't the heart to speak. André was always eager around Fernand. He only ever wanted to be like his father and make him proud, and he's taken an immense liking to William.

But he can't stay. My smile slips, and a wave of sadness crushes me. William will leave, like the many that have come before. André will never again see the pilot with his stories of flying, travel, and university that have fascinated him. He's already lost his father, and doesn't know if he's alive or dead...

Maybe I shouldn't let him keep coming down here. It will break his heart when William is gone. The thought of William leaving makes my heart twist painfully in a way it never has before. I've grown fond of all the soldiers I've hosted, like any caregiver does, but something about his imminent departure feels heavy and sharp, like a knife poised and ready to pierce.

I clear my throat, drawing André's attention. "Aunt Louise!" He grins guiltily, but unapologetic.

He frowns with disappointment when I inform him it's time for chores, but nods, and waves goodbye to the men. I usher him upstairs, not daring to look back even though I feel a pair of ardent blue eyes following me.

All day, I've been able to think of little else but the soldiers beneath our feet. All I can think of to blame my persistent fixation on is the many days they've been here, and André's attachment to them. We never housed any Allied men for more than two weeks, excluding the months the Comet Line's leaders were arrested and we were on our own, but it's already been nine days since they arrived. Nine days that were originally intended to only be a few.

What is going on? I expected the bombings would have interfered with the routes, but it's been three days since the bombs stopped, and Marie hasn't received any news.

The counters are already clean, but still, I find myself anxiously wiping them down a fourth time. Marie and André went to bed hours ago, but neither my mind nor body is ready to lie down to leave tonight's troubles for the morning.

As I am searching for something else to clean, the unmistakable click of the back door opening catches my ears. Ice rushes through my veins and I hold my breath, trembling, as I grab a carving knife. I've always kept a spare key beneath the flowerpots in case the need arises, so it must be someone who knows about the key, but I don't dare make myself known to tonight's intruder. I tiptoe to the door and crack it open to peek into the sitting room.

Two shadows are inside. One ushers the other to sit on the floor, and the ragged breaths coming from the one on the floor accompany the faint scent of blood. Suddenly, the second figure is moving toward the kitchen, and I tighten my grip around the knife, heart thundering.

The figure pulls the door open, and recoils as we come face to face. "Amia!" a woman gasps, and I quickly recognize the Comet Line member who has entered my home.

"Michelle!" I gape, finding myself staring at an equally startled and distressed Michelle Dumon. "What are you doing here? Who else is here?"

"He's been shot," she whispers urgently. "He's an American. I need to dress his wound."

I nod without further question, gathering rags, water, gauze, and a bottle of alcohol from the kitchen for Michelle while she makes sure the doors and windows are locked. As she peels off the man's blood-soaked shirt, I look anxiously out the window. The streets outside are dark and empty. No Germans, flashlights, or dogs. Michelle rolls up a piece of cloth for him to bite down on, and breathes a sigh of relief upon realizing the bullet is not embedded in his shoulder.

"What happened?" I ask, lighting another candle for her.

She frowns deeply and casts me a withering glance before she goes on trying to stop the bleeding. "Gestapo," she mutters. "This was as far as I could bring him. We went through the canal, then the park. We can't be traced here."

"Where did you come from?"

"Can you take him in?" she asks rather than replying. "I'll explain everything, but I can't risk bringing him anywhere else."

Tears of pain and grief fill the soldier's eyes as Michelle washes the gunshot wound, and, as the fire illuminates his glistening eyes, it's difficult to see him as anything but a young boy.

Marie is going to have a fit... I frown but nod. "Of course."

I scrounge up an extra sheet, a bit of bread, and we help him into the cellar. Though we move nearly soundlessly, the men stir as if sensing the unordinary even in sleep. William is the first to wake, locking eyes with the new soldier, and recognition draws his brows together.

"Jack? What are you doing here?" he asks, offering his arm for support as Jack winces with every movement. William looks worriedly at Jack, then back at the others, who are now sitting upright with identical expressions of shock and confusion.

They know each other? How could they—

The air drains from the room, the shadows bear down and crush the breath from my lungs. My eyes snap to Michelle, silently pleading for her to deny the possibility darkening my thoughts, but she only sends me a despondent look, and I follow her back to the kitchen. Suddenly, the promise of an explanation of the abrupt arrival of this soldier who escaped the Gestapo, who knows William, feels like impending oblivion.

"There was an ambush on one of our members tonight," Michelle begins after a deep breath. "I had business with another Line member and saw it happen as I was passing her house. It was Yvonne."

"Oh, God—" I gasp, clutching my tightening chest, barely making it to a chair.

Michelle lays a hand on my shoulder. "I'm sorry, Louise. I wish I could've done something... The Gestapo arrested two of the Americans she was hiding. Only Jack escaped. He said they were going to meet their guide when the Gestapo caught them. I don't know who gave her these instructions, we haven't been in contact with her since before the bombings."

But she was in contact with Pierre Boulain... "An infiltrator?" I suggest shakily.

"I think so. From what Jack said, it seemed like the Gestapo were waiting for them. Did Yvonne mention anything about this to you?"

My stomach turns uneasily. "She said we were supposed to have a different guide to Spain. Marie and I were supposed to meet him too, but Marie switched the day you wanted us to take three of the men, so we never did. Yvonne said it was Pierre Boulain."

Her grip on my shoulder tightens, face growing rigid with contempt. "That *rat!* I told them!" she hisses, head dropping into her hands. "He's a German agent, I've known that for months! When I was briefly arrested, I was able to talk with one of our other members, and she told me it was Pierre who turned her in to the police. I told the British MI9 agents leading Operation Marathon, but they were incredulous when I accused him! 'He's a trusted member,' they said. He was even aiding the operation establishing the forest-camps for Allied airmen to hide in. They were even going to give him money to establish a forest-camp in Belgium! They wouldn't believe me without hard proof, wouldn't even let me warn anyone because they didn't want me to cause *unnecessary* panic! I had no idea he and Yvonne were communicating."

Ice claws down my spine like a serrated knife, and the realization settles over me with terrifying clarity. *Pierre betrayed Yvonne. He wanted to betray us. If Marie hadn't tricked me, we might have been arrested, but we're still not out of danger.*

"Do we need to go underground?" I ask, mentally starting a list of all the things that need to be done. "I know Yvonne would never betray us, but mine and Marie's positions are still compromised now that she's been arrested. They might force her to reveal us. Should I..."

My voice trails away into the dark void of the kitchen. Michelle's eyes have grown heavy with sorrow, the pitiful sadness one feels when looking upon a small child whose parent has died, who doesn't comprehend the finality of death.

"No..." I deny, choking back a sob.

She reaches out to take my trembling hand. "I'm so sorry."

Had a bullet pierced my heart in this moment, the pain would be a welcome relief to that which now seizes my soul in its cold, merciless fists. Soft hands brush away the warmth trailing down my cheeks, and suddenly I am embraced in a pair of comforting arms that remind me all too much of Yvonne.

"Her son? W-where is... Daniel?" I struggle for words between sobs.

"I don't know," Michelle whispers. "I'm going to her home now to see if he's still there. If not, I'll check with their relatives."

I shake my head. "No. Go to her mother first. Yvonne never... she would have taken him to her mother if she had plans for tonight."

"Alright, I will," Michelle says, moving to stand.

I rise quickly with her. "Wait! What about the men? We still have—there's four now. It's been two weeks, Michelle, what's going on? When are they leaving?"

For a fleeting moment, I resent the soldiers downstairs, wishing they would simply disappear and take this dreadful nightmare with them.

She shakes her head apologetically. "I'm sorry, but I don't know. With all the recent bombings, our routes are being disrupted, and trains are being stopped. We don't want to keep risking moving men by foot over long distances. Too many of our helpers have been arrested these past weeks. It's too dangerous to move *anyone* right now. We're going to give things some time to calm down, then we'll send word, hopefully by next month. And Louise"—she grasps my shoulders, her eyes commanding and intense—"do *not* act without instructions explicitly from Max or me. Pierre Boulain is a traitor, but there are sure to be others, remember that."

"I won't forget."

Not again. Yvonne is gone, but God has seen fit to give me another chance. I won't let this happen to Marie or André.

9

MAY 1, 1944

MARIE

It's been difficult to look at André since the Gestapo killed Yvonne. My heart aches to see Louise's puffy, bloodshot eyes as she forces smiles and tries to put on a brave face, but it is André's presence I cannot bear. Despite Michelle's efforts, she couldn't find little Daniel, and the possibility that the Gestapo may have gotten to him first is a reality that breaks my heart, makes me terrified to think it could've been us if I hadn't made the decision to avoid Pierre Boulain.

Louise and I could have been killed like Yvonne. André might have disappeared like Daniel. Fernand and Father, missing and possibly still alive like Yvonne's husband, might have come home to learn of our deaths...

These grim thoughts have been impossible to shake away over the last miserable week, like a dark stain that refuses to be washed away, deepening my resentment for the state of the world and our crumbling lives.

As I bitterly count my wages—which have been cut again—I contemplate just tossing the few worthless francs in the river or the hearth. It's barely anything anyway and couldn't buy me even a few eggs.

When I demanded an explanation from my supervisor, she only acknowledged me when I slammed a fist on her desk. The grievances of a "young, ill-tempered pouffiasse," as she put it, were none of her concern, and I should be grateful to have a job at all. How I would have loved to slap the spectacles off her face, demand she confess that *her* paycheck hadn't been cut in years.

At the market, I take only what is listed on the ration cards. My stomach grumbles in longing as I pass a café where the divine scent of sugar and bread wafts out the windows. Now that there are four soldiers living with us, with my pay being cut again and goods growing scarce, we'll be going hungry for the foreseeable future.

And the foreseeable future only seems to grow bleaker by the day.

A commotion down the street draws my attention. Civilians are gathered outside an apartment building, looking at one another with concern as shouts emanate from a high window. A van and a car are parked on the street along the sidewalk, and three stone-faced Gestapo in their black coats and caps stand astride them. Jeanne's officer, Carl, is among them, indifferent and cold, as if whatever disorder upstairs is naught but a passing inconvenience to him.

BANG!

I flinch at the gunshot, then a woman's wails of misery. I stop with the growing crowd of onlookers, fearful, anxious curiosity winning out over my self-preservation instinct in such close proximity to a group of Nazis.

The doors of the apartment building are kicked open. Soldiers emerge, wrestling a sobbing woman outside as she pleads in vain. More soldiers follow, dragging a man's limp body, which leaves sickening streaks of blood on the sidewalk, and escorting a man, a woman, and a terrified little boy at gunpoint. The last three walk with slumped shoulders that cannot hide the yellow stars sewn to their rumpled clothes.

Jews...

Thousands of them were rounded up like cattle a few years ago, then they all disappeared on trains. Yet it appears that, somehow, some of them managed to hide from the Germans with the help of French civilians.

And look where it's got them, I think, staring at the crimson smears on the ground, the crying Frenchwoman, and the little family that was caught despite her efforts.

The crowd murmurs as everyone including the dead body is shoved into the van. There are silent looks of sympathy and dismay, and then there are jeers and laughter, jokes and insults thrown without care for the fate of Jews or anyone who would dare harbor them.

Jeanne's officer, Carl, announces something to the crowd. Despite his cutting, businesslike tone, the ghost of a sadistic smirk twists his lips.

He's enjoying this...

As he turns to climb into the car with the other Gestapo, his eyes catch mine. He tips his cap in greeting, but the shudder that rakes down my spine makes it feel like a threat. The grinning skull on his cap seems to mock me from above his predatory gaze. *See what happens when you hide enemies of the Reich? See what we'll do to you and your family?*

The van and car disappear, leaving the people to shake away the disturbing events they witnessed to go about their lives. A face among the crowd draws my attention, a young woman already looking at me with concern and a tinge of guilt. For once, I let my contempt for Jeanne show, glaring at her with all the betrayal that's boiled beneath my mask for years.

How have we come to be on opposite sides of this sidewalk? You were my friend, and now I can barely stomach the sight of you. Collaborator.

Without a word or a backwards glance, I push my bike onwards down the street, around the drying pools of blood and Jeanne, ignoring her like the ghost she has become to me.

A flash of color draws my eye, and I am faced with a Vichy STO poster, pasted conveniently beside the door of the STO building. The boy on the poster grins, silently encouraging people to give up their lives here in France to work in Germany, promising better food and pay to anyone who volunteers for the forced labor service rather than be deported against their will. I stare back at him, furious at Jeanne for her disloyalty, at Roger, Léon, and Victor for disappearing from my life, at Louise for her misguided sense of duty to the Allies, at Fernand and Father for leaving us behind, at our government for abandoning us.

My basket is nearly empty, my wages are a soft weight in my pocket, and the thought of the men in our cellar having a share of it makes our poverty all the more miserable.

For years, the Germans have ensured that no matter how much money I make, how much food I buy, steal, and swindle, it's never enough. Louise hasn't helped much on that front either. Maybe if we'd never joined the resistance, there'd be enough to get by, no reason to fear for our lives. If I were to leave, it would be one less mouth to feed, one less person who knows about our connection to the Comet Line, and I could send home more food and money than I could ever hope to make here in Paris.

But would that make me a collaborator? I wonder, curling my fingers tightly around the francs in my pocket. The STO would send me away to aid the German war effort; maybe I'd be assembling bullets the Germans would use to shoot at the Allies, or making uniforms or parachutes. But I'd be providing for Louise and André, even if I'd be helping the enemy at the same time...

It doesn't matter. I'm not like Jeanne. It would be to keep my family safe and fed, not for my own selfish pleasures. I can't do this anymore. I won't. I'm done being helpless, a resistance puppet dreading the day my strings are cut.

If I were ever caught, my knowledge of the Comet Line and all the members I deliver messages to could be turned into a weapon for the Nazis in exchange for my family's safety... I'd rather it not come to that, for it is an option—if offered—I'd take without a second thought. If I am gone, it will be safer for Louise and André; one less liability to worry about, and I will be able to provide them with the money they need.

I push my bike inside the STO building, unwilling to leave it unattended for someone to snatch, but relent and let the doorkeeper mind it as I join the line of men at the reception desk.

My boys would drop dead of shock if they could see me now, I think. Roger, Léon, and Victor would no doubt be having fits if they knew their "fire ant"—as they've vexingly been calling me for years—even entertained the idea of bending to the Germans' will. But they didn't have anyone to look out for. Roger was an orphan, Léon stayed in Paris while his mother and sister left before the invasion, and Victor grew up with his uncle, who was the sort of man who punched first and forgot to ask questions after drowning in alcohol. There was nothing to hold them back. I love them dearly, but they don't have the same responsibility to anyone the way I do to Louise and André.

When I make it to the front there is a pudgy man with spectacles sitting behind the desk, nose buried in a pile of papers. "Summons letter," he requests blandly.

"I don't have one."

My voice gives him pause and he looks up, gauging me with surprise and curiosity.

"My name is Marie Beaufoy. I want to volunteer for the program."

He sputters incredulously at this. "This is very irregular, mademoiselle."

"But not unheard of," I retort. "Women are not forbidden from volunteering. I'm sure I'm not the first."

"Well, no, but... well, regardless, all workers must be of age. I'm sure your father—"

"I'm twenty," I cut him off, producing my documents for proof. "I'm well of age. The law says even women are obligated to serve in whatever way they're needed."

He bristles, lips pressed into a thin line. "Well, yes, but— that's only *theoretically*. Everyone knows that little detail is *rarely* put into practice. The Vichy isn't exactly breaking down doors to whisk women away for work."

Not like they're doing to the men, passes unsaid as I glare at the clerk.

"Well, there aren't many men left to 'whisk away' anymore," I mutter crossly. "So, here I am. One more 'willing' worker who will count toward bringing our prisoners of war home. Three of us for one prisoner, that's the deal, isn't it?"

The clerk shifts uncomfortably. "I think it would be unwise, mademoiselle. War isn't kind to girls. Factory work and hard labor isn't suitable for a young lady."

"War isn't kind to anyone," I mutter, the image of Father and Fernand in some filthy POW camp making me shudder. I hold the clerk's stare with unyielding resolve. At last, when he seems to realize I won't be dissuaded, he shuffles for the proper paperwork. I quickly fill in my information and, once he's verified everything, he stamps a letter that he informs me contains all my instructions.

"Miss Beaufoy," he says stiffly, handing me the letter with reluctance. "Your train departs on May seventh. Don't miss it, or the authorities will be paying you a visit."

Louise is alone when I arrive home with our rations, which I suppose is a good thing. I need to tell her about my joining the

STO program, though as I enter the kitchen, where she is washing the dishes, I consider putting it off. I'll be on a train to Germany in six days, which means for six days she'll be berating me endlessly. She greets me with the usual questions about my day, but her voice is softer than usual, fragile, as it has been since Yvonne died, since there has been no word of what happened to Daniel and Yvonne's mother.

No, it can't wait. My absence will cause a disruption to the resistance; best to let her get it straightened out as soon as possible. Get it over with. "Where is André?"

"He went to go play with the Leclairs' sons. I told him to be home before sundown."

Good. He might not hear us arguing. The poor boy has probably had his fill of it in the last four years... "Louise," I start determinedly, and she grows tense.

"I know that tone," she mumbles, turning to face me. "If this is about the men, I'm—"

I shake my head. "No, it's not about them. Well... not entirely. My wages were cut again today. I couldn't even afford an extra cup of flour."

Her frown deepens. "We'll make it work. I have a little extra saved from my lessons, and there's Jeanne's jewelry we can sell... we'll have to stretch things thin until—"

"Until when?" I interrupt. "There is no *until*. I know you won't give this up, not even now. More men will keep coming, we'll have to stretch our supplies even thinner, my wages will keep getting cut, and it will keep taking food out of our mouths. We can't keep struggling like this. If you want to keep hiding soldiers, *fine*, but that means we need more food, more money, and we can't provide it like this... So, I'm joining the STO program."

"What?" she cries out in shock. "Marie, what are you talking about? You think becoming a slave is how to provide for us? What's wrong with you?"

"I'm not a slave! Volunteer laborers are paid better than either of us combined right now! At least by going away for work I can send money and food home for—"

"No, no, no!" Louise shakes her head furiously, face growing red. "This is ridiculous, Marie! I will not allow it!"

"You don't have to allow it! You're not *our mother*, in case you've forgotten," I snap, and pull the stamped letter from my pocket for her to see. "And it doesn't matter. I've already signed up. I'm leaving for Germany on the seventh."

A strangled sound escapes her, and she grasps for the counter. "Y-you... Marie, you..." She struggles for words, shaking, and then suddenly she explodes. "You idiot! How could you be so rash? What were you thinking? No, don't answer that, I know you weren't thinking of anything! You never do! You are so reckless! What about Fernand and what we promised? Did you not think of André? You never think about *anyone!*"

Louise has always been patient and collected, but now, as her anger boils over and she screams at me, my heart stings in a way I'll never admit aloud.

"Did *I* not think of André?" I demand incredulously. "That's rich, coming from you! *I* am not the one who's been putting his life in danger every day! If anyone has forgotten what we promised Fernand, it's *you!* I've helped you; I've stood by you, but I won't do it anymore! I *never* wanted to. I don't care about any soldiers, I care about providing for this family."

"And you think the best thing to do is run off to Germany? You are so impulsive!"

"Call it what you want! I'm doing what I have to do, since *you* won't! I've always done what I have to do for this family, and I can never tell *you* anything because I know you'll have a fit or ignore me."

She crosses her arms, like a furious mother scolding her child. "Because *maybe* I'd need to talk some sense into you!"

"Stop, just stop! You've always treated me like I'm some

stupid child who doesn't know any better! You're not *our mother!*" I yell again, furiously. "I know that dallying around here isn't putting money in our pockets or food on the table, in case *you* haven't noticed!"

Louise draws up straighter, her eyes narrowed to slits. "You don't have to remind me of our situation. I am more than aware."

"Then if it bothered you," I growl, lowering my voice, "we wouldn't have your Americans in the cellar."

"*My* Americans? They're our allies, they're like Fernand and Father, and they need our help. Do you think I enjoy doing this? I don't! Sometimes I don't even want to, but it's my duty to France and my family."

"Fine! Do your duty to France, *I* will take care of us. Lord knows *you* won't," I seethe, unable to stop the fury of the last three years from exploding all at once. "Keep risking everything for France and the Allies if you want, to hell with me and André, but I am *done* with this and I am *done* with you. I refuse to let us end up like Yvonne and Daniel, no matter how hellbent you are on getting us killed for strangers!"

The tense silence is fit to be cut with a knife. Louise's red-rimmed eyes have grown wide, her dark irises glinting with pain and anger. I've crushed the STO letter in my fist, quivering with rage and the overwhelming weight of our honest feelings now laid bare.

Wordlessly, she steps past me and ascends the stairs. I grit my teeth, forcing the bitterness down, unconvincingly telling myself it doesn't upset me that neither of us are likely to speak to one another for the rest of the night.

10

MAY 7, 1944

LOUISE

The day of Marie's departure arrives much too soon. As André and I walk with her in painful silence to Gare de Lyon, I regret so terribly the three days I refused to look her in the eye.

The thought of seeing that hostile, accusing expression on her face was unbearable. I regret the things I said to her in that rash moment of anger, regret being the cause of the rare flash of hurt in her eyes, but I was too terrified to even think of the words spilling out. We've already lost a brother, and now I'm about to lose my only sister because I failed as a protector and provider. Roles that have consumed my life since our mother passed.

The platform is bustling with people; men with suitcases, women holding tightly to their husbands and sons, children crying as their fathers kneel to embrace them. The air beneath the station canopy is frigid with the cold of the morning and the dread of impending goodbyes.

I wish I could reach out and take Marie's hand, but she clutches her bag with both hands. She seems to purposely be avoiding my gaze, staring down the tracks where the train that will carry her away from us will soon be approaching.

"You have your winter coat? Germany is cold in the winter," I whisper softly to hide the tremor in my voice.

She nods shortly.

"And you remembered the rations I packed you? This will be a long train ride..."

Again, she says nothing, only nods as if to say, *"Yes, I know, Mother."*

"Aunt Marie?" André begins, unusually somber. "You'll come home, won't you?"

Marie's resolve crumples as she looks down at him, her eyes glistening with unshed tears, and I feel my own heart clench. His father vanished four years ago, and, with no word in all that time, he's come to fear—like I do—that those who leave France will never return.

"Of course I will," Marie assures him, wrapping him in a tight hug. "I'm only going for work, and only until the war is over. I'll write to you whenever possible. This will be a good job for all of us. I'll send you all the food and money I get my hands on. Maybe even some chocolate."

He smiles slightly at this, and Marie ruffles his hair.

"Now, you're the man of the house, so you better take care of your aunt while I'm gone. I hope you've found a job. Can I trust you to look after things?" she teases.

He grins and nods with pride, holding his pinky out. "Yes. I promise."

"Good." Marie nods, linking their fingers in agreement. She looks at me hesitantly, still avoiding my gaze. "You've... settled things with Michelle?"

"Yes, I sent her a letter," I say, trying to keep my voice steady. It took me days to write the letter to Michelle, telling her that Marie would be leaving France. Merely thinking the words was agonizing, and having to write reality into existence made the pain unbearable.

"Good..." Marie looks away while I desperately search for words.

We step closer to the tracks, André with his arm around Marie's waist and her arm rested on his shoulders. The scream of a whistle cuts through the air like a bomb siren, and I wish I could hide in the cellar from this nightmare as a train pulls to a stop before us, steam and the scent of metal choking the air. Men and women shuffle toward the conductors with their bags and tickets in hand, bidding their last farewells to crying family members.

Marie steps forward, drawing her ticket and STO letter from her pocket, and the reality of her leaving settles over me like a mourning veil. I rush after her, drawing her back into a crushing embrace, trying not to sob like a mother unable to let her child go.

She is not a child. She is a young woman doing what she believes is best for us.

"I'm sorry, I'm so sorry," I babble, burying my face in her soft, red hair that smells of lavender soap. "I'm not angry with you! I'm just so scared; I don't want to lose you too. I love you so much, and I am *so* proud of you. I know Fernand would be too."

The tension sags from her shoulders. "Thank you," she whispers. "I will come home when this is over, even if I have to walk the whole way, I promise." Her eyes glisten, but she maintains her composure. "I think we've done a fine job so far," she murmurs, nodding toward André a few paces behind us, standing with all the strength and resolve of a young man, so similar to his father it makes my heart hurt.

Fernand... would you hate me for what I'm doing? I only want our family to be together again, and I want the same for others.

"Last call!" a conductor shouts, checking the pocket watch

clipped to his black waistcoat and ushering in the last few straggling passengers.

No, it's too soon!

"Bye, Aunt Marie," André mumbles.

"I'll see you soon, I promise," Marie says, drawing us quickly into her arms one final time.

The warmth abruptly vanishes as she pulls away and approaches a conductor, her fiery hair a perfect match to her red double-breasted Reefer coat as she steps onto the train.

Come back, Marie, please don't leave... I want to cry, grab her and drag her back home where I can make sure she's safe, but the whistle screeches, and the wheels begin to grind against the tracks. From the window, Marie waves at us, like the hundreds of other passengers shouting goodbyes, waving, and throwing kisses to their families.

"See you soon!" André shouts over the deafening chaos.

"Stay safe..." My words are swallowed and lost to the noise, but I hope somehow the wind carries them to her, and she always remembers I'm thinking of her.

We stand for a long time on the platform, watching the empty horizon where the train has disappeared and the trail of smoke lingers in the sky. Eventually, the passengers for the next train begin to gather. André and I turn to leave, and nearly bump into a woman as she darts into the station. She speeds past us and my heart jumps.

Michelle! What is she doing here? What is she running from?

Quickly, I scan the crowd, but find no Gestapo or SS. There are soldiers standing guard in a few places, but they're not out of the ordinary, and don't seem to be looking for anyone.

I've had no reply to the letter I sent her about Marie, no word from any of the Line's members, and I am growing impatient. It's almost as if the Line in Paris still doesn't have any leaders, and I'm floundering in the middle of an ocean circled by sharks like I was months ago.

"André, wait right here," I instruct, indicating for him to sit on a bench. "I'll be back in a moment. Don't move."

I follow after Michelle as discreetly as I can, and catch up with her a little further down the platform, as she is passing through one of the towering archways. She gasps, startled, as I slip my arm through hers and steer her around the corner out of sight.

"Amia! What are you doing?"

"I wanted to ask you the same thing," I whisper.

She looks around, frantically scanning the crowds. "I think I've lost him for now," she says. "I was following Desoubrie. He was meeting with two British MI9 agents. I'm not sure why they were meeting—probably something to do with Operation Marathon—but he saw me spying on him, so I ran."

"Who is Desoubrie?"

"Pierre Boulain," she clarifies, and a shiver rattles through my body. "I've found out recently his real name is Jacques Desoubrie. He's working for the Gestapo. I have what I need to prove he's a double agent, but now I'm leaving France."

"You're leaving?"

Michelle nods reluctantly. "He knows my face now. I was lucky the police released me the first time, but the Gestapo won't take Desoubrie's word lightly—especially since I've already been arrested before. I have to escape while I still can." She tenses, dips her head, and pulls me into another archway. "That's him."

I follow her gaze, finding the man who until now I've only known as Pierre Boulain. A stocky, relatively short man with a pair of spectacles on a flat face that vaguely reminds me of a pug, he is quite unimpressive.

"He may look harmless, but he's dangerous," Michelle whispers, and we weave back in the opposite direction. "I got your letter about Cora. I'll pass it on to Max and Thomas when I see them today. I know you're worried about... well, you know. I am too, but, with the air raids slowing down, the groups should start moving again. Just wait for instructions from Max and *only* Max. Dozens of our helpers have been arrested in the last month, you're one of the few who is still hosting guests at the moment."

Could this day get any worse? Marie is gone to God knows where, Michelle has been compromised and is fleeing, the double agent who betrayed Yvonne and likely hundreds of others is roaming free, and there are no plans to get the Americans in my cellar out of Paris...

I catch a glimpse of André through the crowd, tapping his feet on the platform absent-mindedly and twiddling with his hat. Suddenly, my throat constricts and feverish chills rake over my body.

"Stay safe, Louise. Remember, Pugna Quin Percutias."

I try to return Michelle's farewell of "Fight Without Arms", but simply forcing myself to breathe is becoming an arduous task, and I barely notice her disappear as my head swims with unbearable lightness. My fingers tingle with the beginnings of numbness as André and I leave the station, being sure to avoid anyone who even remotely resembles Jacques Desoubrie.

Breathe... deep breaths, I repeat silently, trying to loosen the tightness in my chest. *In through your nose, out slowly from your mouth. Clear your mind.* That's what Father said he did when he was a young man in the trenches, trying not to panic while shrapnel exploded around him, bodies were falling, and the Germans threw gas canisters as he rushed to pull on a mask.

"Aunt Louise? Are you alright?" André's voice is distant, as if he's speaking to me through glass, and I feel myself being directed toward the sofa.

We're home already? I didn't realize—

My heart clenches painfully, strangling itself like a snake around its prey. Flecks of light streak across my vision like falling comets as I turn toward André's voice. He's too quick, and my spinning mind barely registers a blur of movement as he yanks the curtains closed and retreats down the hall.

What if Desoubrie saw me with Michelle? The Gestapo could be on their way right now, ready to riddle me with bullets, make André vanish like poor little Daniel, drag the men off to some POW camp. And Marie. Oh, God, she'll never know what happened to us! Oh, God, I can't breathe...

A tall figure returns on André's heels. My heart seizes in terror at the sight of the foreign shadow moving toward me.

"André, go get her some water." The voice is familiar, soothing and calm like a somber violin. A gentle hand softly caresses my cheek. "Louise. Louise, look at me. I'm right here. Yes, that's it, look in my eyes. You're panicking. Take deep breaths."

Everything slowly starts to clear, first a flash of the most beautiful blue held by dark lashes, then the steadying movement of lips forming quiet words.

William...

Both of his strong hands have found their way to my face and his thumbs are brushing away tears. "There you are," he whispers, smiling faintly. "Alright, focus on me. Try to breathe slowly with me. In... out..."

Trembling, I grasp his arms, desperate to ground myself to the world. I hold his gaze, letting him guide me through every breath as if he were teaching me something I've never done.

"You're... very good at this," I murmur once my breathing has steadied.

He smiles. "A lot of practice. Not easy to keep your head falling out of an airplane."

André returns promptly from the kitchen with a glass in his hand.

"Thank you, André." William nods gratefully. "I'm glad you came to get me."

"Are you alright?" André asks, reaching out to lay a comforting hand on my shoulder.

"It was probably just the heat. You could be dehydrated. That will make you feel faint," William says dismissively.

André seems calmed by this explanation, and I cast William a look of gratitude as I sip the tepid water. A man who studied medicine knows the real signs of dehydration, more so than a young, concerned nephew, and I'm thankful for his false diagnosis. My weakness shouldn't be among the things concerning André. The only thing a boy his age should be worried about is telling me he got into a fight at school or that he tore his best shirt.

"Oh, I feel much better." I quickly drain the rest of the water. "Thank you, André. And thank you for closing the curtains."

God, that's all I need, some nosy neighbor glancing through the window to find some unfamiliar man in my sitting room. I can hear the Gestapo pounding on the door now...

"You should rest for the day," William says. "Plenty of water and sleep, that's the best way to go. Which also means peace and quiet." He looks at André, smirking. "I know you like to gabber, but I expect you'll roll up your flaps."

I glance between them, confused, either truly faint or missing some underlying meaning.

"Yes, sir, Sergeant." André grins, straightens and salutes. "I'll go study. I'm already learning about adjectives. I'll be upstairs if you need me, Aunt Louise."

"Roll up your flaps?" I wonder as he bounds up the stairs.

"Oh, that." William chuckles quietly. "Soldier talk. Means to stop talking."

"Did you teach him that?"

"No—well, yes, not just me necessarily," William says. "André's been excited to show me he's learning English, so he likes to talk a lot. George finally told us to 'roll up our flaps,' so I've been explaining the things we soldiers say to each other."

"André is a boy, not a soldier." I draw away, terror clawing down my spine. "If he knows what's good for him, he'll never join the military. All it's good for is going missing and getting killed. I won't let him end up like his father."

William frowns, tilting his head in assent. "I apologize, I didn't mean to overstep."

Maybe I should forbid them from speaking. I don't want André to be fascinated by the idea of becoming a soldier. Men fight and die, some go home, then their sons forget the hell their fathers suffered when the next war comes. We've already lost Fernand and Father, and now Marie is gone, and Yvonne is dead and Michelle is running and Desoubrie—

"Louise, calm down. Breathe slowly." William grasps my quivering hands firmly, and only his steady presence at my side allows me to maintain my hold on the earth before the panic can drag me into its treacherous currents.

"I'm sorry," I whisper, unable to look him in the eye. "I didn't mean to snap at you. I'm just..."

"You're overwhelmed, and I'm not surprised," he says gently, brushing his fingers across my cheek, urging me to meet his gaze. "You've been strong for a long time. I know what that's like. Sometimes it means bottling everything up for the sake of others, but it's not good to keep it there. Then it just comes out ten times worse, and at the worst times. Whatever's going on, just let it out. I'll be right here."

Nothing could have endeared me to him as powerfully as his soft, understanding blue eyes, letting me deflate into his arms as the tears fall. Oh, how painfully wonderful it is to cry, to let myself be held and protected, to not have to stay strong when all I want to do is curl up and hide from the world. There is no judgment in his embrace, no reason to be afraid. There is only warmth, safety, and stability. I would be content to remain like this forever, and I wish for a moment that he'd never let go.

Am I just afraid, overwhelmed by how swiftly circumstances are growing more dire, or will I only ever find this wonderful feeling with William?

I've had several boyfriends before, perfect gentlemen who took me for picnics in the park, made me smile and laugh until my cheeks ached, and yet never have I felt something as powerful as this. No other voice has sounded so soothing, no other hands have felt as tender, no man's embrace has ever felt as comforting as his. For now, I push away all thought of this moment inevitably coming to an end and allow myself to bask in the warm feeling of safety and comfort as long as he will hold me.

11

MAY 9, 1944

MARIE

I always wondered how the Nazis made people disappear so easily. Now, I wonder if there will be a trace left of me when this train finally stops. Only God knows where we're going anymore.

A few days ago, I was under the impression that the train from Gare de Lyon was supposed to run directly from Paris to Germany. However, after only an hour we stopped at a station in Creil, where a group of SS ordered everyone with an STO letter to exit the train and board another. After two days, stops at six different stations in France, sitting in a musty, crowded compartment, I am ready to faint from exhaustion. All seven men in our compartment have drifted to sleep. The only other woman slumps beside me, head rested heavily on my shoulder no matter how I try to nudge her off. It is horribly cramped, but, while I have no room to stretch my aching legs and the stifling air grows thinner by the hour, I am grateful to at least have been a volunteer worker.

The train has towed several wooden storage cars. All the

forced laborers—gaunt, unshaven men, resistance members, and criminals from the cities' prisons—were tossed into those cars like cattle, with nothing but a bucket of water and another bucket meant for other, unsanitary purposes.

The groan of the train as it begins to slow has me peering anxiously out the window to see if there is any indication as to our whereabouts. The sky is dark, but my watch indicates it's three o'clock in the morning. No matter which way I strain to look through the foggy window, I see only the inky silhouettes of trees and hills. A few lanterns shed spots of light on a single building and wooden platform situated in the middle of nowhere, and all that assures me this isn't a long-abandoned station are the uniformed SS who stand irate and waiting.

Efficient and obsessive over keeping their schedules as always, the SS throw the storage cars open. Hundreds of slave laborers stumble onto the platform. Each of them is more wretched than the last, thinner, paler, some with horrid stains on their clothes I imagine reek of the filth they've lived in for the last two days. They are divided into groups and sent in numerous different directions through the trees under the aim of armed SS.

Drops of rain have begun to streak down the window by the time our compartment door is opened from the outside. An SS man issues a command, which, when one of the men in the compartment stands and straightens his jacket, I assume is an order to disembark. The SS man moves on to open the other compartments, and we hastily file off the train.

I inhale deeply, filling my lungs with the chill of fresh air, free from the stifling musk of the compartment and unwashed strangers. The coolness of dawn nips through the coat I've been wearing since I left Paris. I step beneath the canopy to escape the drizzle from the clouds that befall day with the illusion of night. Straining to see around the mass of men and several women, I catch a glimpse of a sign by the tracks that reads BAHNHOF KAHL.

So, we're somewhere in Germany... Maybe I should have let Louise teach me German, I think in frustration. *Who volunteers to go to work in Germany and doesn't speak the language? God, she was right. This was rash.*

An SS officer steps out of the station, rigid and impassive. He shouts a command in German, and the soldier beside him repeats the command in another language I recognize as Dutch, then in French. "Everyone be quiet!"

I breathe a sigh of relief. The murmurs of confusion and trepidation die down and everyone turns their attention to the SS.

"Welcome to Kahl! The Reich thanks you for donating your labor, it will be used most productively. As promised by the STO department, food, payment every two weeks, and housing will be provided to you, as well as your work assignments once you have been sorted. You will be divided by skillset and race. If you are German, step to the front of the platform!"

A few dozen Germans break from the cluster of people, to be met by another SS, who beckons them inside the station building.

"If you are French, Belgian, or Dutch, divide yourselves into three groups to the left of the platform and await further instructions!"

Reluctantly, I step from under the canopy into the light shower of rain. We begin to murmur quietly to one another, searching for familiar languages and accents, until we've found our respective countrymen. Once the officers have finished issuing commands to the Poles, Italians, and other nationalities, we are asked to raise our hands if we've had experience in certain professions: auto mechanics, agriculture, electricity, woodwork and metalwork, construction, or medical aid.

Are you skilled or unskilled, I conclude is what they want to know as they separate those who raise their hands from those, like me, who have had too little experience in these fields to be able to lie convincingly. The group I am sorted into consists of fewer than fifty people, mostly men and just four other women, almost all French with a few Belgians in the mix.

Another armed SS man in a group of three addresses us in heavily accented French, and the light of the oil lanterns casts unnerving, heinous shadows over their faces.

Hell is empty and all the devils are here...

"This group will come with us! You will be placed in Lager Six, where you will work in the Reichsmarschall Hermann Göring factory of Walpersberg, also referred to as REIMAHG!"

I'm not sure what I expected from this place. A road? A town with streetlamps? Both reasonable to expect near a factory. However, what I hadn't expected was a long trek across the countryside in darkness under the threat of German rifles. After a miserable hour of walking through patches of woodland, we finally stop at the outskirts of a small village. For miles we've gone without rest, guided only by the light of the lamps and shielding our eyes from the rain.

Any hope of a dry roof over our heads is quickly stamped out as, rather than being ordered to get onto the truck waiting on the first paved road we've seen to be taken to Lager Six, all our belongings are abruptly torn away. "Hand everything over! These things are the property of the Reich!" an SS shouts.

I try to hold on to the only possessions I have in this strange place; my winter clothes and the rations Louise packed for me, but the SS man is stronger. He easily breaks my grip and tosses my bag to the other SS men to riffle through. No one protests; we're all too stunned and fearful to even think of demanding our things back.

How far the mighty have fallen, I think, bitter yet amused as the SS greedily snatch any money, clothes, or food we brought, biting back a smirk as one seriously examines a woman's slip dress in consideration. *Once the scourge of Europe, now reduced to thieving scraps and rags.*

The rest of the walk to Lager Six lasts an hour. Through the cluster of trees and brush, stone structures sprouting green moss from the crevices of the bricks come into view. There are seven buildings organized on either side of a large clearing now turned into an expanse of mud. It strikes me more or less as a prison—the dour structures and strict quiet—and, though it lacks walls or fences, nature serves as an isolating barrier. We are miles from anywhere.

The shouts of German guards break the unsettling silence as we arrive. The latches that seal the stone buildings closed are unlocked, then hundreds of men and women spill out into the clearing. There must be over a thousand, all of whom have emerged from six of the seven buildings. A deathly quiet lingers around the seventh; there are no windows, no locks on the door, and yet I cannot help but think it isn't empty...

"This is Lager Six!" one of our escorts declares as everyone trudges to form rows of ten, and I'm astounded by how many bodies can squeeze into such a limited space. "You will rise every morning at four o'clock and line up for roll call! Afterwards, you will have until half past five for breakfast! Line up—the longer you dally, the less time you'll have to eat!"

The promise of food has my stomach clenching, and we newcomers move to find places in line with the others. The majority are men, just a few women, but they all have the same slumped, filthy appearance, and I wonder again if I've been brought to a prison.

God, what the hell am I doing here? What was I thinking? I should have listened to Louise!

I find a place between two men and stand, tense and freezing as the rain seeps into my clothes. The man on my right is much taller, his shoulders level with my brow. His gaze shifts down to me. He is pale in every aspect. His piercing, emotionless gray eyes seem to reach within my own to pick apart my every thought, his short hair and beard are so blond they are nearly white, his pallid complexion gives him the look of a ghost, and the scattered constellation of scars littering his face is pale as moonlight.

Fearsome is the first word that comes to mind. There is something of a challenge in his empty eyes as I stare back at him, clenching my fists, determined not to be afraid, not to be prey. He inclines his head slightly with something akin to approval.

Roll call seems to drag on for ages. At last, we are dismissed to receive our morning meals, and I bite back a groan as the newcomers are called away. "You five, yes, the women. Step forward," says one of the SS guards. We are each issued a bowl, a spoon, a pair of oversized men's boots, pants, and one cotton shirt. "You five will be lodged in block one, at the very end. Settle your things in your bunks and then you may join the line for your rations."

"Hopefully it's the women's block," a woman mutters as we traipse across the sloshy yard. "Did you notice? There're hardly any women here!"

When we reach block one, the pale bearded man is there, leaning against the wall with his empty bowl dangling from his fingertips. The women fall silent, reluctant to approach. Though he looks half-starved beneath his loose clothing, his height, broad shoulders, and fierce scarred face still make him a formidable man.

I take the lead of our little group determinedly and the others follow timidly behind.

"The doors on the left," the pale man says, his voice low and gravelly with a distinct Russian accent. He sounds younger than I initially thought he was, probably near Louise's age.

As if Nazis weren't enough. Now we have Soviet Communists to deal with.

I narrow my eyes at him. "And why should we listen to you?"

"You are new," he says simply, regarding me in a way that is both indifferent and intense. "Women have the rooms on the left, men have the right."

One of the women gasps in horror. "We're to be housed together?"

His eyes don't move from me. "There aren't many women in this lager, no point in separating. All the doors are locked from the outside at night; you'll be safer then. But still, don't wander outside your rooms."

His face is unreadable, and I cannot tell if his words are a threat or a warning, so I decide they are both. I am under no illusions. Here, I am vulnerable, a pretty young woman vastly outnumbered without any allies or protection, and this man knows it as well.

A knife would be good. If not, maybe a stick. I could make a stake, I think, gripping my new belongings tightly as I brush past him into the dank block. I have no idea what's going on. This place is so different from what I thought it would be, like an isolated prison in the woods, and I must stay on my guard. Perhaps in some ways I am still innocent, but the world has made me harden myself, and I refuse to be crushed by its depravity.

For the hundredth time in the last hour, I regret saving the food Louise gave me. The morning meal was nothing more than beet and cabbage soup, which was watered down in addition to tasting like dirt. It's like we're being given prison rations! I wish I would have eaten the bread, jam, and cheese before we were forced to surrender our possessions.

The long trek to the REIMAHG factory of Walpersberg is several miles to the west through beaten forest trails. We are led between what appear to be two more lagers. The first is much larger than ours, its dozens of barracks built of wood rather than stone, contained by high, barbed-wire fences. The other is much smaller and unrestricted by fences or guards, and the reason for this lax security is apparent when hordes of SS men emerge from the barracks.

"Lager One." The rumbling voice sends shudders down my spine, and I grit my teeth, refusing to acknowledge him. "There will be over twenty lagers when construction is done, they go for miles in every direction. Volunteers, slaves, prisoners. They"—he nods toward the people gathering in Lager One—"are slave laborers. They work with us in the factory."

The pale Russian is following me. After seeing the dismal state of the dirty block and deciding to carry all my distributed possessions from the SS on my person, I was acutely aware of his gray eyes following me as I lined up for breakfast, and when the SS called us into line for the march to the factory he fell into step beside me.

Remnants of an abandoned mine take form through the trees. Gaping holes lead deep into an abyss of tunnels, and the beginnings of cement walls appear to be in the process of developing into bunkers. Sacks of cement sit piled in mountains beneath canopies, shovels and pickaxes stand upright in the dirt, and wheelbarrows are overflowing with rainwater.

What are we doing in a quarry? I wonder, staring in bewilderment at the other laborers, who are assuming positions around the miserable worksite. *We were told we would work in a factory...*

Internally, I chide myself for believing anything the Nazis said to me. Has my entire existence since their infestation been anything but one lie and disappointment after the other? Of all the fickle things to trust, the word of the very people who believe any non-German is inferior! But, for all the lies a serpent's tongue can hiss, it can be trusted in a single regard; it will remain loyal to the interests of its Reich, or itself if all goes to hell. Whatever is expected of us, it will be to aid *their* war effort.

A large hand locks around my arm and draws me forward. I fight to break free, but the pale Russian is frighteningly strong for one who looks half-starved. "Don't draw attention to yourself," he mutters. "Standing idly is a good way to get in trouble."

"Let go of me," I growl, trying to break his grip, to no avail.

"And mind your temper. You look ready to kill."

"I am, but it won't be the SS." The threatening implication of *it will be you* seems to amuse him.

"I'm only a prisoner of war, not an SS. I'm not who you need to worry about, lisichka."

No? No need to worry about a Soviet dragging me to a dark tunnel as long as an SS has his gun trained on me?

"Let. Go!" Grabbing one of his fingers, I draw it backwards in hopes of breaking it.

He flinches, loosening his grip enough for me to pull away. He levels his eyes on me, and the coldness in their empty gray depths pins me in place like steel chains. How could someone's eyes look so dead and yet so weighed down by emotion at the same time?

"You should not have come," he says quietly. "This place will eat up a pretty little thing like you. Why *did* you come?"

"That's none of your concern." I back away, shaking with fear or fury, or perhaps both. "Touch me again, and I'll break your fingers. Do the SS care what happens to Russians?"

"After Stalingrad?" He chuckles humorlessly, indicating his body. "Does it look like they do? Don't fool yourself—you might be a volunteer, but you're no freer than I am. You will be fed more, and your punishments won't be as severe, but you're a slave now. I'm trying to help you."

If there's anyone I need less than the Nazis, it's their former allies who are every bit as, if not more, brutal. Even in Paris, we heard the horror stories of what happened in the territories reclaimed by the Soviets, what they did to the women and little girls they encountered—

I suppress a shudder, wondering how many people have died at this Soviet's hands, what has now made him place his target on me. "I don't want your help."

"I can see that. But you need it," he states. "Come, you need a work assignment before the SS get impatient. Lazy slaves only become dead slaves. This factory won't build itself."

"What?" I blanch, and avoid his hand, to start toward a labor supervisor giving instructions. He hasn't lashed out yet, but I shouldn't be trying my luck with a man who has proved he can easily overpower me.

A knife, a stake, something sharp. Even a piece of slate or cement would do.

"We are considered unskilled laborers. You don't need anything but two good legs and arms to use a shovel or carry stone. That's all we needed when the SS made us build the lagers. We're still digging their factory."

At last, the pale Russian leaves, grabbing a pickaxe and disappearing down into a tunnel in the hill. As my heart slowly settles, the heat of adrenaline is replaced by the frigid rain seeping into my clothes. The supervisor assigns me to a group of laborers hauling wheelbarrows, and I put the Russian's unnerving words out of mind.

By the time the SS blow their whistles for the midday meal, the blue sky beneath the clouds has emerged, painfully bright to look upon. All morning has been spent trudging through the muddy quarry, hauling load after backbreaking load of dirt and stone cleared from the mine—a former sand mine with many underground tunnels, which is being extended several miles. My legs quake, my hands are red and raw, and my entire body aches with hunger. The meal is soup, nothing but bitter water with a few pieces of turnip, and a single ladleful does nothing to slake my thirst or ease my hunger.

The Russians aren't fed. They emerged from the tunnels, dirt caking their faces and ragged clothes; however, after everyone else received soup, there was nothing left to be scraped from the pots. The Russians didn't seem surprised, nor did they complain, although their gaunt faces were ravenous with hunger and shoulders slumped.

The workday drags into the evening, when the sky fades to violet. My feet are aching and soaked with water, my boots have rubbed painful sores against my toes, and I can't do anything without the fragilely clotted blisters on my fingers breaking and bleeding. I dared not ask the SS for bandages, and the other laborers advised me to sacrifice part of my shirt and make do.

At least one good thing came out of today, I remind myself, swallowing the whimpers trying to escape my throat as we trek back to Lager Six. The long, jagged stone in the pocket of my pants beneath my skirt is thin and sharp, a comfortable weight against my thigh.

It's eight o'clock when we arrive at Lager Six, and I nearly scream in frustration when all that is laid in my hands for supper after twelve hours of excruciating labor is a lump of hard bread and a spoonful of jam. We are given an hour and a half for supper, which only enrages me further. Who but a rat needs so long to consume a crust?

As the night grows black and lanterns are lit, the next two hours are spent lingering in the clearing without purpose. Small groups talk quietly among themselves, others have lined up to make official appeals to the SS. I make myself as inconspicuous as possible—which isn't an easy task with strikingly red hair. The pale Russian was right about one thing, at least. I must refrain from drawing attention to myself.

"Good evening, lisichka."

Speak of the bloody devil...

I leave my hand at my side, fingers hovering over the place where my rock is hidden. "What do you want, *Soviet*?"

"My name is Radomir, not Soviet," he says, then pauses as if waiting for me to correct whatever Russian word he's been calling me with my real name.

"I don't care what your name is. Leave me alone."

The ghost of a smile crosses his face, and the way the lamps reflect off his pallid complexion gives him an oddly devilish and yet angelic look. "You are an angry one, like fire, inside and out."

I narrow my eyes, and shift away from where I lean against the block in case he thinks to trap me against it. "Then maybe you should go away. Fire will burn you."

He smiles this time, a small, genuine smile lacking any malice. "I came to bring you this." In his hands he presents a roll of gauze to me. My blisters ache with longing at the mere sight of it, pristine and snowy white, looking so very soft. Then, my stomach churns as I look back up at the one who offers it.

I am a thief, but I only stole from the enemy, and only for my family. I'll be damned if I accept favors from a Soviet soldier. He fought with the Nazis. Stalin invaded Poland with Hitler, abused and exploited Europe's people, and I would rather my hands bleed every day until the end of the war before I treat a Nazi or Soviet with civility.

"I don't want it. I don't want *anything* from you," I snarl, not bothering to hide my disgust or hatred, relieved to be allowed to express it rather than pretending to be meek and docile like for Jeanne's Gestapo officer.

Though his face falls in disappointment, he nods, and slips the gauze into his pocket. "Tomorrow won't be easier. It will only get worse. You'll want it eventually. It's cleaner than anything you'll find around here. And the SS won't give you anything unless for a steep price."

"You mean they won't give *you* anything, Soviet," I retort.

He chuckles. "Where do you think *I* got it? Not many dealers out here except the SS. Men will sell anything to anyone for the right price, even to his enemy."

"I will buy my own when my pay comes," I mutter.

His laugh startles me, a shockingly bitter sound. "That's what they all think at first. Even with your pay, I wouldn't ask the SS for favors. Money isn't the kind of payment they'd want from you, lisichka. And you're not allowed to leave this camp, anyway. Your money will be useless."

"What rubbish are you spouting? I am a volunteer laborer. Why would I not be allowed to use my wages? And even if I can't, I don't intend to keep them. I will send them to—"

"No one," he cuts me off. "You will send nothing to no one because the SS will not allow it. This is no ordinary factory where we may come and go freely. Here, we are prisoners of war, concentration camp prisoners, forced laborers, criminals, some conscripted workers and volunteers. There isn't anyone who wouldn't give both legs to leave. The world doesn't exist to us anymore. Didn't you wonder why we came across no other lagers but one in all the miles to the factory? And beyond the lagers, who can say how far the wilderness goes? The SS want us blind. Not even the Red Cross comes out this far. REIMAHG is the world now."

I thought about this... how the Nazis seemed to be trying to make us disappear...

In volunteering for the forced labor program, I was guaranteed pay, food, and shelter. The blocks are dark and airless, the cramped bunks have only straw mats, the windows have thick metal bars that allow the freezing air to creep inside. The food is minimal: bitter, watered-down soup, and a single ration of bread that tastes of sawdust. And even if I'm truly not allowed to use my pay, as long as I receive it all the promises the STO propaganda gave me have been fulfilled.

God, is this really happening? I truly have been brought to a prison. Am I a slave now?

A whistle pierces the night. My legs numbly carry me inside block one and to a room on the left. As nineteen more women cram inside the suffocating space, the echoes of bars slamming down over the doors seal everyone inside their prison cells.

I'm so sorry, Louise. I wish I would have listened to you; you're the level-headed one. I wish I could hug you now, fight with you, laugh and discuss Shakespeare... What are you going to do when I never write to you, never send any money or food?

She'll go mad with worry for me, but what about André and her soldiers? How will she take care of them all with her meager wages, with only the rations for two people?

As I crawl trembling into a bunk between two fetid strangers, exhausted and dreading the sunrise, I vow that I will go home. I am not a slave. I won't spend every day terrified that my family is starving because the Nazis won't let me provide for them, wondering if every day will be my last, in a place where the most honesty I've received is from a Soviet. I don't belong here.

I belong in Paris, with my sister and my nephew. That's where I've always belonged.

12

MAY 22, 1944

LOUISE

Two weeks have come and gone with no word from Marie. No letters, no curt telegrams to inform us that she arrived at her destination, not even the courtesy note labor camps generally send to families to inform them that an individual is healthy and happy.

I tried to remain calm the first week, tried to convince myself her letter just got lost in the mail. Now, I've begun sitting by the window to watch for the mail courier, like a hawk waiting for its prey to inch closer. Every day, she passes on her bicycle and never stops to deliver something for me. Nothing from Marie and nothing from Max.

Maybe the officials in the STO department will tell me something, I think hopefully. My heart surges as the courier appears, dropping again when she passes without a backwards glance.

What if she's still angry with me? She can hold a grudge for a long time, I worry, rising from the armchair I've moved to the window. I apologized to her the day she left, told her I loved her, though she didn't repeat those words to me... but she said we'd done a fine job raising André, that she would walk the whole way home if she had to.

I smile at the memory of those words, so determined, passionate, and very Marie. Perhaps a bit dramatic, but what more could I expect from a deep lover of Shakespeare?

After our mother died, the invisible barrier that had always stood between us seemed to grow wider. I retreated into my duties around the home, and Marie ran off with Roger, Léon, and Victor, and buried herself in Mother's collection of Shakespeare. For the longest time, it was one of the few things we could connect on, until the day Fernand asked us to take care of André. Then, we joined the Comet Line at my insistence, and the fragile bond we'd slowly built since our mother's death was shattered.

"André!" I call, slipping on a pair of white gloves and a beige cloche with a dainty bow that complements the underlining of my cherry dress.

He comes down the stairs in a hurry. "Yes, Aunt Louise?"

"I have a few errands to run. I'll be gone for a few hours," I say, applying some red lipstick from what is left of the tube I've been conserving for months. "I know you're studying, but please make some time to straighten the house up. I'll have a lot to do tonight."

"Yes ma'am." He grins, saluting like a soldier, speaking in flawless English with the faint tinge of William's accent.

"Very good," I respond in English, attempting to smile.

He'll be heartbroken when the men leave, wondering where in the world William's gone and if he'll even remember the little French family back in Paris.

Or perhaps I'm *the one who will be heartbroken... Lord knows I've grown fonder of these men in the last month than any of the others, William in particular.*

When the evening is late enough that they won't be seen or

heard, I allow the men upstairs, but William always sits with me either in the kitchen or by the hearth. In whispers, we exchange childhood stories—which often have both of us stifling laughter. He speaks fondly of his hometown in Nebraska, his family oil business and estates, the river where he and his cousins go fishing. I offer my own stories about Yvonne and me growing up together, my favorite fabric and flower shops, my time as a teacher, and, even though I consider them mundane, he listens as though nothing could fascinate him more. Sometimes, on quiet nights when the warmth of the fire seems to draw us closer together, our discussions stray into the deep, uncharted waters one's soul wades in. It's so easy to talk with him, to smile and laugh, and sometimes I forget I haven't known him all my life.

"And what do you do if there are Germans at the door?" I ask André, guilt gnawing awfully in the pit of my stomach.

"If I'm downstairs, run out the back door or windows, if I'm upstairs, out the window to the roof and down the tree, then run," he recites without a pause, and his chirpy tone only worries me more.

Once André found out about the soldiers, I had to explain the danger we were in, and plan for what he'd do in the event of the worst. If we were ever betrayed or suspected and soldiers or Gestapo appeared at our home, he would run and find somewhere to hide. I told him to stay away from family friends, fearing the Gestapo might search for him there, and to go to the farmer in the country. He'd be able to get in contact with Max from there and the Comet Line could move him underground.

I grab my empty laundry bag and make my way to the STO building. It's vacant save for the clerks and doorkeepers. My shoes click and echo across the marble floor, and in the silence I can hear the glittering chandelier swaying slightly on its gilded chain, and the scratch of the clerk's pencil on his desk.

"Hello, mademoiselle," the squat clerk greets me.

"Good afternoon, monsieur. I'd like to make an inquiry

about my sister," I say politely. "Her name is Marie Beaufoy. She volunteered for the program on the first, and she left for Germany on the seventh."

He frowns, fidgeting slightly. "Hmm... oh, yes, I remember her. Young girl with red hair, very... *set* on her way."

"Yes, that's her." I nod, smiling at his description. "I've been waiting for word from her, but I think her letters have been lost in transit. Could you tell me where she's been sent to work so I can write to her?"

"No, no, that is not allowed." He shakes his head quickly. "I'm afraid I can't help you."

"What? Why is it not allowed?"

"It's just not permitted, mademoiselle. That information is confidential. It can't be given out to anyone."

"*Anyone?* I am her sister, not some stranger off the street. I'll show you my documents if that's what you need to confirm it."

"I apologize, but that won't make a difference. It's simply not allowed."

"Why not?" I demand, my hands beginning to tremble. "She is a volunteer, not a prisoner. I am her immediate family; I have a right to know where she's gone."

"No, you don't," he says, uncomfortably glancing toward the door as if hoping for someone to enter so he has an excuse to send me away. "If you volunteer your labor to the Reich, that business is between the worker and the STO department. We have no obligation to disclose any information to anyone outside the parties concerned. As much as I would like to help you, there is nothing I can do. You must simply wait for your sister to contact you first."

"That's ridiculous! If she writes to me, I'll see where she's addressed it from anyway," I snap, unable to quiet the anxious shrillness of my voice. "Why can't I be told where she is? What if none of her letters come, then what am I supposed to do?"

"Mademoiselle—" he begins impatiently.

"Is there a problem?" The French is spoken in a heavy German accent. A Wehrmacht officer with war decorations pinned to his perfectly ironed uniform emerges from an office, brow raised in annoyance at the clerk.

"Yes, Herr Hauptfeldwebel," I interject in German, addressing him according to the insignia on his collar and shoulders. Perhaps speaking to him in his language will lend me some credit to make my case.

The clerk tries to insist nothing is wrong, but the officer waves a silencing hand at him. "Fräulein, what is the problem?"

I sigh with relief, and dip my head respectfully. At least *someone* is willing to listen. "I'm sorry for disturbing you, Herr Hauptfeldwebel. I am just very worried. My sister volunteered her service to Germany earlier this month, and I've heard nothing from her. I was hoping to find out where she's working so I could contact her. I just want to know she made it safely."

"I tried to explain our policy to her, but she wouldn't listen to me, Herr—"

The officer cuts the clerk off impatiently. "Fräulein, this is highly irregular. This information is not allowed to be made public. I'm certain your sister will write to you when she has the chance."

"Yes, I understand why it wouldn't be wise to give out this information. But would it be possible for the department to send a letter *for* me?" I try, hoping to keep his attention a little longer. "I wouldn't want to compromise you in any way, but perhaps I could write a letter for her, and you could send it, then I wouldn't know the address."

I hold my breath, encouraged by the officer's contemplative expression. He finally nods his assent. "Very well, Fräulein, write your letter. I will see that it's sent today. *But*," he says pointedly, "I will only do this for you once. I can't be running about doing favors for everyone. After this, you must wait for your sister to write to you."

Not wanting to risk losing his generosity, I keep the letter as short and unproblematic as possible, omitting anything about conditions in Paris as they'll probably be blacked out anyway. At the bottom, I sign, *with all my love, Louise.*

As I make my way home I continuously adjust my bag of laundry, as it is heavier than it was last week. I've recently started my own service to make a little extra money. Years spent washing and mending my family's clothes have made me an excellent laundry attendant and seamstress—one must be especially proficient with a boy as messy and rambunctious as André. I don't charge as much as the tailor, so I've acquired several regular clients who would rather the work get done quickly and can afford to hire someone to do their chores.

Marie's old friend Jeanne was added to my list this week, though I can't imagine why she would prefer I wash and mend her clothes when her Nazi lover spoils her like a queen.

Perhaps she's feeling guilty, I mull, *or maybe a bit petulant. It could be she's hoping to find a friend in me like the one she lost in Marie. Fat chance of that.*

I smile slightly at the thought. I've heard William using that particular American idiom a few times, heard André repeat it, and it seems I too am growing more inclined toward his use of language.

A solid body collides with me as I round the corner, and I stumble and catch myself against the wall, dropping my laundry bag.

"Pardon me," I mutter, quickly kneeling to gather up the clothing that spilled out.

"Oh, no, pardon me, mademoiselle. I didn't mean to knock you over," a man says, taking a knee to help me.

Just as I open my mouth to thank him, the words die in my suddenly dry throat. I send God a vehement thanks that Jacques

Desoubrie is too focused on the clothing to notice my ashen face or trembling hands.

Traitor. Spy. He killed Yvonne. Breathe, deep breaths. Stay calm.

"Thank you, monsieur," I force out, desperate to flee, to cry, to slam his flat, rat-like face against the sidewalk for all the horror he's put me, my friends, and my allies through.

"There, no harm done." He stands and pulls me to my feet, my bag of laundry dangling hostage in his hand. "You may call me Pierre. And what may I call you, lovely lady?"

"Louise."

"A pleasure bumping into you, Louise," he says, placing a sloppy kiss on my knuckles.

Bile rises in my throat, and I fight the urge to jerk my hand back and wipe it on my dress.

"I should be going, monsieur. I need to start supper, and curfew is soon."

As I reach for the bag of laundry, Desoubrie draws it back. "Allow me to escort you. This bag is quite heavy for a young lady. Let me carry it for you."

"Oh, that won't be necessary. I'm sure you have other important business." I try not to let my desperation slip through, briefly looking around for anyone who might see my discomfort and come to my aid. But no one seems to have noticed us, except for one particularly unfriendly-looking man in a long gray coat. He stands across the street, holding a newspaper he isn't reading. His eyes are trained on Desoubrie and me, like a hawk watching its prey, making me shudder.

"I always have time to spare for a lovely lady." Desoubrie grins, offering his free arm. "And look at you shiver! You must be cold. I insist. It's getting late. You shouldn't be walking the streets by yourself."

If I keep saying no, he might wonder why I'm so desperate to escape, and with the Comet Line active in Paris he might get suspicious. He's not very large for a man, but I couldn't overpower him or grab my bag back. I need to play along, smile and nod and be grateful for his help, then send him away with the first flimsy excuse I can think of.

I let him tuck my arm into the crook of his own in defeat, struggling not to cringe in revulsion or give away the distress that has my heart thumping at such a rate and volume I can barely register the bustle of the city.

The evening is growing dim. Parisians running the final errands of the day and leaving work weave through the streets by foot and bicycle, and I purposely lead Desoubrie in the opposite direction of home. I would never let him know where to find me again. There is an hour until curfew, and a few detours will give me the chance to escape while I pretend not to notice when he makes subtly lewd comments.

An uneasy tingle rattles through me, though this time it isn't caused by the spy I'm walking arm in arm with. It is a strange, almost instinctive feeling that makes me think I'm being watched. Desoubrie, so consumed by his own end of the conversation, doesn't notice as I glance around for the other source of my discomfort. A flash of gray has me straining to look over my shoulder.

That man is following us. My heart leaps at the sight of the unfriendly stranger in the gray coat. He's lagging behind several feet, and, even though he isn't looking directly at us, I'm certain he's paying us more attention than he's letting on.

No, maybe I'm just being paranoid. A lot of people are walking this way. Why shouldn't he? Still, I find myself directing Desoubrie off the main street, and am relieved when I look back and see no sign of the man in the gray coat; then my heart drops to the ground as he makes the same turn as us. Desoubrie, feeling me quiver, draws me closer, babbling something about the evening chill that I can't hear over the frantic pounding of my pulse.

Get away. Get away. It's the only thought my mind is capable of forming, only now it isn't just Desoubrie and his unyielding grasp I must escape. Someone is following us, and, with our conflicting statuses in the resistance and the Gestapo, there's no telling who the stranger is stalking.

If only I were like Marie. She'd have made a scene, snapped and shouted at Desoubrie, grabbed her laundry bag and stormed off. She wouldn't have caved in to his proposal to walk her home, she wouldn't have to worry about some stranger following her, she'd have gotten away by now...

After another four streets, ten blocks, and a half-loop around City Hall, I finally look back to see the man in the gray coat has disappeared, though his absence doesn't ease my nervousness. The sun is sinking quickly, and, with our stalker out of sight, I decide I've stalled long enough. "Oh, my! I'm so sorry, monsieur!" I gasp for effect, jerking my arm away from Desoubrie. "I was supposed to pick up my husband's shoes from the tailor, and I've completely forgotten!"

Our abrupt stop has placed us in the center of the sidewalk before towering apartments, and another short, stocky man with dark hair bumps shoulders with Desoubrie.

"Excuse me," the man apologizes, tipping his hat and straightening his checkered jacket.

The resemblance between the two strangers, even their manner of dress, is uncanny. It reminds me of an American picture my father and I saw, a comedy about a boy named Penrod who constantly wound up in trouble when an identical boy moved to his town.

Desoubrie waves dismissively and his doppelganger continues on. "A husband," he says, somewhat testily.

"Yes, I'm terribly sorry, but I must hurry. I'd like to get his shoes before the tailor closes for the night. I've enjoyed talking with you and thank you for carrying my bag."

I reach for my laundry, but he draws back, and I fight to

swallow my nerves as his other hand locks around my fingers. "Why not go in the morning?" he suggests. "My flat is just around the corner, and I'm sure you've had a long day."

I can leave the bag if I get that desperate, but then I'd lose all my customers and he'd be suspicious.

"That's a very kind offer, monsieur." My forced smile begins to wane as his grip on my hand tightens. "But I couldn't leave my husband worrying about me all night." I bring William to the forefront of my mind. The thought of his voice and kind eyes gently soothes my rising panic.

Desoubrie's eyes narrow, and his lips thin in an unsettling twist of offense. "I generously helped you with your things, mademoiselle. I think it's only fair you—"

Just as I consider feigning fainting to make a scene, the man in the gray coat reappears out of the alley, a pistol raised. My scream is swallowed by a gunshot, and I drop to the ground, covering my head. Desoubrie ducks at my side, shielding his own head as he scrambles back, then runs for cover. For a split second, the man in the gray coat doesn't move, eyes wide with shock and disbelief, then he turns and sprints back down the alley. The man who looks like Desoubrie lies on the ground like others who dropped in fear, but he doesn't scramble up and run away in panic. His face remains pressed to the cement, and a crimson stain darkens the ground.

"Oh, my God! Is he alright?" a woman cries.

Several men rush to his side. "He's been shot!" They grab him by the shoulders and flip his limp body over onto his back. "He's dead! Call for the police!"

The mention of police who will no doubt be Gestapo shakes me from my terror. I snatch my laundry bag and rush from the scene. When I have run so far my lungs cannot sustain my pace and the sounds of distress have vanished, I slump heavily against the back of a brick building, panting, too weak to bother wiping my tears.

God, I just saw a man shot! Breathe. Deep breaths. In... out...

I take a few minutes to compose myself. It wouldn't be wise to walk the streets looking as frazzled as I must. The police would certainly question me. Thankfully, I recognize the street I've run to, and I realize the building I lean against is the back of the STO department.

As I straighten, shakily smoothing my dress, a bit of paper catches my attention. Beside the back door is an overflowing rubbish bin. One paper, crumpled in a tight ball, has tumbled from the heap inside the bin, and yet it looks out of place, bright and pristine white among the trash.

I hesitate, loitering in the darkening alley, unsure why this discarded paper has captured my interest. The curiosity, the sinking in my stomach nags uncomfortably, so I lift the ball of paper and unfold it. My heart seizes as I scan the familiar lines, the neat, elegant handwriting my teachers praised, the signature at the bottom of the letter addressed to Marie Beaufoy.

William is waiting for me when I return home, standing behind the barely open cellar door listening for my entrance. He shines me a faint, comforting smile and quietly slips into the house once I've checked to make sure the curtains are drawn.

"André already went up to bed, probably studying," he informs me, mindful to keep his voice low. "He brought us our rations an hour ago, so no need to trouble yourself."

"You're no trouble." I smile wanly, wishing I could muster a more pleasant greeting.

William frowns, taking the laundry bag from my hand. "Are you alright, Louise? You're pale as a ghost," he says, guiding me to the sofa.

Part of me wishes he couldn't see through me so easily, that I could fool him with demure smiles and a calm facade. Even Marie had difficulty seeing through the walls I built to stay strong for her and our family, just like I rarely saw through her walls.

Two bricks cut from the same stone... we've just crumbled to different sides of the obliterated wall...

"Marie," I manage breathlessly, and William patiently waits for me to continue. "I... I haven't heard from her. The STO officials said they would send a letter for me, but..." My fingers tighten around the crushed letter. "They lied. They won't let me contact her or tell me where she is. I'm terrified! I've already lost so many people I love; I can't lose her too!"

Once again, I'm swept into the protective warmth of his arms. The events of the last month spill out without pause; Yvonne's death and her son's disappearance, my argument with Marie, the chance meeting with Desoubrie, who Michelle unmasked as a German spy before she fled, the murder I witnessed, my discarded letter. He doesn't interrupt, though his muscles tense as I speak of Desoubrie. He holds me steady, caressing my back, listening, and I try to draw strength from his calmness.

"It was so sudden..." I mutter, thinking back to the dead man on the street. I can still see it happening, and yet it seems so far away. "I've never seen anyone die... not even my mother."

William's fingers trace the length of my arm. "What happened to her?" he asks softly.

"Complications with pneumonia..."

My mother's face is one I see every day in the mirror. Even when I was a little girl, no mother and daughter had ever looked so similar. I cannot bear to think of her toward the end, deathly pale in the hospital bed, brown eyes weighed down by dark circles, thin beyond health, her blond hair cut to her ears. She asked Father to cut it because she was too weak to brush it herself. That day, Mother cried silently, and Father wept as he took the scissors to her beautiful locks. That was when I knew she was dying. She could barely walk anymore, could barely breathe, and she felt she was a burden to us. Her hair was the last part of herself she could take care of, and once that was gone we knew it was only a matter of time.

Tears spring to my eyes as I picture that day in the hospital, blond hair in a neat mound on the dresser, Marie and me sitting at the edge of the bed, Father on her one side and Fernand on the other. André was two years old, smiling at my mother, who cried as she held him.

"I was fifteen. Marie had just turned ten, André was still a baby..." I go on quietly. "We didn't get to say goodbye. We stayed with her in the hospital all day, we did that a lot in the last few weeks, when we realized she wouldn't get better. She passed away that night... alone."

"I don't believe that," William says, tightening his hold when I move to draw away. "I can see you loved her very much. If a stranger can see that, then I *know* your mother knew it too. She had her family's love with her. I don't believe she was alone, Louise."

Of course, Mother knew she was loved, and perhaps our love gave her comfort when she died, but she was alone. Now I am alone as well, and I hate to think she might have felt this fear, this hopelessness.

"I'm going to make you some tea," William says.

"No," I protest weakly. "I—there's not much left for the month."

"We'll survive. Truth be told—but don't tell them I said so—the guys prefer coffee. Besides, they're *your* rations, and it's good to calm your nerves. Wait here and I'll be right back."

He slips into the kitchen, and the soft rustle of cabinets and the kettle is a cozy, familiar sound. It sounds like home. It's like he and I have lived here all our lives, and he's always made me a cup of tea, and I've come home to melt into his arms and wait for him on the sofa.

Did Mother ever feel this way? I wonder absent-mindedly,

riffling through the cabinet for my sewing box. *She and Father were so close, so familiar... perhaps that was the foundation of their love. Not wild passion or excitement, those can be fleeting. Perhaps it was comfort, ease, and simplicity. I've never felt so at peace with any other man.*

By the time William returns with a steaming cup of tea, I've grabbed my sewing gloves so I can start mending the fragile lace of a gown. He clears his throat and raises a brow in the questioning way a teacher does when they're reprimanding a student caught red-handed. "What are you doing?"

"I have a lot of work to get to tonight. I need to—"

"Do nothing and relax," he cuts in, gently taking my gloves and replacing them with the cup of tea. "You do nothing but work. Work for the resistance, work for your students, work as a seamstress. If anyone is to be put to work tonight, it's me or the guys. Seems unfair the lady of the house works nonstop all day while we sit around doing nothing."

"Well, of course I don't expect you to do anything. You are the ones in hiding."

"And *you* are the one hiding us. I think it's reasonable I do something." He nudges me to the end of the sofa and settles at my side, where he blocks my reach to the piles of clothes.

"William, please, I need to start mending tonight and washing in the morning," I protest, though the sweet aroma of the hot tea is temptingly soothing. "It will all take me days."

He selects a needle from the pincushion, casting me an assuring glance. "Then you do the washing, but I'll do the rest. Don't worry, I won't touch those fine-looking dresses. I doubt you have gloves that would fit me anyhow. Silk and satin don't agree with a soldier's hands."

Stunned, I watch as he expertly threads the black string through the lumen. He takes a tailored suit jacket and carefully traces the seams, searching for holes and tears, and I stare, mesmerized, as he begins to mend the fraying threads near the shoulder.

He is as proficient as a tailor, like Fernand was in his old shop. How did he know not to touch the delicate fabric without gloves to avoid snagging it? That must be a woman's teachings.

He chuckles at the sight of my aghast face. "I'm good for more than just flying planes."

"Who taught you to sew?"

He smiles, eyes gleaming with the tenderness of good memories. "My grandmother, Ethel. She was an old-fashioned woman, went west with my grandfather during the gold rush. He was one of the lucky ones to get a good claim, struck it rich like all the pioneers dreamed. Ethel never let the money change her, though. My grandfather started investing in the railroads, moved the family east to join the oil business, but she stuck to her ways. She always said a man should know how to take care of himself without fame, fortune, or a woman. So, she taught my little sister, Dorothy, and me what our mother calls 'servants' work.'"

We've talked about our lives before, but I didn't realize the high status William's family must have back in America. I've found—like with my father—that it's difficult to equate the smiling man who enjoys the company of others with the soldier who dropped bombs and shot down German Luftwaffe. In a few short years, he's gone from being a wealthy heir to a fugitive acting as man of the household to a French resistance woman and her nephew.

And I never would have met this wonderful man if I hadn't joined the Comet Line...

I sink back into the sofa, sipping my tea, sighing as the warmth and tranquility of the quiet sitting room chases away the worries that lie beyond the door.

I don't understand why the STO department won't tell me anything about Marie. That officer only told me what I wanted to hear to make me leave, but maybe the Comet Line's leaders could help. Perhaps Max or Thomas will be able to help me find some answers, and besides, I need to contact them as soon as possible and find out what plans are being made for the men. But more than anything, I *need* to know what has happened to my sister.

Oh, Marie, please be safe...

13

MAY 22–29, 1944

MARIE

I never truly knew pain before REIMAHG.

Léon accidentally giving me a black eye when we were wrestling, that hurt. Spraining my ankle when my boys and I were playing chase, that was painful. Falling out of a tree and breaking my arm when Jeanne and I were apple-picking when we were twelve, that was excruciating.

But after all those falls and rough games, there was someone to help me up, someone to walk me home, someone to make me soup. And the pain all went away eventually, and then I would be back on my feet, ready for the next romping to get my knees dirty.

There is no rest in REIMAHG, no one who cares if you fall, no one to help you walk back to camp, no food to fill your belly after a long day, no bandages to stop the wounds from bleeding. The pain never stops, and every morning, when you wake to the whistles for another agonizing day of slavery and starvation, the only thing you're ready to do is die.

The sky is clear and bright, the sun scorching down on my face as I haul a sack of cement over one shoulder from the trucks to the tunnel entrance. My skin is burnt and peeling, and the sweat searing down my reddened skin is painful like I've been burned by a hot poker.

No, not like a hot poker. That would be less painful, I think, and my head throbs with the effort. Roger, Léon, Victor, and I once stayed out late to make a bonfire and pretended to be musketeers sword-fighting with burning sticks. We all bear scars where we accidentally burned each other. Now, my entire body feels as though it's on fire.

My ankle rolls and I crumple beneath the weight of the cement. I suck a sharp breath through my teeth as stabbing pain shoots down my leg from where my hip has struck a stone. The other workers assigned to unload the trucks pass me, unwilling to incur the wrath of the SS on my behalf. I struggle to my feet, somehow lift the bag, trudge forward, dump it into the pile, and dread making the trip again. I've already carried eleven bags, and before the truckloads arrived I hauled countless wheelbarrows of rock and dirt that had been cleared out from the mine.

The tunnels grow larger by the day, miles and miles of corridors below our feet.

On my thirteenth trip from the trucks, an overwhelming fatigue assaults me, and suddenly my own weight is too burdensome to carry. The cement bag topples, my knees skin the ground again, but I can hardly be bothered with the pain. Life has been nothing but pain since I came here. The rations are just enough to keep us from starving, my hands, back, and feet are broken and bloody, lice riddle our dirty blocks and bodies, and many have fallen ill.

"You should not have come. This place will eat up a pretty little thing like you."

How I despise that that Soviet was right. I'd be better off in

Paris, barely scraping by. At least then I would be able to take care of Louise and André...

The first two weeks' wages were paid to the volunteers yesterday. The pay was dismal, but by calculating what everything would add up to at the end of the month, it would be more than I made as a mail courier. I went to the SS during appeals, to ask about sending a letter home. They flatly refused. Even upon my insistence that I was a volunteer, they had nothing more to say other than "don't find yourself in any trouble." I knew it was a threat, and retreated to block one, deflated and lost.

A shadow falls over my face, and I almost don't care who's come to punish me, content to endure a beating if I can just stay sitting. An SS shouts nearby, probably brandishing his gun at me, our labor supervisor demands that I get up, then the figure standing before me speaks.

"She's too small for what she's doing. Look at her. She shouldn't be carrying stones. You'll just kill her faster."

My eyes crack open, blinded by the sunlight as it reflects off the pale Soviet like snow.

"I'll decide what she can do," the labor supervisor spits. "You mind yourself, *Soviet*. Go crawl back into the tunnels."

"At least I'm out of the sun," Radomir says impassively. He pulls me up and presents my raw hands to the supervisor. "Are you so weak you need a little girl to work hauling rock for you? She's no good to anyone out here."

The supervisor glares at him. "I didn't ask for your opinion!"

"She can't work quickly enough; she's slowing your group down. You and I both know the SS are getting impatient. What do they do with incompetent supervisors?"

At this, the supervisor's lips press into a thin line, and his eyes flicker almost fearfully to where an SS guard has his gun trained on us.

"You should find a worker who doesn't weigh as much as these bags."

The supervisor makes no retort, and, after a moment's consideration, rolls his shoulders back. "Take her to the tunnels. Maybe you'll make better use of her," he says, and my heart drops as he leaves, content to abandon me at the mercy of a Russian in favor of a new worker.

There were days when Louise and I wouldn't let André listen to the broadcasts, and sometimes she herself could not stomach hearing the horror tales of places reclaimed by the Red Army—people butchered and mutilated, women and little girls raped, tortured, and murdered, homes burned with screaming people trapped inside.

"Stay close to me, lisichka." Radomir's voice startles me from my thoughts. He heaves my bag of cement over his shoulder, still strong for a man weakened by starvation and hard labor, still much stronger than me... I shudder, wondering what inhumanities have been committed at his hands. I am determined that I will not fall beneath them.

I slip my hand into the slit I made in my skirt that makes the sharp rock in my pocket more accessible, and, despite my dizzy, throbbing head and aching muscles, I remain alert as I reluctantly follow him into the tunnels. The immediate darkness is consuming and oppressive, like stepping into a crypt. The lanterns burn low and dim as if they too cannot breathe. The damp scent of dirt and decay reminds me of the day Roger, Léon, Victor, and I discovered an entrance to the tunnels beneath Paris and found ourselves in the catacombs from centuries before.

Will I die down here? Will my skull be placed in the wall, never to see the light again?

Radomir leads me further into the mountain, past workers chiseling at the walls, shoveling dirt into barrows to wheel up to the living world, smashing stones with pickaxes and hammers, and the occasional SS guard where no labor supervisor presides. We come to a small room no more than six feet in length either way. A lantern, a bucket, and a tin cup sit in the corner.

"Drink," Radomir says.

With one hand resting on my rock, I keep my back to the wall, eyes half on him as I grab the tin cup with parched longing. I've only had a few drinks today and, though my throat is raw and dry, I hesitate at the brownish-gray tint of the water in the bucket.

"It's clean enough." Radomir takes a rag from his pocket and uses it like a pouch to scoop some water from the bucket and let a small stream of water trickle into the tin cup. "This is what we've been doing. Trying to filter what we can."

The water in the cup is still dirty, but the cloth has caught most of the larger particles. As I hesitantly move to drink, a wandering hand touches my ankle and lifts my skirt. Gasping, I smash the cup against his face and draw the sharp rock from my pocket.

Radomir draws back, looking more surprised than hurt as he wipes a trickle of blood from his nose. "What was that for?" He sounds genuinely confused. "Did you hurt your ankle too? Have I hurt you?"

"What for?" I demand, shaking with rage and a twinge of fear, trying to edge around him to the entrance he's blocking. "You tried—you lifted my skirt! Do you think I'll let you touch me if you get me out of the sun, give me water? I owe you nothing! Touch me and I'll kill you!"

Realization seems to dawn on him, and he nods. "I didn't mean to scare you. You fell on your knees, and your hip too. I saw. I was going to check for bleeding. You should wash them, so they don't get infected."

I narrow my eyes at him, scoffing skeptically. "I don't want your help, so fuck off."

He chuckles. "I didn't know ladies could have such a foul vocabulary."

"Four brothers," I grumble, thinking of Fernand and my boys.

"Hmm... I only had sisters, but they never picked up such words from me."

"Just leave me alone!" I snap, tightening my grip on the rock. "I know you watch me, I'm not blind, and I'm not helpless either!"

His pale eyes have followed me since I arrived in REIMAHG. I've felt him watching me from afar, though he hasn't approached since the first night I refused his bandages.

His brow quirks, seriousness replacing the amusement. Like a snake, he darts out, snatching my wrist. Terror surges through my body as he grabs the rock from me, drawing me against his broad chest. It all takes less than a second. Stunned by his speed and the ease with which he restrains me, my heart clenches, and I cannot find my voice to even scream.

"Not helpless," he muses, though it doesn't sound like a taunt. "You have power in your hit, but you're at a disadvantage. You're smaller than any opponent you'll fight. Your goal should be to escape, not to win." He releases my arm. Holding my rock, he assumes a defensive position. "See, keep your arms close to your body. You don't want to give anyone the chance to grab you or take your weapon like I just did. Once you strike, bring your arms back to your body."

He offers the rock to me. Dumbfounded, I take it, and he urges me to assume his current position. Hesitantly, I comply, and he nods.

"Good. And remember, always go for the vulnerable spots. Dig your thumbs in their eyes, right here." He demonstrates, his calloused thumbs hovering above the corners of my eyes by my nose. "That could blind them. The nose is good too. Here, give me your hand. Take your palm or fist like this and ram their nose up toward their brow. That will disorient them, could cause head damage too. Or this—" He flattens my hands from the fists he made and places my palms over his ears. "If you find yourself close like this, hit both your hands over their ears. *Hard.* As hard as you can and break their eardrums. The throat is also effective. Punch hard enough, and they won't be able to breathe. Go for the knees too. Kick them back and break them."

"You fight dirty," I mumble half-heartedly.

He shrugs. "There's no such thing as fighting dirty. There's fighting for survival, and there's getting killed. As you can see, I'm still here. I've been hurt plenty of times, so I know you should clean your cuts. You don't want an infection. You won't find much medicine here."

Any medicine here is for the "noble Aryans." There is a hospital for the laborers, Lager Hummelshain, and a few smaller infirmaries exist in the other lagers, but there are few doctors, and the likelihood of recovery is low. Laborers are expendable, so medicine is spent more generously on the SS and German workers.

Radomir turns his back to keep a watchful eye on the other dimly lit tunnels. Blind to my movements and defenseless as he is—though his hands are weapons enough—still I pose no threat to him. He knows it, and so do I. With a sigh, I slip the rock back into my pocket and kneel. I glance at Radomir every now and again as I roll up my skirt and pants to wipe the blood from my knees and hip, but he doesn't turn, nor make any move toward me again.

Work in the tunnels is no easier than above ground. It's worse, shoveling at the tunnel walls to widen them, smashing rocks and quickly becoming winded from the lack of air. But I'm out of the sun and away from the SS. I'm one of few women underground, and the deprived stares of men who've been without women for years and months make me uneasy, but none approach. I remain close to Radomir as he instructed, and his presence alone is deterrent enough.

Better the devil I know, I think foggily, though truly I know Radomir no better than any of the others. I know nothing of his past, of anything he's done in the war, if he's one of the monsters I've heard about on the radio... If I could force my thoughts to align coherently, I might wonder why he's fixated on me. But as I trudge forward through the supper queue back in Lager Six, simply holding my bowl is a struggle, and I slump against the wall of block one. The sight of the small bread crust and glop of margarine makes my stomach roil, and I try to force down the nausea.

"You look ready to fall over, lisichka."

I groan, quickly straightening. The movement leaves me dizzy, and I cannot find the strength to glare as Radomir appraises me.

I want to scream at him to leave me alone, or cry, or try one of his techniques to dissuade him from following me, or... I don't care. Everything is painful, every breath, every thought, and I only want to find somewhere quiet and soft to sleep.

His fingers brush the hair from my face, then press against my forehead. He frowns, unbothered as I shrink from his touch. "You're burning up," he murmurs. "It could be the heat... do you feel ill?"

"What do you want from me?" I ask hoarsely, trying to swallow the cough rising in my throat. My voice lacks any contempt. I am too tired, too sore to waste my energy on him.

He frowns, saying nothing, and, after a glance toward the supper line, sees there is still food left, and moves to be served with the other Russian POWs.

My first instinct is to escape into the block while he's gone, but I discard the idea immediately. I wouldn't dare enter alone until the SS lock us in our segregated rooms. Besides, no one would willingly subject themselves to sleeping on rotting wooden bunks and lice-riddled mats any longer than absolutely necessary. I secure my bright hair beneath my shirt and slip away into the crowd of laborers.

Men and women congregate separately, and I find a place near a milling group of around forty people bargaining for food, clothes, and other goods. Shaking, I try to eat my ration. After several moments of fighting to keep it down, my stomach rejects the bread, and I empty what little food and water was in my body into the mud behind the block. The stench from block seven doesn't help to ease the nausea either, and I determinedly keep my eyes averted from the morgue.

The SS blow their whistles at eleven o'clock, and I reluctantly drag myself into the room I share with nineteen other women. I catch a glimpse of Radomir, who visibly relaxes when our eyes meet. As I squeeze into a bunk for a few precious hours of sleep, I dread the sunrise. Sleep doesn't come, for the groans, coughs, and heaving of starving, ill people are deafening, and I think back to Radomir's concern as I unconsciously scratch the red bites beneath my clothes.

Wailing rather than whistles is what I awaken to in the morning. I attempt to open my eyes, but my head throbs with the effort, so instead I listen as women scream and cry. I don't understand all the languages being spoken, but I needn't know the words to feel their grief, their distress.

The door of our room is thrown open and demanding German voices echo through the block as the other doors are unlocked. The screams grow louder as the SS shout, stinging my temples. A hand settles over my head. I groan, trying to swat it away, and fight to open my eyes.

Radomir's face is paler than usual, lips pressed into a grim frown, and his gray eyes seem to waver with fear. "Fever," he mutters quietly. "You have typhus."

As if to prove his diagnosis, a coughing fit seizes me, leaving my entire burning body trembling. I try to speak, but my throat is too raw and painful.

"There's been a typhus outbreak in our block. Three died last night," he informs me gravely, and I'm too weak to fight him as he draws me out of the bunk and carries me as a man would a bride into another room. "We're under quarantine. The SS won't be opening this block for a week, not for anything."

He carries me to a bunk next to a barred window, and I fill my lungs with the gust of fresh air. For a heartbeat, I am grateful there will be no labor for us, and then despair drags me back beneath the darkness of exhaustion as Radomir pulls the hair back from my face, and I can form only one terrifying thought as I lose consciousness.

I am completely at his mercy...

So soft...

It's the first thing I'm aware of after the unbearable heat. My hands feel soft, and I caress the delicate fabric that surrounds my palms and fingers. Gentle hands run through my hair, braiding the locks away from my burning cheeks, and I sigh with contentment. When did someone last brush my hair?

Mother... oh, Mother, you were the last one to do this for me. Is it you now? Are we in heaven? Or is it you, Louise? You always wanted to, but I never let you...

"Louise..." I murmur, reaching blindly for her.

The hands pause, then one slips into my grasp. They are far too large to be my sister, far too real to be my mother, and yet they are no less tender.

I force my eyes open, and am met with darkness and a pallid, bearded man gazing down at me. I know him, I'm sure I do, but my mind cannot form the name. As I struggle to sit up, the ache in every limb roars to life like an inferno and I slump, biting my cheeks in pain.

"Don't do that." His hands leave my hair to urge my jaw to loosen.

As the pain ebbs, the tension fades, and I breathe slowly, tasting the faint traces of blood.

He raises a pouch to my lips, and the earthy scent of beets and turnips brings the nausea crashing back. I seal my lips, turning away like a child refusing supper, but he forces my mouth open and tips the cold soup down my throat. I sputter, narrow my eyes, and try to crawl away, though there isn't anywhere to go. I am against the stone wall, his body separating me from the others on the top bunk, and I don't have the strength to get down.

"Stop it," he demands gruffly. "Eat. Believe me, starving is *not* the way you want to go."

"I don't need..." I groan, unable to continue. *I don't need you.*

My head is heavy as a brick, crushed so terribly from all sides that tears stream down my face, and for a moment I believe I see comets shooting across the ceiling like the night sky.

"Swallow your pride, it isn't good for survival," he says, forcing me to drink and swallow again. "You are strong, and proud. That is good, but you do nothing for yourself by refusing help. There is no shame in needing someone."

I don't need my enemy. If Hitler hadn't attacked Stalin, he'd still be fighting with the Germans. He isn't a friend... And yet, I cannot find my voice to speak, for my eyes are slipping closed, and the last thing I see are my own hands held by his, wrapped in clean white bandages.

. . .

The days come and go in agony and humiliation. What little food and water is forced down my throat comes back out one way or the other, and I have no control over either. At some point, Radomir suggested he remove my undergarments so I wouldn't soil them. I cried and screamed and fought him when he said it, fearing I'd endure the brutality that I had heard girls suffered at the hands of the Russian army, but he put his hands up in surrender and didn't touch me. Soon, the stench became too much to bear, and I couldn't stand to be unable to wash myself in such a state. I must have been delirious, but I can vaguely recall nodding when he asked again, and he removed my pants and skirt, then used a blanket to cover my partial nakedness.

Sometimes I lie awake, listening to the groans of pain, the occasional panicked screams of women trying to bar their doors while several men try to force their way in. Other days, the only sound is the heavy dragging of bodies being hauled to the designated morgue room at the end of the block. The SS won't open the door for anything, not to feed us, not to let us relieve ourselves, not even to remove the dead. When I am conscious, I can hear Radomir talking to me. Even though I don't understand, something about the Russian words is calming. Once or twice, I've awoken to his voice rising in a murderous shout, felt hands being torn off me, then cries of pain have carried me back to the dizzying realm between sleep and the present like a lullaby.

What I wouldn't give to hear my mother's lullabies... Mother had the loveliest voice, so angelic and soft. Louise would sing with her while they did chores, and I remember I was jealous of how beautiful they sounded together. How I wish I could hear Louise now...

"I'm so sorry, Louise," I hear myself whimper, my heart clenching in regret. After our mother died, I couldn't stand to hear Louise sing. When I was thirteen, I shouted at her when she started singing Mother's favorite song, 'Mon Homme', and after that I never heard her sing again.

What an awful sister I am! How could I have left them? Louise is so much smarter, so much stronger than me, a far better daughter than I ever was...

She was closest to our parents. People used to say she was our mother's twin daughter, and she and Father bonded over their shared love of teaching... perhaps I was jealous of that. I took everything for granted, never spent enough time with them while I had them, and now here I am once again, abandoning everyone when I'm needed the most...

"But you didn't abandon us, dear."

My breath catches in disbelief, and I have the faintest sensation that someone is shaking me. But I am alone now, and weightless as I sit up. Across from me on a bunk, two people are sitting together, their hands intertwined, watching me.

"Mother... Father..." I whisper.

They smile, beautiful, kind smiles I haven't seen in many years.

"How are you—what are you doing here?" I gasp, a grin breaking across my face.

Father slips his arm around Mother's waist. "We're waiting for you, dear."

Mother nods. "I've wanted to hold you for so long, my little girl. Come back with us." Her arms extend to me, and the little girl in me wants nothing more than to throw myself into her warmth.

And yet this all feels wrong. The world is so bright, so painless, like a heavenly light smiles down on us, but something isn't right. There is another voice reaching for me from beyond the light, a deep, masculine voice, and the sense of cold hands caressing my face.

"Please, come home with us, Marie," Father says, offering his hand.

I want to go with them, be the daughter I should have been years ago. But why are Louise and Fernand not here? What about André? Mother's and Father's welcoming, loving gazes are so tempting that I could discard the thought of anyone else and simply go home with them. Mother begins to sing the words of 'Mon Homme' like an angel as the light grows brighter. I draw away.

Louise and André need me... they are waiting at home.

Mother's love song is overtaken by another, a quieter, lamenting melody in some language I don't understand. The light dies, darkness engulfs me, and suddenly I am gasping for air as though I haven't breathed in days, and all the warmth that remains is the fleeting sense of a kiss on my forehead. My heavy eyes fly open, to be met with a startling, heartbreaking sight. Radomir's face hovers above me, the evidence of tears tracking down his pale, dirty cheeks to his beard, and the mournful Russian song I just heard ends abruptly.

For a while he only stares at me, his trembling hands still holding my face. "I thought you were gone this time..." he whispers. "But you're a fighter. I think you'll survive, after all."

Gone? Mother, Father... Was it a dream, another hallucination? Or was it real?

To think too much about whatever I saw makes my head throb painfully with confusion, so I push it away. This moment is what I must focus on, today and tomorrow and whatever it takes to get home. *And if it weren't for him, I wouldn't be able to think of getting home right now.*

Typhus has ravaged me brutally. I haven't been able to feed myself, relieve myself, let alone defend myself. All this time, Radomir has protected me, never once abused his power over me. Instead, he's bound my wounds, cleaned the messes I couldn't control, cried over me when he thought I was dead... and it was his voice that drew me back from the light. I might have died if not for him. But I refuse to die. I didn't come all this way to die on enemy soil of a damn fever.

"Marie," I rasp, realizing I have never told him my name. "My name is Marie."

In the shadows of the block, a sliver of light from the window illuminates his face as a fragile, genuine smile graces his lips, and he lifts a tin of water to my dry, cracked lips. I manage to keep it down without vomiting.

"That is a lovely name, lisichka."

14

JUNE 1, 1944

LOUISE

The little café Yvonne and I once frequented is empty. When we joined the Comet Line, we came here for the secrecy as the small business never attracted the attention of the Germans. When life was simpler, we came here as young girls to have cookies and giggle over handsome boys at school, share inconsequential gossip, and plan our futures.

Oh, Yvonne, how different things have turned out to be. Back then, we never would have guessed our lives would turn out this way, or end as yours did...

Swallowing the lump in my throat, I approach the counter and smile at the young girl polishing the wood.

"Good morning, mademoiselle," she greets me happily.

I glance at the vase of red roses. "How lovely," I observe, and the girl pauses, holding her breath as if anticipating something more. "But I think lilies would look beautiful as well."

The girl nods in recognition of the code phrase and slips me a piece of paper.

I finally managed to get a message to Max, and the piece of

paper will hold the address of our meeting place. I only linger long enough to memorize the address, slip the paper into my pocket to burn later, then I'm on my way to an old bookshop on Rue Bouret that was once a restaurant with a wine cellar accessible from a stairwell outside.

The oak door at the bottom of the stairs is locked from within. I give a quick knock, wait several seconds, then knock three more times in quick succession. After a moment, the click of the latch opens. Oil lanterns have been forgone in favor of dimmer, odorless candles, and I move to take a seat on a dusty crate as Max slides the door's lock back into place.

"It's good to see you," Max whispers, though we are far out of earshot of anyone even had they pressed their ear to the cellar door.

I nod curtly, my concerns taking precedence over courtesy. "It's been over a month, Max." *Forty-six days to be exact.* "What's going on? I've never housed any soldiers for so long. We're all at risk the longer they stay here. Have any plans been made yet?"

His shoulders sag with a sigh. "Nothing concrete. I promise, we'll get them out as soon as possible, but there are complications. Michelle told me one of the Americans you're hiding was shot?"

My throat constricts, and I am drawn back into the darkness of the kitchen with a bleeding soldier in the cellar, and Michelle Dumon's sad, sympathetic gaze on me. "Yes, Jack was shot in the shoulder. He's still in pain, no matter what he does."

Max frowns. "I don't want to risk moving him until he's fully healed. He'll slow down any group he leaves with, and I'm sure I don't need to say why he'd pose a problem if the SS or Gestapo suspected and searched him."

"And what about the other three?" I press on. "Marie has gone to Germany, and I've heard nothing from her. I'm providing for all of them on my own now. I don't know how much longer I can sustain it. Please, I need to know what plans are being made for them."

"It's not that simple. There are other members who've been hiding airmen for just as long as you. The Gestapo are doubling their efforts. We're rooting out their spies as quickly as we can, but the raids just keep coming. We have to be extra cautious, me especially." Max sighs, wipes his brow and replaces his hat over his inky black hair. "I've managed to keep them off me so far, but I think the authorities are having me followed. They don't know I'm our main guide, or else I'd have been arrested by now. I think they might be waiting to observe who I have contact with."

My breath catches and I clutch my skirt reflexively. Taking Max out of the picture would be catastrophic for the Line. He is the one all our members know, the one who knows all the routes from Belgium to France to Spain, the most experienced guide we have.

"I'm arranging for more guides; it wouldn't be good for me to leave the city now. Taking too many extended trips is like asking for the Gestapo to catch me. We've only managed to move about a dozen airmen into the forest-camps in the last month, but you and I both know those camps are more vulnerable to discovery than our safehouses. I'd rather not move anyone out there unless absolutely necessary. But I promise you, we're working to get everyone out of Paris as soon as possible."

I nod reluctantly, but his answer doesn't assure me in the slightest. Promises are all I've had since the Americans first came, the promise they'll only stay for a few days, that they'll be escaping as soon as possible, and I'm still in danger of discovery.

Contemplating arrest brings my thoughts back to Jacques Desoubrie. A spy could just as easily be my downfall as a Gestapo raid. "And what about Jacques Desoubrie?" I ask. "Has Michelle been able to prove his allegiance now?"

Max's face darkens with contempt at the mention of the

name. "Oh. Yes, Michelle proved his status. But no need to worry about him anymore. He's been dealt with."

"Dealt with?" I venture.

"He's dead," Max states with dark indifference. "The British MI9 agents asked the French Forces of the Interior to shoot him a few days back."

Every hair on my body tingles and rises. I want to be relieved by this development that the FFI resistance fighters killed Desoubrie, and yet the warning clench in my stomach makes me doubtful. The shooting was only a week ago. The killer was following Desoubrie and me that day, and Desoubrie said we were near his home... *What are the odds?*

"Was it last week? On May twenty-second?" I ask warily.

His brows rise in surprise and my heart plummets. "How do you know that?"

Suddenly, the man in the gray coat's reaction when he shot that man doesn't seem so odd. He looked shocked, and, ever since, I've wondered why he would be so when he clearly meant to kill someone. He was expecting Desoubrie to walk by, not the man dressed like him.

"I saw it happen," I choke out. "But it wasn't Desoubrie. I was with him. He insisted on walking me home and I couldn't get away. There was another man there who looked just like him, he was even wearing the same coat. He was the one shot, and Desoubrie ran off."

Max's face pales. "You're sure?"

"Of course I'm sure! I watched it happen! Someone was following us, shot him, and ran away after Desoubrie escaped!"

"Alright, alright! I believe you. I just—" Max stops abruptly, his words trailing away as it appears his thoughts are fighting to align. "Damn him!" he exclaims at last, slamming his cap on the floor in frustration. "We should've known he messed up when he gave the FFI some shit excuse to leave Paris! Right after the shooting, he just couldn't get away fast enough! Damn coward didn't want to admit he screwed up! Oh, if he were here, I'd wring his bloody—"

"Max!" I interrupt his tirade, looking sharply, worriedly to the door. "Lower your voice! You never know who might hear you. There's nothing to be done about it now."

He huffs angrily, pinching the bridge of his nose. "Desoubrie is a lucky rat... I'll inform our members and the MI9. We need to be cautious. Desoubrie is bound to lie low for a while if he suspects we had anything to do with it. And you said Marie has left?"

"Yes, she joined the STO program. I wanted to ask you a favor. The STO department won't let me find out where she is. Her papers said she was going to Germany, but I haven't heard from her, and I'm getting worried. Is there any way you could find out where she is?"

I should probably feel guilty for asking a favor from him when he already has so much to deal with, but my heart doesn't bother to twist. I have to know where Marie is.

"I'm not sure." Max frowns. "We don't have any members in the STO department. I'll see what I can do, but I don't want you to get your hopes up. I don't know if I'll be able to find her."

"All I'm asking is for you to try."

"I will try," he promises, but, as our discussion ends and we space our departures so neither can be connected to the other in case of stalking spies, my hopes aren't high.

For once, André isn't studying in his room when I return home; he is kicking a flat ball back and forth with the other boys, and I muse over the irony of it. At one point, that boy had to be dragged inside by his ear, made every excuse not to study, and lately, I've hardly been able to get him to abandon his books, so it comes as a surprise to finally see him outside again.

I put on a kettle as I store away our rations of flour, eggs, coffee, beef, cheese, and two jars of jam—the extra cost me thirty francs. Pearls, like silk, are scarce but in high demand among the upper class, so the pearl necklace Marie stole from Jeanne went for a good price on the black market, and I've had a little extra money for food. However, no amount of money could change that not a single teaspoon of sugar or butter was to be found in the market.

I pour four half-cups of coffee and take the tray into the cellar.

William is the only one awake while the others have dozed off, the same arrangement I usually come down to. He is the oldest of them at twenty-nine; George is twenty-five like me, and Robert and Jack are both barely nineteen, and William considers them his responsibility, just as an older brother would think of his siblings. Like Fernand regarded Marie and me... William nudges them awake.

"How is your shoulder?" I ask, handing a cup to Jack.

"Never better." He smiles, wincing as he takes the coffee, and Robert snickers at him.

"There's no infection," William offers quietly.

A poor standard of health. Even without stitches, Jack's shoulder has almost completely healed, but he is still in terrible pain. Privately, William has expressed concerns that Jack's bones may have been damaged. If that's the case, he won't recover without proper surgery, and the only medical attention I can offer him is clean gauze and alcohol.

"I'll try to get you some medicine for the pain."

"Don't trouble yourself. I'm fine," Jack protests, but I see the prospect makes him yearn for relief.

"Is there any word about the Allies?" George asks, unable to contain his curiosity.

I shake my head. "Nothing reliable. The papers and radio just say more of the same. Germany is on the brink of victory, the Allies are already defeated. I've heard a few rumors; people expect there will be an Allied landing soon."

"Will we be moved soon?" Robert asks hopefully, looking every bit the teenager he is.

"There are some complications. I'm hoping a new guide will be arranged soon. I'm sorry I don't have any concrete plans to give you right now, but we're doing everything we can."

Their faces, while fallen with disappointment, remain optimistic. As I gather their cups, wondering where I might be able to buy aspirin or morphine for Jack, William arranges the tray.

"I'll help you with this," he says, his eyes flashing with the silent request to talk alone.

I nod. As William follows me upstairs I notice the others smirking and nudging one another. I lock the doors and draw all the curtains shut. The evening is late enough that no one will see our silhouettes inside, but he is careful to stay far from the windows.

"What do you want to talk about?" I ask quietly.

"I wanted to know if you've heard anything from your sister yet."

Breathing deeply, I force down the distress that hasn't released me since the moment Marie's train disappeared. "No. I've spoken with one of the Line's members, and I'm hoping he'll be able to help me find her."

He settles a comforting hand on my shoulder. "You'll find her, Louise. And if not, then she'll find you. I know I don't know her that well, but I can tell she's the persistent sort. She loves you; she'll find a way to get back."

She loves you... Those few words break down all my semblance of control. I feel my face crumple, and I turn away, hiding my tears. I can't remember a time in my life when I cried so much. I wept for days after my mother died, but since then I've made myself stay strong for the family; but lately it seems the smallest things bring all my fears and grief to the surface.

This is your fault, I think, half in fondness and half in accusation, as William draws me into his arms. I was perfectly fine before we met. My days were quiet, albeit filled with fear, and I resolved to be strong, to keep my family together though we often seemed to be fraying at the seams. Then, he came waltzing into my life with his beautiful eyes, kind words, and warm arms, shattering all my illusions and plans like glass, making me realize that for so long I'd been suffocating, then teaching me it was alright to breathe.

"It's always been hard for Marie and me," I mutter into his chest. "Our mother said sisters were supposed to be close, but we never were. It got worse after she died. I took over the house and family, and Marie became so distant and cold. We just kept drifting apart... but I've always loved her, no matter what. Sometimes she makes me furious and sometimes she can be so hurtful, but I *do* love her. I don't think I've ever heard her say it. I know she does, but..."

"I know the feeling," William murmurs. "My little sister, Dorothy, and I aren't two peas in a pod. We didn't even *start* to get along until after I left for university, and that was when I realized how much I missed having her around to argue with and tease.

"But no matter how many times we fought, called each other names, or got each other in trouble, we were still brother and sister before anything else. We'd always be there for each other, and, even if we'd never say it, we loved each other—though you'll have a hell of a time getting Dorothy to admit it."

"You admit it easily," I tease at the begrudging fondness in his voice.

He chuckles, and the sound rumbles from his chest to my heart. "Life is fragile. I don't see any reason to waste time when we already have so little of it. When I get home, the first thing I'll do is take Dorothy to see Ella Fitzgerald. Ella's been her favorite musician for years."

"When my brother comes home, the first thing I'll do is cook him a banquet of his favorite meals. I don't imagine army or prison rations are that good."

"I don't know what it's like for the French, but ours weren't usually too bad. The navy is spoiled, though. Did you know we have entire ships whose only purpose is to make ice cream?"

"Ice cream ships?" I laugh in disbelief. "Europe can barely scrape up enough food for one person, and you Americans have ice cream ships?"

"Just the navy." He grins. "Where is your brother? André mentioned he's a soldier, but I've never heard you talk about him."

"Fernand," I murmur, my heart falling. "I don't know where he is. He and my father joined the army four years ago. We haven't seen or heard from them since. I can only hope they're alive, maybe in a prison camp somewhere..."

William brushes away the tear that slips down my cheek. "If they're anything like you and Marie, they're incredibly strong. They're alive, Louise, I'm sure of it."

They have to be alive. Father survived the Great War, Fernand will do whatever it takes to return to his son, and Marie... well, Marie has never done well with authority. She'll come home, if for no other reason than to spite whoever doesn't want her to.

But part of me will always worry. Marie and I have lost each other so many times over the years, fought and ignored each other for days, but her room was always right down the hallway. Maybe, if I'd taken better care of the family, if I hadn't driven a wedge between us with my work for the Comet Line, she would have stayed.

15

JUNE 5, 1944

MARIE

If the choice ever comes down to starvation or a bullet, I'd rather be shot.

Two weeks have gone since the beginning of our quarantine. I have eaten for only half of those days, and the crushing weakness in my limbs, the blurry, unfocused state of my mind, the unbearable pain of my body turning against itself from within, is torturous.

Typhus has taken the lives of over thirty people of the hundred and twenty in our block, though for some of them I'm sure starvation and dehydration got to them first. The SS only gave food and water occasionally through the windows, and only the people strong enough to fight for it were able to eat. Had Radomir not been strong enough to fight for the rare rations, to defend me in my vulnerable state, I wouldn't have eaten at all—or might have come to some worse fate.

The block entrance is thrown open, and the morning light is so blinding it stings my eyes. I turn my gaze away toward Radomir's body, trembling with the effort standing takes, and cannot find the strength nor will to remove his supportive arm keeping me upright.

Two weeks spent relying on him and living on the brink of death has somewhat softened my callousness toward him. My suspicion of his objectives still remains, but I have grown less wary of him. After all, if he wanted to hurt me, he'd have done it by now.

Now that quarantine is over, those of us who survived will be returning to our usual labor schedule. For now, that inevitable hell is overshadowed by the ability to fill my lungs with the cool, fresh scent of pine and earth and feel the sun warming my clammy face.

"Never thought I'd be so happy to stand in this lineup," I groan as we shuffle to join roll call and Radomir chuckles low in his throat.

I never want to enter another building again. If only I could be allowed to sleep on the ground outside, rain, snow, and wild animals be damned. Oh, God, I don't want to go back into the tunnels!

Lager Six is divided into two groups. The first heads directly for the quarry, but group two—consisting of all the POWs and the surviving inhabitants of block one—are instructed to follow our SS guards and supervisors into the forest. After an hour, we make it to a small clearing in the trees. Fallen trees lie in stacks alongside hatchets and handsaws, split logs sit in discarded piles bound together with rope.

"It seems we're lumberjacks today," Radomir mutters. As the SS divide the Russian POWs from everyone else, he gives my hand a reassuring squeeze. "Just keep your head down. This is better than the mines," he whispers, then joins the other Russians, grabs a hatchet and vanishes into the woods with multiple SS men, their guns already drawn and aimed in case of trouble.

The hours pass in relative quiet, aside from the occasional

shouted order and the serrated saws dragging back and forth across branches as we strip them from the fallen trees. Every now and again a bird twitters in annoyance at us for having cut down their home. The men are left with the hardest work, cutting down trees, tying ropes around the logs after we chop the branches off, and hauling them miles to different locations to build additional lagers.

I might have been grateful for the opportunity to work outside of the tomb that is the mine, shaded from the sun and heat, but I haven't fully recovered. Crushing exhaustion makes every drag of the saw as burdensome as carrying cement, my legs wobble, and the only relief is that Radomir's bandages have kept my hands relatively protected, though the sores are still raw.

The evening bread—while barely a few bites—feels heavy in my palm, and my stomach still cannot handle more than a nibble or two. I find myself glancing about the clearing in search of my large, pale shadow, as he is usually somewhere nearby, but I haven't seen him since we returned to Lager Six an hour ago.

"Missing me, lisichka?" His deep accent rumbles almost teasingly as he approaches from around the corner of a block, making me jump.

"What are you doing? There's still food." I nod toward the supper line where the relieved Russians are taking their rations. "Aren't you going to eat?"

He shakes his head. "Not tonight, I can go without."

I eye him skeptically with a twinge of concern. "How could you just go without?"

He shrugs, beckoning me to follow him. "I've been in *real* prisoner of war camps. I've learned how to never eat. After that, a place like this isn't half bad."

As we slip back around the block the way he came, I'm

drawn back to our quarantine, when he forced me to eat and told me that starving wasn't the way I would want to die. He, like all the other Russians, is thin beyond health, especially for a man of twenty-six. I can't imagine what he must have gone through in the Nazi prison camps. A man as tall and broad as he is, even while starving, must have been an incredibly well-built soldier.

I wonder how he was captured. Even now, I think he could take on multiple SS and win.

Radomir withdraws a small burlap bag that has been hidden under his thin shirt. From it, he takes a soft, golden dinner roll and two white tablets. "Aspirin," he explains. "Eat the bread first, then the medicine. I have more tablets for the next few days if you're still in pain."

"Where did you get this?" I blurt in shock.

"Some of the SS went to the Lindig village for their day off yesterday. A few of them sometimes bring back things to sell to the workers. Now, don't waste that, they charge a Russian twice as much."

The fluffy bread is too tempting to refuse even if my appetite has dissipated, and I quickly swallow the tiny aspirin tablets.

"Why aren't you eating?" I ask at the audible grumble of his stomach.

"Because the SS are bastar—" He clears his throat abruptly, as if realizing he was about to curse in front of a lady. "If you're Russian, and you want to trade, you get a choice. Nightly rations, or whatever you can buy, but not both. The way they see it, there's no point in wasting twice as much on dead men."

"You're not eating because of me?" The soft bread is suddenly fighting to come back up, and a pang of guilt wrenches my gut as I look over his body. "Just eat my ration, you idiot!"

He smiles, and his dim eyes shimmer faintly like stars. "There you are, lisichka. Fiery as always. Trust me, there are worse things to eat than nothing. I can live for another six hours without food. Besides, we need to save what we can."

Save what we can? I wonder, prepared to ask what we're saving, why we're saving it, and why it's *we*. But then something else he said confuses me.

"You're a prisoner of war," I say, brow drawn. "You're not paid anything. How could you have bought bread and aspirin from the SS?"

He scans our surroundings with the intensity and practiced efficiency of a sniper, then jerks his head in a silent command to follow, and I fall into step behind him as we creep to the back of the blocks. The others are still making appeals, socializing, and eating, and the SS are busy keeping watchful eyes on them, so Radomir and I are left completely unguarded.

How easy it would be to run away, I think, gaze focused on the treeline ten yards away. *I could escape, slip away while the SS are distracted and never look back.*

"Quickly, be quiet," Radomir whispers, his large fingers curling around my wrist, and my heart stutters in disbelief as my body numbly follows as he runs to the woods.

It is cool and dark beneath the trees, and the evening wind carries with it the songs of owls and crickets. One could almost forget the lager behind us, the quarry, and the SS, but then I am struck by the unfamiliarity of this serene place.

None of us are allowed contact with the other lagers besides the ones we work with, and our knowledge of the land is restricted to the paths to our worksites. We are completely blind, isolated from the rest of the world even though it's at our fingertips. Radomir helped build the REIMAHG camps, so he knows there are lagers in every direction, uncharted miles of German land I've never seen. If I were to run away, I would need a map and a miracle.

"What are we doing? Are you mad?" I hiss as he leads me so far into the woods I no longer fear the SS will hear the twigs snapping beneath my feet. The lanterns on our stone blocks have vanished and we are left beneath the luminous glow of a full moon, but Radomir knows his way effortlessly, even in the dark.

Finally, we stop, but my heart still pounds harshly against my chest, though I have no idea whether in fear or excitement. Louise would say it was both, then call me a reckless thrill-seeker. A smile gentles my apprehension at the thought. What I wouldn't give to hurl insults at each other again.

"Well? Care to explain?" I whisper, sounding more like Louise than I'll ever admit.

Radomir kneels at the base of an oak tree. "You're about to be furious at me," he begins, using a stick to dig. "But try not to shout. Come here, and I'll explain it."

Suspicious, I kneel beside him and peer curiously into the hole he's dug. A foot into the earth, his stick strikes tin with a clink, and he lifts a rusted metal box.

"I took your wages to bribe the SS. That's how I bought it," he says.

My hands fly to my pockets in disbelief, frantically digging in search of the marks, but there is only my sharp rock. He must have stolen it during quarantine, when I was too sick to see or think straight. "You no-good thief! I should've expected it!" I fume, the back of my hand stinging his cheek. Before I can slap him again, he catches my wrist.

"It was no good anyway," he whispers forcefully, pinning me in place with his steely gaze. "Unless you have some secret way of getting into the village, your money is useless here."

He's right, I know that, but my money wasn't his to take and spend as he sees fit. My glare doesn't waver, and my heart thumps so loudly with rage I wonder if he can hear it too.

"But it will do us good later. With money, we can bargain in towns, or with the SS," he goes on, opening the tin he buried to stuff the bag from under his shirt inside it. In the dark, I glimpse several dozen rations of bread, a jar of jam, a roll of gauze, a dinner knife, and a wad of German marks.

He's getting ready to run, I realize, then my heart skips a beat. *No. We're getting ready to run. Why else would he have told me this, shown me where he's hoarding his supplies? But since when have I become part of his plans?*

"Why did you show me this?" I demand, short of breath. "Aren't you worried I'll report you to the SS?"

His brow quirks in a way that says he seriously doubts my suggestion. "Would you?"

Of course not, is my immediate thought. I'd become a Russian citizen and declare my undying devotion to Stalin before I betrayed *anyone* to the Nazis.

Radomir takes my silence as his answer. "When I was sixteen, I was imprisoned in a gulag. After that, I joined the Red Army, and that was my prison until I was captured at the Siege of Sevastopol two years ago. Ever since, I've been in Nazi camps. I've been a prisoner almost all my life. I refuse to die a prisoner, and you are the same."

"What do you mean? You don't know anything about me."

"I know you're strong. You have a fire here," he says, touching his finger to the place above my heart. "During quarantine, I kept thinking you were going to die. Your fever got worse, you couldn't eat, and sometimes I couldn't wake you up. But then you would speak to someone named Louise, then you'd wake, and I could see the fight in your eyes. You're not the kind of woman to go quietly with your head bowed. Am I wrong? Do you plan to wait for rescue from the Allies or die here?"

"No." My voice is stern and defiant, and indeed a fire burns in my chest, like he described. "Louise is my sister. She and our nephew are in Paris. Coming here was supposed to be a way to provide for them, but if I can't do that, then no. I won't stay here. I certainly won't die here."

And the possibility of death is more dire than I ever realized it could be. With the meager rations we're fed, we'll all be on the brink of starvation soon. Our deplorable living and sanitary conditions make us vulnerable to disease, and the SS have made it abundantly clear they don't care whether or not we die. And if none of that kills me, exposure and slave labor can kill as efficiently as a bullet. Mother Nature and neglect have no need for help from Nazis in killing.

"You'll come with me then?" Radomir asks.

There is no point in staying in REIMAHG. I'd rather take my chances with Radomir. He knows the land, he is strong, and he is the only one offering me a way out. "Yes. I'm coming."

"Good. Save any food you can spare and all your wages. We need to travel light."

"When were you going to run?"

"Before, probably in the next few weeks. We'll wait for another few months until we have enough provisions to last us long enough to get far away from here. It will work in our favor. The higher-ups are getting impatient with the slow construction of the factory and bunkers. Soon, the SS will probably be bringing in thousands more people to speed up the work and start production of the Luftwaffe fighter jets. With those distractions, it will be easier to escape."

Why would he postpone his plans for me? Years spent as a prisoner, loath to remain so, and yet willing to wait to help me escape too... What does he want from me?

The questions are on the tip of my tongue, but I'm not sure he'd answer honestly. I can make assumptions about what he wants. I'm not naive—I've seen how his eyes roam over me—but I know desire alone cannot be the reason he wants to help me. He's had plenty of chances if my body was all he wanted. And yet his touch has always been gentle, somewhat hesitant, just as it is now, his hand engulfing mine, keeping me steady as he leads me safely through the night back to Lager Six.

16

JUNE 6, 1944

LOUISE

"Thank you," Jeanne murmurs after I've returned her freshly washed and mended clothing, and hands over thirty-five francs.

I nod wordlessly, wondering what she'd say if I told her an American soldier is the one who expertly fixed the stitches on the lovely Dior dress she is wearing. She might faint dead away, and I press my lips together to fight the amusement that image brings.

From somewhere in the lavish house, the Gestapo officer, Carl, calls for her, making my stomach turn uneasily. She smiles and bids me goodbye, and I'm grateful she doesn't notice how my hands quiver as I depart to finish my deliveries.

Just under a shirt in my laundry bag there lies a folded piece of paper I must deliver to another Line member, whose code name is Alfred, under the guise of returning clothing. Max has confirmed his suspicions of being watched, though he's not sure who the spies are working for. He's arranged for new temporary guides, and the map I picked up from the bookshop where Max and I met a few days ago contains the new route to Tours. Eager to be rid of it, I pick up my pace.

"Madam?"

The whispered English word makes my heart stop and I gasp, whirling to face the shadows of an alley between the apartment buildings. A pair of tired eyes peer at me from a man's stubbled face, a hat pulled low over his brow, his shabby coat ill-fitting on his thin body.

"Please, are you Louise?"

I clutch my bag tightly, glancing up and down the street for witnesses, but we're alone, and the apartment windows face the road, not the alley, so he is invisible to anyone but me.

Why is he speaking English? Why is he hiding? How does he know my name?

"Who are you?" I demand in French, my mind racing.

He manages a few broken words in French, but as I begin to back away he becomes panicked and quickly mutters, "Max! Max," and then, "Soldier!"

Don't trust him, is my first thought, and I pointedly ignore how much it sounds like Marie.

"Who are you? What do you want?" I demand in English and his eyes fill with relief.

"Max sent me. My name is Henry White," he says, reaching into his pocket to reveal his identification papers. The picture is him, but the name written is Marcel Bernard.

False documents... is he really a soldier?

"Please, madam, my men and I need your help," he whispers urgently, then startles when a dove coos from a tree and rustles the leaves.

I'm being watched, Marie's paranoia tells me. *Max is being watched, and he would have given him the false name Amia, not Louise... What if someone saw me with Max and now I'm under suspicion? What would Marie do?*

I force my face to remain neutral. "You're American?"

He nods quickly. "Yes, my plane went down during our last air raid. Max said you were one of his helpers and you would hide us."

Max never would have sent him to me, knowing Marie is gone and I'm struggling to provide for four men. There are other helpers in Paris he could have sent this man to.

"How many of you are there?"

"Three," he whispers shakily, unconsciously indicating the number with his hand. With his thumb, index, and middle finger. Like a German would signal three. An American would use his middle fingers to indicate three, I've met enough American men to know that.

He's a spy.

"Stay here," I say, glad for the steadiness of my voice; he doesn't seem to realize the conclusion I've come to. "I need to make some preparations, then I'll come back for you."

The spy smiles. "Thank you, madam. God bless you."

I hurry down the street, past Alfred's closed, waiting door, dreading the thought of what could have happened if I'd been seen there. I can't bring the map to Alfred yet; he'd be implicated with me no matter what, now that my loyalties have been tested.

I need to find another way, perhaps through Henry in City Hall, or one of the couriers in the mail office, I think as I pick up my pace, and terror prickles across my body as I hastily shove the map down my shirt. A German police station comes into view, and I frantically turn over the role I must play again and again in my head like an actress ill-prepared to go on stage. *Terrified, loyal young woman, that's what Marie would pretend to be.*

"Help! Please, someone help!" I cry out in genuine panic as I run through the door of the station. The startled faces of SS and Gestapo turn as I burst inside, grinning skulls staring down at me with malice from their black caps. "Down the road, in the alley! There's a soldier! An American! He spoke to me in *English!*"

All at once, every Gestapo's expression shifts from one of irritation to a vicious twist of predatory excitement and fury, and I don't have to feign the way my hands tremble.

Is this what Yvonne saw when she died? These... monsters, their eyes and skulls filled with bloodlust. I nearly pity the spy waiting for me in the alley, and then a much darker thought intrudes. *Hopefully, it'll be too late by the time they realize he's one of them...*

A Gestapo captain steps forward, the red patch on his arm like a bloodstain on his impeccable black uniform. "Calm down, Fräulein," he murmurs in a way that must be intended as a comfort, although his approach is like the shadow of the devil engulfing me.

I try to speak, but my mouth refuses to cooperate. The Gestapo is much taller up close, towering over me as William does, but William has never instilled such raw terror in me, like a petrified rat that's run directly into the cat's jaws.

"Fräulein. You said there is an enemy soldier in the city, yes?"

I nod quickly, lowering my eyes, the single piece of paper burning hot and heavy beneath my blouse. The captain's hand extends. For a panicked heartbeat, I think he's somehow sensed the map I'm carrying—which contains the new route and multiple safehouses. His cold fingers tilt my chin upwards so I must look upon his face, and the lives of the Line members within the map are a crushing weight over my heart.

"There is no need to be afraid," he says with practiced, false earnestness. "You're not in any trouble. You've done the right thing by coming to us. Now, this soldier. How do you know he's American?"

"He said so," I manage breathily. "He showed me fake papers and asked me to hide him."

"Such is the way of vermin," he sneers. "They truly have no shame, begging women to save them." He sends a sharp glance over his shoulder and three more Gestapo step up to his side, hands already poised over their pistols.

After I describe where the spy is hidden, the captain instructs his men to bring him to the station alive, and they depart with far too much excitement at the prospect of the task ahead. To my absolute horror, as I move to step away the Gestapo winds an arm around my back and directs me toward an office.

Morning light bathes the office, glinting off the polished wooden desk, the knobs of the silent radio, glowing through the crimson drapes. The captain takes a seat in the cushioned chair behind the desk, indicating the hard wooden chair opposite him. "Sit," he says, and it is a command rather than an invitation.

Deep breaths, deep breaths, I recite as I take a seat, the Gestapo's dark shadow blocking the sunlight as it falls over me. Father could stay calm in the trenches, bullets and gas cans flying at him. William could stay calm jumping out of his own airplane and hurtling toward the ground. I can stay calm now, a Gestapo officer sitting across from me, using his mere presence as a threatening tool to toy with me.

"It's all procedure, you understand," he finally says, flashing a smile that reminds me of a dog baring its teeth in warning. "You'll have to identify this soldier, if there is in fact a soldier. You wouldn't lie to me, would you, Fräulein? Dishonesty is a great sin."

"Of course not," I insist. "I am a good Catholic woman, I would never knowingly tell a lie, especially to you."

"I hope not. And, unfortunately, there is always the chance —small though it is—that resistance puppets could be trying to draw us into traps." He pauses, staring at me with such coldness that a shiver rattles through me. When the silence is verging on oppressive, he chuckles, leaning back in his chair nonchalantly. "Of course, not that I'm accusing *you* of anything..."

But the threat lingers in the thick air. If I'm a resistance member and, if my act was to lead them to a trap, he's not letting me escape.

I force the lump in my throat down, attempting a smile to conceal my fraying nerves, twisting my fingers into my laundry bag.

His eyes, like a predator, narrow on the bag in my lap. "And what is that?"

"Laundry, sir."

His brow arches in suspicion. "You carry your laundry around the city?"

"Not mine, I wash and mend clothes for others. I'm returning them to their owners."

He hums, lights a cigarette and takes a few long drags, and I wrinkle my nose at the smell that settles heavily over my chest.

"Give me the bag," he demands.

I place the bag before him, thanking God I had the foresight to hide the map in my shirt. One by one, he turns everything inside out, checks every pocket, every pair of trousers, every dress, every set of socks, until I consider washing everything a second time to remove his bloody fingerprints. When he reaches the bottom, I startle at a knock before the office door swings open, but don't dare look over my shoulder.

The captain's brows rise to his cap. "And what's this?" he asks around his cigarette.

Two men shuffle into view, one of the Gestapo who went to investigate, and the spy who claimed to be an American.

"False alarm, Herr Kriminalkommissar," the Gestapo says gruffly, laying two folds of documents on the desk.

The captain scrutinizes the papers, flicking ash absent-mindedly onto my laundry, before glancing up to the spy, then to me. "Is this the man who approached you?"

I look up at the spy, whose eyes already stare back at me, no longer fearful and pleading, but cold and hard like steel. His lip is bleeding, and the red ghost of a hand is taking form on his face, no doubt the reward of a struggle before he convinced the Nazis he was one of them.

I nod. "Yes, Herr Kriminalkommissar."

"No need to fear." The captain hands the documents back to the spy. "He's not American, but I'm glad you came to us. Allied men are very cunning. They seek out the young and vulnerable to protect them, and there are sympathizers among us. One can never be too careful."

I can feel sweat beginning to dampen my skin and the map, but thankfully the Gestapo lets me gather my laundry and flee without further questioning.

Before I collapse onto the sofa, I shove the map as far as I can reach into the chimney between the bricks. My hands still tremble violently, and I cannot find the strength to kick off my shoes. I drop my laundry bag, uncaring that it reeks of cigarettes, trying to collect my thoughts.

Alfred is expecting the map today. When I don't turn up, he'll assume there was a complication and get word to Max. I won't be able to risk doing it myself. The Nazis' suspicions are not so easily curbed. They might think I realized it was a spy and turned him over to clear my name. It's likely I'll be watched over the next few weeks. And to think that scenario is the best I could hope for! If they had any concrete suspicion, I'd have been arrested already.

I wonder if Desoubrie was the one to suspect me... He's working for the Gestapo, he knows my name, and I was anxious to get away from him the day he was nearly assassinated—

A knock almost makes me tumble off the sofa before I calm myself. The clink of the letter box has me rushing to the door. A single envelope lies on the hardwood floor, covered in a multitude of stamps, suggesting it's been lost for a long time. It's come from Germany, and, with a jolt of excitement, I hope it's from Marie. I tear it open.

January 2, 1941

Dear Louise, Marie, and André,

We hope this letter finds you well and in good time. We miss you very much and we hope you all have your health. We are alive and well and reside in a camp under the inspection of the Red Cross. We are eating plenty and staying healthy. Our dearest sisters and daughters, son and grandson, we are thinking of you and love you very much.

Sincerely, Fernand and Father, Dad and Grandpa

I sob, my knees stinging the floor, and I can no longer read the letter, for tears of joy blur my vision. Fernand and Father survived and were taken to a prison camp *alive*! For so long, their deaths have been an agonizing possibility, and now, at last there is proof they lived! This letter was written over three years ago, and though we've received no others, it doesn't mean there's no hope. Who knows how many others were sent and lost like this one?

"André! André!" I call, scrambling to my feet and bounding up the stairs. His bedroom is empty and there are no boys in the street playing, so I run back down the stairs, close the curtains, and barrel into the cellar.

"Aunt Louise!" André gasps, colliding with me at the

bottom of the stairs. My haste has nearly knocked both of us to the ground.

"André, you'll never believe—"

"Shh!" André's hand shoots up to cover my mouth, stunning me to silence. "We're lis—"

"André! Did you just shush your aunt?" William's stern, reprimanding voice cuts André off as he did to me. "You better not disrespect her that way again. Apologize."

I've never heard him so commanding, never seen his expression so firm as he and the other men sit gathered around the radio. It's the voice of a soldier ordering his troops, the face of a father disciplining his son.

"I'm sorry, Aunt Louise," André murmurs meekly. "We're listening to the radio. There's a report from the Allies." He grabs my hand and tugs me to the radio.

"We've got the BBC," William whispers.

Hearts thundering, we listen with bated breath until an American's voice reaches through the garbled noise with incredible clarity.

Here is a special bulletin read by John Snagge.

D-Day has come. Early this morning the Allies began the assault on the north-western face of Hitler's European Fortress. The first official news came just after half past nine, when Supreme Headquarters of the Allied Expeditionary Force— usually called SHAEF from its initials—issued Communiqué Number One. This said:

"Under the Command of General Eisenhower, Allied naval forces, supported by strong air forces, began landing Allied armies this morning on the northern coast of France."

Shudders tingle across my body, and, with sobs of joy choking my every word, I translate what the reporter said for André. The men grin victoriously and jostle one another, and hope lights the dark, dank basement brighter than a hundred suns could ever dream of doing.

"We've landed!" Robert exclaims in whispered excitement, and even Jack's injury isn't enough to dull his sudden energy as he grins and throws his arms around his friends.

"Goddamn it! We're missing it!" George groans. "I bet they're giving the Krauts hell!"

William elbows George for his foul language, and Robert and Jack laugh heartily. Overcome, we embrace one another, languages and nationalities thrown aside in light of this wonderful news, this moment of victory. I hug each of them tightly as though they were my own brothers—and, after all this time, indeed I have come to care for them as such. William's arms are open to receive me as I pull him to my chest, laughing blissfully. Hesitantly, his smiling lips press a kiss to my cheek, and his face flushes slightly as I grin and return the gesture.

Father and Fernand could be alive! The Allies have launched their invasion! The end of this war might be in sight!

"André!" I whirl around and grasp his hands. "We've just got a letter! It's old, but it's from your father." I smile through my tears and present the letter from the Red Cross, trying to smooth the crinkles from where I clutched it in my fist.

André says nothing as he reads the letter. His face crumples and he throws himself into my arms with such force we fall back in a heap of tears and glee. "Papa's alive!" he cries, and I don't have the heart to voice my sudden dread. Anything could have happened in three years... are there years' worth of letters for us lost somewhere in the world, or was this the only one?

The joyful, whispered words of an American song have me peering over the unruly hair André and Fernand share, across the candle and the radio, where the Allied broadcast continues, to where George, Robert, and Jack have begun to sing "I'll Get By as Long as I Have You". William hums along with them, a low rumble that harmonizes beautifully with their song.

André jumps from my lap and bounds to William. He babbles in broken sentences of French and English, excitedly presenting him with his father's letter, proof at last that Fernand might be alive. William's eyes meet mine, and, as I am held in their comforting blue depths, no other place in the world than in this cellar with my nephew and my soldiers has ever felt so warm, so safe, and the inevitability of one day saying goodbye to him forever crushes something deep within my heart.

17

JUNE 27, 1944

MARIE

Whatever bodes direly for the Nazis is certainly good for us. Rations are dwindling, and the Russians are fed less and less as the days drag on. Construction of the underground bunkers, the workshops, and assembly halls above ground for the Germans' airplanes has been forced to speed up. Though whatever shift in the war is deteriorating our already dismal conditions, we know it's beneficial to us in the grand scheme of things.

Though I think we should take what little we have and run before our situation becomes any worse, Radomir refuses every time. He says we're not prepared enough to escape into the German wilderness that surrounds REIMAHG, but I've begun to wonder how much longer he can last. The SS have never been civil with the Russian POWs, but lately they've become even crueler. He refuses to let me do any trade with them—which I wasn't eager to do when I suggested it—and he grows thinner, and bruises and cuts randomly appear all over his body.

I wipe sweat and dirt from my brow, wishing there were some way to get soap. I haven't bathed properly since the night before I left Paris, over a month ago. I've cut fabric from my red coat to cover my hair, hoping to keep it a little cleaner. Beside me, Radomir works with a pickaxe at the wall of an underground bunker. Dim lantern light glows against the bright red fabric wrapped around his large, calloused and blistered hands.

Not for the first time, I try to convince myself my rationale in giving it to him was strictly practical. After all, he is protecting me, he knows the layout of the camp complex, and I need his help to escape—and yet I thought of none of those things when I wrapped his hands.

A whistle echoes through the tunnels, signaling the midday meal. People drop their tools, abandon wheelbarrows, and rush from underground for turnip soup. The thought alone leaves a bitter taste in my mouth. The scent and taste of dirt is so deeply embedded in my senses—both from the mines and the food—that I doubt I'll ever eat a turnip again once I escape this place.

Radomir catches my arm as I make to follow the others. "What say you to something more filling?" he whispers.

My stomach rumbles in response, and we slip away from the hundreds of laborers returning to the surface and further into the tunnels. I've seen many fights break out over small things like a slice of cheese, especially between Russians, to whom eating twice a day is lucky, so if one comes across something extra it's best to keep it secret.

We come to one of the half-completed bunkers in the miles of tunnels, where a lantern shines faintly and bags of cement lie scattered around.

From his pocket, Radomir reveals an entire sausage, and hands it to me. My mouth waters at the mere sight and I look up at him questioningly.

"I traded for it with one of the Poles."

As I begin to tear the meat in half, Radomir shakes his head. "No, you have it and save what you want. I—"

"Had better eat, or I will force you," I cut in sharply.

His brows rise. "You think you can make me do anything, lisichka?"

"I might be able to if you get any thinner. You need to eat. And if you say you can go without, so help me God, I'll make you eat the entire thing. Why are you so hellbent on starving for me?"

No matter what it is—a piece of bread, a mouthful of soup, a bite of cheese, or a link of sausage—he always insists I eat everything—even at his own expense.

"I'm only making sure you don't," he mutters softly. I've never heard his voice sound so fragile, as if one sharp word would shatter him.

"Well, I don't plan on starving." I try to take on the caring tone Louise would have used. "And I'm not keen on you starving either."

He smiles at this and something warm flickers in his dull eyes. But almost immediately they are hardened, as his gaze moves over my shoulder. He snatches my arm in a fierce grip and drags me behind him as he reaches down for a shovel.

Every muscle in my body tenses at the sight of two men at the bunker's entrance. The glow of the lantern glints on the sharp edge of a long, broken pair of tailor scissors and the blunt point of a pickaxe like the sun on shiny steel. My hand slips into my pocket for my rock, and the only thoughts in my increasingly panicked mind as the men take predatory steps closer are Radomir's words.

Go for the vulnerable spots.

One of the men speaks and, though I don't understand the language, I've listened to Radomir enough to realize they're Russian. The man with the pickaxe indicates toward me, the second begins to edge away from his comrade, like wolves circling their prey. Their eyes are just as ravenous. Radomir makes no response to their demand other than a low, warning growl. They're starving, like all the other Russian POWs.

Perhaps they want the sausage we have, and a girl caught outnumbered in an isolated bunker is the cherry on top of the cake...

Radomir backs us further away as the men close in. "Marie, the first chance you get—"

The pickaxe slices the air and Radomir barely stops it from entering his body with the shovel. The second man charges straight for me. I raise my rock, ready to stab him, but then Radomir's arm shoots out to shove him back as he fends off the first man.

"Marie, run!" Radomir's furious shout rumbles through the mine like a deadly quake in the earth. With both men now focused on eliminating the strongest obstacle, the entrance of the bunker is wide open for my escape.

The pickaxe swipes near Radomir's face and he staggers back, the shovel his only shield. The second man raises his scissors like a knife and suddenly all thought of fleeing is gone. I tackle him from behind, knocking the blade from his hand as I bring the sharp tip of my rock down with all the strength I can muster, and he howls in pain. My back strikes cement as he slams us back, knocking the air from my lungs, then his calloused hands are strangling me. I kick for his knees, but he is too close, the odorous heat of his breath overwhelming my senses.

Vulnerable spots! Throat! Ears! Eyes!

My palms slam against his ears and he yelps, stunned. His hold loosens, and he lets out a chilling, anguished scream as I shove my thumbs into his eyes. He drops me, stumbling back, and I gasp for air, then scramble from his reach and grab the broken scissors before he can recover. One of his eyes remains closed, blood smeared across his cheek and nose, and he barrels blindly—murderously—toward me. A shovel slams into the back of his head, sending him sprawling to the ground. Radomir, trembling violently with rage, hurls the shovel away and lands a vicious stomp to the man's face. The crack of bone is deafening. Both men lie motionless and silent. I'm not sure if they are unconscious or dead.

"Are you hurt?" Radomir asks shakily, grasping my face, searching for signs of injury.

I manage to shake my head, though tremors still rack me. He brushes the loose strands of hair from my face, then draws me to his chest, where his heart pounds rapidly. There is not a hint of the violence I just witnessed from him. Despite the rough feel of his skin, the ferocity he defended me with, how he dwarfs me in a way that would make any woman feel small and vulnerable, he is unbelievably gentle. And I don't feel vulnerable now. I feel... safe.

All too soon he draws away and starts moving between the two Russians and riffling through their belongings. I watch, confused, and still stiffened with adrenaline, as he pockets a spoon and an extra pair of socks. He compares shoe sizes with one of the men, and I realize he's wearing shoes that aren't his. Last night, he had leather boots, but now he wears simple shoes with worn soles. He swaps his damaged pair for the Russian's boots.

Are these not his countrymen? I have no pity for them, but why would he side with me over them? He's known me for barely more than a month. These Russians are his fellow soldiers, who he may have served with in the war, who he has certainly suffered the camps with...

"Keep that in your pocket. It will do better than your rock," he says, nodding to the sharp, broken scissors still clutched in my fist.

The Russian who attacked me died in the tunnel. If the shovel wasn't enough, then surely Radomir's foot ended his life. The second Russian lived, but not for long. The SS, unwilling to waste medical treatment on a Soviet, ended his suffering with a quick shot after dragging him into the woods. I couldn't bring myself to feel remorse for their fates, but Radomir's reaction—or rather his lack of—worried me. A soldier is used to killing, that is his job in war, but Radomir didn't even flinch. He simply went on eating his share of the sausage as if he hadn't heard the crack of rifle fire.

When evening falls, I take my nightly bread from the supper line and return to Radomir, who waits between blocks six and seven. We've taken to this spot lately as it's more private. No one usually treads near the morgue block unless necessary. Silently, I watch as his eyes absent-mindedly follow a bird in the treetops. It's a little off-putting. All day, I've refrained from commenting on his emotionlessness. How does one broach this sort of topic?

"Thank you. For saving me today," I say quietly. That is true, regardless of my misgivings. I couldn't have escaped those men if I was alone.

Radomir nods, seeming lost in his mind, gaze roaming Lager Six without purpose. I hate that look. The emptiness, the lifelessness that often fills his gray irises. Sometimes there is a flicker of emotion; amusement, happiness, anger, and what I've decided is fondness when I forcefully insist he care about his well-being. But now the void is back, and, even if he is pale and defined enough to be a marble statue, I never want to see that cold, stone abyss in him.

"Why did you do it?"

He focuses on me, brows drawn in confusion. "What do you mean, lisichka?"

"You defended me. You didn't have to. You could have let them have what they wanted. Why didn't you?"

His eyes narrow. "That is not a question. I would never have let them hurt you. How dare you suggest it is even an option."

"Because it was," I insist. "Just because you didn't choose it doesn't mean it wasn't an option. You *chose* to defend me. Why? You barely even know me."

"Only because you haven't told me about you."

"That's not the point. You've been protecting me since the day I arrived. But today was different. Weren't those men your comrades? You have no obligation to me like you do to your own men. Why would you protect me from them?"

"Why didn't you run?" he retorts sharply, jaw tense. "You have no obligation to me, but I saw you fighting him. Why did you defend me?"

I've been wondering as much all day. I could have escaped unscathed. I could have listened to him and run, let him be overpowered and maybe killed. If he were gone, I'd still have the supplies, I could still try to escape on my own... and yet, when I saw one of the men about to hurt him, running wasn't a consideration.

Oh, God... do I care about him? Is that why I'm so insistent he eats enough, why I've shared my own things with him, why I didn't flee today?

Caring is a dangerous thing. It's only ever led me to heartache, and, whether willingly or not, everyone I've ever loved has abandoned me. I couldn't think of a less opportune time or place than wartime on enemy soil to begin caring about someone. And yet, loath as I am to admit it, I cannot lie to myself. Perhaps once he was the dangerous enigma of an enemy, then a common sufferer like everyone else in REIMAHG, but now....

"I'd like to think that... you're my friend." I mumble, gaze trained on the hardened earth.

He crosses the distance between us and leans against block six beside me, his arm brushing mine. "I am your friend, and you are mine. That is why I fight for you."

"But what about them?"

He sighs, a heavy, painful breath that seems to come from

his soul, and the exhaustion carved in the scars of his face appears to deepen. "We haven't been comrades in a long time. War will do that; it makes your bonds stronger or crushes them. We stayed strong and loyal to each other as long as we could, but... some things are too horrible for one's soul to survive. Theirs were dead before today, like mine."

"What do you mean?" I ask, then regret my words as his eyes grow distant and haunted.

"When I was captured at the Siege of Sevastopol in '42, I was the only one in the 25th Rifle Division to survive. Ever since, I've been moved between POW camps. Russians have suffered worse than the other Allies. Of course, no one had it good, but the Nazis said Russians weren't protected by the Geneva Conventions because our government never ratified it, so they could treat us how they liked...

"We didn't have shelter. Sometimes, in the snow or rain, we'd dig holes to sleep in just to be out of the weather. Many died of disease. Thousands every day. The Nazis tortured us... beatings, floggings"—his hand rises, indicating the scars across his face that I now realize must have come from a whip— "mass shootings, some men were burned alive. And that wasn't the worst of it. Most of us died of starvation. The Nazis barely fed us. We would trade our only clothes to the British and French just for a scrap of food. Many got so desperate to end it all they'd ask the Nazis to kill them..."

Radomir looks down at me and somehow this man who's always seemed so large, so powerful, looks fragile as glass.

"I have begged men to kill me..." he whispers in shame. "I have been on my knees in front of SS, pleading with them to shoot me because I couldn't bear the starvation anymore. They wouldn't do it, as a punishment, said it was their decision when I would die, not mine. Eventually, we all hit a breaking point. Your body feels like it's eating itself alive, the dead piled up faster than they could be disposed of, and some of us resorted to... It was the only meat we'd seen in months, and we thought, why let it go to waste?"

Suddenly, his words that seemed inconsequential a few weeks ago take on a horrific new meaning. *"Trust me, there are worse things to eat than nothing."*

Forcing down bile and tears, I reach out and tightly grasp his hand. I am reluctant to look at him, not out of revulsion, but for fear of seeing the heaviness in his haunted eyes, the nightmares I could never imagine, realities I am terrified to know of.

"That is why my countrymen are strangers to me," he goes on quietly. "The things we've suffered have broken their spirits beyond saving. Loyalty, sympathy, all that's been killed in them. All that matters now is survival, there's no room for anything else."

"But what about you?" I breathe shakily.

His hand moves to link our fingers. "Sometimes I don't think I survived," he mumbles distantly. "Sometimes I wake up and I think I'm still in one of those damn holes trying to hide from the snow, sometimes I'm afraid to eat because for a moment I think my bread is actually... Sometimes I forget I'm still a man. But I don't want to be what the Nazis tried to make me. Maybe it's spite or pride, or maybe I'm foolish, but I refuse to let them win. When the war is over, I will be a man, not a savage."

Finally, I raise my gaze, finding his troubled, determined gray eyes trained on me.

"I think that is why I was drawn to you. You have very expressive eyes. They are sad and angry, like me," he says, fingers ghosting across my cheek. "But they are strong, too. We've both suffered, maybe not in the same way, but we have. You and I are more alike than you realize. Neither of us intend to go quietly, if for no other reason than to spite whoever tries to make us."

I smile slightly at this. His eyes grow lighter as I do, gentle with affection, and I decide in this moment that I'll do whatever I can to ensure they're never deadened by misery. I cannot bear to see him in pain, any more than I could have Louise or André.

Maybe I'm a fool to care about him, but he's right. We are similar; in our hatred of this war, the Germans and all they've done to us, our determination to escape, to survive and be stronger than whatever hardships are thrown at us, to make something good of our lives.

18

JULY 2, 1944

LOUISE

The stomp of shoes startles me, and I accidentally flick a spoonful of boiling water from my pot. André shouts a quick greeting as he runs upstairs, and I collapse against the counter, clutching my chest, eyes screwed shut against my tears.

I've driven myself insane with paranoia this last month since the Allies landed at Normandy. Every creak in the floorboards, every stranger who glances my way on the street, is a threat, an enemy, someone waiting to drag me off to prison, arrest my soldiers, and make my nephew disappear. Although the Nazi propaganda would have us believe they're butchering the Allies, the Germans have become more agitated.

Resistance organizations are being weeded out every week. People simply suspected of resistance activity are suddenly dragged from the streets as they walk or have their doors broken down by the Gestapo in broad daylight, and are shoved into vans and never heard from again. Henry was arrested two weeks ago, a few days before him it was one of the Comet Line's couriers, and yesterday the old farmer Marie and I used to trade with was arrested for his black-market food dealings and his home burned to the ground. Every appallingly endless day, I can't stop dreading that we're next. My willingness to turn that spy over to the Gestapo may very well be the only thing saving me right now.

And there are still no plans to get the men out of Paris... The thought is bitter, turning my terror at the Nazis' growing ferocity into anger with the Comet Line. We were only supposed to host these soldiers for a few days, and now it has been nearly three months. The silence from both Marie and the resistance is driving me to madness.

Trembling, I turn back to my pot, and stir the two chopped potatoes I managed to buy yesterday. Food and rations are becoming scarcer, and I spent the last of the money from Jeanne's jewelry to get a bit of extra food for the month—which didn't amount to much. None of my students attend their lessons anymore, and so my only source of pay is from the few wealthier households, doing laundry and mending for them. Families can barely afford food now, let alone private tutoring. But even if it was affordable, fear of the Nazis' mounting ruthlessness has driven many parents to set stricter rules for their children, as I have done for André. My heart quickens to a painful throb in my chest whenever he is out of my sight for more than a few minutes.

André comes back down the stairs with a pile of books and papers. "I'm ready for school," he chirps in English with an even more distinct tinge of William's Nebraska accent.

Leaving my measly potatoes to boil, I take a seat at the table across from him. "Alright. Did you study your history last night like I asked?"

He nods, smiling unconvincingly.

"Well, that's good. How do you feel about a test?"

His face falls immediately, and I chuckle as he tries to stutter out a half-hearted excuse. The next few hours pass quietly, as I alternate between cooking and helping André memorize events and solve mathematical equations, but my mind is disturbed, constantly drawn to the door as I dread a sudden pounding and the shouts of Gestapo. As usual, our afternoon ends with a small meal and a quick goodbye as André goes to find his friends down the street. I sit in silence, staring after him long after he's gone, as my mind spirals into the dark again.

What the hell am I waiting for? For Gestapo to storm the house, discover the men, kill my family? What am I doing sitting here? Max, what's going on?

It's been a month since the incident with the spy. I managed to slip the map to the courier before she was arrested, and can only hope she managed to get it to Alfred first. If not, it would make sense why Max hasn't contacted me. He'd have to find completely new routes, more guides if he's still being watched... and that hardly makes a difference to me anymore. As the days drag on, I find I understand Marie's frustration, how utterly alone she must have felt...

How could I ever have thought I could do this on my own? I wonder, pacing upstairs, each step unbearably heavy. *I couldn't have done it without Marie; she was strong, she was smart, she would know what to do right now. She would—*

I glance across the hall at her closed bedroom door. I haven't gone inside since she left. There's been no reason. No one is here to use it anymore.

She would leave. She would never wait around for the worst to happen to us. Even if she had to abandon the soldiers, the Comet Line, and me, she would do what she had to do for André.

Quietly, as if I am trying not to wake her in the morning, I slip into her room. I crawl beneath the soft blanket of her bed and bury my face in the pillow that still smells of lavender, determinedly swallowing my tears. Marie never cried. Only when our mother died, but since then nothing has been enough to bring the tears. She was stronger than me, and she wouldn't cry right now if our positions were reversed.

Because she felt alone... Marie never let her resolve slip because, even though she wasn't, she felt alone, just as I do now. Oh, Marie, I wish you were here. I wish I could hug you and listen to your sarcastic quips. You wouldn't be in my room, falling to pieces. You would know what to do.

Supper is quieter than usual, and Marie's empty chair next to André keeps luring my attention. Her absence serves as a cruel twist of guilt for the direction my thoughts have taken over the last few days.

I am tired. Not only of the war and occupation, but of the constant dread I've lived with since I joined the resistance. Since the Comet Line was formed, I've aided one hundred and seven Allied men and guided nineteen of them to safehouses myself. I have never lost count. But I am tired of waiting. Waiting for Max to contact me, waiting for the Gestapo to break my door down, waiting for letters that may never come, waiting for the bomb siren, waiting and waiting and never doing anything. I am tired of being helpless.

André clears his plate without my asking and disappears. I am left in silence, drumming my fingers anxiously against the table.

I'm tired of waiting for the Line to do something. Leaving is not a question of if. I am capable of being a guide to Spain. But such a long absence would be unexplainable in the eyes of the authorities if I were to take the men to Spain, and I can't leave André alone for so long, so he'd have to come. And if André and I were to go underground, I couldn't leave the men here alone. The Line would have to risk moving them to another safehouse, risk them being caught and tortured for information... If we leave, we cannot come back. I'd be accused of resistance activities and arrested with or without evidence, but we're all in danger the longer we stay here.

"Louise?" William's voice washes over me like a calming breeze. "André said you didn't seem well," he says, checking to ensure the curtains are drawn before he enters the kitchen.

I offer a small smile. "And you're here to heal me, Dr. Chappell?"

"Hopefully there's no need. Is everything alright?"

With a heavy sigh, I slump in my chair, and he takes a seat across from me, his eyes patient and soft. He listens wordlessly as I express to him all my fears and frustrations, the thoughts I've had of taking André and going underground, the guilt that tears at me for even thinking of leaving my sister and the people who may still need me...

"Louise," William begins gently, reaching to take one of my fidgeting hands. "Have you ever considered... maybe you spend too much time worrying about others."

"What?"

"I don't mean that in a bad way. You are loving and selfless and I greatly admire that about you, but don't you think you've done enough? You've helped countless men escape the Germans, risked your life for years. Could it be you've been putting all of that above yourself?"

His eyes seem to silently ask me other questions as well. Could it be you're trying to save your brother and father by saving others? Could it be you've lost sight of yourself since your mother died? Could it be you're hiding behind the love you have for others?

I draw away and pace to the counter, furiously rubbing my eyes. How dare he barge into my life and bring all these realities to the surface! How dare he disrupt my peace, make me feel vulnerable and protected in a way I haven't felt in years! How dare he—

"You've already saved so many people," he whispers, his

arms slipping around my waist from behind, chin brushing against my blond curls. "Many of your members have been arrested, and you told me so, the Nazis are suspicious of you. What if someone gives you up? The Gestapo will do anything to get the information they want. Even if my men and I leave, you and André will still be in danger. Right now, you need to think about what's best for you and André, not the resistance or anything else. I can't stand the thought of you staying here."

"You don't understand. Marie is still missing. I can't leave her behind because *I'm* not safe. I can't abandon her! And it isn't just Marie. It is our home, the life and memories we've made. Once we leave, there is no returning."

And I don't want to leave you... Once we all leave, there is no more living in our little sphere of peace. You will return to your troops, go back to the war, and I'll never see you again...

His grip tightens. "I do understand. I've lost a lot of friends in this war, and some of them I had to leave behind even when it killed me to do it. I was the pilot of a Boeing B-17, I had a crew of nine men. I say 'men,' but most of those boys were barely twenty. When we were hit, three of my gunners were killed. The rest of us had to parachute out.

"Robert couldn't even get his parachute on; he was so terrified. The poor damn boy was crying like a baby, kept screaming that he wanted to go home, that he wanted his mom and dad. By the time I was ready to jump, it was too late to strap him up. I had to hold on to him for dear life and pray to God the chute would hold both of us... My copilot broke his legs when he hit the ground, the others landed so far away I couldn't find them. George, Robert, and I had to leave them and escape while we had the chance... I had to do what was best for the men I still had."

And how long do I still have a chance to do what is best for André and the men? Days? Hours? How long before it's too late to save them because I didn't leave?

For a long time, neither of us speak. There are no words that could adequately express the guilt and agony for all the things we have and haven't done, the awful choices life presents us with, and the inevitability that we must choose sooner or later.

"The Allies are moving closer," he whispers. "The war will be over soon. You've done more than anyone else can say they've done. Please, get out of here while you still have the chance, wait the rest of this madness out, and, once you and André are safe, find Marie. You can't do anything for her here, but you can do something for André."

Though it pains me terribly, I know he's right. I can barely support us anymore without Marie, and I'm not helping anything by worrying myself to death. The Nazis are growing more vicious, more paranoid as the tide of the war turns, and I am already under suspicion. How long before my willingness to turn over the spy to the Gestapo is no longer enough for the authorities, or one of our many members who've been arrested gives up my name under torture?

William turns my shoulders to face him. "What would Marie do? What would she want you to do?"

"She would leave... she'd probably be shouting at me to leave right now." The reality of those words spoken aloud is like a kick in my stomach.

Marie would trust me to take care of myself, set aside her own feelings to get André to safety. She wouldn't wait for our resistance leaders to do something. She would take André and run, leave the Line to deal with the soldiers. Patience was never a virtue of hers, and now my hesitancy to leave is endangering us all. The members I am most connected to have been arrested, and, if they break under torture, it could just be a matter of time before the Gestapo comes for me, comes for André and the men. Marie wouldn't take that risk, even if she had to leave me behind... and my heart aches to realize I can't risk it either.

"I used to think she was so... cold. After our mother died,

and Fernand and our father left, she took it as her responsibility to be the 'man' of the family... I chastised her for it, but her strength gave me the ability to care about others. I didn't have to be strong because she was..."

William tilts my chin to meet his gaze. "You *are* strong, Louise, only in a different way. You're soft and kind, and you give your heart fully to everyone. Marie reminds me of my grandmother. She's strong because she's stubborn and tough, and she'll do anything for the people she loves. Those are all good things, but... sometimes we have to be strong in ways we don't think we can, because it's all we can do."

By leaving our families behind to fight, to provide. By letting go of friends we can't help in order to save the ones we still have. But I can't leave the men. I care about them too much to abandon them to an uncertain fate with the resistance, and I can't stay here anymore. It's too dangerous now, and I must do what is best for the loved ones I still have. Abandon the work I've dedicated my life to, that Yvonne gave her life for, abandon my home, my family all missing somewhere where I can't help or protect them.

I'm so sorry, Marie...

19

JULY 10, 1944

MARIE

Radomir and I have begun two additional stockpiles in the woods. If one is discovered by animals or SS, it's best we have something to fall back on when the time comes to run.

The bunkers are not even close to completion, but the SS seem to be growing desperate in their impatience, and materials and equipment that will be used to build the Nazis' fighter jets are already arriving by train. Luckily for Radomir and me, Lager Six has been tasked with unloading everything into the tunnels; lots of materials and tools that would be useful on the run, such a large quantity no one notices when a few things go missing.

A hundred yards from where Radomir is making contributions to the first provision hole, I empty my pockets into a second. We didn't get the chance to sneak away last night, so, by the dimness of dawn, while the others of our lager are lined up for breakfast, Radomir and I bury stolen tin cups, rope, nails, knives, and scraps of burlap. If only I could get my hands on some sinew, I'd be able to sew some of our burlap into a sturdy bag to carry our things.

The thought makes me stiffen. When did they become *our* things? We are friends, of course, but there is a sort of... intimacy in thinking that way. We haven't discussed where we're going when we escape. I will return to Paris but, between work and survival, it didn't occur to me to ask what his plans are. Somehow, the thought of separating makes me feel horribly morose, and I resolve to put to rest my questions once we are alone as we start the trek to the factory.

The Russians aren't fed, and for once Radomir doesn't protest when I shove a spare ration of bread from our stockpile into his hands.

There isn't a chance to speak with Radomir for the first six hours of the workday. A train carrying tons of aluminum, steel, tree logs cut down in the nearby lagers, and hundreds of engine systems has arrived and needs to be unloaded.

By the time the SS blow their whistles, my back aches from carrying hundreds of pounds of materials, and my head spins with the heat and lack of water. The Russians don't bother to approach the soup line, instead seeking out what little shade there is to sit and stare hungrily, dejectedly at the pots of soup. Radomir sits in the entrance of a tunnel, swiping dust from his beard and hair, and a strange warmth blooms in my chest. I quickly turn my eyes away.

A thin woman with short blond hair a few people ahead of me steps out of line after receiving her ration. My heart leaps in disbelief, for I imagine she is Louise. The woman turns and limps away, her blue eyes downcast and dull. Aside from her hair, she doesn't bear much resemblance to my sister at all.

Perhaps it's the heat, I think, shielding my eyes from the glaring sun. Still, I find myself casting glances back at the woman. She sits alone near the treeline, far from the SS and prisoners who gather during their meals. Something tugs at my heart as I observe her slouched form, her desolate expression as she mindlessly swirls her bowl of soup. She looks... horribly alone.

It makes me think of Louise. I wonder if she's sitting alone in the kitchen, anxiously looking for something to clean. I wonder if there are new soldiers in the cellar, or if the Gestapo—

I shake the thought away before it can form. I won't think about it; I refuse to believe anything bad has happened to them. Louise is smart—even if her compassion sometimes gets in the way—and André will be her priority.

A spoonful of turnip soup is slopped into my bowl, and I make to approach Radomir but then hesitate, glancing back at the blond woman. *If you don't show her kindness, there may not be anyone else who will*, Louise's conscience tells me, and her voice is vexingly difficult to ignore. She would never turn away from someone in need. I've never been a giver like her, but I understand what it's like to feel alone.

With a huff, I start toward the woman and sit on the shriveled grass across from her.

She looks up, startled, seeming at a loss for words. As she stares at me, I realize I hadn't thought of anything to say either.

"Do you speak French?" I ask.

"A little," she says with a thick Polish accent.

I sip my soup as if it were delectable tea, as if it were not completely out of the ordinary to approach a stranger for conversation. "Where are you from?"

She pauses, thinking. "I am from Poland. Warsaw."

"I am from France. Paris."

Silence falls and she lowers her gaze like a child expecting to be reprimanded, like someone who has not experienced kindness in so long that any gesture of compassion is suspect.

I reach into my pocket. Only half of my bread ration remains from last night, but it's the only peace offering I have to give. "My name is Marie Beaufoy," I say, offering her the bread.

Her eyes widen in disbelief, then she quickly blinks away the gathering tears. With a quaking hand, she accepts it. "Thank you," she whispers. "My name is Bronisława Rabinowitz."

"It's nice to meet you."

Her smile is soft and brittle, as though she cannot quite believe her eyes. For the second time today, I see a flicker of Louise as the heaviness over Bronisława's shoulders lessens, and I finally think I understand why Louise cares so much about people. Being the reason the gloom in Bronisława's eyes lightens is a deep, humbling feeling I cannot describe.

As our break draws closer to its end and our somewhat constricted conversation fades, I bid Bronisława goodbye and join Radomir, who still sits in the tunnel entrance.

"You could have sat with us," I say.

He shakes his head. "I don't think she would have liked that."

I pause, glancing around for anyone who might be listening to us. "Radomir, we've never discussed our plans. I was wondering—"

The buzz of a distant siren, reminiscent of the bomb sirens in Paris, interrupts me. It is utter chaos as several gunshots are fired into the air. Everyone jumps up, trying to hear the Germans' commands over the shouts of confusion, rushing here and there like cattle spooked by howling wolves.

Radomir grabs my hand, pulling me away from the swarm of panic as the rumbling drone of airplanes echoes across the forest. We duck behind a mound of rock, avoiding an anxious SS man's notice as they struggle to herd the laborers into the mine. We rush into the trees the first chance we get, and run for several dozen yards, until Radomir stops to catch his breath.

"Don't worry, we're safe. They won't bomb us. They can't see the factory where it is, there's no advantage in a bombardment here. And if they do, I don't want to be trapped underground," he says, quietly scouting for a place to hide.

I nod, though it hadn't occurred to me to worry. I worried about the bombs in Paris, but I trust Radomir. It never crossed my mind that he would lead me anywhere but to safety. What a liberating feeling it is. To place complete trust in someone else, to not be afraid because you're sure they'll protect you.

"If the SS call for a roll call, we'll sneak back," Radomir says. He's slipped into a nook in the earth, and gestures for me to join him. "But if not, we can hide and rest here for the day."

I lie down beside him and relax against the cool, soft earth, wishing I could sleep outside instead of in the block. But the persistent sirens and distant vibration of falling bombs make it difficult to close my eyes peacefully. Radomir is eerily still, his eyes consumed with that awful blankness, the look of a man spiraling into the darkness of his past.

"Did you know I'm from Paris?" I whisper, thinking back to those long hours in the cellar when that American soldier was able to calm André with stories of his life. I try to do the same, distract Radomir with stories of my own life and inconsequential things. I tell him about the beautiful Butte-du-Chapeau-Rouge Park, my boys and I constantly inventing new ways to get into trouble, even about Jeanne and a time when we used to do one another's hair and make silent jokes behind our teacher's backs. I tell him about my mother; how I would stand at the counter helping her make dough while she and Louise sang, the way my father would spontaneously take her hand and spin her around to the songs on the record player.

After a while, his body begins to relax against mine and he looks down at me with gratitude, listening intently to every word.

"I worked in the mail office as a courier. My supervisor was a nasty woman, but I liked the job. It made it easier to carry letters for the resistance too."

His eyes widen, and I can't believe I let the confession slip. But it would be pointless to try to take it back, so I go on. "Louise and I joined the Comet Line in '41. We hid Allied airmen in our cellar and helped them escape into Spain. Things started getting very bad a few months ago. My pay was being cut; prices kept rising. We couldn't provide for ourselves like that, definitely not for the soldiers. That's why I came here, so I would have better pay to send them."

"You're very brave, lisichka."

"What does that mean?" I ask. "You hardly ever call me Marie."

"It means little fox," he explains, twirling a few loose strands of hair that have tumbled from beneath my scarf. "Your hair reminds me of a fox. And they are strong, clever creatures. In our folklore, they outsmart anyone who tries to hurt them. They use their minds instead of brawn, and that is smart."

"I'm not brave," I mutter. "I didn't want to do it. Louise is the brave one. She wanted to help the Allies, I wanted to stay out of trouble and take care of André. I only agreed to it so I could make it easier for her."

"And *that* is brave," Radomir says. "It's easy to do nothing, but it's hard to get involved, especially when you just want to be left alone."

I sigh. "Louise and I don't get along. We've never understood each other... but I could never have let her do it alone. I still love her very much."

"I miss my sisters," he murmurs.

"What are their names?"

He is quiet for a while, eyes turned toward the canopy of trees, sunlight reflecting across his pale, scarred face like in the depths of calm water. "Alya and Inessa," he says at last.

"Are you close in age?"

"No. We're ten years apart. Alya and Inessa are... would be sixteen by now."

A wisp of wind unnaturally cold for summer makes me shudder. I snuggle closer and wind my arms around him, wishing I could think of something to say or do to make him better. "I'm so sorry," I whisper.

"They were twins," he goes on quietly. "My parents' land was taken and put in a collective farm when I was ten. Stalin thought he would industrialize the Soviet Union, but it just led to famine. My sisters were born into it. They used to scream and cry for hours, but we had nothing to feed them. Whenever I found food, I made them eat it. I was older, bigger, I could go without. It didn't matter in the end. They were just too little, and they starved. They were three."

I bury my face in his chest to hide my tears. Suddenly, it doesn't seem so odd that—even though starvation once drove him to beg for death—he feeds me anything extra he has. He's not afraid to starve to death, he's afraid of watching someone else he cares about starve.

"My mother never got over it. I wish I could have been there for her. Anyone who couldn't work as efficiently as Stalin wanted was executed or imprisoned. My mother fell ill with dysentery when I was sixteen, and my father couldn't work well enough because he was trying to take care of her, so he was shot, and I was put in a gulag. It wasn't much different than the Nazi camps. I was released when I was eighteen, in 1936. That was when I found out my mother died a few weeks after I was taken. There was nothing left for me, so I joined the army... My life hasn't had a purpose in a long time."

With a deep sigh, he buries his face in my hair, as if ashamed to let me see the tears I can feel shaking his chest. I tighten my hold around him as both my heart and my soul ache. In this moment, I am consumed only by the need to protect him and see him happy. I've never cared for someone this way before. It isn't sisterly like for Louise, or any other familial or friendly sense. If anything, it's reminiscent of the girlish crush I once had on Victor, though the comparison hardly does justice to what I feel now. Victor was tall, older, had such a wonderful smile, and as a teenager I couldn't help but blush whenever he looked my way when we all snuck out after dark to swim in the river or sneak into restaurants to snatch a bottle of wine. But now, holding Radomir... the feeling is far more powerful, and my chest constricts with the intensity.

"We'll get out of here," I promise him, acutely aware of the way his large form molds perfectly to mine. "Once the time is right, like you say. And you'll never be a prisoner again."

Damn it, why must my heart choose now *to care about someone?* Either of us could die of disease, starvation, dehydration, crushing labor, or an angry SS man's whim. And if by some miracle we both live to escape, what then? "Will you go back to Russia when we escape?" I ask.

He scoffs at the suggestion. "Fuck Stalin. I will go east, join the Russian or Belarusian partisans, fight the Nazis again."

His answer terrifies me. Laborers who speak German have overheard rumors from the SS men who visit the village. They say the Allies have landed on the continent, the Soviets in the east are pushing the German army back, and, if they're true, I cannot bear to think of Radomir running headlong into the fighting like Fernand and my father did, or Roger, Léon, and Victor...

"There are partisans in France, too, and you speak French. You could fight with them. The Nazis still occupy France," I ramble, internally chiding myself for sounding so desperate.

"But the Russians are closer," he says, shaking his head. "France is hundreds of miles from here. And we're less likely to be caught in an Allied bombardment if we go east."

"*I'm* not going east," I say stiffly. "I trust *you*, but there's no way I'll go near Russian troops. Is it true? The things they say the Red Army do..."

He doesn't need me to clarify. His face darkens, but he says nothing, and his grip around me tightens protectively. It's the only answer I need.

"I'm going home to Paris. I have to get back to Louise and André, they need me."

The siren dies away, and the silence is tense, filled only with the cheerful twittering of birds, which is unfit for the melancholy that has settled over us.

I am taken by the sudden urge to escape, to run away right now and never look back. Run home to Paris, where everything —though chaotic—makes sense, somewhere far from this moment when my heart sinks at the thought of leaving Radomir, somewhere I don't have to care.

There wasn't time to care in Paris, not with a sister, a nephew, hiding soldiers, treasonous Parisians, and Nazis to worry about. I didn't depend on anyone. All too often, people are disappointing. If someone had told me a few months ago I'd share my only possessions with a Russian, give my only bread to a stranger, go out of my way for anyone not my family, I would have scoffed. And yet, despite all we face here, I have felt protected as I haven't in a long time.

This is your fault, I think, glancing at Radomir as soreness and exhaustion tug my eyes closed. How *dare* he barge into my life and make me care about him! How *dare* he make me lower my walls as I haven't done even for Louise! How *dare* he—

A thought interrupts my internal frustration, and it's as if I am seeing my sister clearly for the first time. *Did I make Louise feel safe?* I spared a thought for Bronisława and let Radomir into my life because, now, there is someone who protects me, someone who makes me feel safe, and in that security, in the small hope that not everyone will leave me, I have found I still have room in my heart for others.

20

JULY 11, 1944

LOUISE

Tuesday. Four o'clock. The usual place.

I reread the brief instructions once again before folding the piece of paper and slipping it into my glove.

Getting word to Max that I had urgent matters to discuss was a trickier task than I had anticipated. With the usual courier gone, there was no indirect way to contact him. In the end, I tracked him down in person. I made my laundry rounds on Marie's bike—mine and William's little business now extends through the nineteenth, tenth, and twentieth arrondissements—and took detours past safehouses I knew he frequented. It took two days, but, when I finally caught him sneaking out of an antique shop owned by a Line member, I pretended he was one of my customers and slipped him my note. Not my most sophisticated plan, but I had no alternative.

And you were impatient, I think, pacing around the sitting room, fussing with the curls coming undone from my blue snood, anxiously checking the mahogany clock on the wall. I'm tempted to rush off to the "usual place," which is the bookshop Max and I met at last time we spoke, an hour early. I stop myself and take several calming breaths, slowly in and out, like William helps me do when my panic takes me over.

As if summoned by mere thought, a light knock on the cellar door reveals William waiting patiently on the other side.

I chuckle nervously. "Am I that loud?"

"A bit." He offers a sheepish smile. "I could hear you pacing. Are you alright?"

His blue eyes, usually calm and steadying like the deep ocean, flicker nervously. I glance down into the cellar behind him at the sound of shuffling, and catch sight of young Jack and Robert giggling at one another like gossiping schoolgirls. William determinedly, purposely ignores them.

"No," I tell him honestly. "I'm afraid something is going to go wrong. And I feel so guilty..."

To leave France, the Comet Line, and my sister was not a decision I made lightly, and it's already the most difficult thing I've ever had to do, but I must. We're not safe, food and necessities grow scarcer every day the Allies move further into the continent, and I can't risk André's, the men's, or my life for the resistance anymore. William has been my constant companion through my turmoil, and now he easily sees what troubles me, reaching out to take my hand.

"You're doing the right thing," he assures me. "Marie wouldn't want you to stay here."

The words, "*I* don't want you to stay here" pass silently between us. He hesitates, rolling something small between his fingers. "You look beautiful, Louise," he says quietly, abashedly. "Well, you always do—" He abruptly clears his throat, and, even cast in shadow, I see his cheeks darken. "I almost feel guilty for ruining it—no, not ruining, that's not what I meant. Nothing could do that. I meant—"

Robert and Jack stifle laughs, then duck out of sight when William looks sharply at them.

"You've done so much for us, and we don't have anything to repay you with," he tries again, holding up the little object he was fiddling with. It's a bracelet made of white cloth that has been woven with a few brown beads. "I made it. I know it's not very pretty... The cloth is from my parachute. We managed to save a bit of it before we escaped. The beads were a gift. When my parents sent me my first care package, Dorothy helped pack it. She put one of her necklaces in it, a reminder of home. I always kept it in my pocket, but while we were on the run it broke, and I lost most of the beads. I still had a few, and I didn't want this to be so plain—"

"It's beautiful," I whisper, drawing him into my arms, fighting back tears. I roll down my glove and, as he gently ties the bracelet around my wrist, his eyes gleam with a tenderness that steals my breath. Father used to look at Mother like this, like she was his entire world.

One night, a few years after Mother passed, I came into Father's room with tea. When he looked at me, he suddenly began to sob. I sat with him while he poured out his grief to me. He told me that, for a moment, he thought I was *really* her returning to him. That was when I truly realized what her loss had done to him. She was his peace, all that grounded him after the hell he endured in the Great War. I never saw any man look at a woman like my father did my mother.

"The parachute saved mine and Robert's lives once," William murmurs, rolling my glove back over the bracelet. "Hopefully, it will bring you luck too."

In this moment, held in a trance by his gentle eyes and handsome smile, his fingers still lingering on mine, I know my heart is lost to him. There will never be another man who makes me feel as warm and safe, never another I want to sit up with for hours talking about nothing and everything, never another I long to hold or have a life with. But what comes after this day, this moment we share? He'll return to America, we'll never see each other again, and—

Stop, you'll drive yourself mad. I imagine that is what Marie would tell me, to stop worrying over all the endless "what ifs."

Softly, I trace the line of his jaw, and he holds his breath. I press a kiss to his cheek, lingering longer than necessary, and I barely fight the urge to turn and feel his lips beneath mine. "Thank you, William."

It's ten past four o'clock by the time I make it to the bookshop. A little boy running errands for his mother shyly approached and asked for help finding the department store, so I took a few minutes to show him the way before hurrying to the meeting place.

Though the sky is still bright, evening has nearly vacated the streets and shuttered the windows, leaving only the whispers of wind to rustle the long-shriveled flowerbeds. Many citizens have taken to retiring to their homes before curfew. The Nazis seem to grow in number by the day, not only within their own ranks but with their sympathizers. It used to be they were lax about certain rules, but since the Allied landing at Normandy they've increased their patrols, become stricter in their authority, and there are at least five arrests every day— many of which are only possible because of collaborators.

I stop short a mere ten yards from the stairwell to the bookshop cellar, and hastily slip into a nook between two brick buildings. I can't be sure if he saw me, but I saw him. It was only a glimpse as he crossed the street into an alley like the rat he is, but I know it was him. Jacques Desoubrie is standing directly across from the bookshop cellar. And I'm late—only by a few minutes, but Max is probably waiting for me inside. Desoubrie knows that, I'm certain of it.

This man—if he can even be called that—who is responsible for the arrests of hundreds of Comet Line members, for killing my best friend and likely her son and mother, is following Max, waiting to see who he's meeting. Waiting for me. Rage burns within me, consuming every sense with an intensity I've never felt before. I won't let him hurt us, not André, not my men, not Max.

"Monsieur! Monsieur Boulain!" I shout, stepping out of my hiding spot and waving enthusiastically. He startles, whipping around to stare at me with wide, alarmed eyes. I set off at a brisk pace toward him. "Boulain! Pierre Boulain, is that you? I thought it was! It's been far too long!" I exclaim loudly enough for anyone within three streets to hear, hopefully loud enough for Max to hear who I am greeting.

"No need to shout, mademoiselle," he hisses. "I'm right here! What do you want?"

"To talk, of course! Oh, don't tell me you don't remember me! We walked and talked for quite some time!" I slip my arm into his; I barely suppress a shudder of disgust, but continue to grin sweetly. The contact gives me the leverage to turn our bodies away from the bookshop, diverting his attention.

Playing damsel in distress for Gestapo officers, stalking the Comet Line's main guide in broad daylight, boldly approaching a Nazi spy like an old friend. All without properly thinking them through. Marie would be proud of me, I think, but the thought is fond, not bitter.

"I don't know you, mademoiselle," he huffs impatiently, though his eyes briefly narrow in recognition. "I'm quite busy at the moment, and I'm in no mood to entertain."

Our interaction lasts only a few seconds, but it's long enough for Max, with a cap pulled low over his face, to silently slip from the bookshop stairwell and out of sight.

If Desoubrie hasn't yet made a connection between the Comet Line member he's following and my sudden appearance, he will once he realizes Max evaded him. Then he'll be convinced of my involvement, especially if he was the one who sent that German spy to act as an American soldier. If my position wasn't compromised before, it is now. And yet, a small part of me doesn't care.

At least Max has gotten away. His position is far more important than mine is. Not that it matters anymore. I made up my mind days ago; I'm taking André and my men and we're escaping while we still have the chance. And with the assurance of never seeing Desoubrie again, I glare openly with hatred. For all the suffering he's caused, a little pain is only a drop of water compared to an ocean.

"Very well. Goodbye, monsieur," I manage through gritted teeth. "But what is that? You have something on your face, by your eye. A little higher. No, not there, it's right—there!"

He yelps, recoiling in pain as I jab a fingertip into his eye. I don't bother with a feigned apology, just leave him swearing and rubbing his eye, and can imagine Marie cheering me on.

Max is waiting for me in a deserted alley at the corner of a towering apartment building, puffing anxiously on a Graycliff cigar. "Thank you, Louise. I didn't realize he was following me, damn rat. I think I'm going to lie low for a while, let him think I've left Paris."

"I need to go underground," I say bluntly. "That's what I wanted to talk to you about. I have to get my nephew out of the country, it's too dangerous for us now."

"And Desoubrie knows your face." Max nods, offering me the cigar, but I refuse. "He'll put two and two together soon enough and assume we're involved. I hate to lose you, you've done so much for us, but I agree. We'll move you to a safehouse tonight. I'll try to have a guide arranged for you in the next—"

"No. We don't need a guide," I cut in firmly. "I've led soldiers before, and I know the routes. I will be our guide."

"But you've never gone all the way to Spain, and you've

never traveled by day in the open!" Max says incredulously. "It's dangerous. I know you're a capable woman, but don't be rash. Wait at the safehouse for a little while and be patient—"

"I'm done being patient, Max. I'm done waiting to be saved!" I snap at him. "I've given years of my life for this, I've saved over a hundred Allied men, I've lost allies, friends, and my sister. I won't lose my nephew too, so don't ask me to wait around for that to happen."

Max's troubled eyes appraise me, and he sighs in defeat. "You sound like your sister."

Perhaps that isn't a bad thing, I think somberly. "You never did find out anything about where she went, did you?"

He shakes his head. "No, I'm sorry. I tried, but there was absolutely no record of her after her train arrived in Creil."

My breath catches. "She's still in France?"

Max shrugs. "I don't know. My contact in Creil said trains make frequent stops to pick up more people, prisoners, laborers and such. Where they're actually going is anyone's guess. I'm sorry I don't have better news. But Marie is tough. Wherever she is, I'm sure she's alright."

I can only nod in acknowledgment, but my worry and guilt aren't eased in the slightest. This time when he offers his cigar, I gladly take several puffs, and smother the subsequent coughing fit that burns my lungs.

"I'll have our photographer at your house within the hour, he'll get new documents put together for you," Max says. "It's best not to use your real identity. The Gestapo will be keeping an eye out for you once Desoubrie informs them about you."

The photographer, a thin, old gentleman, came and went several hours ago. He clicked a few pictures of André and me, then promised he'd have our new documents ready in time to send them with Max when he came later in the night to take us to the safehouse.

We made what little preparations we could as quickly as possible. André and I each packed a suitcase of clothes and all the remaining food rations. For the men, I sought out the suitcases from my parents' room and stuffed them full of Father's old clothes. To get to Spain, we must also travel by day, and that means keeping up the pretense of being ordinary civilians.

It's seven o'clock by the time the evening shadows overtake the city. The cellar door is cracked open, and the men sit at the top of the stairs, waiting. I am too restless to sit and have taken to pacing the entire house. I go over everything we packed, panic when I think I've forgotten something, then relax slightly when I find it safely accounted for. I count the lines on the clock, watch the hands drag agonizingly slowly, then watch the street outside like a hawk.

Marie... I can't believe I'm doing this. Why did I let you go? I'm so sorry, but I have to do this. We promised Fernand we'd take care of André together. I can't do it alone. I need you.

The guilt wrenches in my heart, fierce and ruthless, and I find myself ascending the stairs to her bedroom. The last of the receding sunlight shines on her writing desk, where notebooks and pencils sit idly. I settle on her bed and take up her writing materials. She would understand, I know she would. To her, survival meant taking control, acting on a whim, being willing to make sacrifices she didn't want to make. By the time I've finished my letter to her, Max has arrived. Under the cover of darkness—and with too many close calls with German patrols—Max and I lead André and the men out of the city to a cattle rancher's home.

"Good luck, Louise. Stay safe," Max whispers as he hands over our new identities and the map of our route, then makes the sign of a cross over his chest. "Pugna Quin Percutias."

"Pugna Quin Percutias," I repeat softly, and slip my letter to

Marie into his hand. "If Marie comes back, please give this to her. Tell her I'm sorry."

By the light of a nearly full moon, we trek quietly into the countryside toward another safehouse thirty miles away, leaving Paris and the Comet Line behind. I look up to the sky freckled with stars, watch a shooting star streak across the inky black, squeeze André's hand, and follow its path into the night.

21

JULY 17, 1944

MARIE

Production of the first fighter jets has begun in the underground bunkers, but it's moving slowly. We've been tasked with assembling the jets, from complicated tasks like building the engines to simple things like putting nails into the airframes. Nazi propaganda says that twelve hundred jets will leave the mountain every month.

Radomir scoffed at that in amusement and incredulity. "They'll be lucky if we get a hundred planes out of this mountain," he said. His prediction has turned out to be right so far. The SS want the first test flight to be done by August, but the tunnels and bunkers still haven't been completed, and I am of the opinion—like Radomir—that their unfeasible demands are fueled by fear of the increasingly bleak state of the war.

The underground bunker I've been working in for the last few days is only half-completed, and has a low, domed ceiling and long wooden tables filled with metal and glass parts for assembling the jet instrument panels. The switches and indicators must be fitted into the correct places on the panels and, before that, they must be put together. Afterwards, they're taken to a finished workshop above ground to be checked and have the wiring installed by the conscripted German workers.

The Russians aren't allowed to contribute to the manufacturing of the jets. Their jobs change daily; cutting down trees for construction, leveling the top of Walpersberg hill for the launch site, and building the ramp that will be used to lift the jets to the runway. With our now separate worksites, Radomir and I only see each other in the mornings and evenings for a few hours, and every time I see him I breathe a sigh of relief.

A gentle nudge draws me from my thoughts. Bronisława, who stands beside me at the assembly table, arches a brow.

"What?" I ask in Polish, resuming my task of fitting the needle onto an airspeed indicator.

Learning to understand each other over the last week has been a struggle, but her basic knowledge of French helps us communicate.

Bronisława pauses, searching for the correct French words. "You are thinking hard," she says. "It is that man?"

I shake my head, feeling a flush rise to my cheeks, unable to stutter a coherent denial.

Bronisława chuckles softly. "I know. I have a man. Husband. Avraham." She smiles lovingly, but there is a hint of sadness and uncertainty in her eyes.

"I have no man," I tell her in Polish.

She eyes me doubtfully and tries to piece together a sentence in French, but it seems the words are too complicated. She sighs, patting my hand affectionately like a mother who has yet to convince her child of a simple truth. "Serce nie sługa," she repeats a few times, then says in French, "You will know."

Though our conversations are limited, Bronisława is an incredibly kind woman, caring in an older-sisterly fashion, like Louise—a likeness that isn't surprising as she also has a little sister named Eliana, as well as an older brother. Sometimes, I still find it difficult to believe there is such compassion in strangers for other strangers, especially someone who has suffered as Bronisława has. Her frail body, pallid skin, and the lines on her face are testaments to her struggles, and make her look older than twenty-four. She was quiet and brittle when we met, like an empty seashell; beauty worn down by the ocean, chipped and cracked in too many places.

It's been difficult not to think of Louise every time I look at her.

Our friendship is still relatively new, but I think it's helped her to have someone to talk to. If Louise were here, I know she would be pleased with this recent development.

She would probably have a heart attack too, I think, chuckling to myself. Of course, I had my family, my friends… but no one ever stays for very long, they all disappoint eventually. Jeanne, Roger, Léon, and Victor all left me, Fernand and Father left us behind, my mother… and Louise… With each abandonment, each betrayal, the distance between my heart and the world has grown. If only Louise could see me now, opening my life to strangers like she does, allowing myself to consider them friends rather than keeping them at a distance. She might think a doppelganger has replaced me.

And maybe one has, I muse quietly. Maybe, when I left Paris, a part of Louise came with me, a part I never gave myself the chance to understand.

The sun is sinking at an alarming rate. Evening rations were given an hour ago, and the Russians haven't returned to Lager Six. Radomir and the other Russians didn't come to the factory with the rest of us after roll call, and I have no idea where the SS took them.

I try to focus on the patch of dirt between blocks six and seven that Bronisława and I have cleared for the purpose of teaching one another our languages. We take turns drawing pictures, then exchange the proper words. Tonight, however, I cannot keep my mind straight, and my gaze is continuously drawn to the treeline.

Bronisława waves a hand in front of my face, snatching my attention. She flashes a soft, sympathetic smile, then points to the picture of a heart she's drawn. We each repeat the word in Polish and French until we master the pronunciation, then try to use it in a sentence.

Bronisława goes first in French. "The heart is not... a..." She pauses, gesturing in frustration as if hoping to beckon the word to her. Eventually, she shakes her head and settles for the Polish word. "Sługa. Not a sługa."

I expect we'll manage to clarify what 'sługa' is eventually, like other French words I still haven't taught her, so we move on.

"My sister has a"—I begin, then realize I don't know the Polish word for big, and so make a large gesture with my hands —"heart."

Bronisława smiles, nodding with understanding. We go on like this for another hour, drawing pictures and learning words until the SS light the lanterns. Darkness descends like a mourning veil, seeping deeper into my heart the longer Radomir's absence goes unexplained.

Where is he? This has never happened before. Has he been hurt? Have the SS done something? Oh, Radomir, please be safe...

Just as Bronisława is about to attempt a sentence with the word bird, her eyes flicker over my shoulder, and the words die in her throat.

My heart leaps when I turn to see a group of men entering Lager Six with the armed SS guards, but it sinks with dread as they move closer, and the lanterns illuminate them. Fresh bruises and open wounds caked with blood litter the swollen faces of the Russian POWs. They wince and limp with every step, and several men are being dragged by their hands and feet.

The Russians dragging the dead weight of their comrades drop them at the entrance of the morgue block, then disperse without a backward glance. But I only have eyes for one of them.

"Radomir," I choke, scrambling to where he lies motionless and bloody on the ground. The array of colors in his usual paleness makes my entire body grow cold. His fair blond hair and beard are stained with brown dirt and the hideous black of dried blood, trickles of red are smeared beneath his broken nose, and awful shades of yellow and purple bruises mar his scarred face.

"Radomir! Please, open your eyes! Can you hear me? Radomir!" I beg, dropping to my knees at his side, ripping the scarf off my head to try to clean his face. For a terrifying, unending moment, my heart stops. After an eternity that might only be a few seconds, Radomir's swollen eyes crack open. "You're alive!" I sob with relief, lying my head against his chest in a quick embrace to hear his heartbeat.

He moans in discomfort, and I hastily let him go. "Now there is a sight for sore eyes," he groans, smiling with blood-stained teeth.

"Marie," Bronisława says urgently, grabbing my shoulder. She helplessly stutters for words I can understand. "I go—I... I will..." She hurries away without finishing, limping.

Radomir strains to sit up, but he is too weak, and I move so he may lay his head on my lap. "What happened to you?"

"The SS," he grits through clenched teeth as I try to comb the grime from his hair. His gray eyes remain focused on my face, glinting up at me like pale stars. "They took us to repair the railways hit with a bombardment... they punished and beat us for *everything*, anything they could make up. I... I can't remember what the reasons were right now."

Blinding hatred consumes me, quickens my heart until I want nothing more than to see every despicable Nazi who hurt him meet a painful end. But looking down into his agonized eyes, filled with such softness as he watches me, I am calmed.

"I got luckier than them. I think some of them are dead... or maybe that makes them the lucky ones," he says, swallowing a groan of pain.

I refuse to let my eyes wander to the other Russians lying feet from us. I don't want to know their fates. All that matters is that the man I'm holding is alive.

"Why did they treat you so horribly today? They've never cared for Russians, but this..."

"I know revenge when I see it... I think the Red Army is making some moves against the Nazis right now. There are probably thousands of Germans dead on the Eastern Front, and the SS want to make *us* pay for that."

"Bastards," I spit with venom. "I hope they all get sent to the Eastern Front and have their fucking heads blown off."

A laugh rumbles his chest, and he winces. "Such foul language from such a beautiful lady. I love your voice. Today, I wasn't sure I would hear it again. I'm so happy I get to see you."

I cannot find the strength to let him go and dry my tears. "I'm happy I get to see you too."

What now?

His comrades left him for dead to await the SS guards to stack his body inside the morgue. I think back on the things he told me about the POW camps, and his explanation of his fellow Russians' loss of humanity takes on a new, terrifying reality. If Radomir goes back to the Russian living quarters in this state, what's to stop them from hurting him, stealing from him, killing him...

A few moments later, Bronisława returns with two Polish men. One is tall and thin, and the other has a shaved head. Bronisława says something to them in Polish, indicating Radomir and me. The taller man looks down at us, unsympathetic. "Is he Russian?" he asks in French.

"He is my friend," I say instead.

The tall man's eyes narrow and he looks sharply at Bronisława, lips curled in distaste.

"Please, will you help me move him?" I plead. "If he stays here, they'll put him in the morgue. I need to bandage his—"

"Help him? Bronisława said her friend's friend was hurt by the SS," the taller man sneers at me. "She didn't say it was a Soviet."

"He isn't a soldier anymore! He is a prisoner, like all of us! He has been nothing but kind to me, and he has protected me. He isn't a bad person. What does it matter if he is Russian?"

"Ask Poland what it matters. Your country was never divvied up between the Nazis and the Soviets." The tall man spits with contempt, turns on his heel, and leaves Bronisława and me staring after him helplessly.

"I know you," the bald man says to Radomir. He raises his pants to reveal brown leather boots. They are Radomir's. The day the Russians attacked us in the tunnels, I noticed he wasn't wearing his boots. "You traded me your boots and socks for sausage. My name is Gaweł. That was Nikodem." He nods at his furiously retreating friend. "He doesn't care for Russians. His wife and children were killed by Soviets back in 1939."

"My family was killed by Soviets, too," Radomir mutters. "I am Radomir."

"And you are?" Gaweł asks.

"Marie," I say hopefully, begging him without words to take sympathy on my... on Radomir. "He can't stay in the Russian quarters tonight. He's too weak, they'll—I don't want to know what they might do."

Gaweł nods. "There's space in block three. I don't think the others will mind too much. I'd take a Russian over a German any day. Enemy of my enemy, you know. Can he stand?"

Getting Radomir to his feet is a strenuous task. Gaweł helps him stand and I support him on the other side as we hobble to block three, where many of the Poles and Dutch are housed.

When we get inside, Radomir's face is taut with pain, and he has no strength to climb into the bunk. Instead, he slides down the wall until he is slumped against the floor.

I fish out the broken half-scissors from my pocket and press it into his rough hands. "You'll be alright," I say, unsure if it's meant to convince him or me.

"I'm already alright," he rasps, taking my hand and pressing a kiss to my fingertips.

This tender, affectionate act makes my heart skip, and suddenly I am struggling to breathe. I slip off my red coat, which has begun to turn burgundy as there is no way to wash anything, and place it in his hands.

"No, you'll get cold—" he begins to protest, but I shush him.

I clean his face with my scarf, being as gentle as possible. If my attentions cause him pain, he doesn't show it. He watches me intently, seeming soothed by my touch, and soon I become aware of his battered hand against my leg. It isn't demanding or invasive, and there is no expectation as his fingers softly caress me. It is... comforting, delicate, and I am reluctant to draw away when the SS blow their whistles.

"I'll be here in the morning."

He smiles faintly. "And I'll be waiting for you."

Sleep doesn't take me. When I restlessly lie down on the wooden bunk, every groan, cough, and snore, every patter of rat feet across the floor, echoes like a bomb siren. I lie awake when the lanterns are extinguished, when the falling temperatures nip at my skin and I hope Radomir is warm, when the morning whistles screech and my eyes burn with fatigue.

The moment the doors are open again, I am the first to rush into the dark, humid morning. I run to block three and fight my way through the one hundred and twenty men trying to exit the block for roll call, and into the room where I left Radomir.

Gaweł kneels at Radomir's side where he is curled on the floor, my coat serving as his pillow, and suddenly I am terrified he has died. But then, just as tears have sprung to my eyes and I gently take his scarred, bruised face into my hands, his eyes open and he smiles.

"Good morning, lisichka."

I decide the first thing I'll do when I go home is apologize to Louise. It isn't easy to care about people, to let others beyond your family into your life and heart. It is terrifying, more burdensome than caring about only yourself could ever be. It requires more courage and sacrifice than I ever gave Louise credit for.

"Gaweł," I whisper shakily. "What does sługa mean?"

His brow quirks curiously. "Servant."

"*You will know*," Bronisława told me yesterday. "*Serce nie sługa.*" The heart is not a servant. She tried to tell me when I denied Radomir was mine in any way. She knew what I hadn't accepted yet, what part of me still doesn't want to accept.

22

JULY 20, 1944

LOUISE

Our journey thus far has gone without incident.

The setting sun glares blindingly through the train window and I squint, keeping my head turned toward William's shoulder. André has drifted off to sleep and leans against the window beside me, legs tucked under him. Across from us, George, Robert, and Jack are awake, though Jack is beginning to nod off every now and again, and Robert allows him to slump against him since his injured shoulder is still in horrible pain.

We've come nearly five hundred miles from Paris in the last nine days, traveling by foot, bus, or train, by day and sometimes by night. Once we reach the station in Nouvelle-Aquitaine and the last safehouse, we'll begin the final twenty miles to the border of Spain and then through the Pyrenees mountains, and I am relieved that we'll have a guide. I wouldn't risk attempting to cross those treacherous mountains on my own unless certain death was chasing us. Only that would drive me to face the steep, jagged cliffs and the dangerous, unknown wilderness.

Mine and André's false documents were made to match

William's, so it appears we are parents traveling with our son, and the others we pretend are relatives. The pretense has been complicated to maintain on account of their lack of French, but no one has questioned our story.

William's hand settles comfortingly over mine, stopping my fingers from nervously tapping. I nod and take several long breaths, though it doesn't slow my quickly beating heart. We're so close... and yet the closer to freedom we get, the more anxious I become, and the more horrible I feel for leaving Marie behind.

Shades of crimson and violet are bleeding across the sky like spilled paint by the time the train slows to a halt and everyone carries their suitcases down onto the Gare de Biarritz platform. Our train is the last of the evening to arrive, so the platform is empty save for German guards and a few people awaiting the arriving passengers. I scan faces, not quite sure who I'm looking for but knowing they'll be wearing something to help me identify them as a Comet Line helper, perhaps a ring over their glove, or a tie with a peculiar pattern.

A petite, older woman catches my attention. Her hair has gone white, and a few stray strands peek out from below her black widow's cap. There's nothing conspicuous about her, but, as she lifts a wrinkled hand to adjust her hair, I see the ring on her middle finger is turned backwards, flashing the small ruby in our direction.

"Hello, my dear," the woman greets me as we approach her. She reaches up to hold my cheek like a grandmother, then kisses the other side. As she does, she whispers the Comet Line's motto, "Pugna Quin Percutias."

"Fight without arms," I whisper in return.

"It's lovely to see you all." She smiles, and gives the same affectionate grandmotherly greeting to the others. "Thank you for coming. Lord knows I need the company since your grandfather..."

"Of course, Grandmère," I say somberly. No one stops to question us or check our documents as we quietly leave the station, but I cannot shake the unnerving sensation prickling across my skin, like we're being watched.

The old woman, who calls herself Anna, guides us west down a scarcely populated dirt road, then a half-mile down Rue Philippe Veyrin. The further south we move from the city, the fewer inhabitants there are. A few lonely homes dot the land withered by the summer heat, and the warm wind carries a heaviness that makes everything feel abandoned. Even the birds are silent, like they too sense the solemn veil overhanging their home.

Anna's home, near the edge of Lac de Mouriscot, is a quiet, quaint cottage overlooking the lake. A few speckled chickens peck outside the door. There are only two rooms inside; Anna's bedroom, with a sheet substituting for a door, and the living area, which holds a woodstove and worn, antique furniture. A back door opens to a porch, letting the calming aroma of flowers and the distant ocean fill the house. George and Robert settle on the floor by the back door, deeply inhaling the sweet scent. Jack, wincing with every movement, settles into an armchair with a sigh.

"You must be hungry. I know you've had a long journey," Anna says, passing around bread and jam. We all murmur our thanks. "I don't have much space. The men can sleep out here tonight, and you, dear, you and your boy can stay in my room. Or perhaps you'd like to stay out here too..."

Her gaze is trained on William and me standing together by the window overlooking the lake, and it takes me a moment to realize how close we truly are, his arm brushing mine. A blush darkens my cheeks, but neither of us answer or move to create distance.

"Sleeping arrangements are up to you, but I will be in my room. In any case, you'll leave at dawn. Your guide is a man we call Cousin Frank. There haven't been many crossings into Spain since D-Day, you're the first in almost a month," Anna goes on, rummaging in a cupboard and withdrawing a piece of paper. She unfolds it, revealing a vague drawing of Lac de Mouriscot and the surroundings. "Cousin Frank drew this. Just a harmless drawing so, if any Germans get their hands on it, only people with the instructions know how to read it." She indicates a small line at the edge of the water on the opposite side of the lake. "This is a dock. Here, there will be plant potters full of soil and flowers. At the bottom of one, there will be a paper with an address where you will meet Cousin Frank. You'll have to go yourselves; my legs can't manage that hike. From there, he'll take you across the Pyrenees."

"We'll manage. Thank you, Anna."

Yawning, Anna retreats to her bedroom, and within minutes she is lightly snoring. André, eyes drooping, quickly dozes off in one of the armchairs, curled up with a sheet.

"We're almost there," William says softly in French, gazing at the lake.

Once again, the awful guilt assaults me, aching deep in my heart and knotting my stomach. This entire journey, I've felt ready to keel over with sickness. I am abandoning my home, the Comet Line, and the soldiers who might need my help. I am abandoning my little sister. No matter how many times I tell myself this is what's best, I can't stop thinking about Marie, missing God knows where, like Fernand and Father.

"What will you do when the war is over?" William asks. The question draws me into fonder memories from times that seem so long ago; the primary school and my colorful classroom, my students who often gifted me the art projects we made, playing football with Marie and André in the street, the few rare times Marie and I curled up on her bed reading Shakespeare.

"I'd like to be a teacher again. I loved spending time with my students, like my father and I did when I was young. I miss those days so much." Sighing, I look out over the water with him, at the gentle waves as the wind ripples the surface and the fading sunlight reflects off it, making it glow violet and rose. "And maybe then, I can have my own little ones."

William turns, smiling softly, but I can't meet his eyes. "How many children do you want?"

"At least two," I mutter quietly, blushing as I wonder if he wants children. "And if I only have girls, hopefully they'll get along better than Marie and I do."

"You're a kind, wonderful woman, I'm sure our—" He clears his throat abruptly, looking thoroughly mortified, and quickly says, "*Your* children will get along fine."

My heart skips and I clasp my hands to keep from fidgeting. "And what are your plans?"

He doesn't have to think about it for long. "I want to finish university. I was studying medicine before the war, but now I'd like to study psychology too. I've... seen and been through a lot, so have all the other troops. I've seen what it does to a person. Maybe, if I become a doctor, I can help them get through it.

"I'm supposed to take over for my father. He's tried to groom me into the perfect heir to the family industry since I was a teenager, not that I ever listened. Dorothy has always been more invested in the family business. She's actually the manager of one of our small oil rigs, and she runs it better than anyone. I think I'll step aside and let her take over when the time comes. Might give my father a heart attack, but she'll run the business better than I ever could."

"That sounds wonderful."

"And I'd like to have my own family. A wife, children... I don't mind how many. I'm used to a big family." He laughs quietly, then takes my hand, gently twisting the bracelet made of his parachute. "I'd like a cozy house like this, somewhere quiet by the water, and my wife and I can teach the children to swim and read."

"It sounds..." *Perfect*, I want to say, but settle instead for, "peaceful."

As he holds my hand, he trembles, and my heart begins to race with his nervousness.

"Come back to America with me," he breathes shakily, and I gasp, my eyes shooting up to his, which bore into me with an intensity that makes my body burn. "You are the kindest, bravest, most beautiful woman I've ever known. I've never tried to hide that I admire you, how grateful I am to you, but it's more than that. So often in this war, I've thought I won't be able to survive it, but you make me feel strong again. You are my peace, my hope, and now, you are my heart... I will never love another as I love you, Louise. I can't see a future without you anymore."

My heart constricts and bursts with his every word. Oh, how deeply I have come to need and care for him, and never in my sweetest dreams could I have envisioned this moment. He makes me feel strong and safe as I haven't in a long time, makes the world feel brighter and full of color again, makes me want to throw caution to the wind and take a leap of faith, to say yes.

"And you are my peace, my heart," I whisper, reaching up to hold his face. He smiles, slowly leaning down, and for a hopeful heartbeat I think he means to kiss me, but he hesitates, and brushes his lips against my cheek instead.

"You missed," I murmur playfully. "Should pilots not have better aim?"

He laughs, breathless, and at last captures my lips in a soft kiss that weakens my knees and consumes me with warmth. "Come with me," he pleads again without drawing away.

"Yes," I murmur, feeling his lips smile against mine as our embrace deepens, and the rest of the world melts away. Perhaps it's rash to agree, but I've spent so much of my life worrying over "what ifs," and I've lost so many people I love. Our lives are fleeting things, mere blinks in the eyes of the universe, comets streaking across the sky for a second in the eternal stretch of time. We have only one life, and must go with time quickly, seize what makes our short existence worth existing, and hold on with all our hearts.

"Ha! I told you he'd make the first move! You owe me two dollars!" Robert's triumphant gloating rips us back to the present.

Across the room, Jack looks as though he's swallowed something sour. "The hell I do!" he protests indignantly. "She clearly initiated it, that counts as her making the first move! You don't need to speak French to know that!"

"You girls keep squabbling, but you owe me three dollars each," George cuts in, smirking. "I bet it would happen before we got to Spain."

William and I laugh as they bicker, and I snuggle against his chest as he caresses my back.

"William…" I whisper, and he hums with contentment. "I will come with you, but I have to find Marie first."

"I'd expect nothing less," he says, leaning his head against the top of mine. "Once we regroup with our troops in Britain, I'll talk to my superiors and see if there's anything they can do to help find her. If I end up deployed again, I'll find a place in London for you and André to stay. I doubt I will, we'll all likely be discharged. But just in case. I think André will like it there."

I must hold my breath to keep from crying as I glance over at André, soundly asleep. He's been without his father for so long, and yet William has managed to somewhat fill the void Fernand left behind, and it only makes me love him more.

. . .

Near midnight, I sit propped against the wall in the front room with André's head resting on my lap, but, no matter how the darkness and silence try to lull me to sleep, something will not let me close my eyes. I try to pass it off as nerves. After all, we're so close to freedom, but hardly anything in life ever goes exactly to plan, and we've been so lucky thus far.

Outside, the chickens begin to cluck. They've been quiet so far tonight, and whatever has woken them makes my skin prickle with alarm. I crawl to the windowsill and peek through a crack in the drapes. I see nothing, only the pitch black of a moonless sky. Then I hear it. A bark. Then, there is a flicker of a flashlight.

I rush to William's side. "Wake up! Get up!" I hiss, roughly jolting him awake. For a moment he is dazed and confused, but his eyes fly wide open in panic when I say, "The SS are coming!"

I shake André awake and rush to Anna's room while William wakes the others.

"Anna, get up! The SS are coming with dogs! We have to go *now!*"

She startles, her face paling with terror. And yet, when I struggle to pull her out of bed, she shakes her head. "No, I can't go that far. You take everyone and go out the back door. You know where to go, and how to find Cousin Frank. I'll try to stall them."

"What? No, we're not going to leave you!"

"Amia, there's no time!" she snaps. "I will slow you down. Go, save yourselves."

"Louise, Anna!" William appears in the doorway, gripping the drawing Anna gave us in one hand and André's shoulder in the other.

"Please, go!" Anna begs. "Don't let this all have been for nothing!"

I swallow my tears, and we rush into the hot, black night.

The clucking of terrified chickens is shredded by the vicious snarl of dogs, and the front door is broken down. Gunshots pierce the air, and I whirl around, hoping to see Anna following us. A Dobermann, ears flattened and pearly teeth bared, charges. Everything moves in a blur in a matter of seconds. First the dog, then a searing agony in my leg, and bloody teeth snapping in warning at my throat as I stare up at the sky.

Keep running! Don't look back! I force a scream down my throat so, hopefully, the others don't realize I'm on the ground. Suddenly, the dog's weight is knocked off my chest, and Robert's silhouette against the flashlights stabs the dog's neck. With a yelp and a whimper, the dog is dead, and Robert reaches down for me. The panic in his eyes is a testament to the young boy he really is. "Louise, hurry! Come—" Suddenly, his eyes are blank. Thick warmth spatters my face and he falls in a heap beside me, dead eyes staring at nothing, blood gushing from the hole in his head.

I barely hear an enraged German shouting, "Nein! Idiot! Cease fire! I want them alive!"

A second Dobermann skids to a halt beside us, sniffing the body of its companion.

"Aunt Louise!" André shrieks. Dread consumes me as the dog's ears perk to attention. In Robert's limp hand, there lies a bloody army knife. It must be what he used to kill the first dog. His last act in this world was to save me... and mine will be to save the others.

I snatch the knife and lunge at the dog before it can run after André, stabbing the blade into its eye. A steel grip snatches my wrist, twisting my arm, and I drop the knife. A flashlight blinds me, and I barely catch a glimpse of William and André, near the treeline.

"Take him! Run!" I scream at William, and a boot knocks the breath from my body as several SS men chase the others.

For a horrifying heartbeat, William hesitates, and I fear he means to run back for me, SS be damned. Then, with tears streaking down a face twisted in anguish, he grabs my kicking, sobbing, screaming nephew and hauls him into the forest.

I sob with relief, and fall limp into the grass, still struggling to breathe. They will escape, I'm sure of it. William speaks French, they know who to find and how, and the SS don't have any more dogs with them. They'll be long gone before they can get more dogs to track the scent.

The SS haul me to my feet and I cry out in agony. Blood where the Dobermann mauled my leg soaks through my skirt. As I am forced to walk away from Robert's body, past Anna's body that lies in the doorway, I push away the thought of André and the others.

They will make it. They're out of your hands now. Just focus on surviving the SS.

And I think I might have a chance of surviving. They don't have my sister, my nephew, or the man I love to hold over me. I will not break for anyone else, not for Michelle Dumon, Max, or any other Comet Line member. The ones I love are out of their reach, and that thought is the only thing giving me the strength to limp back to the city, my hands bound behind my back.

23

AUGUST 1–25, 1944

MARIE

"Twelve hundred jets a month," I snicker under my breath as we march back to Lager Six, and Bronisława suppresses a giggle.

The first test flight was supposed to take place today, but the launch site at the top of Walpersberg mountain is still under construction, and not a single jet has been completed yet.

"The war must be bad for them," Bronisława whispers in Polish, and this time it only takes me a few seconds to internally translate what she's said. Having Gaweł as a go-between over the last two weeks has made our progress in understanding one another grow exponentially, and we're quickly knocking down our language barrier.

"I wonder what's happening," I say, wishing there were some way to contact the outside world. All we have are rumors overheard from the SS who visit Lindig village on the weekends.

Bronisława is silent, chewing her lip in consideration. "Gaweł can tell us, maybe," she says quietly, but doesn't elaborate. She glances around at the hundreds of others marching back to Lager Six with us, and I nod in understanding. Whatever she has to say should be kept private.

After taking our nightly bread, rather than finding Radomir we weave our way toward block three, where Gaweł and many other Poles live. I offer Bronisława my arm and she takes it gratefully to keep her weight off her left leg so she doesn't have to limp as much.

"Gaweł was in a camp. He can make..." She trails off, tapping her chin thoughtfully until she remembers the word in French. "Radio. Yes, a radio. I heard him talk about it."

That would certainly be helpful. If we can gain some insight into the state of the war, Radomir and I can work out an opportune time to escape. With the thought of escape, the inevitability of splitting up, my interest is dampened slightly.

Gaweł, the Polish man named Nikodem, and two others stand at the entrance of block three.

"Bronisława, Marie," Gaweł greets us kindly. "What can I do for you?"

"Do you have a radio?" Bronisława asks quietly, and all four men seem taken aback.

Nikodem scowls darkly. "What are you talking about?" he spits.

Bronisława shrinks slightly under his fierce gaze. "I heard you talk about a radio. We want to know about the war."

Gaweł considers this, casting uncertain glances at his companions, then nods and beckons us to follow him into the block.

"Are you stupid? You want to tell them something this important?" Nikodem demands. "That one"—Nikodem's glare turns furiously on me—"will run off and tell her Russian, then they'll go to the SS! Then we'll all be dead!"

"I won't tell them," I grit out, insulted by the insinuation that I'd betray anyone to the Nazis.

Before Nikodem can say anything else, Gaweł ushers

everyone inside. "Let's not argue in the open for all to see," he says.

Instinctually, I reach into my pocket and grab the scissors. Bronisława and I slip inside one of the living quarters with the men and they close the door, leaving the six of us alone.

"Nikodem, we are equals here," Gaweł starts sternly. "Polish, French, Belgian, Russian, it doesn't matter. We all want news. We all want this to be over. So, I will tell them, and if you don't like that you can leave and know nothing. I trust them. And they could help us."

Nikodem's face is burning dark red, and I wonder if he is going to explode. Thankfully, Gaweł doesn't give him the opportunity.

"I was taken as a war prisoner in 1939 after the Germans took Poland, to a prison camp," Gaweł says to Bronisława and me. "I learned from some Italian soldiers to make a radio. They call it a foxhole radio. It's simple, and I only need a few things; a safety pin, wire, a razor blade, and some wood and nails. You girls work underground with the jet's electric panels. Could you get any of that?"

Bronisława and I share a glance, uncertain, but determined to know what is happening outside our prison.

"We might be able to get some wire," I say. All the wire for the instrument panels is in the aboveground workshops. The only time anyone but the SS and conscripted German laborers are allowed inside is when workers bring the completed panels to the workshop. Maybe, if Bronisława or I are the ones to bring the panels to them, we could steal some...

Gaweł nods. "Good. We need headphones too. Those will be hard to get, but it can wait until we have everything else."

The door swings open, and several dirty, gaunt men step inside. They halt, taken aback at the sight of women in their sleeping quarters. One eyes us with intrigue, but, before anything can be said or done, Gaweł stands and leads us outside. To no one's surprise, a tall, pale Russian is standing directly outside the door.

"What were you doing?" Radomir asks, though the question seems directed at Gaweł rather than us and there is a hint of hostility in his voice.

Gaweł glances at me, a knowing gleam in his eyes. "I'm sure she'll tell you."

As he disappears back into the block, Radomir looks at me, awaiting an explanation. "I was waiting for you," he says. "But it didn't seem like you needed help. You are alright?"

Bronisława nudges me, smirking. "You have no man?" she asks, amused, this time in Polish so Radomir cannot understand her, and I nudge her back, blushing.

God, how I've forgotten what it's like to have friends, to need and trust someone. Our situation is less than ideal, but in speaking of inconsequential things, teasing one another over schoolgirl things, and telling stories of times before the war, even the worst things can be made more bearable.

I turn to Radomir, who has stepped closer protectively. "Could you help us make a radio?"

Getting wire took less planning than I had anticipated. Bronisława and I came up with an idea to get inside the workshop, which Gaweł was happy to aid us in. He and a few Poles staged a brawl and, when the SS guards at the workshop entrance rushed to stop the fight, I snuck inside. The vast cement structure was filled with piles of instrument panels, lines upon lines of assembly tables and tools, and hundreds of crates of materials. I snatched three small coils of wire and rushed back outside.

Radomir promised he would get us the wood and nails. It wasn't too difficult, since the rail runway intended to lift the jets to the launch site was still being built and the Russians were doing the construction. The day after our meeting in block three with Gaweł, Radomir, with a mischievous grin, presented a small plank of wood and seven nails. A few days after that, he brought us two bent sets of headphones. When the crates were unloaded into a workshop, he managed to purposely damage a few headphones enough that they were still usable but discarded after examination.

Finding a razor blade was a struggle for a week. Eventually, Gaweł managed to get one from a young Dutch woman who worked measuring, cutting, and sewing the jets' leather seats.

The safety pin was the most difficult thing to find. After three weeks, Nikodem found some completely by accident, and partly because of me.

He hasn't let go of his animosity for Radomir, nor for me for associating with him. Often, our interactions consist of glares and sneered insults, but one evening during the march back to Lager Six, he was in a fouler mood than usual. After growling some rather unsavory insults about Russians, he spat on Radomir. At that moment, I—just innocently adjusting my stride—happened to lift my foot and catch Nikodem's, making him lose his balance and fall face first into the dirt. Naturally, seeing as he was now part of the path, I walked over him and ground my heel into his hand. He probably would've liked to throttle me, but he'd sprained his wrist and I'd broken two of his fingers. He returned from the hospital in Lager Hummelshain with three safety pins in the bandage on his wrist.

As they say, all's well that ends well.

Sunday afternoon, when we have the day off and many of the SS guards have gone to Lindig, Bronisława, Radomir, and I have congregated between blocks six and seven. Gaweł approaches us.

"We're ready," he says simply. There have been few chances

to listen to the radio in the last five days, since we gathered everything Gaweł would need to construct it; our forced labor hours, the food line, and appeals leave little time in the day. Instead, Gaweł has spent that time practicing building and dismantling the radio. By now, he is able to build it in under a minute, and also able to deconstruct and hide it in the same time.

Most of the laborers have gathered outside, eager to enjoy a day of relaxation in the warmth of the sun, the fresh breeze, and the laxer security.

We slip inside block three, Bronisława and I with our heads down, Radomir and Gaweł protectively on either side of us to keep the attention of the other men off us. One man stands guard outside the door of the sleeping quarters, and nine men, in addition to Nikodem, wait inside. Nikodem shoots Radomir and me a scornful glare. I narrow my eyes at him, then smirk, tapping my nose in mockery of his own. When I tripped him, he skinned a good portion of his face, and his nose is scabbed and slightly crooked.

Perhaps it's unwise to taunt him, but Radomir's large, imposing frame has become my second shadow, and it's rare now that I feel genuine fear of another person. We are a well-known pair of companions, and no one has ever dared to harm me, for fear of incurring the wrath of the man they consider a vicious Russian.

We all watch in fascination as Gaweł quickly assembles the radio, his hands moving in an efficient blur. At last, he connects the damaged headphones, hands one pair to a German-speaking Pole and slips the other over his own ears.

For several minutes, no one speaks, no one breathes, then suddenly Gaweł freezes and the Pole quickly grabs a broken piece of pencil and a pad of paper they bought from a more lenient SS guard. His hand poised to scribble out whatever is being said, he and Gaweł share looks of confusion. "Russian?" Gaweł guesses.

At this, Radomir crosses the room. The Pole removes his headphones and Radomir slips them on. Immediately, he nods, confirming, "Russian," then grabs the pencil and paper and quickly scrawls what he hears. We wait, desperate to know whether it's good or bad news. At last, he pauses, and my heart leaps when he grins.

"The Red Army is in Poland," Radomir says. "The Russian front is advancing fast. They've crossed the Carpathian Mountains in Czechoslovakia, they're near Warsaw."

A strangled sob of joy escapes Bronisława, and I excitedly crush her in my arms. The Nazis are being pushed out of her home! Gaweł quickly translates into Polish for the other men, and they all celebrate with smiles and silent prayers of thanks. Nikodem, however, is frowning, and his eyes are filled with rage and anguish.

I remember what Gaweł told me about Nikodem's family, and suddenly my heart is heavy for him. The prospect of Russians taking Poland must not be a welcome one to him. After a moment of hesitation, I move across the room to sit beside him. He glares at me, fists clenched, but I say nothing. What *can* I say?

Perhaps he is rude and spiteful, but he isn't a bad person. He's a man who's been through too much, who's lost too much...

Tentatively, I lay a hand over his trembling fist, wishing I knew how to offer comforting words like Louise. He blinks at me in confusion with red-rimmed eyes, teeth grinding together, and then, he deflates. A heavy sigh escapes him, and he lowers his gaze and runs a bandaged hand down his face in exhaustion.

"I'm sorry," I whisper in Polish, nodding toward his hand. I find myself wondering what his life was like before the war. What did his wife look like? How many children did he have, how old were they? Did his world fall apart when he lost them, like ours did when we lost my mother?

"French! An Allied broadcast!" Gaweł's hushed words draw my attention. He beckons me over and I put on the headphones Radomir hands me and prepare to write down what I hear. It takes me a moment to adjust to the crude, garbled sound, but soon the Frenchman's speech becomes clearer.

> *Paris martyred! But Paris liberated! Liberated by itself, liberated by its people with the help of the French armies, with the support and the help of all France, of the France that fights, of the only France, of the real France, of the eternal France!*

"Liberated! Paris is liberated," I choke, tears rolling down my cheeks, and my hand trembles as I hasten to write.

> *Since the enemy that held Paris has capitulated into our hands, France returns to Paris, to her home. She returns bloody, but quite resolute. She returns there enlightened by the immense lesson, but more certain than ever of her duties and of her rights.*
>
> *I speak of her duties first, and I will sum them all up by saying that, for now, it is a matter of the duties of war. The enemy is staggering, but he is not beaten yet. He remains on our soil.*

To hell with the enemies still on our soil! I think in elation, muffling the laughter that threatens to overwhelm me. Paris is free! After so many long, bloody years of terror and occupation, Paris is free! Louise and André are free!

Gaweł takes over jotting down notes, for my vision is too blurred by tears to see clearly.

"Louise and André!" I sob, grasping Radomir's hands.

"They're free! Paris is free! No more Gestapo, no more soldiers, no more resistance! They're free!"

He smiles brightly at me, squeezing my hands. I return my attention to the radio and, as the speech draws to an end, my heart is bursting with joy and relief.

We, who have lived the greatest hours of our history, we have nothing else to wish than to show ourselves, up to the end, worthy of France. Long live France!

"Long live France," I quietly echo.

I have a home to return to, a home safe from the Nazis! My family will no longer fear for their lives! Louise will never have to hide another Allied man, for they will walk freely down our streets rather than hiding beneath them!

Grinning, I wrap Radomir in my arms while the others try to search for another radio wave. His grip around me tightens as if some fear has occurred to him, as if he is afraid of letting me go, and I hope he doesn't.

24

AUGUST 16–20, 1944

LOUISE

No amount of water has been able to wash away the feeling of Robert's blood. No matter how often the Gestapo lay a towel over my face and pour buckets of water over me, I can still feel the warm spatters on my cheeks, still taste the metallic bitterness in my mouth. I feel as though I am drowning in blood.

My cell is dark and quiet, with an odd, damp stench that hangs in the air, a mixture of blood, wet stones, and mold. I flex my fingers as I lie on the floor, relieved to find I still have all of them, even though several are broken, like my ribs.

I don't know where I am anymore; I lost track a few days ago. Or maybe it was a few weeks, or perhaps only hours. At some point between beatings and floggings, everything became a blur.

The first few days weren't bad. The SS called me in for interrogation in cozy offices. They offered me tea, expressed sympathy for my injured leg, sought to create a false bond of trust by steering the conversations away from the resistance. The SS interrogator told me about his wife in Berlin, his son who'd been promoted to SS-Obersturmführer, and his daughter learning to play the violin. He even showed me pictures of them. What a lovely, normal family they looked like.

It almost worked. I almost started crying. Talk of his family made me think of my own, lost God knows where and hopefully safe, and I almost talked to him. Then, he said I should tell him what I knew, since I, as a parent, should understand what it was like to love their child, to do what they must to protect them.

A mistake on his part. Once he tried to appeal to me as a parent, I knew André and the men had escaped, or else he would know I was not a mother. After four days, when I still refused to talk, the SS decided they were done with me. That was when they handed me over to the Gestapo. That was when the real interrogation began.

A shiver runs through my bruised, battered body. I started lying on my stomach at some point over the last few days—at least I think it was days. I've been fading in and out of consciousness ever since they finally let me sleep after forcing me to stay awake for three days. I prefer the pain of lying on my broken ribs to the pain from the lashes that flayed my back. Waterboarding has been the worst. It is absolute hell, to lie under a towel and be held down as I flail and fight to breathe. Oh, how people take for granted the air they breathe! I think that's how I sprained my wrists, fighting to break out of the handcuffs because I thought I was surely about to drown.

And the wait is torture. Every second, I wait for the door with the little barred window to open and let a sliver of light inside my airless cell. I wait for the Gestapo man who tortures me and screams his questions in my ears. I wait for the other Gestapo man, who bandages my wounds and tries to gently coax information out of me.

The door creaks and, not for the first time, I wish I were dead.

I groan, whimpering as someone roughly lifts my body over

their shoulder like a sack of flour, and sob as the position stabs my ribs and forces the air from my lungs.

Perhaps I'll be executed now, I think, half in hope and half in despair. They're probably done wasting their efforts by now. With that thought, of death, of a noose or a firing squad, I think of my family. Of André's face as he screamed for me, of hugging Marie goodbye at the train station, of kissing Fernand and Father before they disappeared, of lying next to my mother in the hospital bed the morning before she died, of William and the way he held me and made me believe everything would be alright.

Please, take care of André, I pray as tears roll down my face. *Find Marie and Fernand for him, become a doctor and take Dorothy to see Ella Fitzgerald, find that quiet house by the water, teach your little ones to read and swim, and be happy with another...*

Suddenly, I am weightless, and I scream in pain as I land on a wooden platform in the darkness. I force my eyes open, squinting as they painfully adjust to the daylight, and catch a glimpse of a Gestapo man closing the entrance of a cattle car.

"You look like hell," a woman's voice rasps in German. I strain to see her, and barely make out her form crawling toward me from a corner where there is a pile of hay and a dozen other women. On the other side of the cattle car, barely illuminated by the barred window, there is an overturned bucket that reeks of urine and feces, and two people lying face down. I avert my eyes, forcing away the thought of Robert, kind, rambunctious young Robert...

"Where are we?" I force out.

"Still in France, God knows where we're going," she says. "Probably a prison camp."

But she's German. What is she doing here? "But you're German," I manage to whisper.

"Not to the Reich. I am a 'race defiler;' my husband was a

Jew. Before they shot him. We are all criminals to the Reich; French, German, Polish, doesn't matter to them."

Suddenly the cattle car jerks, and then we're moving. The bucket in the corner rolls much too close for comfort and I gag, whimpering as knives slice through my stomach. The German woman drags me to the group in the corner. The world is fading, the light is dying, and the lingering agony of my weeks of torture is dragging me into the void of unconsciousness. "I'm sorry about your husband," I hear myself whisper, then I know no more.

The train never seems to stop. Sometimes, when I open my eyes, there are more women crammed inside, and the German woman shares the bit of food and water the SS occasionally throw inside. By the time I'm able to drag myself into a seated position, we've been on the train for four days.

The train slows and, abruptly, we jerk to a halt. No one moves or speaks; we are all straining to hear anything of the outside world. A woman wobbles to her feet and peers out the barred window. "We're at a station," she rasps, voice dry from lack of water. "The sign says Ravensbrück."

"I've heard of this place. We're in Germany," an older woman mutters. "It's a camp for women and undesirables."

Undesirables... My mind turns over the list of those the Nazis deem sub-human. *Race defilers, collaborators, political opponents, homosexuals, Jehovah's Witnesses, Romani, Jews...*

The cattle car door clatters open. To my shock, it is a woman who stands before us. Her uniform is grayish green, and my throat constricts at the sight of the SS insignia and Nazi eagle. Suddenly I'm back in the dungeon, drowning under the towel. Heart quickening, I desperately suck down as much air as possible, terrified I'll never breathe again.

"Everyone, get out! Hurry up!" the SS guard commands,

covering her nose with a handkerchief. She turns to someone I cannot see. "Good God, even dog shit doesn't smell this bad!"

We all struggle down from the cattle car to the platform, squinting as the sunlight blinds us, stumbling, as we have been able to do nothing but crawl for the last few days. SS women holding whips, pistols, and leashed German Shepherds with flattened ears and bared teeth stand guard. Knives slice through my torn leg, and I fight the urge to run screaming in terror from the dogs.

As we are directed down a long dirt road, I bite my cheeks to keep from crying or screaming. A woman at the head of the line trips, landing on her knees. The woman beside her leans to help her up. Suddenly, she too is knocked down by an SS woman. The guard raises her whip and brings it down with savage force on each of the collapsed women, kicking them as they scream and cry. Threatening us with their own whips, the other SS guards force us to continue past the horrific beating, and the women's wails chase us down the road.

"Don't stick yourselves where you don't belong, and you whores will all get along fine!" an SS woman shouts mockingly.

The meaning of those words, this unspoken rule in this place called Ravensbrück, makes me quiver. *Don't help others, it's a punishable offense.*

We are herded into a long, spacious building for disinfection, moving as quickly as we can from the whips and the dogs nipping at our heels.

"Empty your pockets, take off your clothes, and line up!" a blond SS officer commands.

We all exchange stunned looks, eyes wide, as we search for somewhere to undress. I waver, suddenly light-headed, and cover my chest as if my clothes were already stripped off. There is nowhere for privacy. Impatiently, the SS woman snaps at us again to undress and give up our possessions. Trembling, afraid of enduring the same punishment as the others who fell, we comply.

As I unbutton the cuff of my blouse, I freeze. For some reason, the Gestapo didn't take it, or perhaps they didn't notice it, but I now realize I still have William's bracelet.

Give it up? I wonder with dread, glancing first at the SS women and then at my fellow arrivals as they lay the contents of their pockets on the growing mound of clothes. *How could I ever give up something so precious to me? The parachute that saved his life, the beads that served as a reminder of the loved ones waiting for him... No, I won't let it go.*

As I shrug off my blouse and the cool air nips at my exposed skin, I tuck the bracelet under my tongue. When we've all completely stripped, we huddle together, shielding our breasts, heads dipped and avoiding one another's eyes in shame. The SS order us to line up and we hasten to obey. When I reach the end of the line, there are piles of blond, brown, and black hair on the floor, short curls and long braids, and, as a pair of shears are taken to my sunny blond locks, I almost don't care. After the Gestapo, having my head shaved is the kindest thing I've endured since my arrest.

Afterwards, we are ushered into a communal shower room. I choke as icy water spurts from the pipes lining the ceiling. A woman yelps as I fall backwards into her, sending both of us tumbling to the tiles as I scramble to escape the water, to breathe. Someone grabs my wrists, strong and unyielding like handcuffs as the water beats against my bruised, broken body.

Breathe! Breathe! I can't breathe!

"Take deep breaths," someone tells me. Slowly, the panic and flashes of the prison cell fade. The German woman who first spoke to me in the cattle car kneels on the tiles with me, holding me steady, and, together, we take slow breaths until my heart has steadied. She helps me to my feet and, with tears clouding my eyes, freezing water piercing my skin like millions of tiny bullets, I quickly wash away the hair, blood, and grime.

After our shower, we are issued thin, striped cotton dresses, a pair of shoes, and a bowl. Colored triangles and patches with numbers are placed in our hands, and we are instructed to sew them onto our uniforms later. My triangle is solid red, the symbol of a political criminal, like most of the other women, but I—unlike the others—have a large red cross painted across the back and arms of my prison dress. None of our possessions are returned to us, and, when I deem it's safe, I take the bracelet from my mouth and hide it under my arm.

The doors at the opposite end of the disinfection building are thrown open. The world we emerge into is a vast, dull expanse of wooden barracks, mud, thousands of prisoners and lines of tall, barbed wire, and beyond the watchtowers is a lake and an endless stretch of dark forest. There is a heaviness over this place, a crushing darkness that tries to drag me back to the Gestapo dungeons, the awful helplessness, the agony, the terror... I look over my shoulder at the building whence we came, hoping that some flicker of the real world will be there. But there are only the SS guards.

A screeching whistle pierces the chilly wind. Suddenly, the prisoners who were milling in groups are jerked to attention, and all rush to the wide-open square of mud before the SS command buildings. The SS women shove us to join the growing swarm of thousands of prisoners, shouting, "Line up! Appell! Roll call!"

I find myself several rows behind the front, standing alongside a woman with the same red markings on her arms and back as me. All at once, silence falls. The abrupt shift from the chaos of thousands of women in the crowded square to strict quiet is foreboding.

"Don't react, no matter what happens," the woman at my side whispers, her voice so low I nearly don't hear her. Stealing a quick glance around, I realize everyone has lowered their heads and is standing as still as possible. I mirror their stance.

Movement at the front of the square catches my attention. An SS officer has arrived, a whip in one hand, a leashed dog in the other. A delicate-looking woman with blue eyes and round cheeks framed by blond hair, she seems like the type of girl who would offer you cookies and tea. And yet, her presence carries something eerie, something that has made the voices of all Ravensbrück's prisoners die at once.

As the guards conduct roll call, the pretty SS officer walks the length of the lines. Her dog remains obediently at her side, though it eagerly sniffs the prisoners, growling at anyone its mistress pauses beside. The SS woman stops in front of the German woman who came on the train with me. She looks her up and down, demands to see her identification patch, and, upon seeing the mark of a race defiler—a yellow triangle overlapping a black triangle to form a Star of David—frowns deeply. She whistles. The dog lunges. The German woman lets out a bloodcurdling scream as the dog tears into her leg and drags her to the ground.

Someone snatches my arm as I jerk in terror, forcing me to stay still.

The SS woman watches in amusement as her dog savages the sobbing, shrieking woman, and then, after several unending minutes, whistles again. The dog, face stained with the German woman's blood, happily leans into its mistress's hand as she coos in approval. She kicks the brutalized woman on the ground again and again with vicious force, until the German has stopped crying, stopped moving. Then, she wipes her bloody boot on the woman's prisoner dress, straightens her hair, and strides away as if nothing happened.

It isn't until roll call has ended several hours later that anyone speaks. The woman with the same markings as me, who grabbed my arm, turns to me. "That was Dorothea Binz," she says in German, though her accent indicates she is British. "She's the deputy chief wardess. Never look her in the eye or show her weakness. She can sense it like a hound, and she likes to punish it."

"Why... why did she do that?" I ask weakly.

The woman shrugs grimly. "She likes to... She's the worst of them all. Binz used to oversee the torture bunker."

I can't breathe. My vision swims and tremors rack me as I look at the crumpled body of the stranger who showed me kindness being dragged to a wooden cart piled high with corpses. The image of Dorothea Binz's deceptively gentle, beautiful face clouds my mind, and bile rises in my throat. Of all the faces for evil to wear, innocence is by far the most terrifying.

"Take deep breaths," the woman reminds me, laying a comforting, motherly hand on my shoulder.

"Is she alright, Mum?" A girl who couldn't be older than sixteen, with the same red markings on her arms, steps closer.

"She'll be fine," the woman says. "My name is Fiona, this is my daughter, Isla. And you are?"

It takes several moments before I can force my voice above a whisper. "Louise."

"French?" Isla inquires, and I nod.

"Resistance by the looks of it, too," Fiona adds. She smiles sympathetically when she feels me tense. "Don't be afraid, dear. We're resistance fighters too." She indicates the red crosses on her arms and back. "This is how they separate us from the regular political criminals. Under the Nacht und Nebel decree, people like us who rebel in Nazi-occupied territories are supposed to either disappear or be executed."

And the Nazis are so good at making people disappear...

"Come with us. We'll help you sew your patches onto your uniform," Fiona says, and I let her guide me to a wooden barrack. Windows allow the sun to cast sickly light over three-tier wooden bunks and a long heating channel running through the center of the building. Hundreds of women shuffle to lie in the bunks or sit on the cement channel or floor, bundled in as many articles of clothing as they have. The frigid wind digs below my thin dress, and I'm suddenly aware that none of us were given undergarments.

Fiona, Isla, and I take seats beside another small group of women on the floor by the heating channel. They are Jews, wearing bright yellow triangles. They speak softly, and I am taken aback to hear they're teaching one another mathematics equations. Isla slips a wad of frayed rope out of her pocket and braids the strands into a little bracelet. All around us, the ill, starving prisoners are quietly telling stories, giving history and mathematics lessons, making jewelry and little dolls from scraps of fabric and straw.

I cast Fiona a bewildered look. How are they acting so nonchalantly? How are they not going mad, when I am already losing my grip on my mind after what I just saw?

Fiona flashes me a brittle smile. "Trust me, this is how to survive. The SS might have our bodies and dignity, but they can't have our souls. We have to hide it from the SS, we're not supposed to care about each other."

"They don't like it when we come together," Isla says quietly.

Fiona nods. "I think it reminds them that we're human. And that we're stronger than them, even if we don't have guns or whips."

"Fight without arms," Isla murmurs in English, and Fiona echoes the words.

My heart jumps. *Could it be coincidence? They said they were resistance fighters, but now to speak the Comet Line's motto...*

"Pugna Quin Percutias," I whisper with uncertainty, and suddenly their faces are aglow with shock and happiness.

"You worked for the Comet Line!" Fiona grabs my hand

and squeezes it tightly. "We were some of their helpers, too! We were betrayed in 1941—an infiltrator in Belgium turned us over to the Gestapo. We've been here ever since. What happened to you?"

Hatred darkens my mind as I think of Jacques Desoubrie, the despicable rat who got Yvonne killed, who betrayed countless Comet Line members, whose deceit has caused me so much fear and grief, and I wish I had poked both his eyes out when I had the chance. There haven't been many people I've genuinely wished ill on, but I hope Jacques Desoubrie gets everything that's coming to him and worse.

"I was compromised by a German agent in Paris. I tried to escape to Spain with my nephew and four Americans. We almost made it, but the SS caught me near the border. My nephew escaped with the others, thank God."

"That's one good thing to think about. Hold on to it," Fiona says with an encouraging smile. "He's safe, and that's something the SS can't take from you."

If Fiona and Isla can survive Ravensbrück for three years, then so can I. If they can hold on to hope despite the horrors I've already witnessed, then so can I. So much is uncertain, the fates of the ones I love, my life, this war—but I refuse to die.

I will survive to know that André and Fernand are together again.

I will survive to find Marie.

I will survive to see William again.

Silently, I make these vows to myself, and push away the thought of anything else but the women around me keeping one another's hope alive.

25

OCTOBER 28–29, 1944

MARIE

Over five months in REIMAHG and today is finally the day. The timing is perfect. The first jet has been completed, there are thousands of laborers—despite the high mortality rate—to provide a distraction to the SS, and our supplies have remained undiscovered. Originally, REIMAHG was supposed to produce Fw 190 and Ta 152 fighter jets, but—in what we all consider a rash last-moment decision brought on by insanity—Hitler ordered production to be switched to an entirely different jet. The Messerschmitt Me 262. Over the last few weeks, the SS have rushed to have the first prototype completed.

Tonight, I repeat to myself for the thousandth time. No matter how many times I think it, my heart clenches with fear and excitement. We decided to wait until Saturday to make our escape; the SS guards are laxer on the weekends. After the nightly roll call, there will be a several-hour window in which we can slip away.

The afternoon is the coolest it's been in weeks. A bright, cloudless sky looks down on the thousands of laborers gathered before the workshops, underground factory, and bunkers as the first Me 262 prototype is slowly raised up the ramp to the launch site. It's an impressive plane, even I must admit it. With a wingspan of over forty feet, armed with autocannons, and the ability to carry bombs weighing over five hundred pounds, it leaves everyone in awe. And yet, there is an air of uncertainty overhanging this day, even for the SS. Construction of the tunnels and bunkers has fallen abysmally behind in the last months, and we can all sense that the Nazis are growing increasingly desperate. This prototype jet wasn't supposed to be completed so soon, nor should there be a test flight today.

Some of the SS have been overheard voicing their anxiousness over pressure from the higher-ups to speed up construction, as well as their concerns over this jet—which, as far as we're aware, their superiors haven't been informed of. Unless takeoff today is a success, the existence of this rushed prototype won't even be documented.

"It can only be success or failure," Radomir told me the day the launch site was completed. Even after the trees were cleared and the hill was leveled, the runway was too small for a plane to launch from and land at again. If takeoff today is a success, the jet must be flown to another location. The only other outcome is that the jet doesn't make it off the hill at all.

The latter possibility is the one all of us silently hope for, even if it means the product of our labor going up in flames.

Beside me, Bronisława shifts uncomfortably. Now that we speak one another's languages fluently enough, she's managed to explain that her limp is from a childhood injury, when she broke her ankle and it never healed properly. It doesn't usually pain her unless she's been standing on it for too long, like now. I offer my arm and she gladly accepts the extra support.

The jet reaches the top of the hill. I cross my fingers, hoping for anything but success, then, quite suddenly, a strange wave of guilt washes over me. It's easy to put a person beneath the broader canopy of "enemy" or "ally," "German" or "American," and forget that the nameless, faceless ones beneath those terms are still human.

Internally, I chide myself. I pass these thoughts off as Louise's, a product of all these months spent missing her and beginning to understand her for the first time in my life. She would worry for the man in the cockpit, worry for the mother waiting for her son, wonder if he had children or siblings he couldn't wait to see again. That's what Louise would think of, not me. And yet, I uncross my fingers.

"Damn it, Louise," I mutter under my breath.

Radomir casts me a curious look, but I shake my head. There's no point explaining my conflict, especially to him, who probably wishes to see the jet crash and burn. Thinking of him in the prison camps, resorting to horrific means to survive, I try to beat down the twinge of sympathy in my heart.

The telltale rumble of an engine coming to life echoes across the valley. We all watch, unblinking. Even from the bottom of the mountain we can see that the jet seems to shiver as it begins to pick up speed, swiftly losing ground on the perilously short ramp.

"He's not going to make it," Bronisława whispers, gripping my arm tighter, sounding torn between hope for both outcomes, like I am.

The jet raises its nose, seeking the sky. I draw in a sharp breath as it rattles, lowers slightly, then shoots into the air. The tail clips the treetops, and, like a bird knocked out of the sky, spirals downwards. Everyone gasps and yelps in surprise, hoots with triumph, stares in shock as the jet wrecks against the hill. By either a miracle or misfortune—depending on one's perspective—the Luftwaffe man crawls out of the jet.

Radomir leans down, his breath ghosting against my ear and making me shiver. "This is a good omen for us, lisichka."

The enemy is staggering, but he is not beaten yet. The

Nazis can no longer keep it secret that the war isn't progressing in their favor. They are exhausted, injured, starving, and desperate. I doubt they can continue this war much longer.

Tonight, I tell myself again. *After tonight, I'll be gone, and I'll never be subjected to the Nazis again.* But the thought doesn't bring as much excitement as it should. Radomir stands close behind me, a comforting, protective veil I've become so accustomed to that the prospect of not having him after today, when he goes east to the partisans and I return to Paris, is akin to the feeling of leaving Louise. My gaze flickers reluctantly to Bronisława, a woman I've laughed and suffered with, who has become one of my dearest friends, who reminds me so much of my sister...

How can I leave them behind?

My happiness at the prospect of escape is overshadowed for the rest of the day by the inevitability of separation.

Radomir is still determined to reach the partisans in the east. I stopped trying to convince him to come with me after the third time he refused. We are both stubborn people, and I know well enough that, once my mind is made up, there is little that can change it.

Bronisława has known about our plans for over a month. It took a long time for me to work up the courage and trust to tell her, but when I finally did it was like a weight taken off my chest. I tried to convince her to come with me too, but she just smiled somberly, shook her head, and said she would slow me down. She would rather stay behind and give us the chance to escape. The only consolation it has given me is that she will have Gaweł to look out for her.

As Bronisława and I line up for supper, Radomir slips off to the woods to dig up our supplies. I can barely hear anything over the frantic pounding of my heart. The closer to freedom we get, the more terrifying each new "what if" becomes. What if I get injured on the way to Paris? What if I'm caught by a German patrol? What if—

Bronisława nudges me. "Are you alright?"

Months ago, I would have dismissively assured her nothing was wrong. That is what my sense of self-preservation would dictate I do... and yet, gazing into her kind, worried eyes, I think of all the times Louise looked at me this way, all the times the hurt flashed across her face when I shut her out. My shoulders sink, and I shake my head.

Bronisława slips her arm through mine, and we make our way to the secluded place between blocks six and seven. "Tell me what's wrong," she says.

I look around for eavesdroppers, then lower my voice. "I'm afraid... I've always been afraid of a lot of things, I just never let it show. That's the only way I know how to be strong. I stopped letting people close to me... but you're right. Serce nie sługa."

"The heart is not a servant," she says in French, smiling softly, knowingly.

"I'm used to being in control of myself." I lower my gaze, swallowing thickly. "I care about him... I didn't even mean to, I just *did*. It wasn't something I could control. It scares me."

"I know what that's like. When I met Avraham, I didn't think I would love him," Bronisława says. "But we had a lot in common, even though he was Jewish and I was Catholic. When I went to buy fabric from his store, I stayed longer and longer each time, and we talked about everything. Then, one day, I realized I was in love with him, and I hadn't even meant to fall in love. I was scared. I knew my parents wouldn't allow it. My little sister, Eliana, married a Jewish man and moved to Kraków the year before, and our parents cast her out of the house for it... I said no when he asked me to marry him."

I wind an arm around her waist as she wipes the tears that have sprung to her eyes.

"I tried to make myself stop loving him, but I couldn't. Eliana was the one who stood by me through it. When she married Toviel, I couldn't believe she'd let herself be so swept away by a man, but with Avraham, I understood. You can't command your heart, and I'd wasted so much time worried about what others would think. I'd hurt the one man I loved. And so, I went back to Avraham, and *I* proposed. We got married a few months later. Then Warsaw fell to the Germans, and he was taken to the ghetto in October of 1940... I don't know what happened after that. I was arrested for my brother's involvement in the resistance the same month, and I've been through prison and labor camps since then." Bronisława's blue eyes shine with pain and understanding. "I pray every day to see him again. I know what you feel for Radomir. Please don't make the same mistake I did. Don't be afraid, and don't let go. Our lives are too short for such things."

"But I have to go home. My family needs me. And he wants to fight with the partisans..."

"I see how he looks at you," she says quietly. "If he has any sense, he won't let go either."

And yet, most people in my life have let me go. Fernand and Father left for war. Roger, Léon, and Victor left for the resistance. Jeanne left for her officer. Louise left for the Comet Line, even though I followed her down that path. Everyone leaves eventually...

"Are you certain you won't come?" I ask, wishing I could hide the gloom in my voice.

Silently, she offers a wan smile. She tears her bread ration in half, then offers me the piece with the most margarine. "For good luck?"

I swallow the lump in my throat, pull Bronisława into my arms and hold her as tightly as the day Louise held me when I left Paris. When we part, I take the piece of bread she offers and place my entire ration into her trembling fingers. She smiles and rises to her toes to kiss my cheeks, then limps back toward the supper line to stand with Gaweł and Nikodem.

I slip away to the back of the stone blocks and wait a few minutes for the SS men to lower their guard. The sky began to fade to violet some time ago, and a warm autumn breeze rustles the trees. I silently slip into the treeline, weaving my way through the darkening woods. I check the first two supply holes and, finding them empty, make my way to the last hole, praying Radomir was able to evade the SS too.

I breathe a sigh of relief upon seeing his large form kneeling at the last provision hole, carefully dividing rations and supplies into the bags I made from leather and thread I stole from a workshop. REIMAHG is unlike any prison or camp I would have imagined; there are few guard towers or patrols, but the mountains and forests serve as their own guard walls, and even Radomir doesn't know what lies beyond the complex of lagers. For months, we've prepared for this moment, stolen, saved, and hoarded all the food and supplies we could possibly carry to escape the unknown wilderness. And yet, now that the long-awaited day has arrived... My heart twists as I pause behind the undergrowth, committing Radomir's face to memory, wishing that I'd never let myself care about him.

"Are you coming or are you just going to stand there?" his voice rumbles quietly.

Resolutely, I step forward, steeling myself against the inevitable. I sling one bag over my shoulder, not bothering to check what is inside yet. He's never cheated or taken advantage of me before—excluding the time he stole my wages to buy me medicine from the SS—and I want to put as much distance between myself and this place as possible.

"Here, you can take this one," he says, slipping a map out of his pocket. When the launch ramp was under construction, he stole one of the less detailed maps of the REIMAHG complex and made a copy of it so we could each have one. Frowning deeply, he hands me the original.

For a while we stand in silence, and I determinedly keep my eyes averted, whereas I can feel his gaze seeking mine. I've said goodbye to a lot of people over the years; my parents, my brother, my sister, my nephew, my friends—saying goodbye to him should be no different. And yet, when the crushing silence becomes too much to bear, when I turn to make my way into the forest, my soul is heavy in a way I haven't felt in a long time.

His hands suddenly grasp my shoulders, and my heart skips as he draws me back. Gently, his fingers caress my cheeks, then softly twirl the stray red locks of hair peeking from below my scarf. His eyes smolder like white flames, and their heat burns through my body like an inferno.

"Paris..." he whispers, the word ghosting across my lips. "I'd hate to let you go alone."

Hopeful tears spring to my eyes. I slip my arms around his back, a silent plea to stay with me, to come with me. "Then don't," I whisper. *Please, don't leave me too.*

A weight seems to be lifted from him and he sighs, his eyes slipping closed as he presses his forehead to mine. I would be content to never leave this moment, to always live within this sphere of warmth and tranquility where there is nothing else but us.

He murmurs something in Russian, but I don't need to understand the words to feel their devotion, their passion, to know there is a promise in them. "Let us go quickly," he says, his large hand engulfing mine, and the absolute joy filling my heart leaves no room for me to question why he changed his mind. Perhaps I will ask him soon, when we're safe and there is all the time in the world. For now, we are within an hourglass, and we must be far from this place when the SS realize two prisoners are missing.

Each minute stretches into hours as Radomir leads us south-west through the woods, where there are miles between the other lagers and less chances of coming across watchtowers or patrols, but the absolute need for invisibility seems to magnify every crunch of a leaf or twig beneath my feet. We reach a dirt road a few hours later, and the pleasant quiet of night and all its creatures has remained undisturbed by German shouts, sirens, or dogs. Still, my heart races, and Radomir's presence at my side, holding me steady and leading me to freedom, is all that keeps me calm.

Suddenly, Radomir snatches my arm, jerking me away from the road and into the brush. His large hand presses over my lips in a command to be silent.

Crunching gravel not far off makes my breath hitch. Someone is coming down the road, though I can't be sure how many, for I can hear nothing but my heart pounding in my ears. Two lights pass before where we sit crouched in the forest, illuminating two SS patrolmen and a dog.

A dog! My chest constricts, sheer terror threatening to draw a whimper from my throat. Radomir's fingers tighten over my mouth as the dog halts, sniffing the air, ears perking to attention. The SS men stop, tiredly rubbing their eyes, lazily flicking their flashlights into the woods. The light passes over us and, even invisible in the foliage, I feel bare beneath the blinding light. The SS try to tug their dog onwards, but it remains in place, lips curling in a low growl.

Out of the corner of my eye, I catch the faint glint of steel. Radomir has drawn a knife, and a cold, deadly calm has overtaken him. Like a predator rather than prey in hiding, he eyes the dog as it strains toward the trees, the SS men sharing tense looks as their hands move to their pistols. *He's killed for me before*, I think as he releases me, freeing both his hands as the SS let their dog pace forward, as he prepares for a fight. *He won't hesitate to kill them.*

The agitated dog continues to snarl, setting its masters

further on edge. I hold my breath, praying to God and begging as I have never done before. *God, please don't let them find us, let them walk away. We're so close to freedom.* The SS are only feet from the treeline, so close I can see the scuffs on their black boots reflected by the flashlights.

Rustling a few feet away snatches their attention. A fox darts out of the brush and across the road. The dog, snarling viciously, lunges for it, dragging a startled SS man into the dirt. Swearing, the SS jerks the dog's leash, struggling to his feet. Even as the dog immediately shifts its attention back to where Radomir and I quietly crouch, the SS men pay it no further mind. Likely annoyed at having gotten worked up over what they now think was just a fox, they drag the dog with them as they continue their patrol, ignoring its growls as it strains to run back to us.

Not until the flicker of flashlights, the tired muttering of German voices, and the insistent howls of the patrol dog vanish do I allow myself to breathe, tears pricking my eyes.

Radomir slips the knife back into his pocket and reaches to take my hand and help me to my feet. Soothingly, he murmurs something in Russian, although I recognize the word lisichka.

"Saved by a little fox," I manage breathily, and the moonlight illuminates Radomir's scarred face just enough for me to see him smile fondly.

Shaken but relieved, we continue on, thankfully encountering no other patrols, just occasionally glimpsing the faint lights from watchtowers in other lagers of the REIMAHG complex miles away. The land morphs into rolling hills thick with forest, and the blackness of midnight is brightened by a full moon that lights our path. As I glance up through the protective arms of the trees, several comets burn trails across the night in the direction of France, reminding me of Louise, of home, of the man still holding my hand.

Dawn breaks near five o'clock, and, when Radomir

announces we're several miles from Storchsdorf and twenty-five miles from REIMAHG, we take to the forest floor in exhaustion.

"We've been lucky," Radomir says as he lies in a nook of earth beside a fallen tree. "The SS might just be noticing we're missing, if they feel like taking roll call on a Sunday morning."

Smiling softly, I lie down beside him, my eyes heavy and feet aching from a night of walking. Though the ground is damp and chilly, and each little sound startles me, I snuggle comfortably into his arms, warm. He sighs with contentment, drawing me closer, and, as I drift off to sleep, I feel his lips press gently against my forehead, and think that perhaps I don't need to ask him why he changed his mind.

26

NOVEMBER, 1944

LOUISE

Pugna Quin Percutias. Fight Without Arms.

Silent resistance has been the only way I've ever been able to fight. Ignoring the Germans when they took Paris like they were ghosts, making deals for more food than the occupying authorities dictated we could have, smuggling soldiers right out from under the Nazis' noses. If I had more nerve, Marie's temperament, I might have gotten involved with the resistance groups who fought with guns and sabotage.

Perhaps it's a blessing Marie and I are so different. My insistence on fighting combined with her short temper. We'd wreak havoc! I muse silently as I sit outside, leaning against the wall of the block with Fiona and Isla. Thankfully, my caution tempered her impulsiveness, and her quick action saved us when I was too consumed with hypotheticals and "what ifs."

There is no labor on Sunday, and so everyone mills idly outside their blocks and in the roll call square. God forbid the SS allow us to remain inside and sleep, not that anyone would prefer to be inside, cramped head to feet on the wooden bunks, unable to move, breathe, festering in the filth and illness of over a thousand other prisoners.

The wind nips our cheeks and the muddy ground soaks through our clothes where we've taken to sitting. Blisters have torn open along my fingers and all of my nails are broken. I, along with Fiona and Isla, have spent the last two months slaving in the fields outside the Siemens factory, digging up the crops and planting new ones, and dragging boulders to pave new roads with my bare hands. There is little food, and my stomach is constantly aching. All that keeps my mind off my body and the obsessive hunger is silent resistance.

William's bracelet is always tucked beneath my headscarf. It's all I have left of him, of my life before this place. To have a piece of him so close is a comfort, something to remind me to breathe and stay strong, that there is still a life beyond the barbed wire.

Isla sits with a small wad of rope, hunched to keep the bracelet she's making hidden. It's incredible what she can do with fraying strings, weaving them into beautiful, intricate braids to fit any woman she makes them for. Fiona speaks in hushed tones to two young Jewish women, teaching them words in English, and they teach her words in Yiddish.

Despite the unwritten rule that helping anyone is forbidden, we disregard it. Regardless of ethnicity, religion, or why we were brought here, we are all sisters, daughters, mothers, aunts, friends—no longer strangers, but common victims of the Nazis—and we do whatever we can to keep one another alive. At night, I listen as women softly sing, recite poetry, and tell childhood bedtime stories, and we watch one another put on plays and conduct school lessons. Medicine is smuggled in for the poor women who are forced to work in the brothel, and they are gifted with soap, handmade jewelry, drawings, and other little keepsakes. Everyone covets these gifts as if they were gold and silver, and women band together to keep them hidden from the

SS, sometimes at the risk of their own lives. After roll call, we use our own clothes to clean the wounds of the women who are beaten and flogged, and share whatever scraps of food we have.

Fighting in silence is the only thing we can do anymore, all that keeps us strong.

I slip the little drawing book from under my shirt when I've confirmed there are no SS nearby. Fiona, Isla, and I made it from the SS's discarded newspapers. We call it our Book of Good Deeds, and today it's my turn to carry it. Whenever we see someone do something good, we draw it. We don't write down anyone's name or the good thing they did; it would get them sent to the torture bunker if the SS ever found the book.

I flip through the many pictures we've contributed to the book. Women helping one another stay standing when the SS aren't paying attention. A woman sharing her soup. A secretive smile passing between a young woman and a male prisoner as they are marched off for work. Handmade paper flowers being playfully placed behind ears. Women exchanging family recipes and holiday traditions—all of which everyone promises to include in their own lives when they're free again. Each image brings tears to my eyes, and I clutch the book tighter, as if this sole reminder that goodness can survive even in hell will be snatched from me.

A whistle causes everyone to tense, but we relax slightly when we realize it signals the arrival of a train, not roll call. A while later, we look pityingly on a large group of women being ushered into the camp. Though they're all identical, with shaved heads, striped dresses, and looks of shame, terror, and loss, one in particular draws my eye. A thin woman with a limp and a bruised face has the same red markings on her uniform that Fiona, Isla, and I have.

The red crosses are like targets. Other prisoners are wary of those marked under the Nacht und Nebel decree because they are presumed marked for death, and the SS are more likely to single them out for extreme punishment. My back is still raw from an incident last week when an SS woman said my footing wavered during roll call and stripped me bare for all of God and Ravensbrück to see, then whipped me until everything went black.

The woman looks in every direction, shoulders taut and fists clenched, determined not to let her fear show. She reminds me of Marie...

With difficulty, I rise to my feet, hide the book, and make my way to her. Her gaze jerks to me, startled, as I offer a friendly smile. "Do you speak French?" I ask.

This seems to make her eyes brighten. "Yes," she says with a thick Polish accent. Her expression remains guarded, like she expects me to lash out at any moment.

I reach into my pocket for what's left of the bread ration I've saved. My stomach contracts in pain as I offer it to her. We're all starving. Women die every day, their skeletal bodies carted away, and my body protests my giving away of a means of survival.

The woman's eyes fill with tears, and her lips tremble in a smile as she accepts the crust.

"My name is Louise."

"Thank you," she whispers shakily, holding the bread to her heart. "I am Bronisława."

Fiona, Isla, and the two Jewish women greet Bronisława kindly as I lead her back to our group. Isla fishes a spool of thread from her pocket along with a needle, so Bronisława can sew her classification patch and number to her uniform.

I take the needle and thread. "I'll do it for you. It's easier for someone else to do it."

My breath hitches when she lays the mark of a race defiler in my hand. I am drawn back to the cattle car, the showers, the German woman who helped me, the first roll call, the malicious look in Dorothea Binz's eyes and her dog... I desperately shake the memories away.

"Why do you have this mark?" I ask. "You're Polish."

"Mostly Polish. My mother is part German. My father and his family are Polish. I..." She trails off, hesitating, then continues quietly. "The Nazis don't consider me 'Aryan', but also not 'degenerate', not until I got married. My husband is a Jew."

"Is that why you were sent here?" I ask, gesturing to the red marks on her arms.

Bronisława shakes her head, pressing her lips into a firm line. The sudden hardening of her eyes reminds me of Marie. How many times did I try to get her to open up to me? How many times did my heart jump, seeing her exterior soften, only for her to slam the door shut on me?

Perhaps if I had been more understanding... if I didn't unwittingly push her away...

"I won't judge you," I assure Bronisława, then indicate my own markings, and Fiona's and Isla's. "We're 'criminals' too, that's no secret. We worked for resistance groups. Surely your crime is like ours?"

She considers this in silence, then gives a slight nod. "A crime against the Nazis, yes, but I wasn't a resistance fighter. My brother joined the resistance in Warsaw, but I stayed out of it. I just wanted to see my husband and make sure he was safe after he was sent to the ghetto. When my brother was found out, I was arrested too, then sent to a labor camp."

So much like Marie... just wanted the ones she loved to be taken care of, where she is now because someone else got her entangled in their fight.

"I was only sent here because I helped some people escape the last labor camp I was in," Bronisława adds, and a small, winsome smile graces her face.

Thankfully, Isla interjects, for I am valiantly trying to fight away the tears behind my eyes. "We helped people escape too. Allied soldiers."

Fiona nods. "Yes, we all worked for the Comet Line."

A stunned gasp parts Bronisława's lips and her eyes widen, suddenly aglow with happiness. "I knew a girl who worked for the Comet Line! I met her in the REIMAHG factory. She was from Paris. She taught me to speak French, and I taught her Polish. Her name was Marie."

My heart stops, the world blurs, and I latch on to Bronisława's arm, unable to control the way my entire body trembles. *The Comet Line. Paris. Marie. It can't be coincidence.* "Marie Beaufoy? Was that her name? Was it? Marie Beaufoy?" I plead desperately.

Bronisława's eyes flicker with recognition. "Yes. Marie Beaufoy. That was her name."

"Oh, thank God!" I cry, throwing myself into Bronisława's stunned embrace. "Thank you! Thank you!"

All these agonizing months of not knowing where she is or if she's safe, and now, at last, there is *something*!

"My name is Louise Beaufoy." I sniffle, unable to dry my tears for I am holding Bronisława's hands, this beautiful angel who has brought me news of Marie. "Marie is my little sister. She left France to work, but I never heard from her again. Is she alright? Is she safe?"

Bronisława's eyes fill with tears. "It's you! Marie told me about you, and your nephew! Don't worry, she's alright, I hope. I told you I helped some people escape. It was Marie. Almost two weeks ago, she escaped the camp with a Russian POW. I'm sure they made it a long way. They ran away in the evening, and I helped make sure their absence went unnoticed. It wasn't until seven o'clock the next night during roll call that the SS realized they were gone. They assumed I helped them get away, since we were close. It was hours before they got a patrol together.

Two runaways weren't a priority, not with the construction of the jets falling behind."

Escaped! Thank God! How like her! No one could ever make Marie do something she didn't want to do, at least, not without giving them hell over it.

"Marie wanted me to come with them," Bronisława says fondly. "But I didn't want to slow them down—my ankle never healed right after I broke it when I was little—and I wanted to make sure they had time to get away. And still she kept insisting I should come, until the moment she was about to run. She was a wonderful friend."

I pause as the initial shock fades, letting the rest of her words sink in. "You said she escaped with someone? A Russian? That doesn't sound like something she'd do unless she absolutely had to. She's very... independent. She doesn't trust easily."

Bronisława smiles in a nearly teasing manner, like Yvonne once did when she had gossip to share. "She didn't trust him easily, but he earned it. You'd have to be blind not to see the way they look at each other."

I gape, stunned beyond words. Marie never let anyone into her heart. To think she may have fallen in love seems as unlikely as her willingly becoming a German's mistress. But Bronisława seems so certain—and I haven't seen Marie in almost six months. How could I know how she's changed? I'm sure she'd be shocked to learn I've abandoned the Comet Line. Perhaps, in our separation, we've both changed more than the other could have foreseen.

"Thank you, Bronisława," I whisper, wiping my cheeks. "Thank you for helping her. I wish I could see her now... I wish I could be there for her."

Bronisława squeezes my hand. "Marie once told me that you had a big heart. I see it is true. She always spoke very highly of you."

A dam breaks inside me, and then I am sobbing as Bronisława hugs me, wishing that it were Marie I were holding, wishing I could tell her how much I love her, how much I miss her.

Please, make it home to France, stay safe, I pray silently, and the knowledge that she is out there somewhere, alive, determined to return home, renews my own strength and resolve to do the same.

27

NOVEMBER–DECEMBER, 1944

MARIE

A lake stretches placidly before us, a little island sprouting vegetation near the center, reminding me of the Buttes Chaumont Park back home. I inhale deeply, and the scent of spruce trees, the calming sight of gentle waves licking at the sandy edge, make me want to dive in despite the chill of the early morning.

"We're near Goldisthal," Radomir says, tucking the map into his pocket. After a careful examination of our surroundings, he seems satisfied with the location. "Let's make camp here for the morning."

We've been traveling by night and resting by day, staying a safe distance from villages or open flatland, sticking to the woods and hills, where it's easier to hide. If we're lucky, we can find an abandoned barn to take refuge in, but otherwise we make camp in the open. Radomir builds shelter to shield us from the rain and cold, digging holes into hills and using branches to make a canopy. He hasn't said it, but I can see the glaze fall over his eyes when he digs holes for us to sleep in, as he is taken back to the hell of the prison camps. I always press myself close into his arms, hopefully offering him comfort from the memories, a reminder that he is safe with me, and, always, he settles his arms around me and buries his face in my hair.

The treeline dips toward the lake in the crevice of the sloping hill, keeping us well hidden from any unwanted attention. I settle in the shade of a spruce tree, sighing with relief and immediately pulling off my boots. We each eat two rations of bread and drink the rest of the water in our canteens. Our bags are still filled with food after nearly five months of hoarding it in REIMAHG and over two weeks on the run, but water wasn't something we could easily store in the camp. Catching the rainwater, drinking from creeks, and drinking boiled water when Radomir deems it's safe to make a fire has been sustaining our pace.

Radomir also pulls off his boots, but he doesn't stop there. He turns away from me, shrugs off his shirt, then reaches for his pants.

"What are you doing?" I demand shrilly, swiftly averting my gaze, cheeks burning.

"I haven't been able to bathe properly in months," he says unashamedly, chuckling. "This place is perfectly hidden. And who knows when we'll get another chance?"

The water sloshes as he dives in. Discreetly, I glance over as he rises for air, thankfully still half-submerged. A shiver tingles my spine and, unsuccessfully, I try to convince myself it's caused by the wind. Although the years spent in captivity have left him gaunt and scarred he is still undeniably handsome, like a pale Roman statue carved from marble, and my heart skips at the sight of him.

Stop gawking at him! I inwardly scold myself, hastily looking away as he combs his hands through his light-blond hair, but no matter how I try to keep myself occupied my eyes are drawn to him.

"Is it cold?" I ask, somewhat breathless.

"You'll get used to it." He shrugs, his piercing gray eyes raising to mine. "Shall I turn around?"

The prospect of being clean is tempting despite the cool wind. Dirt from the mines still cakes my skin and hair. My clothes could certainly do with a wash, then they could dry in the sun. But should I? Even Louise has never seen me without clothes. But my hygiene is telling my modesty to get lost. I trust him with my life, and for once I've felt that it's alright to be vulnerable, because I know he would never use it against me. Part of me wants to have this familiarity with him.

"Yes, turn around." I nod, blushing. He chuckles and turns his back.

I leave my clothes neatly folded by the edge, and the wind tickling my bare skin makes me shiver. The frigid water as I place one foot on the rocky bottom makes me gasp.

"Dive in. It's better to get it over with quickly," Radomir says, wading out a little deeper.

After several moments, the freezing burn of the water is replaced by a slight numbness. I close my eyes, hold my breath, and dive in. The world is dark and quiet under the surface, peaceful like the night, and I think if I were conscious in sleep this is what it would feel like. As I swim deeper, push myself further into the unknown, my life and all its possibilities seem limitless, and I want nothing more than to grasp them all and make the most of everything. I rise, taking a deep, refreshing breath.

Radomir, as always, is waiting for me. I smile bashfully as my teeth chatter, sinking a little deeper so the water is at my chin.

"Ah, my poor lisichka." He laughs, and the sound makes my

entire body burn. "Your lips are turning blue. It's the Frenchwoman in you, not used to this kind of cold. Bathe quickly and I'll make you a fire."

As I wash, he builds a small fire, and, after I wrap myself in the cotton blanket we found in a barn a few days ago, he sets about scrubbing our clothes and then leaves them out to dry. I lie down, tired and refreshed, with my clean hair braided, and watch him. I admire the slight waviness of his soaking hair, the way his broad shoulders are relaxed, and the sight of him so at ease warms my heart as I drift to sleep.

Damn it, you idiot, be careful! I think with a nervous huff, as I sit crouched in the undergrowth several yards from a farmhouse while Radomir stealthily creeps up on the chickens plucking at the ground. The pastures are empty; all of the livestock has likely been taken for the German army. I bite my knuckles as he gets closer, anxiously watching the windows for anyone inside.

They might not have gone to bed yet—if anyone still lives here. A lot of houses have been abandoned. But what if this one isn't? What if they have a dog? What if the chickens start crowing and get someone's attention?

This paranoia is driving me to madness. As I watch Radomir snatch a chicken, snap its neck, and sprint back for cover, I cannot help but appreciate the way Louise overanalyzed everything. For every rash decision I made—even if the consequences would only have fallen on my head—she was right behind me, agonizing over the trouble I could be getting myself into and how to keep me out of it. She was always looking out for me, like I was for her, even if we were both too caught up in our own heads and problems to acknowledge it.

We've come a long way in the last month, and now we are near Volkach, a small town a little over fifty miles from Nuremburg and halfway to France's border from REIMAHG. The days have slipped by quickly, turning into weeks as the weather grows colder during the night and the days grow shorter. We've stretched our saved rations as thin as they will go, but, as December begins, scavenging and stealing has become necessary. The further south-west we travel, the more villages and farmland we come across, and often we've taken long detours to avoid coming into contact with anyone. Not that I mind not seeing anyone. Although I miss Bronisława, and I even miss Gaweł and the other Poles who were reliable in a pinch—part of me doesn't want these days of solitude to end; curling against Radomir's chest at night, pretending to be asleep when he wraps his arms around me and whispers softly in Russian.

Radomir grins, triumphantly presenting the chicken. "Mademoiselle, I've caught your breakfast."

We retreat into the woods, where our little fire is crackling in a hole, and Radomir sets about roasting the chicken. While I have time, I pull off my boots, wincing, and re-wrap my feet again. We're moving quickly, eager to be out of Germany and away from the tremors that wake us when Allied planes bombard the country. Blisters have formed where my feet rub in my boots, and wrapping them in cloth is the only way to ease the pain a little.

"We'll go slowly tonight," Radomir says. True to his word, after we've eaten and stomped out the fire and the sky has darkened, we set out at an almost leisurely pace, and we break more often than usual over the next few hours. As midnight nears, I am biting my cheeks to keep from whimpering; I can feel dampness where my toe must be bleeding. Radomir seems to instinctively know I'm in pain, and, when we come across a tiny, seemingly abandoned shack in the hills, he lights a wax candle and announces that we're stopping for the night.

There isn't much inside, just barren floor, half-charred

sticks in the hearth, and a table missing a leg balanced on the end of a small bed.

"Oh, they still have a bed!" I sigh happily, sinking onto the mattress in relief. In the few homes we've come across where families have fled, they have always taken their mattresses.

Before I can reach for my boots, Radomir kneels and gently slips them off my feet. The bandages are indeed red again and, without a word, Radomir tends to them, pouring water into his hands, running them delicately across my skin and massaging the ache away, eliciting a sigh of pleasure from me. I quickly snap my mouth shut in embarrassment.

Our position is quite improper, and so is the heat spreading through me at his touch, but then again so has our entire relationship been, since the moment we met. My feet are long clean when he finally binds them in cloth, and the way his calloused fingers caress me is leaps past the line of propriety, and yet I yearn to follow wherever he leads.

"Radomir," I whisper, mesmerized by the way the candlelight dances across his face. "Why did you change your mind? You were so set on reaching the partisans and fighting. Why did you decide to come with me?"

I'm not naive. I know he desires me. If I'd been confused before, the last month spent together would have alleviated that curiosity. But he's never pushed me, never demanded anything, and so I know there must be something more than physical attraction. God knows I feel it too.

He is quiet for a while in his thoughts. "When I gave you the map and you turned to walk away, it hit me. I was being a fool," he says. Even from his place on the floor, his pale eyes are level with mine, and the intensity in them makes my breath catch. "I was so focused on revenge that I didn't realize... for the first time since I was eighteen, walking out of the gulag, my life had a purpose. I'd lost too much to just stand there and watch you walk away. And for what? For revenge? For getting killed getting it? No. That is meaningless." He takes my face into his hands and leans his forehead against mine. "With you, I am at peace. You make me believe I am still a man... you make me whole again, make me want to live."

And you make me feel safe, I think, melting into his arms as tears slip from my eyes, relishing his comforting scent of the forest and home. *You let me be a woman, not in a way that is demeaning or domineering, but in a way that makes me feel strong, makes me feel cherished, gives me relief because, for the first time in a long time, I can be vulnerable without being weak.*

"Marie..." he starts hesitantly after a long silence, his eyes betraying fear for the heart he's placed in my hands. "Will you say something?"

There are so many things I want to say to him, so many feelings and desires I cannot think of which to express first. In the end, I settle on a few words, a truth that has consumed my heart even when my mind was oblivious, has made me dread losing him, has made me think that, perhaps, this world isn't such an awful place after all.

"I love you," I murmur, trailing my fingers across his scarred cheeks and beard.

For a moment I think I have seen tears in his eyes, but I cannot be sure, for in the next second his lips are pressed fervently to mine, and he is whispering the same words against my mouth. "I love you, Marie."

Heat consumes me, smolders within my chest, blazes across my skin where his fingers trail upwards from my back and into my hair, leaves me breathless as his kiss burns against my lips, my cheeks, my neck. I am indeed like fire, like he once told me, but it will be his flames I am devoured by. His passion gentles, and when he reluctantly draws away there is an unspoken question in his eyes, one I answer by drawing him back to me, drawing him over me as we lie down. As the candle burns low, with every touch, every kiss, every breath of pleasure, we become one in a way I will never be with another, lay bare our souls, make a promise of forever.

And so, when dawn is breaking and we still lie fitted perfectly together as if God had crafted each of us only for the other, when he asks, "When we reach Paris... will you marry me?", I smile, and murmur against his lips, "Yes."

28

DECEMBER 1944

LOUISE

I have begun counting my reasons to live.

I have to apologize to Marie. I have to finish teaching André English. I have to tell William I love him. Whenever my mind is drawn into the dark, I repeat some variation of these reasons to survive to myself. And, if that doesn't help, I flip through the pictures in the Book of Good Deeds, and every kind act I've witnessed is one more reason not to die.

A light snow has fallen, coating the earth like powdered sugar over a cake. Vaguely, as I kneel beside Bronisława in the fields, trying to dig up the carrots from the frozen ground, I think of all the things I used to bake at home, and decide I'll make André an apple cake.

"Look at this! Pathetic! You've been at it for hours, and this is what you have to show for it?" A few yards away, an SS woman kicks over a bucket, scattering the few tiny carrots inside across the icy ground. The Jewish prisoner who dug them up shrinks away, and screams when the SS woman stomps on her red, freezing fingers, likely breaking them.

I glance inside mine and Bronisława's bucket as the woman is whipped. We planted new crops—beets, radishes, and carrots—back in early September, but winter came early, and the dropping temperatures have shriveled the plants that didn't die as seedlings. It's barely half full after three hours, and what we've managed to pull from the ground is small and discolored.

The failure of the crops has been attributed to our "laziness" rather than the weather, and leather whips and wooden batons beat us more often than the endless bullets of rain.

My entire body tenses subconsciously before I even hear the crunch of snow beneath boots right behind me. I try to dig faster, but my hands are numb, the ground is solid with ice, and the next carrot I unearth is thinner than my bony fingers.

"And what is this?" an SS woman demands. "Could you filthy hags work any slower?" Spitting at us, she overturns the bucket, then hurls it at my head.

I've learned not to react to their insults, their abuse, for that only makes it ten times worse. I've learned not to cry when they hit or whip me, not to show any emotion when I am called a whore or a hag, to become numb. But Bronisława flinches.

Without a word or warning, the guard draws her whip, and Bronisława cries out, crumpling, as half a dozen leather strips crack against her back. I hurl myself over her, gritting my teeth as the next lash strikes me across the face. Her boot stings my ribs. She is furious that I would dare intervene. But she isn't picky when it comes to bodies to abuse, and flogs me mercilessly. Bronisława softly cries beneath me, begging me to move away and let her be punished instead.

I hold her tighter, refusing to move as the agonizing minutes drag on. I barely have any friends in the world anymore. Bronisława, Fiona, and Isla are the few I have left, who have shown me kindness when others wished me nothing but an existence of misery until death.

Enraged, the SS woman rips the back of my dress and flays

my bare skin. *I have been beaten by men twice your size, twice as strong, and they couldn't break me,* I think foggily. *You are vicious and cruel, you have nothing and no one in this world, and so inflicting pain is all you have. You are nothing. You will have nothing from me, not my tears, not my screams, and not my friend.*

I am someone, I am something to this world, to people who I love and who love me. No whip, no hateful words, and no murderous SS can destroy that. I screw my eyes shut and remain huddled over Bronisława until the SS woman exhausts herself and walks away.

I have to tell Marie it was me who lost her copy of Hamlet. *I have to get André a new football. I have to tell Fernand about the time when André was nine, when he lost his shoes in the river and didn't want to tell me, so he wore one of Fernand's old pairs and insisted they were his.*

My list grows longer as the days drag into weeks. Any little thing I can think of, no matter how mundane or unimportant, becomes a reason to keep living.

There's still laundry in André's room I need to wash. I haven't dusted the house in weeks and the floors need to be polished. My flowers need to be watered.

"Sorry," Bronisława says hastily when I wince. The lashes on my back are starting to scab over, and every evening she does her best to clean them. She's a gentle woman, and when she brings the damp cloth to my back it's as if she's touching a newborn.

"You'll be a good mother one day," I murmur quietly.

"I hope so—" Bronisława starts, then smothers a harsh cough. "Avraham has always wanted girls, so he can spoil them. I'd like that, but I want a boy too."

"Then you'll have to have them all," Fiona teases, and lays

an arm around her daughter's waist. "One is enough for me, though. Well, Isla, will I ever be a grandmother? I know you liked that boy. John, was it? What a nice young man."

Isla rolls her eyes. "That was three years ago, Mum! I was thirteen, and we only danced once at the town picnic."

"Oh, you'll find someone." Fiona sighs dreamily. "You'll look so beautiful in white one day. I wish your father could be here to see it. Will you let me walk you down the aisle?"

Isla smiles, tears pricking her eyes, and leans further into her mother's arms. "Of course, Mummy," she murmurs.

"Do you think you'll be a mother one day?" Bronisława asks, wincing as she tries to sit comfortably against the heating channel.

William's face returns to my mind. Even as the months go on, the image remains as vivid as if he were right in front of me, his dark hair and deep blue eyes, his kind smile and how warm and soft it felt against my own lips... *I have to know what our children will look like*, I think, adding the reason to my list.

"I hope so," I say, slipping the bracelet out of my headscarf to show her. "Before I was caught, there was an American soldier I was hiding. William. He asked me to come back to America with him, and I said yes. He escaped with André; I know he did. I can see he thinks of André like his own son. He would never let anything happen to him. When we're free again, I want to marry him."

"That's wonderful." Bronisława smiles. "I've never been to a wedding, besides my own. My parents wouldn't let me go to Eliana's... I wish I'd have been there for her. And she still came to my wedding, when even our parents didn't."

"I suppose sisters can be very forgiving," I whisper, hoping my own little sister will accept me with open arms when I find her again. I refuse to think "if." I *will* find her.

Bronisława quickly swipes at her eyes. "I haven't seen

Eliana in over four years now. The last letter I got from her was in 1940, a few months before I was arrested."

"You'll see her again," I say resolutely. "If what you heard over that radio in the camp was right, then Poland could be liberated by now. Stay positive. She'll be looking for you."

Like Marie will be looking for me. I must force down tears at the thought, of Marie finally coming home to find our house empty, to be given the news that the last members of her family could be dead...

Isla shuffles closer, lowering her voice. "Can I have the book? I have something to draw."

I hand the book to her, and she begins to sketch. We try to draw at least one picture a day, and, when we're not absorbed in stories of our lives before the war or describing in great detail our favorite meals and the first things we'll eat when we're free, we repeat the stories behind the drawings over and over.

Fiona loves to talk about older prisoners approaching the new arrivals, offering them comfort and friendship. We were all once like them, and to have a stranger bring you kindness rather than pain is an unbelievable relief. Isla's favorite story is of two young women, one Jewish and one German, who used to be in the camp, who sang American songs, taught others the western swing dances, and, in moments of grief and despair, could be heard to hopefully say, "we will dance again." Bronisława tells every story, with no favorites; prisoners comforting one another after the death of a friend or family member, helping to hide each other's keepsakes from the SS during barrack inspections.

"Done," Isla whispers, turning the book around to show a picture of Bronisława and me, sitting with our arms linked as we're doing now, smiling, and talking.

Whistles announce that it's time for silence, but Ravensbrück is never quiet. Soft cries, hoarse coughs, and whispers fill the night, the morning is consumed with whistles, shouting, vicious dogs growling, screams as women are beaten or torn into by the dogs. Even the wind moans in misery as if it shares in our torment.

As we crawl into the crowded bunks, Bronisława forces down another dry cough. She trembles and I offer my arm, worried that she will fall over. Sleep doesn't find many of the thousand women in our barrack, and they lie groaning and coughing, as they've been doing for the last few days. Similarly, I stare into the dark, trying not to scratch the red flea bites, trying to ignore the maddeningly irritating tingles as lice and fleas jump from body to body, trying to convince myself that my throat doesn't burn.

29

DECEMBER 1944

MARIE

The weeks pass relatively uneventfully, save for a few close calls while stealing from farmers and stumbling across two German battalions. Even without news from the outside world, the barrenness of the fields, the gauntness of every civilian and soldier, speaks for itself. The war is turning devastatingly against the Nazis. Two lowly fugitives are no one's priority, and it's made for a somewhat peaceful journey.

The forest has been eerily quiet today. Now that we're so close to France we've started sleeping from dawn until noon, then pressing onwards. We passed through a small city called Kaiserslautern a little while ago, finding it almost entirely devoid of residents, the majority of the buildings bombed into piles of rubble.

Radomir's hand tightens around mine, and we slow our pace, calculating each step to avoid snapping twigs or leaving footprints in the snow or mud. The quiet has left us on edge, and I tug my scarf tighter around my head. Though I tried to refuse, Radomir would hear none of my protests when it began to snow, and he tugged his second shirt over me and wrapped my feet in so much cloth that my oversized boots now fit snugly. His overprotectiveness should irk me, probably would have before I left France, but now I find it endearing. I never let Roger, Léon, or Victor coddle me.

I hope they're alright... Lately, I've been thinking about the night my boys came to say goodbye to me. It was dark when they appeared at the front door, and I couldn't fully see their faces in the moonlight, but I remember how their eyes gleamed as they hugged me. I was sixteen at the time. I remember I was so angry at them. The Nazis were forcing them to abandon me, like I'd been abandoned by Fernand and Father when they left for war, by Louise after our mother died...

I slip my hand out of Radomir's and link our arms, suddenly afraid he too will disappear if I let him go. People have come and gone from my life, but I've never tried to hold on. I saw no point. Bronisława certainly knew that. She had her own regrets about her sister, about her husband, about pushing the ones she loved away out of fear. She didn't want me to make the same mistakes. *"Don't let go. Our lives are too short for such things."* I remember fondly, an ache deep in my heart, longing to see her again.

"Stop," Radomir whispers, bringing us to a sudden halt. I hold my breath and try to listen for what has caught his attention.

I lower my voice, pressing closer to him reflexively. "What is it?"

"Get down. There's something out there," he commands, snatching my hand and dragging me back through the brush into a dell. I cannot find my voice to ask him what's wrong, and instead sit nestled in the dry riverbed while he crouches protectively beside me.

A rustling catches my ear, a disturbance in the foliage a few dozen yards away. There are no birdsongs, no startled retreats as we happen across an animal's path. The inhabitants of the forest have long fled, sensing something amiss. Everything is still, and the afternoon sun glimmers down at us through the trees. A blast of gunfire shatters the silence. Then the earth trembles as a grenade explodes. Startled, terrified shouts are drowned by more guns.

Radomir dives over me, cradling my head to his chest and shielding my body from whatever mayhem has erupted. I cling tightly to him, trying to draw strength from his steady voice as he whispers, "You're alright, lisichka. It's alright. I won't let anything hurt you. Never."

Machine gun fire makes me start and bury my face in the crook of his neck. Loud crashes tumble through the forest and, through the hysteria, I pick out the panicked voices of Germans, then a few French whooping in triumph. A few yards away, I catch a glimpse of German soldiers retreating for their lives, then men in commoner clothing giving chase.

I gasp hopefully. "How close are we to France? Are they partisans?"

Before Radomir can respond, more gunshots puncture the air, and several Germans tumble down the hill. The first lands face down and doesn't move. The second takes a few bloody, gurgling breaths before he goes still. The third lands directly on top of us. The fearful yelp from the German as Radomir hurls him away and reaches for the pistol he dropped sounds more like a child than a man. The German scrambles backwards, his oversized helmet slipping over his wide, terrified eyes. He barely looks fourteen.

He's a little boy. Like André. Not a soldier. Not an enemy. I have no war with this boy.

Tears spill down the boy's round, rosy cheeks as Radomir trains the pistol on him.

"Wait!" I grasp Radomir's arm. "Please, don't kill him," I

beg. "He's just a boy... please, someone loves him too, someone is waiting for him."

Radomir is silent. His eyes are cold and distant, somewhere far away in the war.

"Please," I whimper, gripping him tighter, fearing that he will kill the boy anyway. Then, slowly, the numbness softens. Radomir looks at the young German and waves the gun in an order to run.

The boy lets out a sob of disbelief, grasping a silver cross around his neck. "Thank you! Thank you!" he cries, then vanishes over the hill.

"Marie!" Suddenly, Radomir hurls me to the ground and huddles over me, then fires several shots at a man who's run into the riverbed, rifle aimed at us. The man ducks for cover behind a boulder. Dozens of others are crossing the area after the Germans, and we are exposed to the bullets and grenades rattling the battleground.

"French!" I scream over the deafening gunshots as Radomir fires back at the man shooting at us. If they are partisans, this may be our only chance. "Please, help! We are French!"

For several unending seconds my plea is met with nothing, then a man yells in French, "Where from?"

"Paris!" I shout. "We've escaped a labor camp!"

Again, a long pause. "Put down your guns! I won't shoot if you don't!"

Radomir hesitates but obliges. The man steps out from around the boulder, rifle at his side. A growl rumbles from Radomir's chest as he gets closer, and he places himself defensively before me. But something about the Frenchman makes my heart stop. I stare wide-eyed at the mess of sandy-blond hair beneath his cap and the faint outline of a burn mark under his left eye. The place I accidentally burned Roger when my boys and I were playing musketeers with burning sticks.

"R-Roger?" I stutter in disbelief.

This makes the man stop in his tracks, and his hazel eyes widen with shock. "How do you—wait... Marie?"

"Roger!" I cry with joy, then I rise and run into his arms. He laughs, lifting and twirling me the way he used to do before they ran away, and this simple gesture makes me break down in tears. Oh, how I have missed my boys! How terrified I have been for them, all these years of not knowing if they're alive or dead.

"Little fire ant! You're alright!" Roger ruffles my hair, giving a lopsided grin, then his expression grows thunderous, and he seizes my shoulders. "What the hell! I could have killed you! What are you doing out here?"

"We were in a labor camp, we escaped when we heard Paris was liberated," I say, nodding back to Radomir who hasn't risen from his knees. "We've been on the run for almost two months."

Roger sighs shakily. "Well... you're safe now."

"Are Léon and Victor here?" I ask, imagining their faces when they see me. Léon will be giddy, bouncing on his heels like he always did when he was excited, and Victor will talk my ears off with a million stories, and we'll all laugh and roll our eyes at the embellished details.

But Roger doesn't say anything. His eyes are heavier than I ever remember them being. They are the eyes of a soldier who has seen and lost too much, eyes I see in Radomir...

My heart shatters like glass within my chest, and the broken shards slice me open, leaving my soul crushed and bleeding. "Don't," I whisper, unable to bear hearing the truth spoken into existence. I pull Roger into my arms, muffling my sobs as I cling to my last friend, and he returns my crushing embrace like it's all that's keeping him tethered to sanity.

"Marie..." Radomir says hesitantly, and his use of my name rather than lisichka makes me tense. I turn, growing light-headed when I see the dark crimson stains on his shoulder and leg.

"Oh, God! You've been shot!" I gasp, rushing back to his side.

"It's alright, I'll live," he assures me with a gentle smile. "I'm just in a lot of pain."

"Shit, I'm sorry," Roger mutters behind us. "Don't worry. We've got a damn good medic. I'll go get a few guys and we'll help you back to our camp. You're both safe now."

Grief, fear, and relief rage for dominance within me, and I can only nod, unable to find my voice.

Radomir's hand rises to cradle my face and he touches his forehead to mine. "I'm so sorry, lisichka," he whispers.

We are free... I hold on to that thought with all I have and press my lips to his. We are alive. We are safe. My heart will ache for Léon and Victor for the rest of my life, and there will be time to grieve them, but now I need to focus on what is real. We are free, Roger is going to get a medic, the Germans are retreating, and Radomir's hands, which have settled around my waist, are the only things holding my world in one piece.

30

JANUARY 14, 1945

MARIE

Léon's and Victor's graves lie in a field of daisies, miles from Paris, miles from home. Léon, who was always the first to suggest some wild new adventure, was killed two years ago. Victor, the unappointed leader of our group, who could talk his way out of anything, died of meningitis a month before I found Roger.

After a few days in the partisans' camp, then another few weeks in Kaiserslautern, where the partisans captured the rest of the German soldiers, Roger and I made plans to travel to their graves. Radomir, though still injured, was reluctant to let me out of his sight, but agreed the trip was something I should do with Roger, not him.

I don't remember the last time I cried so much. Maybe not since my mother died. Roger and I sat by the wooden crosses engraved with their names for hours, and I was too inconsolable to do anything but sob while he kept an arm around my shoulders. Over the next few days, I listened as Roger recounted all they'd done together after they ran away. By the fourth day of camping out, I began to smile as we reminisced about the good old days; when Victor taught me how to bait a hook when they took me fishing, and how, after a socialite heir snubbed Léon after the gardening he'd done, we stole a number of pigs and unleashed them in his manor house during a fancy party. The shrieks of those high-class, grown men, undistinguishable from the women's, had us dying of laughter for hours.

Those thoughts of happier times are the ones I let fill my mind as our train draws into the station. We spent a month in Kaiserslautern while Radomir recovered from the gunshot wounds, and now, finally, we're arriving in Paris. Many of the railways have been bombed, but a few are still operational. Passengers and Allied soldiers enter the city together, smiling and talking, and convoys of French farmers and Allied soldiers haul food supplies and medicine in carts and trucks. How wonderful it is to see them out in the open, not hiding from the Nazis! All those long months of fear and uncertainty in REIMAHG, and I am determined to remain in good spirits.

I have a home to return to. Paris is free. We are alive. And we're getting married!

My heart jumps with joy and excitement every time I think of it, and I try to imagine the look on Louise's face. She'll be surprised to see me at the door, but she might faint when she sees I've brought home a man.

The train stops and we disembark, and I shiver, drawing the winter coat Roger gave me tighter around my body, and slip my arm through Radomir's. The afternoon is crisp and clear, filled with the scent of freshly baked bread. I close my eyes and allow everything to wash over me; the bustle of the station, the foreign accents of allies and not enemies, the brisk steps of women carrying full baskets of groceries, relaxed men smoking cigars, carefree children playing and laughing together. A dark shadow has been lifted from Paris, from the shoulders and hearts of her people, revealing a free city like the one I remember.

"Welcome to Paris." I smile brightly up at Radomir. As we start down the busy streets, I find myself smiling and nodding to anyone who looks in our direction, whether they be soldier or civilian, unable to contain the excitement that has put a spring in my step.

I'm home, Louise! I promised you I would come home!

I frantically turn over everything I need to say to Louise in my head. So many apologies, so many stories, so many things fighting for consideration that my mind won't align. But all thought ceases abruptly when I lay eyes on my home for the first time in seven months, and I can't breathe.

No...

The windows are shattered, the flowerpots have been smashed, and the door barely hangs to the frame by a hinge.

"Louise! André!" I shout and run inside. The house is unrecognizable. The curtains, rugs, and furniture are gone. Glass litters the floor, glinting in the light like broken stars. Every cupboard is empty, antiques inlaid with gold and silver are missing, all my mother's jewelry has been stolen from my parents' bedroom, the clothes are gone from the armoires. Everything is gone, from my collection of Shakespeare to Louise's sewing box.

Did they escape? Was the house looted after they left? Or were they arrested? Did the Gestapo seize everything? Did they take my family away?

"Marie, stay calm. Look at me. Take deep breaths." Radomir is holding my face, brushing the tears from my cheeks. I do as he says, taking several shaky breaths to compose myself.

"T-there're some people I need to talk to. Other Comet Line members," I stammer quietly. "I have to know what's happened. T-they might know where Louise is. Maybe she's hiding."

His eyes are gloomy, like I am but a little girl denying that her dog has died, insisting he's just sleeping.

I set a running pace, straight to one of the mail offices. There were other couriers working for the Line besides me, but when I approach the desk the supervisor informs me the woman I am looking for was arrested six months earlier. At City Hall I bypass the line of people, who rebuke me in irritation, and all but beg to know where Henry, the Line member who passed me the false documents for the Americans, is. Perhaps it's my stricken, desperate expression, but the clerk sighs with pity, questions his colleagues, and regretfully informs me that Henry was arrested by the Gestapo. Panicking as my list of known members grows shorter, I sprint toward the outskirts of the city. A group of British soldiers on a lorry stop me, and one asks with concern if I'm alright. After a quick explanation, they happily give Radomir and me a ride to the city limits, from where we run to a farm. But the little farmhouse is gone, burnt to the ground, and there is no sign of the farmer Roger, Léon, Victor, and I used to help. My last resort is a photography shop in the third arrondissement. The sight of the elderly photographer adjusting his spectacles has me sobbing with joy, and I embrace the stunned little old man.

"Cora!" He gasps. "I've not seen you in—"

"My sister! Amia! Her real name is Louise!" I cut him off. "Do you know where she is?"

He frowns, brow furrowed. "Oh, yes! I remember! Max asked me to take Amia's and her boy's pictures for their documents. That was back in July. He said she'd been compromised and had to run."

I don't know whether to be crushed or elated at the news. She and André escaped Paris... Did they make it to Spain? Max will know. He has contacts all throughout the continent. If anyone knows where she is, it's him.

"Is Max still in the city? I need to talk to him."

The old photographer nods. "Yes, he's staying at one of the old safehouses in the tenth arrondissement. I'll give you the address. Michelle Dumon has come out of hiding too. She came back to France not long after the liberation."

Just as I turn to leave, the old man smiles and says, "Long live France!"

"Long live France," I mutter, though it doesn't fill me with as much joy as it did when I still thought Louise was waiting there for me.

At the safehouse in the tenth arrondissement, I am greeted with the same shock I received from the photographer. It is Michelle Dumon who opens the door when I knock.

"Marie!" she gasps. "When did you return to France? Louise said—"

"Do you know where she is?"

"I... Why don't you come inside? It's freezing out here."

The house is warmed by the flames in the fireplace and the stove in the kitchen, but the cold refuses to leave my bones. Max, who sits at the table with several other men, looks up as we enter the kitchen, and his eyes widen. "Marie—I didn't think... It's good to see you."

"I've just been to see the photographer," I start, ignoring the others. "He said you asked him to make new documents for Louise and my nephew. Where is she? Who was her guide? Did they make it to Spain?"

Max's eyes reflect the same sad reluctance that Radomir's did a few hours ago. He excuses himself from the men, then escorts us into the sitting room. "Perhaps you should sit—"

"Where is she?" I demand hoarsely, clenching my fists as I begin to shake.

"I don't know," Max says regretfully. "She was compromised by Pierre Boulain and had to go underground. She decided she was going to be the guide and left with André and four soldiers in July. I... I got word a few weeks later that the SS raided a safehouse where they were staying near the border with Spain. My contact said one of our helpers was killed and another was arrested. I don't know which one Louise was..."

Dead or tortured and executed. Dead or tortured and imprisoned. Rage and grief consume me, obscure any rational thought but the horrifying image of her face—so kind and beautiful like our mother—bruised and bloody, the sound of her sweet voice not singing, instead screaming in agony.

The world falls from beneath my feet. "How could you not know?" I scream, lunging at him. "You have contacts everywhere! What else did your contact see? What happened to my sister?"

This can't be happening! We went undiscovered for years, and now, when everything is so close to being over, she's gone! God, please, she can't be dead!

Powerful arms restrain me, force my hands that seek to strangle Max to my sides, crush me to a broad chest while I sob, scream, and fight to get away. All my strength drains away, and I go limp. Radomir takes a knee, holding me tightly as I sit weeping in his arms. I don't know how long we remain like this. Maybe for hours. All of time and space seems to be crawling. When my head begins to pound with such unbearable pain it aches through my whole body, I try to breathe steadily, and finally become aware of a deep, tender voice whispering in Russian against my ear. Michelle has come to my side as well, her pained eyes downcast as she rubs my back.

"A-André," I force out, breathless. "Where is he?"

"He made it," she says softly. "Three of the soldiers escaped. Only one person was arrested. I believe André was with the men who got away."

This isn't how it was supposed to be... We were supposed to take care of him together, and now Louise is missing, and I have no idea where my nephew is or who he is with.

"I will find him," I vow, struggling back to my feet. Fernand entrusted his son to his sisters, and I refuse to let him down any more than I already have. And Louise, wherever she is, would want me to focus on finding him.

Max reappears from an adjacent room, an envelope in his hand. "Marie..." he begins, offering it to me. "Louise asked me to give this to you when she left. She wanted me to tell you she's sorry."

I take it with trembling hands. With Louise's letter pressed over my heart, I numbly turn to leave without a goodbye, somehow feeling heavy yet hollow as I wordlessly start down the sidewalk in search of the nearest Red Cross office. It's the only thing I can think to do. Perhaps André's name is in their files, where he's been documented as a refugee or an orphan...

A crushing, unbearable weight is bearing down on me. My sister is gone. I have no idea where she is or what fate she has come to, and there is nothing I can do for her. Nothing but imagine and dread the worst, nothing but hope, nothing but stay in Paris and wait, and this absolute loss of control makes me break down in tears anew.

Radomir guides me to a bench, but he doesn't speak. What is there to say? Any words of assurance would be meaningless. Every shuddering breath that becomes a misty white cloud is numbing my face, and I force myself to stop crying. As I gaze down at the envelope in my hands and break the seal with quivering fingers, a guilt-sharpened knife twists in my heart. I hate to think this is the agonizing uncertainty and fear I put Louise through when I left.

My dearest Marie,

If you're reading this, then you've made it home and I'm gone. I hope André and I will be safe in Spain or maybe Britain by now. I'm sorry. I have no choice, but I'm so sorry. I feel like I'm abandoning you. It's no longer safe for us in France, and I have to get André away.

I have been terrified every day since you left. Every day, I worry for you, and every day is awful not knowing where you are. I'm sorry I can't be there for you, and I'm sorry I wasn't there for you even when you were home. Even though we've never gotten along well, you've always been here for me. You were strong for me, looking out for me, and I didn't appreciate that. I think I understand now, because lately I have felt so alone without you, felt that I must bear the weight of everything because I am the only one who can... You're stronger than me, the strongest person I know. You would take care of André, like Fernand trusted us to do.

And I'm sorry for forgetting that too. I let myself get so caught up in the Comet Line, in helping others the way I wished someone helped Fernand and Father, I lost sight of what mattered most. I got a letter from the Red Cross from Fernand and Father. They're alive. The letter was from a few years ago, but they were taken to a prison camp, and they're alive. I have to believe that.

I promise, once André is safe, I will find you. I'm not sure how, but I will find a way. Until then, know that I miss you terribly, and—though I don't say it enough—I love you so much.

With all my love, always, Louise

"I love you too, Louise," I murmur. I wish I could tell her I'm sorry, that there were times I wasn't there for her either, that I understand her need to care for others, that I've learned people aren't as awful as I used to believe, and I don't blame her for leaving.

I'll tell her one day. I will find her, or she will find me, and we'll find André... I have to believe that. I stand, resolving to stay strong for her, for André, and for myself.

Across the street, a bald woman in a ragged brown dress catches my attention, and I'm drawn back to the first time I saw Bronisława. She looks away from everyone in shame, and those who don't ignore her hurl insults and spit at her. I've seen women like her, their heads shaved in disgrace for sleeping with Germans. But something is familiar about this woman.

"Wait here," I say to Radomir, and follow the woman as she retreats down a deserted road where she won't be accosted. She turns, hearing my pursuit, and we both gasp at the sight of the other.

With bruised, dirt-stained cheeks, and a split lip, Jeanne stares back at me with stunned, despairing eyes. Her thick black hair has been shaved to the skin, all the finery she used to wear is gone, and I barely recognize her. She sniffles and squeezes her eyes shut with a sigh of resignation, as if anticipating a slap. "Please, get it over with, Marie," she whimpers.

Maybe I should scream at her, call her a traitor, let out all my pent-up rage and grief on her like the Marie she knows would do. And yet I don't see a collaborator in front of me. I see the girl who was my friend, who I used to have snowball fights with, who brought my family a pot of beef stew after my mother died, who now expects me to abuse her.

If Yvonne had taken a German as a lover, I think Louise would still have pity for her, still love her in some way. Somehow, Jeanne still has a place in my heart. Perhaps she never truly lost that place. Perhaps it's the loss of Léon, Victor, and Bronisława, Louise and André, Fernand and Father, but I find I don't have it within me to be angry at her.

I step forward, arms outstretched, and she flinches. Delicately, I pull her to my chest, feeling her stiffen in shock at this small kindness, and she breaks. Fierce sobs rack her body, and she holds me tightly like a woman lost at sea, hanging on to the only piece of driftwood.

And perhaps she is lost. She was barely seventeen when she became involved with Carl, she was young, impressionable... I wonder if she believed she was in love, believed he loved her. There is very little we wouldn't do for the people we love.

I draw away to undo my headscarf and tie it over her baldness. I don't know if I can forgive her, but I can show her compassion. That's what Louise would do.

31

JANUARY–FEBRUARY 1945

LOUISE

The days crawl, like a soldier with his legs blown off desperately trying to drag himself away from certain death. I think of Fernand and Father, wonder if they were injured that horribly, if they were taken to a place like this, doubting they're alive anymore... *I have to take fresh flowers to my mother's grave. I have to learn the swing dance routine Isla has been trying to teach us. I have—*

A hoarse coughing fit interrupts my train of thought, and Bronisława clutches her aching stomach. Isla is in a similar state, face screwed up in pain. Fiona cradles her daughter, looking as though she wishes she could take all her pain upon herself instead, and quietly sings English lullabies, wiping a damp rag over Isla's head, which is burning with fever.

Our friends, family, and strangers have become our keepsakes. As the months grow colder and the snow falls deeper, the diseases that have always swept Ravensbrück have become epidemics of typhus, dysentery, and malaria. When the SS come to inspect our barracks, it's not just our drawings or jewelry we must hide. Should the SS see the women who are gravely ill and decide they're showing too many symptoms of sickness, they'll take them to the sickbays.

But there are no real doctors. There is no medicine. We've all been warned to stay far from the sickbays, for that is where the sadistic SS doctors kill their patients with lethal injections or other horrific experiments.

I gently dab a cloth over Bronisława's brow. Her fever is rising and shivers shake her entire body. She cried when I made her take off one of her two sets of clothes, but her temperature was getting too high, so I didn't let her protests dissuade me.

I have to find us some food, I think, rising unsteadily to my feet. Fiona and I are the strongest of our little group, the only ones well enough to stand and walk. I look down at my hands. I am now able to trace the lines of my bones. I must suppress a cough when I emerge into the freezing morning, but it isn't illness that claws viciously up my throat. Against my will, my eyes seek out the newly constructed chimney across the electrified barbed wire, the plume of black smoke that chokes the clouds with the stench of burnt bodies...

When the transports of Jewish women began arriving from Auschwitz, they described a living nightmare. I didn't believe them at first. Starvation, disease, horrific abuse, I could believe them about all that. We've suffered the same in Ravensbrück. But chambers where people are murdered with gas? Crematoriums where thousands of bodies are burned every day? How could I possibly believe those horror stories they told us?

And yet, here I stand, staring at the chimney of Ravensbrück's new crematorium, sickened to think such a horrific creation of man would explain where all the Jews of Paris disappeared to.

Mentally, I add new reasons to my list. *I have to breathe fresh air again. I have to see clear, blue skies again.*

I force myself to step into the snow, avert my gaze from the chimney, and trudge to the neighboring barrack. Skeletal corpses lie in heaps outside the door of every block, so pale and gaunt one would think they've been dead for weeks, but the living don't look any different. There are large hollows in the spaces between my neck and collarbone, my limbs have become thin like matches, every day my body shrinks around my ribs, revealing the sharp edges of my hips. My striped dress, once snug, hangs off me like a woman's dress on a child.

The women in the first few blocks have nothing to trade. There is so little food that, even if they did have any, they'd already have eaten it before I came along. Still, I scavenge, offering a pair of wool socks for any scraps of food. I make my way to the fence that separates us from the men's camp. I wouldn't normally risk coming this way, but the SS workshops are empty today, and the SS women are locked up in their cozy houses at the opposite end of the camp, out of the misery of last night's blizzard.

Ever since the beginning of January, thousands upon thousands of people have been arriving from other concentration camps. There are more women, likely near fifty thousand crammed into the barracks along with several hundred children, but only a few thousand men reside across the fence from us. A few gaunt figures limp near the men's blocks.

"Do you have food? To trade?" I call out quietly, letting the wind carry my voice to them.

After a moment, a man calls back weakly, "Some bread... What do you have?"

"Wool socks. They don't have any holes, and they're very warm."

I wait for his answer, shivering, trying to shield my head from the snow. A few seconds later, some crusts of bread are hurled over the fences. I scramble to gather them up. "Thank you! God bless you." I choke with tears as I throw the socks with all my strength over the fence. He shouts his thanks and blessings in Yiddish—which I've learned from some of the Jewish women—and we retreat to our barracks. I stop short, catching a glimpse of someone both strange and familiar in a window. It takes me a moment before I realize it is me.

I pace closer to the glass, studying my hollow cheeks, the dark circles under my brown eyes, the prickly strands of blond hair cut to my scalp, the sickly pallid tinge of my skin. I am... I am my mother. My mother was so beautiful but, near the end when she lay wasting away in the hospital, dying of pneumonia, she looked much as I do now. Except for the hideous scars now marring my face where an SS woman whipped me. I've always looked just like her... and suddenly, I have a new reason to live.

I will live to see my mother's face beautiful again. I will live to see her defeat her illness and be healthy again. I will live to see my mother's face grow old.

I slip into my block and give Fiona a crust for her and Isla when she wakes, then sit next to Bronisława on the floor. There is no room in the bunks anymore. Every block is overflowing with people, most of whom are gravely ill. I nudge Bronisława and her eyes crack open, suddenly aglow and burning with hunger at the sight of bread. With my help, she manages to eat.

"I got it from a man across the fence," I whisper. "I offered to trade him socks, and he threw the bread to me, trusting me even though he didn't know me and could barely see me. 'God bless you!' I called to him, and I gave him the socks, and he said to me, 'Thank you! Hashem bless you! L'chaim! To life!'"

A soft smile graces Bronisława's gaunt face at the sound of the words, and I know she is thinking of her husband. Fiona smiles and slips the Book of Good Deeds from under her shirt to draw the scene I've described.

"Raus! Schnell! Appell! Roll call! Everyone outside!"

These words, accompanied by whistles, have become the

bane of my existence. I dread them every day more than I dreaded being caught by the Gestapo in France.

In a rush, thousands of women stampede into the roll call square, and dead silence falls immediately when Dorothea Binz appears. She doesn't have her dog anymore. It died some time ago, and it was the first time we'd ever seen her express sorrow.

She cries for a dog, brings flowers to his grave, and yet she smiles as she beats a human being to death...

We line up to be counted. It takes several hours and my feet burn in the snow, then go numb, and my legs tremble. Women collapse, are beaten and forced to stand, collapse again, for their sick, starving bodies cannot support themselves, and are dragged to a group at the other end of the square. All the while, I keep my head down. I try to block out the weeping and despairing wails of the women across the square, try to ignore the SS women who whip them for being too loud, try to forget they'll soon be taken to the gas chamber.

If only I could save them. I've saved so many people, and now I'm powerless. I glance at Bronisława out of the corner of my eye. Her eyes are drooping, and, several times when I'm sure no SS are looking, I must shake her back to reality. There are others around me who are just as ill, who cannot stay standing, and though part of me longs to reach out and help them... I don't. I can't. I have my own little family to look after.

By the end of roll call, several dozen women have been picked out of line and taken to die. The rest of us survivors return to our barracks.

"My wedding dress will be made of silk, like William's parachute, and I will carry a bouquet of irises," I whisper to Bronisława, and she smiles despite her pain.

"Mine was lace... Avraham owned a fabric shop. We both picked the material, and Eliana helped me make the dress. My bouquet was yellow roses and white lilies."

"I wore my mother's dress," Fiona says, smiling. "It was a

linen gown, with lace trim, and my bouquet was made of dandelions and shamrocks from the field behind our house."

"I want... a blue dress," Isla murmurs dreamily, half delirious in her illness. "Blue like the sky, and I'll have white roses like clouds... Daddy loved blue. His favorite suit was blue, and he kept the handkerchief I embroidered for him in his pocket... Will you make me a blue dress, Mummy, so Daddy can be with me?"

Barely seventeen, having spent over three years in this place, since she was only thirteen—after she and her mother were arrested, and her father was executed—Isla looks far from what a young woman should be. Weakened by typhus, curled in her mother's arms like a baby, she looks dreadfully tiny.

Fiona swipes tears from her eyes. "Of course, my little bird. Mummy will make you any color dress you want. You'll be the most beautiful bride in all the world."

Around us, other women chime in, fondly describing the gowns they wore on their wedding days or the dresses they'd like to wear if they survive the war. For a little while, we all let ourselves be drawn into one another's dreams and memories, imagining the scents of a dozen different flowers, the wonderful tastes of a myriad of German, French, Polish, Jewish, Russian, and British meals. For a little while, we forget the diseases claiming dozens of lives a night, the lice and fleas that infest our bunks and bodies, the freezing nights that leave us weak, shivering, and blue, our stomachs that have not had solid food in days.

The bunks grow empty as the weeks drag on, and the sky clouds with black smoke.

For the first time in days, Bronisława is able to sit up on her own, and she stubbornly insists on accompanying me in search of food. I offer her my arm and we trudge to the barrack entrance, slower than usual as her limp has become more painful, but she is determined to walk.

Outside, the first thing I notice after the piercing cold is the shouting, rising from the SS command center, unintelligible, but enraged. Their voices seem to merge together as my mind swims with aching hunger and overbearing fatigue.

"Should we stay inside?" Bronisława asks tentatively.

I shake my head. "Wait a moment. I want to try and listen." The SS sound furious, but also incredulous, perhaps even panicked. We've heard no airplanes, bomb sirens, or artillery, so it can't be an immediate danger. I strain my ears, forcing my mind to focus, but I can only pick out a few words.

"They're saying something about the Ardennes. And they keep saying 'the Allies'."

"Do you think the Allies are attacking?" Bronisława asks hopefully. "I'm sure France is free by now, and the Soviets are pushing back in the east. The Nazis are surrounded on all sides."

Could it be possible? Is this war coming to an end? Just as my spirits are lifted by the possible turn of events, they crumble. I've seen an SS woman whip a prisoner to death because she sneezed when the SS were talking. Shudders claw down my spine as I imagine what violence they could come up with given real provocation, like their army being butchered by the Allies.

Whistles signal a roll call. Bronisława's grip tightens around my arm, and my legs are heavy as lead as we watch SS women emerge from the command area, screaming, "Raus! Appell! Schnell! Outside you lazy, worthless pigs!"

Tens of thousands of women stumble into the snow and crowd in the square. The SS don't count us. Instead, they drag away prisoners of their choosing, kicking and punching them. The SS don't grin or laugh like they usually do. Their faces are grave, furious, and a collective dread washes over us all. Today, our pain and deaths will not be for their amusement, it will be for revenge.

I swallow thickly, wipe all emotion from my face, and stare blankly at the ground.

I have to live, I think as the girls in front of me are pulled out of line. *I have to see Marie again*, I think as shots are fired indiscriminately into the prisoners and bodies drop. *I have to find André*, I think as a woman is struck with a baton and beaten to a bloody heap where she stands. *I have to tell William I love him*, I think as the SS unleash their dogs and women scream as fangs rip into their flesh. *I have to—*

My train of thought ends at the sight of the beautiful Dorothea Binz. I clench my fists to stop from trembling. While her subordinates carry out floggings, beatings, and executions with rifles, Binz marches to the front line. She draws a Browning pistol and levels it with our faces. "One, two, three, you," she counts, emptying a bullet into the fourth girl's head. "One, two, three, you," she goes on, over and over again, shooting every fourth prisoner. Frantically, I try to count how many women are between myself, my friends, and Binz.

One of us is going to die... I feel myself sway, sickened by the realization. It doesn't matter where Binz stops because we're all lined up beside each other.

"One, two, three," Binz counts aloud, and stops when the barrel glares at Isla. "You." Binz pulls the trigger, but it clicks. She keeps pulling it, indifferent to Isla's gray, terrified face. The gun, out of bullets, keeps clicking. Binz curses, grabs Isla's arm, and shoves her toward the women selected for the gas chamber.

Fiona wails and rushes to grab her daughter and draw her protectively to her side. "Please, Deputy Chief Wardess, don't take her! Her illness is passing!" she begs desperately. "Please, please, not my little girl! Don't take my baby! Please, she is a good girl, a strong girl! She will get better soon!"

The world seems to go silent. For a moment, I see the

German woman, the nameless stranger who showed me kindness before Binz beat her to death during our first roll call. For a moment, Fiona's voice is all I hear, that first day when she told me to never show Dorothea Binz weakness, and now, as she cries to the beast for mercy...

Dorothea Binz doesn't look at Fiona as she begs for her daughter's life. She is too busy acquiring another gun from an SS guard. Freshly armed, she turns back to Fiona and Isla.

"You think she will get better soon?" Binz asks, softly, as if she did not just shoot and murder ten women, and my heart freezes. Something flickers in Binz's eyes and, for half a heartbeat, I think she will show mercy. Then, the pistol is between Isla's eyes. A bullet knocks her head back, and blood sprays over both Binz's and Fiona's faces. "There, now she's definitely not sick anymore," Binz sneers.

Robert is reaching for me, trying to save me, blood is splattering on my face, André is screaming. A woman's scream pierces my senses as my mind searches for reality. Fiona has crumpled, cradling Isla's body as dark blood pools in the snow. "NO! My baby!" Fiona wails.

I have to live, I repeat to myself as one of my friends lies dead, as one of my friends cries in misery. My heart is screaming at me to do something—anything—besides stand here like an unfeeling statue. But I can't help them, and, if I did, I'd be killed for showing compassion. I've risked my life to save others before... but I don't want to die. I can't die. My entire family is scattered somewhere in this world, surviving for each other, and I have to find them.

Suddenly, Fiona howls in fury and hurls herself at Binz with a strength inhuman for her malnourished body. Binz yelps in shock as she and Fiona tumble into the snow, and fires a desperate shot. Fiona rakes her nails down Binz's face, grabs her perfectly styled hair and slams her head against the ground over and over again, smashes her fists against Binz's face in a blind rage. The attack seems to last for hours as we all watch, horrified and mesmerized. Rifle fire silences Fiona's screams. She goes limp against her daughter's murderer, fists stained with blood. Binz shoves Fiona's body off and scrambles to her feet, disheveled, then furiously unloads the rest of her bullets into Fiona's face.

I stare down at my friends' bodies, so impossibly thin and brittle, and a part of me—a motherly part that has always cared about everyone, that never would have refused a hand begging for help—fractures and dies. Roll call ends. Nearly a hundred women are carted off to the gas chamber. We are ordered to pile the dead into carts to be taken to the crematorium. I step toward Fiona's body. I owe her this; a friend, not a stranger, to bear her body. She is unrecognizable. Pieces of bone show through the blood as I look into the place her eyes used to be. My vision swims, but I force myself to hold on to reality for fear of the SS women watching us. With violently shaking hands, I drag her to the carts. Bronisława, weak though she is, hobbles to me with Isla's body, silently sobbing. Together, we lift our friends onto a cart.

I should look away, but I find myself staring at Isla, so young and beautiful despite the abuse she endured here, and anguish washes over me as I look into her eyes. They are blue. Blue like the wedding dress she wanted her mother to make for her, a wedding dress she will never wear to a wedding that will never be. Another prisoner nudges me out of the way as she throws another body onto the heap, over Isla and Fiona.

"Louise," Bronisława whimpers. "Please, let's go."

Why are people so vile? I think bitterly as Bronisława cries, trying to tug me away. *I have been tortured, starved, made into a slave, witnessed too many murders to count, and the ones who force these cruelties upon us do it gladly. How can there be any goodness in such an evil world?*

Something snatches my attention among the bodies, something tucked into Isla's waistband. I pull out of Bronisława's grasp and reach for it, and—remembering that today was Isla's day to carry it—find the bloodstained Book of Good Deeds.

I have to make jewelry like Isla did, I begin a new list. *I have to make the smoked salmon Fiona said she loved to have on Christmas. I have to memorize every story in this book, because it is proof that, no matter how powerful evil is, kindness and love will find a way to endure.*

32

FEBRUARY 4–28, 1945

MARIE

I am going insane. I've taken to sitting at the shattered window, where the freezing winter air lashes at my cheeks when I peer through the threadbare rug Radomir nailed up to keep the cold out, waiting for the courier like a hawk waiting for an unsuspecting mouse. Every day, she passes without a letter for me, and then I make my way to the Red Cross office. The officials are growing weary of me, I see it in their exasperated expressions when I appear twice a day. After all, there are millions of missing people, millions of people searching for their loved ones, not just me.

A pair of arms slip around my waist from behind, and Radomir brushes a kiss against my temple as he draws me back against him. He follows my gaze out the window at the snowy streets. Little boys and girls laugh, build snowmen, throw snowballs, and a few soldiers caught in the crossfire of their games playfully toss snow back at them.

It's been so long since I last played with André in the street, even longer since Louise, Fernand, and I were children, laughing and playing without the slightest idea that one day we'd all wonder if we'd ever see each other again.

"Do you want to check with the Red Cross? We haven't gone today," Radomir says softly.

I almost refuse. The last month has been nothing but disappointment, and I don't want to leave the sphere of peace that envelops me whenever Radomir is near. But, with a sigh and a nod, I tell myself that today will be the day the Red Cross has something for me, just as I've told myself day after day.

Radomir holds my coat for me to slip on before he dons his own, and I let him carefully adjust my scarf. Such attentiveness would have miffed me at one point, but now my heart warms at his gentleness. Even though I've already agreed to marry him, he seems determined to prove himself to me, prove that he can take care of me. He's taken a job in a concrete factory during the week and has been helping the locals tend their ranches.

Now that France is free of the Nazis, everyone is starting to get back to their normal lives. The military has been extraordinary in getting aid into the country, and there have been no shortages of food or medicine. I've returned to my old job in the mail office, but I feel as though the world is moving on without me. I have no idea where my family is, if any of them are alive, and even liberation cannot return any sense of security and normalcy to me.

The Red Cross office is empty when Radomir and I step inside. Alice, a Red Cross worker I've come to know in the last month since I've been pestering the organization, glances up from her desk in the corner. Before I can get a word out, she beckons to me. "Miss Beaufoy! I have something for you," she says, shuffling in a stack of papers.

My heart leaps. "You do?" I choke out, rushing to her desk. "What is it? Is it my sister? My nephew? Have you found them?"

"Slow down, dear. I'm sorry, but I'm afraid I don't have news about them." Alice shakes her head. "Actually, *you* are the one we've found."

My brow furrows. "Found me? What do you mean?"

"We put your sister's and nephew's names into our files, but it appears you aren't the only one looking for them," Alice says, finally finding the paper she needs. "A man in Britain also had their names taken down back in September. The name Marie Beaufoy was documented, along with Louise and André Beaufoy. Do you know a man named William Chappell?"

That name sounds familiar, but I'm not sure... If he's in Britain, maybe he was a soldier, maybe we helped him and that's how he knows us.

I nod. "Yes, I know him. He's a... a family friend."

Alice smiles. "Would you like us to notify him of your whereabouts?"

Maybe he knows something about Louise and André. It can't hurt to find out who he is and hear what he has to say.

"Yes. Thank you, Alice. Do you have an address for me?"

She hands me an address in London, and, once she has sent a telegram to their office in the same city, I hurry home to start a letter to William Chappell, desperately trying to remember who he is and how I know him.

The weeks pass the same as they have since January; I stare out the window in hopes of a letter, check at the Red Cross office, except this time there is a twinge of hope in my heart. Weeks ago, I didn't know what I was waiting for, didn't know if there was anything to wait for at all, and now—even if I still can't recall who he is—I know there is someone looking for me and my family, someone to await a letter from.

The sky is blue and cloudless for miles, and the bright sun warms my cheeks as I step out of the mail office. The snow is finally beginning to melt, and with the passing of winter comes the sweet promise of spring.

I make my way toward the Red Cross office. Once again, Alice shakes her head at me when she sees me poke my head in through the door, and I sigh with disappointment. Rather than head straight home, I decide to take a long walk. Radomir won't be home from the factory for hours, and I want the opportunity to clear my head, perhaps talk with other people. With the constant anxiety of not knowing where Louise and André are, waiting for a possible lead from some stranger, I've found that Paris is terribly lonely. Of course, I am never lonely in Radomir's arms, and with him all my fear melts away, but in moments like these everything and everyone feel so far away—

"Aunt Marie!"

The world tilts and I stumble, barely catching myself. Heart racing, I whirl around in search of the boy who shouted, scanning the swarm of people who have emerged from the train station I was passing. Did I hear that right? Did someone call me? Is he here?

The boy shouts again, and this time an arm shoots into the air, waving enthusiastically to draw my attention. "Aunt Marie!"

I hold my breath as the boy weaves out of the crowd, dreading that I am only imagining things. And then he is there. Taller than I remember, his dark, unruly hair neatly trimmed, wearing a brown, British-style suit, André emerges with a grin on his face.

"André!" I cry out, slipping and sliding on the icy sidewalk as I run to him. His arms snap around me, and I crush him in my embrace. At last, I breathe, sobbing with relief and disbelief. He is here! I wasn't mistaken, I wasn't seeing things. André is here. He is safe and he is crying against my shoulder. When did he get tall enough to rest his head on my shoulder? God, it's been almost a year since I last saw him! He's thirteen now. He's grown up so much!

"Where have you been?" we both ask at once, then laugh through our tears.

André wipes his face. "I've been in London," he says, and the English tinge in his accent confirms it. "I'm fluent in English now. Aunt Louise will be proud, don't you think?"

"I know she will be," I whisper, and her absence punctures my happiness like a knife popping a balloon. "How did you get to London?"

"I brought him, mademoiselle," a man says. A tall, dark-haired man with two suitcases has appeared beside André. "My name is William Chappell. I don't know if you remember..."

A stunned breath escapes me. "The American. You were one of our soldiers." The sight of his face revives the memories I didn't realize belonged to that name.

William nods, smiling somberly. "One of the many soldiers, from what I know. I assume you..." His voice wavers and he blinks back tears. "You know about Louise?"

"I've heard things, but I don't know for sure," I say, winding an arm around André's shoulder and swallowing thickly. "Thank you so much for keeping André safe."

"It was the least I could do," he says. "I wish I could have done something for Louise. I'm so sorry I didn't protect her."

"Is she alive?" I whisper, holding my breath. Max's words have weighed heavy on me for weeks. One member killed, one arrested... William's hesitation makes my heart sink, and the world tilts, the fragile hope that held it together beginning to crack and crumble.

William breathes shakily. "I hope so. The SS caught us near Spain and arrested her."

All the air escapes me in relief and I grasp André's shoulder for balance, tears falling from my eyes as I look to the sky, thanking God in heaven for that small consolation. There's still a chance she's alive out there somewhere!

"I didn't want to go," André interjects quietly, eyes downcast. "I'm sorry, I didn't want to leave. Aunt Louise—"

"André, nothing is your fault. Don't make me say it again, young man," William says sternly, laying a fatherly hand on André's shoulder, then looks back at me. "Louise wanted us to run. I didn't want to leave her, but I had to get everyone away from the SS. I found the guide and we crossed into Spain that night, then from there we made it to Britain and were discharged from service. That's when I gave your names to the Red Cross. André has been with me since then. We've been looking for you, Louise, or even your brother... You're the first one we've had word of. We got on the first boat heading to France after I got the telegram."

A gust of frigid wind carries away his words, leaves us standing in an awful silence riddled with regret, the despair of uncertainty, and tentative hope.

"We will find her," William assures us, though I can hear the fear behind his words.

He loves her... that's why he's so afraid, why he took care of André, why he's standing in front of me right now... why the awful possibility that although she was arrested alive she might not be anymore is unbearable...

I draw my coat more snugly around me and find myself adjusting André's coat like a fretful mother, like Louise. "Let's all get inside, or we'll catch colds out here. I'll make everyone warm soup and tea." The three of us make our way back to the nineteenth arrondissement, never uttering a word, though I'm sure the same thought plays across all our minds.

We will find her.

And for my own sanity, for André's sake, I have to stay

hopeful. Like Louise said in her letter, *I will find you. I'm not sure how, but I will find a way.* If there's one aspect Louise and I are alike in, it's our stubbornness. I am going to find my sister.

Or I will find out what happened to her, I think grimly, and must fight not to break down in tears in front of André.

33

MARCH 5–11, 1945

LOUISE

The end is near. Whether that end will be liberation or death is still undecided. For thousands, the latter has been their fate. Those of us still clinging to life try to view the agitation of the SS as a sign of military defeat. We aren't being taken to work as often anymore, and the roll calls grow shorter. And the SS are trying to kill us faster. Black vans arrive every day after evening roll call and the SS doctors enter several barracks, emerging with hundreds of sick women who are then shoved into the windowless vans and vanish.

As the evening grows dim, the rumble of planes echoes overhead, and we run to our blocks for shelter. It has become routine. Planes swarm in the air, bombs can be felt from miles around, and prisoners rush to hide wherever they can. Bronisława and I crowd in a corner of the barrack with dozens of others, barely able to breathe, we are pressed so tightly together. We link hands and bow our heads. While the religious among us pray and sing, Bronisława and I take turns repeating stories from the Book of Good Deeds. I've never been particularly religious, but the small, bloodstained stack of drawings has become a bible, and I tell the story of a group of women hiding and caring for the baby another gave birth to six months after she arrived.

When the planes disappear and the night returns to the cricket songs, whistles sound across the camp. Evening roll call has already passed, and we all share looks of fearful uncertainty.

Bronisława and I painfully pinch each other's cheeks. It makes our gaunt faces flush pink, giving us the illusion of health. She's somewhat recovered from typhus, and my symptoms thankfully never deteriorated into illness, but we are both thin and weak, our pale skin marked by thousands of lice and rat bites.

The dreaded sound of approaching vans makes my bones ache with terror. Through the blinding glare of floodlights, I make out the silhouettes of vehicles. But it isn't SS doctors that emerge from them. The SS women approach the vans and meet Red Cross workers.

Are they the real Red Cross, or is this a trick?

Though we are absolutely silent, I cannot make out the words Dorothea Binz is exchanging with one of the Red Cross people over the whistles, snarling dogs, and shouting SS guards. The guards begin to call out numbers from a sheet of paper, and prisoners step forward with trepidation when their numbers are called. They are ordered to show their arms and legs and, with approval from the SS, ushered into the vans.

"They're looking for the Polish girls," someone whispers urgently nearby, and, after a moment of shuffling, a girl limps away to hide. In the years before I came to Ravensbrück, the SS doctors conducted horrific experimental surgeries on Polish resistance women and girls, who they called "rabbits." I've seen some of their legs, gruesome and distorted beyond recognition. By now, the SS have killed most of the patients who could have revealed the Nazis' brutality, but some have escaped by hiding and exchanging numbers with others, and now the SS are making sure none of their "rabbits" are put in the vans...

This is the real Red Cross. The Nazis wouldn't care if the Polish girls were sent if it was just a trick to kill us.

More numbers are called, more women are checked by the SS for any indication they are "rabbits" and are given to the Red Cross if they're not. The same is being done at other blocks. One by one, the vans fill up with mostly French women, and are driven to the gates.

I have to get into one of these vans. This is salvation, I am sure of it. This is my chance to escape, get home to Marie. I've promised myself I will survive, and I can't remain here if that is my wish. Even if the SS don't kill us, the Red Army is swiftly pushing the Nazis back, and I'd rather be dead than be here when the Soviets arrive.

Bronisława wobbles and grabs my hand, stifling a whimper of pain.

No, we have to get into one of these vans, I think, squeezing her hand. She is my last friend. We've taken care of each other, laughed, cried, and endured hell together. She is the only one I'm not willing to leave behind.

Another number is called, but no one steps forward. The prisoner is likely dead. Without a plan or regard for the consequences, I step up to the SS guard and Red Cross worker, pulling Bronisława with me, heart lodged in my throat.

"I didn't call you," the SS woman snarls at me. "What do you want?"

"That number is dead. But we're not, and we're not rabbits. We're not even Polish."

The Red Cross official arches a brow. "Rabbits?" he asks, glancing at the SS woman in question, but she doesn't look at him. She levels a glare on each of us as she settles her hand on her pistol. "I. Didn't. Call. You," she growls in warning.

I don't speak or move. I'm gambling on the chance that she won't shoot us in front of the Red Cross.

"I don't have time for this," the Red Cross official snaps impatiently at the SS woman, his Swedish accent making his words difficult to understand.

"They're criminals, so they don't leave." She shakes her head, indicating our red patches and crosses that mark us under the Nacht und Nebel decree.

The Red Cross official's eyes shift between the SS woman and Bronisława and me, appraising our appearance—two starving and dirty, the other healthy and wearing an impeccable uniform. "*They* are the criminals? Are you French, madam?" he inquires, and, at my nod, gestures in the direction of a van. "The deputy chief wardress said so herself—your orders are to hand over several hundred of these women to us tonight so we may evacuate them. Several people you've called are not present. Where are they?"

The SS woman's face grows red with indignation. "As you can see, we are short on medicine, and there has been a lot of disease," she mutters defensively.

"We have space to fill, and I will not leave until every van is full, and we will return to fill them up again. Your numbers and lists are irrelevant to me. Get in the van, madam." The man takes my wrist and tugs me forward. Bronisława's hand slips from mine.

"No!" I jerk away and reach for Bronisława. "I won't go without her. You have to bring her too! She is also French."

The SS woman draws her gun. "Don't push your luck with me. I see how she's limping. You're trying to help one of your rabbits escape, aren't you? Anyone can see she's Polish. Come here, pig!"

Bronisława cries out as she is torn from my side, and whimpers as she lands on her ankle.

"She is French, she is my sister! She isn't Polish!" I beg,

refraining from making any quick movements that might mean a bullet in my head. Forcing myself to breathe steadily, I straighten and say with as much confidence as I can muster, "Check our files."

The Red Cross is in a rush, maybe they won't bother, maybe I sound sure enough of myself...

"Enough!" The Red Cross official stares wide-eyed in shock at the gun pointed at us. "They've done nothing to warrant this treatment! What is wrong with you?"

The SS woman purses her lips, face growing redder by the second, and her finger twitches over the trigger of her pistol. Furiously, she turns on Bronisława. "Show me your legs!" she commands, ignoring the Red Cross official when he questions her reasons for needing to see Bronisława's legs. Bronisława shakily draws up her skirt. Though her legs are thin and frail, there is no flesh missing, no horrid wounds inflicted by the SS doctors' operations to recreate war injuries.

I am sickened to think that Bronisława would have been one of the "rabbits" had she come to Ravensbrück a few years sooner.

"It's true. My name is Blanche, I'm twenty-four, and I'm from Paris. We came here during the autumn last year," Bronisława says in flawless French, perfectly imitating my accent. With watering eyes, I thank God for Marie.

"For God's sake, put your gun down!" the Red Cross official exclaims angrily. "I told you; I will fill up these vans if I have to stay all night and ram the gates open to get out! You heard them, she's French. Give her to me."

I hold my breath as reluctance flashes across the SS woman's face.

"Gerda! What are you doing?" Dorothea Binz's shout rips through my body like jagged hooks, and I can sense every prisoner curl in upon themselves as her black boots storm toward us.

"Deputy Chief Wardess, I was just checking for—" The SS

woman's words trail away and she quickly holsters her gun at the sight of Binz's enraged expression. There are unspoken orders in Binz's narrowed eyes, commands to protect their damning secrets and not raise more concerns by acting so viciously. Suddenly quiet and composed, she flips through a list of numbers I assume are the "rabbits," then mutters to the Red Cross official, "Take them."

I fear that relief will render my legs useless as I help Bronisława back to her feet and we struggle into a van.

We are going to live… I almost don't believe it. How, after so long, after enduring so much, are we going to live? Of all the people who've passed through Ravensbrück's gates, never to see the outside world beyond its barbed-wire fences again, how could *we* be the ones to make it out alive?

More women climb up into the van, the doors are shut, we wait in silence with bated breath, the engine starts up, and we pass through the gates of Ravensbrück into the night. I let out a shuddering breath, weak and trembling, not having realized until now that, as we waited, I didn't breathe. The van seems to speed down the road like a jet, whisking us away from the depths of hell as reality truly begins to settle in. We are going to live.

We are free… I hold on to that thought with all I have, hug Bronisława, and let myself be lulled by the bumps in the road as the distance between us and death grows mile by mile. Slowly, my mind numbs, the aches in my body and heart fade, and for once I drift away unplagued by the thought of the ones I've lost, by fear or regret, and sleep.

As the days go on, we are given water and food, but barely anyone can keep it down. We are given the opportunity to bathe, but few have the strength to stand, and the new clothes we are given are immediately infested with lice. The only difference is that our new supervisors carry medicine rather than whips. But lack of cruelty alone will not heal us. Many of us were ill during the last disease outbreak, and with every dry cough, every feverish shiver, it grows more apparent that no one ever defeated typhus, just fought it off long enough for it to now return with renewed strength.

Death has not been left behind in Ravensbrück. It has followed us for miles, and, of the twenty women who were in the van with Bronisława and me, only fourteen remain.

Sweat has broken across Bronisława's brow, and I wipe her head, then swat her cheeks when I realize her eyes have rolled back. "Wake up! Look at me, Bronisława. Drink some more water."

Delirious, she barely seems to hear me, but drinks as I place a canteen of water at her lips.

"Don't worry, we'll get you a doctor soon," I whisper to her, biting my lip nervously. Her typhus symptoms have come back over the last few days, despite our improved situation.

As if he has heard my thoughts, the Swedish driver of our van calls back to us, "It won't be long now, ladies!"

We're almost there. We're going to live. I will find Marie and André. I will see William again... Their faces swim before me as I slump over in exhaustion. As I drift into dreams of a life before this, my fingers curl around the bracelet I have kept all this time, a hope for survival, a promise of life after this and the loved ones still waiting...

So warm...

It's the first thing I'm aware of after the silence. My eyes crack open and find a canvas tent rather than the van. Daylight shines in from the opened entrance upon rows of fifty cots spaced about the enormous tent. Red Cross nurses flit quietly about like angelic butterflies, helping their patients spoon water and broth into their mouths, brushing lice from their hair, offering small candies to go with the medicine.

I roll onto my side, tempted to snuggle into my lovely coarse canvas bedding, but then lift myself in search of Bronisława. She is in the cot to my right, so thin and pale, with sunken eyes like a corpse, that my heart seizes. I scramble up, grab her shoulders and shake her until she awakes with a fearful gasp. I laugh and sob with relief, kissing her now-clean cheeks. "We made it! We made it, Bronisława!"

A brittle smile graces her face. "All of us," she whispers, shakily drawing her blanket back to reveal the Book of Good Deeds tucked beside her like a treasured childhood stuffed animal.

Yes... we've all made it.

Bronisława, me, Fiona, Isla, the women who sang hymns to keep their hopes alive, made jewelry for their friends and strangers, composed plays to make one another smile. Every face in this book will survive even if their bodies don't, because the memory of their love and kindness will remain.

"Mademoiselle, would you like to bathe? I can help you, and then we'll have your name put into the files so we can help you find your family." A Red Cross nurse has approached and is looking at me with eyes full of such gentleness it makes me want to cry.

It's been ages since I last had a warm bath, but I am too afraid to get in the tub. The torture in the Gestapo dungeons has never truly left me. In the end, I sit outside the tub and wash myself with a cloth. When I am finished and try to get up, I have no strength, and the nurse must help me stand and dress. She keeps her eyes modestly averted, but I see the way worry creases her face.

I must be a horrible sight, head shaved, hideous scars across every inch of my emaciated body, and for a moment I lament my lost beauty. I haven't thought of such superficial things in a long time. For nearly seven months surviving the camp has been my only concern, but, now that I have reemerged from hell, alive, I wonder if I will ever be able to escape it. Will my mind, body, and soul ever recover? Will the people I love recognize me anymore? I have survived Ravensbrück, but I am not the woman who first passed through its gates so long ago, and my heart breaks to know I will never be her again.

34

MARCH 20–APRIL 14, 1945

LOUISE

The Book of Good Deeds is twice its original size. We ran out of pages after we arrived at the Red Cross hospital camp in France, and the nurses were gracious enough to provide us with paper and pencils to make new drawings. Although I am the only one making contributions to the book now. Bronisława can hardly find the strength to walk, much less lift her arms and draw, so, day after day, I remain beside her cot while we tell new stories of kindness.

A nurse tying a scarf over a frail, bald woman's head. A nurse helping a woman walk. Nurses feeding soup and medicine to those too ill to fend for themselves. A nurse sitting with a woman who she just delivered the news to that her family was killed in a bombing, comforting her and crying with her. Truly, these Red Cross women are angels.

Bronisława coughs, cutting off my retelling of the day when dozens of prisoners came together during a barrack inspection to hide a sick young child from the SS. Coughs rack her and she grasps her chest, face screwed up in pain. After a few minutes it passes, but she still trembles, each breath coming in short rasps.

"Would you like me to get you some soup?" I ask.

She shakes her head. "No, I'm not hungry."

I rub circles over her back, looking worriedly down at her chalky skin. "You haven't eaten since yesterday afternoon. You should try to eat a little." My hands quiver as I trail my fingers over her thin wisps of blond hair, and my heart aches so horribly it makes me weak.

Eleven years ago, when I was fifteen, my mother lay in her hospital bed like this, blond hair cut off, coughing and shivering as pneumonia ate away at her. Eleven years ago, I sat at my mother's side like this, quietly asking her if she wanted me to fetch the doctor to bring her soup, but she shook her head.

Bronisława frowns, and I follow her gaze to Rosa, a kind Red Cross nurse from the Netherlands who has cared for both of us since our arrival over a week ago. My urge to smile in greeting is dampened by Rosa's solemn expression, and my breath catches when I notice the opened envelope in her hand.

She doesn't have good news... Which of us is she coming for? Is it Marie or André? Or Eliana, Bronisława's little sister?

Rosa's gaze moves regretfully to Bronisława. She reaches for my hand, trembling, and I squeeze it tightly. "What is it?" Bronisława asks breathlessly.

Rosa's eyes are reluctant, like she is afraid any bad news will kill her already ill patient. The silence is deafening, and it seems to drag on for an eternity before Rosa finally takes a deep breath. "We found your husband," she says.

It should be good news, something spoken with joy and a smile, but Rosa's eyes are full of gloom. Bronisława lets out a low moan of agony, of denial, and turns away as if to block out reality.

"I'm so sorry, dear—"

"No, no!" Bronisława cries, shaking her head. "Avraham is strong! He—he is..."

He is a Jew... Even in Ravensbrück, when we witnessed what was being done to the Jews around us, when we began to hear the horror stories of what was happening to the Jews in Auschwitz, Dachau, Gross-Rosen, Majdanek, Treblinka, and so many other camps, Bronisława refused to give up hope for Avraham... Now, she sobs against me, and I hold her with all my strength as her grief brings tears down my own cheeks.

"What happened?" Bronisława manages through her tears. "What did they do to him?"

Rosa wipes her teary eyes and sniffles. "He was deported from Warsaw to Treblinka on October thirtieth, 1942... he died on November seventeenth, 1942. The listed cause was typhus."

The listed cause... because there are no natural deaths in extermination camps, and no way to know how he truly died.

"All this time," Bronisława cries as she sinks back into her cot. "I've been living to see him, to hold him again! All these camps, all these years, and... and he died weeks after I was arrested! All along, he's been gone..."

I wish so desperately as her entire being crumbles before my eyes that I could find the words to make her better. I wish there were more I could do besides curl up beside her and cry with her, cradling her head against my chest the way I did for my father so many years ago, when, even years after my mother's death, her loss destroyed him. But there is nothing to say, nothing to do, just as there was nothing I could have said or done back then.

Bronisława has stopped eating. The typhus she suffered in Ravensbrück returned, and has swiftly deteriorated into pneumonia. No amount of medicine the nurses force-feed her is having any effect, she grows thinner by the day, and even her hair has grown so brittle it falls away when I try to brush it. It's like I'm watching my mother die all over again.

"You can't make someone live once they've given up," Rosa whispered to me several days ago, when, furiously, I had cried and begged Bronisława to take a sip of broth. Stunned, I shoved Rosa away, screamed that she was the one giving up. How dare these people who saved us, who cared for us, give up on her?

But nothing is working. Nothing will make Bronisława's eyes glow with life again. No matter how many stories I tell her, how much food and water I feed her, how often I tell her she must hold on to hope for her brother and sister, she doesn't respond. She is numb to the world, even when I cry and beg her to look at me, to acknowledge that she is alive.

By the third week after Rosa brought us the news of Avraham's death, my pleas have turned to shouts, and anger is blooming from my desperation.

"Bronisława, look at me!" I scream, rising from my stool, the bowl of cold soup sloshing in my shaking hands. I've been talking to her for an hour, trying to spoon liquid into her mouth, but all she does is blink up at the tent ceiling. "Why won't you look at me? For God's sake, say something! Anything! I don't care what! Damn it, Bronisława, just say something!"

Bronisława doesn't even flinch when I slam the bowl onto my stool, doesn't look at me as I pace, nearly ripping fistfuls of hair from my head in frustration.

"Louise, be quiet, you're not helping her," Rosa says gently, untangling my fingers from my wisps of growing hair and escorting me from the tent. Bronisława doesn't acknowledge my departure.

"You've given up on her," I accuse, refusing to look Rosa in the eye.

Rosa sighs. "Do you think I want her to die? Do you think I want to see her wasting away like this? I've taken care of many like Bronisława, people who have lost so much they cannot see a life beyond anymore. To them, death is welcome."

"But she *does* have a life beyond! She has a brother, and a little sister, like me! How could she give up? It's not right!"

Rosa lays her hands on my shoulders. "Louise... I know you don't want to let her go. Believe me, I know what it's like to lose someone you care about, but sometimes we need to accept there's nothing we can do."

There's nothing we can do...

I remember when the doctors quietly muttered those words to my father. Back then, I thought that maybe if I sat with my mother a little longer, talked with her a little more, believed a little stronger, that maybe she'd get better. But she never did. Now, I'm watching those horrid days repeat themselves, and once again I'm only screaming at the storm to stop raining. The world doesn't bend to the will of a heartbroken girl, whether she be fifteen or twenty-six...

"After all we've been through... how could she leave me?" I sob, collapsing into Rosa's arms. She holds me until I have no tears left to cry, gently petting my head like my mother used to do until my bleeding heart slows.

"She still needs you," Rosa whispers. "Please, you must be strong for her. Be there for her when the time comes."

I clutch my bracelet, closing my eyes to imagine William's face, his calming voice. He once convinced me to let Paris and the Comet Line go for André's sake, to let Marie go for the time being. To be strong in a way I didn't think I could be.

Saturday morning finds me once again reading from the Book of Good Deeds at Bronisława's side. Splotches of tears stain the pages where the remnants of Fiona's and Isla's blood is spattered, and I cannot stop the tears that trail down my face and smudge the drawings.

Four days have passed since I last spoke to Rosa. The nurses have been giving us a wide berth, like the doctors in the hospital did whenever we came to visit my mother.

As I turn the page and start a new story, I look up, and gasp when I realize Bronisława's large, vivid blue eyes are focused on me, bright and gleaming. I drop the book and kneel beside her cot.

"Bronisława! How are you feeling? Would you like some soup? Some water? I'll go and get the nurses. I could even have them draw you a warm bath! Would you like that?" I babble, feeling my heart leap with hope.

She stares at me with awe, as if I were an angel descended before her, and then, her pale lips form a smile. "I met Marie like I met you."

"What do you mean?" I ask softly.

"I was so alone... so hopeless. She came and gave me her bread. A stranger gave me her bread when we were all starving... Then, I knew the world was still good," Bronisława says, reaching weakly for me, and I take her hand. "So, we became friends... like sisters, like my little Eliana... Then, fate brought me to Ravensbrück, and somehow, you were the one to come and give me bread, like Marie did..."

She breathes shallowly. I bite my cheeks, forcing back tears. She blinks slowly, smiling. My mother smiled the last day we visited her, before she died that night. This is the first time I've seen Bronisława smile since the Red Cross brought us here.

I crawl into the cot beside her—like I once crawled up beside my mother in her sickbed—and nuzzle my face in the crook of her neck, still holding her hand.

"You are my angels," Bronisława goes on after catching her breath. "The world is such a bright place with you in it... you both made my world so much happier, even when I was in the darkest of places. I believe again that people can be good... I never knew how much small kindnesses could do... If only—"

Her voice wavers and I clutch her hand tighter, muffling a sob as I draw her impossibly frail body closer.

"If only everyone would do just one kindness for a stranger, this world would be a wonderful place... Louise?"

"Yes, Bronisława?" I whimper.

She pauses for so long that I hold my breath to hear her breathing, and her grip loosens. "I... I feel..."

"Bronisława?" I whisper after a long silence, but she doesn't respond. "Bronisława..." I try again, my voice hoarse and forceful, begging her to speak, to squeeze my hand, but she doesn't... "Bronisława! Please, Bronisława, tell me what you feel! I'm listening!" I cry, curling around her body. The silence is agonizing, for the void no longer filled with her voice or heartbeat is overwhelmed by the sobbing child within me begging my mother to wake up.

"Louise! It's your sister! We've found her! We've—"

The voice is Rosa's, filled with such excitement as she rushes into the tent. I hear her sharp intake of breath, know she is making the sign of the cross over her heart, and I sob in misery.

How dare you bring me good news when my friend is gone, when she *didn't get to have good news! Why didn't you come sooner? Why didn't you let her hear that Marie is alive?* I want to scream at Rosa. I want Bronisława to open her beautiful, vivid blue eyes and say she can't wait to see Marie again... I want so many things that can never be. I want the dead to live again. I want the pain to become happiness again. I want time to turn backwards to a world that made sense.

And I can only cry.

35

APRIL 16, 1945

LOUISE

Time refuses to register anymore. How long has it been since I lay curled on the ground, clutching the Book of Good Deeds, watching the Red Cross workers dig the grave? Hours? Days? Part of me wishes for the pain and confusion I endured in the Gestapo's custody. I knew that pain would fade eventually, the wounds would heal. Now, everything feels so numb. I trudge through time as if I am dragging a stone, a burden weighing me down deep in my soul. Rosa tries to comfort me, or at least I think that's what she's doing. She speaks, and I hear, but I don't truly listen.

I have to remember.

I keep repeating this to myself. Of all the reasons to survive that I came up with in Ravensbrück, I tell myself I have to live because I have to remember. Yvonne is gone. Robert is gone. Fiona and Isla are gone. Bronisława is gone, so close and yet so far away.

If life has taught me anything, it is that it's unbearably fickle. So much uncertainty, so much that can change in an instant, and the only thing that remains constant is my mind. If I live, then I can remember, and if I remember, if I have the Book of Good Deeds—which I haven't let go of since Bronisława's death—then everything that is gone still exists.

I find myself once again sitting before a mound of loose dirt and a cross, unable to remember how I got here, reading aloud the kind things Bronisława did. When she cleaned the lashes on my back after I took a beating for her. When she would tell women about Avraham's fabric store and describe the beautiful dresses she would make for them when we were free.

Footsteps approach me. Whoever it is says nothing, so I go on reading. Another story passes: Bronisława risking her life to trade prisoner numbers with one of the Polish "rabbits" so the SS wouldn't find her and kill her. The feet make themselves known again by shuffling.

"Louise?" The word is barely a hesitant whisper.

My breath catches.

The voice is not that of any nurse in the hospital camp. I turn. It takes my mind several seconds to register what my eyes are seeing. Her gaze falls upon my scarred face, and she breaks down in sobs, drops to her knees, and my senses are engulfed in flaming red hair that smells so sweetly of lavender.

"M-Marie?"

Is this real? Am I dreaming? So many long months of pain and regret... is she truly here? Is this what Rosa has been trying to tell me?

"Louise!" she cries. My little sister's arms are around me, and her tears dampen my face as she kisses my cheeks. I wonder if she recognizes me anymore—I certainly don't.

"I'm so sorry!" we both cry at once. Our eyes lock, then we burst into laughter. She drags me into her arms, and we tumble back into the grass, crying and laughing. I hold her like I should have done eleven months ago when she got on the train, and vow I'll never let her go again.

"Life is fragile. I don't see any reason to waste time when we already have so little of it," I remember William once told me. My mind is drawn to Bronisława, a best friend who, by some incredible odds, Marie and I shared, who now lies in the earth so close to us, who always believed in life's dual preciousness and fragility.

Slowly, silence falls, and Marie and I lie side by side looking up at the clear blue sky, listening to the birds sing, basking in the warm breeze as it carries the scent of wildflowers. Were she and I ever at such peace with each other?

"I'm so sorry, Louise..." Marie murmurs, grasping my hand. "I never tried to understand you. You're the strongest person I know. I never realized how hard it was to care about people. You were always the kind, generous one, and, because you were, I never had to care about anyone but us, but... I understand now. Life means so much more when you have others to share it with."

Tears sting my eyes and my heart clenches so tightly it steals my breath. How I've agonized for years over how to break down the wall between us. Somehow, all these awful months apart have changed both of us, made us see the world through the other's eyes, and now I understand why I feel at peace with my sister as I never have before.

"I'm sorry too," I whisper, the first words I've spoken to anyone but Bronisława's grave in days. "You were strong for me... I never knew how much I relied on you until you were gone. I don't think I could have survived the resistance without you. You were my rock, and then I was so alone... I didn't know how hard it would be to *not* care. There were people in the camp I didn't help because I only had room for the ones close to me. I left Paris, the Comet Line, you... It killed me to do it. But that was the only way I could protect—"

André! Oh, God, Marie is here! What about André?

"André!" I gasp, sitting bolt upright. "Have you found out

anything? He escaped with William when I was arrested! Have you—"

"He's here," Marie says, her voice soothing and gentle in a way I've never heard it. "He's with William. They came with me."

The weight of the world falls away and I fall lightly back onto the grass. "Thank God."

"I'm so sorry," she continues. "I never should have left; I realize that now. I abandoned you too... we've both done it a lot over the years... I'm sorry. I wanted to write to you, or send you *something*, but I wasn't allowed to. I escaped as soon as I could to get back home."

"I know you did." I offer her a smile. "Bronisława told me. I think she loved us like sisters... I wish..."

I wish she would have lived. I wish she could have seen Marie again. I wish she could have found her brother and sister.

Silence falls again, though this time it's not as comfortable. Marie's gaze is drawn to the cross a few feet from us. Her eyes are vulnerable, shimmering with tears, and the pain etched in her face makes it clear she too has known her share of struggles and heartache since our parting.

"I missed her by a few days. If I'd been here sooner..." she murmurs to herself, her voice so fragile it breaks my heart.

"She told me how you met. You gave her your bread... She told me you made her believe the world was good again."

Marie turns away. "I never had faith in people... It's ridiculous, isn't it?" she sniffles, muffling sobs. "Me, of all people! How could *I* have been the one to give her hope?"

When have I ever known Marie to cry? The time we've spent apart has softened her heart, as it has hardened mine, and I embrace her as she cries. We hold one another for a long time, mourning our friend, silently grieving the losses we haven't shared with each other yet—and perhaps never will. I'm not sure a day will come that I will tell her about Fiona and Isla, how my face came to be scarred, or why I'm now terrified of water. For now, I rest my chin on her shoulder and caress her hair, my eyes fixed on the Book of Good Deeds, which I dropped when I heard her voice.

I must think of the good things, the things that made me survive another day, of what I have right now. Marie is with me. William and André are alive. I am looking at a smokeless sky. I—

The appearance of two people from a Red Cross tent makes my breath hitch, and I begin to tremble. They're here. That kind, handsome pilot whose bracelet is around my bony wrist, that scrawny boy with a mess of untamable hair who looks so much like Fernand...

I duck my head behind Marie, tears trailing down my face as I hide from them.

"No, not like this," I whimper. "Please, tell them to leave. Don't let them see me like this..."

Starved, nearly bald and scarred, marked with the evidence of disease and neglect. Shame and fear burn deep within my heart, and I cannot bear the thought of their horrified, pitying eyes.

"Louise," Marie whispers gently. She cups my cheeks. "I love you."

I sob, feeling a dark void in my heart flood with light at her words. "I love you too."

"And they love you. We've been so worried, waiting for word of where you were, or what... might have happened," she struggles to say, shuddering at her own suggestion of my death. "All we care about is that you're alive. I can have them come over one at a time. Please?"

I want to tell her no. I want the earth to open and swallow me whole. But how could I deny them this? I had the comfort of knowing they escaped, but, the last time they saw me, Robert was dead beside me, blood was on my face, an SS had me in his grasp, and there was no hope for me...

I take several long, deep breaths, then give a hesitant nod. Marie calls out for André. I lower my head, closing my eyes so I don't have to see his look of sadness, but moments later I am almost knocked to the ground as he throws himself into my arms, crying with joy.

"Aunt Louise! I love you! I love you! I'm so happy you're alright!" he babbles in English. I am stunned by the perfection of his speech; my heart swells with pride, and I find myself smiling.

"I love you too, André," I murmur. "You've gotten so big... God, you've grown up so much. And your English is perfect! That's wonderful! I can't believe you're thirteen now! I'm so sorry we missed your birthday..."

André laughs, wiping his tears. "That's okay, I don't care about that. But we can have cake when we get home. Aunt Marie has been baking a lot since Will and I got back from London."

"London?"

André nods. "They've got a military base out there. After we escaped France, we went to London. Will was discharged, so we got a flat in the city, and visited the base a lot. That's how my English got so good."

"I'm so happy you've been safe." I smile, ruffling his hair. "And Marie? You've been *baking*? I can't imagine you ever wanting anything to do with a kitchen."

"It's not as easy as stealing from Germans, but I'm learning," she jokes, glancing at André. "At least *I* haven't nearly burned the kitchen down yet."

"It was an accident!" André protests, blushing.

I laugh until my sides sting and my cheeks ache from grinning. It's wonderful to laugh, to smile. I notice Marie smiling softly toward where William stands. A second man has joined him in silent observance of our reunion. He is taller than William, broad and blond with a scarred face. I assume he's the

Russian Bronisława said Marie escaped with. Though I don't know him, I'm glad to see him. Marie, while still the strong-minded girl I remember, has grown into a more compassionate woman, and, in the midst of this awful war that has stained our lives with pain and bloodshed, I'm happy she's found someone to love, someone to bring her peace.

Marie nudges me. "Would it be alright if I send for William?"

My throat constricts and I lower my head, brushing away the sudden itch below my eye, unable to avoid feeling the lash mark across my face.

"He really wants to see you." This time, it is André who speaks. His face is serious, reflecting a strength and resolve too mature for a boy his age. "We prayed for you every day. We never stopped thinking about you. Please?"

Tears spring to my eyes. Wordlessly, I nod. As we get to our feet, I grab the Book of Good Deeds, summoning the memory of every kind story to the forefront of my mind like a shield against any pain or fear. I barely hear Marie saying she'll find me some soup as she and André leave. My eyes refuse to raise from the ground when, moments later, footsteps come striding toward me.

Familiar hands rise to gently caress my cheeks, and I am drawn back to every moment we shared, every tender touch, every quiet word, every silent exchange of glances. This single touch gives me the strength to look into his blue eyes. There is no disgust, no hesitation, only love so overwhelming that my heart bursts.

William breathes shakily, fighting back tears. "You are so beautiful."

For the first time in what feels like an eternity, I am safe in his arms, feeling the world melt away as he kisses me gently.

"I love you," I murmur, and smile when I feel him whispering the same words against my lips. He peppers my face with kisses; my nose, my eyes, my forehead, gently tracing the path of my scar, and with his acceptance, the assurance of his love, I let myself dream of a future.

I will have a silk wedding gown and a bouquet of irises. I will be a teacher again and have my own children. I will go to America, and we will have a cozy home by the water.

"Thank you," I whisper.

William lets out a breath of disbelief. "For what? You can't possibly be thanking me, Louise. I've done nothing. *You* are the one who saved us, did everything for us and I... I left you to the SS a-and... whatever you've been through..."

I cradle his face in my hands. The pain and guilt are plain in his eyes. I've seen that dark glaze in my own eyes, felt it deep in my heart when I abandoned Marie, when I lost my friends...

"You saved André. And you saved me too," I say, presenting my wrist, and his eyes widen at the sight of the bracelet made from his parachute.

"You still have it," he whispers in disbelief, rolling the beads between his fingers.

"I'd never give it up... I promised myself a lot of things in the camp, but this was your promise to me. This was the only thing from my old life I managed to keep. And it helped me survive. Because it was a promise there was still a life waiting for me, that there were still people who cared about me... I wasn't sure I'd survive, but then I would remember our bracelet, I would read—" I stop myself, clutching the Book of Good Deeds in a fierce grip.

No. Not yet. Maybe someday I will show him, tell him everything, but I cannot bear it now.

"It gave me hope," I go on. "You've always made me feel so much stronger."

His hands tremble, and he kisses each of my knuckles before he lowers himself to one knee. "I want to make you another promise, Louise," he begins softly. "I will never leave you again.

No matter what, I will protect you, I will do everything I can to always make you feel strong. It may have taken a war for me to find you, but I thank God every day that I did. I love you. I know I've asked you to come home with me, but I haven't—Will you be my wife?"

My heart soars, and, even emaciated and scarred as I am, the reverence in his eyes makes me feel like the most beautiful woman in the world. "Of course I will."

He frowns, cheeks flushing with a sudden realization. "I'm sorry I don't have a ring—"

I don't let him finish and kneel to embrace him. After so many years of fear and uncertainty, I remember the feeling of true peace and security. There is no more resistance, no more fearing discovery by the Nazis, this war is surely nearing its end, André is safe, Marie is alright and has someone she loves, William is here, and I will never have to say goodbye to him.

William helps me back to my feet and, before we return to the tents to find Marie and André, I make one final whispered goodbye to my friend. I wish her peace and happiness, an existence free from pain, a life where she has no regrets and always holds tightly to those she loves.

And perhaps it is my own battered, desperate heart fooling me, but the breeze suddenly feels warm like a pair of arms embracing me, and I feel that she is wishing Marie and me the same.

EPILOGUE

MARCH 19, 1949

LOUISE

Germany surrendered on May seventh. Four months later, Japan surrendered. Six years of destruction, and the war was finally ended. Although the fighting was done, the war had taken pieces of us all, and our battles were far from over. We sought comfort in each other, in the knowledge of what we still had; friends, family, food, clothing. But the uncertainty plagued all of us.

There was no word of Fernand or Father. We didn't need tales of the prison and death camps to know what they most likely endured. I'd suffered one of the camps, Marie lived in a labor camp and vaguely alluded to her fiancé, Radomir, having been in POW camps.

By December of 1945, we had all reached an awful, unspoken agreement. Fernand and Father were dead. All our names were in the Red Cross lists, but no one was looking for us, and no one had come home to Paris. It was time to accept reality, no matter how much I wanted to deny it and keep waiting. It was time to rebuild our lives away from the painful memories of the war.

We acquired American citizenship within a month of applying, mostly due to William. As a Chappell whose family had a large influence in the country, he was able to have our applications pushed through quickly. Marie and Radomir married before we departed in late January, and William and I were married in March after we reached Nebraska. His family welcomed us with open arms, and Dorothy, a small, quick-witted woman like Marie, was especially thrilled to finally have sisters.

I've recently begun my own vegetable garden. Slowly, but surely, we are all working to heal the wounds left by the war. When I finally planted my lettuce, pumpkins, and tomatoes, my hands trembled as I pictured planting and digging up the crops in Ravensbrück. But as time goes on I find that, in facing those bad memories, they no longer have the power to rule my life. I'm still trying to find the courage to swim—which is a slow work in progress—but life is peaceful. William moved us out to one of his family estates, where we have a pond, and after a year Marie and Radomir found their own apartment in the city, André is at ease with his new life, and—

"Mommy! Bubba! Look what I drew!"

And we have our sweet little Alisa.

From where we kneel in my garden, André and I look up to the house. A two-year-old little girl with long, golden-blond hair and ocean-blue eyes dashes down the stone path, and my heart melts at the sight of her. My little girl. With a bright, eager smile, she skids to a halt and proudly presents a detailed drawing of her and André feeding the ducks in the pond. She has a brilliant mind and talents beyond her few short years. Alisa, my pride and joy, never ceases to amaze me.

André praises the drawing, making Alisa giggle and plop

down beside him on a pumpkin. Though he is her cousin, she has always referred to him as Bubba, and he makes a wonderful, protective big brother to her, like Fernand was to Marie and me...

André is seventeen now, and he looks exactly like Fernand. He works as an apprentice in a tailor shop. He's learned and perfected his father's trade, and William—who stepped up to be a father figure in André's life—is planning to help him open his own business. I know Fernand would be proud of the young man André has become.

With our baskets full, André and I carry the vegetables inside. Alisa, kind and helpful as always, trots ahead with her little arms full of a head of lettuce.

The sweet aroma of my cooling apple cake fills the sitting room, where William lounges on the sofa across from Radomir, discussing the Sunday paper while a record plays from the adjacent library. I hum along to the original version of 'I'll Get By as Long as I Have You', the song that so long ago, in a basement in Paris, my soldiers sang when we got the news of D-Day. Alisa drops her lettuce in the kitchen and runs back to the coffee table, where dozens of her drawings are scattered at her father's feet. Marie I find in the kitchen, eating the sugarcoated apple slices I intended to place on my cake.

"Marie!" I reprimand her, though it lacks any real annoyance.

"Hush, leave me be, woman!" she says, smiling, words muffled by an apple slice. "I'm craving fruit lately. You can't get mad at me, I'm—"

"Pregnant, yes, I know." I chuckle, overcome suddenly with such emotion that tears prick my eyes. My little sister, a mother!

While André sets about washing the vegetables for me, Marie and I rejoin our husbands to relax to the homely, amusing sound of their conversation.

Yes, life is peaceful. It's the little things that make us content. Pleasant surprises in the form of tickets to an evening picture, or an early, eagerly awaited newspaper. The perfect crimson shade of the apples on our tree, which make delicious desserts. The way Alisa tucks her stuffed animals into bed and kisses them before she goes to sleep. The tranquility of simplicity is a peace like no other.

"Here, Daddy. Please, put this in my book," Alisa says, swiveling on her knees to hand William another drawing. He smiles and obediently takes it. His eyes have never been so bright, full of so much love—except, perhaps, when he looks at me. From the day we first discovered I was pregnant, Alisa stole his heart, and now he is helplessly wound around her tiny, dainty finger.

He lifts another stack of Alisa's drawings, which he's bound into a flipbook for her, and adds the new one. She calls it her Book of Happy Drawings.

I'll never forget the day William first read my Book of Good Deeds. It's the only time I've been genuinely furious with him. Somehow, Alisa, being a curious little baby, managed to find the book hidden in a drawer. I was out running errands and William, curious about what she had gotten into, read it. After the war, I wrote out the stories on the back of each drawing so that, even when I was old and maybe losing my memory, I would never forget the meanings behind the drawings. I never told William what I suffered in Ravensbrück. I was never ready for him to know. When he told me he'd seen it, his face was pale and his eyes were haunted. I screamed at him, cried, and refused to let him near me or speak to him for days.

Then he reminded me of something he told me in Paris, when I was breaking down after Yvonne was killed, Marie had left, and years of turmoil were crushing me all at once. *"You've been strong for a long time. Sometimes it means bottling everything up for the sake of others, but it's not good to keep it there. Whatever's going on, just let it out. I'll be right here."* And I couldn't be angry at him anymore. He'd never done anything with the intention of hurting me; and so, I told him everything.

Looking back, I'm glad Alisa found the book. It helped me to let go of some of my guilt and pain, but it also inspired her to start her own book. She draws every happy memory she makes; helping me in the garden, playing with Marie when they visit for Sunday supper, eating her favorite desserts, seeing pretty birds and butterflies from the window.

Every drawing in her book is proof I'm doing something right. And, in a way, all the kindnesses I made a point to remember and honor have given Alisa an appreciation for the little things that make life meaningful. Through the Book of Good Deeds, through me, and through Alisa, who believes in the best of the world, love will always survive. Bronisława, Fiona, Isla, Yvonne, Robert, and all the nameless strangers who do right by others will survive.

William and I flip through her book, lingering for a long time on the newest drawing. Our entire family, smiling, holding hands. I nuzzle into William's side, looking fondly at our daughter, and he kisses my head.

"Aunt Louise! Aunt Marie!" André shouts, making everyone startle at the abrupt interruption of the peace. He emerges from the kitchen, eyes wide, face ashen.

"André? What's wrong? Are you alright?" I ask worriedly.

"I-I don't—I... there's—I saw..." He struggles to speak, blinking rapidly, and his hands tremble so violently I worry he is having a fit.

Marie steadies his hands. "André, just take a deep breath and tell us what's wrong."

"There's a man. He's coming up the road..." His voice is small, fearful, and raw, and it reminds me of the little boy who once stared in fascination at the German soldiers marching through Paris and asked hopefully when his father was coming home.

Apprehensive about what has disturbed him, I look out the foyer window. Marie joins me and André, who grew taller than us some time ago, looks over our heads.

There is a man walking down the long, unpaved road to the house, a bag slung over his shoulder. It's difficult to make out any features, but he is tall and thin with dark hair. He shields his eyes from the sun as he looks up, and the daylight glints off a pair of spectacles. My heart stops.

Marie tenses, latching onto my arm for support. We need not exchange any words. I know we've both seen the same thing and are not daring to hope.

André is breathless as he tries to ask, "Is... is that..."

It can't be him... Nine years of never knowing, believing the worst, and now... Could it be?

André sprints from the house, Marie and I close on his heels.

"Mommy, what's wrong?" Alisa calls, and William sweeps her up as he and Radomir follow to see what has rattled us. But I can't form any thoughts, can't make my voice work to explain to my husband and daughter that the man in the driveway—

I grasp Marie's hand, not daring to blink, fearing this dream will turn out to be just that. A dream. The man has stopped dead in his tracks. André stands several yards away, frozen. They stare at one another, silent, questioning, hoping.

Finally, the man speaks. "André?" he says with disbelief.

All the air and strength are drained from my body, and I sink to my knees in tears. I don't recognize his face anymore, the way for a long time I barely recognized myself. The war broke us all, and whatever this man has been through has so changed him that only the sound of his voice confirms what my heart wanted to believe.

Fernand is alive.

André sobs, no longer the young man ready to open a tailor shop but the little boy who waved goodbye when his father marched to war and never came back. André runs to meet Fernand, Fernand drops his bag, arms open wide, and father and son collide together in a fierce embrace.

"Papa! Papa!" André cries, sounding impossibly young.

Fernand's entire body shakes with the force of his grief and joy. "My boy! My son! You're all grown up!" he exclaims, sobbing, holding André's face. "My little boy, you're a man now! You look just like me! You still have your freckles, though, just like your mother…"

Marie kneels beside me, weeping, and we hold one another tightly. How I long to run to my brother and hug him; but the sight of André crying in his father's arms holds me back. He needs this moment just for him and his father. For a long time, no one moves. André and Fernand stand with their arms around one another, unwilling and afraid to let go.

Alisa squirms in William's arms, and tentatively breaks the quiet. "Mommy?"

Her little voice draws Fernand's attention, and his eyes lift from over André's shoulder, finding Marie and me.

My first night in Ravensbrück, I made three promises to myself; that I would survive to find Marie, to see William again, and to see André and Fernand reunited. With the fulfillment of each promise, an aging crack in my heart heals. Our father's absence strikes me like a hammer slamming a stake into my heart, but I push away the pain for now.

He has Mother again… He was never truly happy without her.

Hesitantly, like he is afraid we are an illusion that will disappear if he disturbs us, Fernand steps forward.

"Fernand," Marie cries, raising her arms like a child bidding her father to pick her up. His face crumples, he kneels, and, for the first time in almost ten years, he is holding us again.

"Louise, Marie!' he manages through his tears. "My lovely little sisters, you're alright! I've missed you so much!"

"Where have you been?" Marie gasps between sobs.

"A lot of places... I was liberated in 1945, but then I had to stay in hospital camps to recover. By the time I made it back to Paris it was already 1947, and you were all gone."

I bury my face in the crook of his neck. "We thought you were dead," I whisper.

"I almost was. I checked with every relief organization and never stopped looking for you. I met a woman named Michelle Dumon a few months ago, and she told me everything."

I tense, a cold wave of fear overwhelming me. I've never regretted our work for the Comet Line, but I never thought the day would come that Fernand would know of it. We promised to take care of André, and I got us involved in the resistance...

I brace myself for his anger, his disappointment, but he only kisses our cheeks and whispers, "I'm so proud of you, girls. I'm happy you found it in your hearts to help others. Lord knows the war would have been much different if we all helped someone."

I can barely believe my ears. Fernand is alive, he is here, and he doesn't hate me for endangering us when he left for war.

"Thank you..." He draws away, wiping his eyes, and grasps André's hand when he settles it on his father's shoulder. "You've raised him well. I knew I could trust you." Fernand looks up at William and Radomir standing in the doorway, silent and smiling. "You must be William and Radomir. Thank you, for taking care of my sisters, and my son."

"You are most welcome. We've heard a lot about you," William says, adjusting Alisa in his arms so he may shake Fernand's hand.

"I'm afraid I can't say the same," Fernand jokes.

William chuckles. "I suppose that means we all have a lot to talk about. Would you like to come in?"

"Yes, yes, come in!" I nod quickly, eager to cook all of his favorite meals, snuggle into the sofa, talk long into the night, and never let this reunion end. "Our home is yours, Fernand."

Together, we all step inside, still crying, but this time they are not tears of despair as they were when we said goodbye in France. And this time, there are no goodbyes, only new beginnings.

A LETTER FROM S.E. RUTLEDGE

Dear Reader,

I am very grateful you decided to read *The Girl Who Saved Them* and I sincerely hope you enjoyed it. If you want to keep up to date with my current releases, you can sign up at the following link. Your email address will never be shared and you can unsubscribe at any time.

www.bookouture.com/s-e-rutledge

A brief note on history: the Reichsmarschall Hermann Göring Factory, also known as REIMAHG, was one of the numerous underground factories and tunnel systems built by the Germans during the Second World War that utilized conscripted German workers, but also forced laborers and concentration camp prisoners. REIMAHG's original purpose was to mass-produce the Fw 190 and Ta 152 fighter jets, but in October Hitler ordered production to be switched to the Messerschmitt Me 262 fighter jet. During REIMAHG's brief existence between 1944 and 1945, only between seventeen and twenty-seven jets left the factory. Conditions in these underground forced labor factories were beyond dismal, and it is estimated that between nine hundred and several thousand workers died in REIMAHG.

The test flight conducted in late October in this story is completely fictional, as the actual first test flights of the Me 262 jets in REIMAHG were not conducted until January of 1945. The purpose of the fictional flight in this story is only to serve as an example of the Nazis' growing fears and desperation as the end of the war grows closer and it is clear they will not be victorious.

Both Michelle Dumon and Jacques Desoubrie were real people. Michelle, a brave young woman who aided the Comet Line resistance group, revealed Desoubrie to be a German agent working for the Gestapo. I have slightly altered and depicted several events fictitiously that did in fact occur. Michelle Dumon was briefly arrested and, before being released, spoke with another Comet Line member being held, and learned that Desoubrie was her betrayer. On May 7th, Jacques Desoubrie met with two MI9 agents when he caught Michelle Dumon spying on him, and she ran into a Metro station to hide before fleeing France. Another incident that is debated is the attempted assassination of Desoubrie on May 22nd, 1944. MI9 agents asked the resistance group French Forces of the Interior (FFI) to assassinate Desoubrie. Though the FFI claimed it was done, Desoubrie lived, and it is unclear whether the FFI lied or killed the wrong man. After the war, Desoubrie fled to Germany but was later captured by the Allies and executed.

Dorothea Binz worked at the Ravensbrück concentration camp from 1939 to 1945. She was one of the cruelest female guards, who was known to beat, whip, shoot, and sexually abuse prisoners. Both survivors of the Holocaust and the female guards Binz trained have made testimonies about her sadism and crimes during the war. Binz was later captured by the British in Hamburg after fleeing Ravensbrück. She was tried for war crimes in 1947, found guilty, and executed.

The Book of Good Deeds was inspired by true stories of Ravensbrück prisoners. Small gestures of kindness like drawing pictures, making dolls, putting on plays, and teaching one another were often critical to survival for the women of Ravensbrück. When faced with torture, starvation, and the utter loss of humanity in their worlds, faith in one another was all that kept their hope and will to survive alive.

Thank you again for reading *The Girl Who Saved Them* and I hope you loved it. If so, I would love to read your review. It's wonderful to see what readers think and makes such a difference helping new readers discover one of my books for the first time.

Thank you,

Savannah

facebook.com/savannah.rutledge.18
x.com/SE_Rutledge
instagram.com/s.e.rutledge

ACKNOWLEDGMENTS

I would like to begin by thanking my wonderful editor, Lucy. She has been incredibly supportive from the very beginning and her guidance has helped me in shaping this story to its full potential. I would also like to thank the Bookouture publicity team, who have been very supportive and welcoming. I am very grateful for the opportunity to work with them now and hopefully in the future.

I am beyond grateful to my mom and dad, who have always supported me in my dreams, and who tell anyone whether they be family or stranger that their "amazing daughter" writes books! They have always been the first to hear about my stories, which are often long tirades that I'm glad for their patience in listening to, and have never stopped encouraging me to continue writing. And, of course, they are my most supportive—and outspoken—fans!

To my best friend and sister, Felicia, I want to thank you for all your love and support over the years. Even if we don't talk every day or don't see each other for months, nothing ever changes. You've always been there for me and I am glad to have you in my life.

I am very happy to have my little brother's support. Although Kenny and I have very different hobbies and he is inclined toward motorcycles the way I am toward writing, he always finds the time to ask me about what I'm writing now.

I would also like to thank the many English and history teachers I've had throughout the years. They have all encouraged me in their own ways to pursue my love of both subjects, and have made me strive to better myself and my skills.

Finally, I want to extend my gratitude and respect to all those who lived the stories we now tell today. Words alone cannot express the extraordinary strength and courage of those incredible individuals. It is through suffering, bravery, and sacrifice that transcends age and generations that we can learn from them. It connects us all through love and understanding in a way that is too powerful to name. Their lives and stories, the happinesses and tragedies, the failures and triumphs, continue to inspire us all and teach us every day the wonderful value and preciousness of life.

PUBLISHING TEAM

Turning a manuscript into a book requires the efforts of many people. The publishing team at Bookouture would like to acknowledge everyone who contributed to this publication.

Commercial
Lauren Morrissette
Hannah Richmond
Imogen Allport

Cover design
Debbie Clement

Data and analysis
Mark Alder
Mohamed Bussuri

Editorial
Lucy Frederick
Melissa Tran

Copyeditor
Jacqui Lewis

Proofreader
Anne O'Brien

Marketing
Alex Crow
Melanie Price
Occy Carr
Cíara Rosney
Martyna Młynarska

Operations and distribution
Marina Valles
Stephanie Straub
Joe Morris

Production
Hannah Snetsinger
Mandy Kullar
Jen Shannon
Ria Clare

Publicity
Kim Nash
Noelle Holten
Jess Readett
Sarah Hardy

Rights and contracts
Peta Nightingale
Richard King
Saidah Graham

Printed in Great Britain
by Amazon